LIE STILL
—THE—
DEAD

LIE STILL
—THE—
DEAD

Matthew Heilman
& Ryan Henry

STYGIAN
PRESS

PITTSBURGH, PENNSYLVANIA

PUBLISHER'S NOTE:
This book is a work of fiction. Names, characters, places, and
incidents either are products of the authors' imaginations or are
used fictitiously. Any resemblance to actual persons, living or dead,
events, organizations, or locales is entirely coincidental.

Book Design and Cover Artwork by Craig Hines,
using stock content under license from Adobe Stock and Envato

Edited by Kimberly Henry and Marjorie Vania

PUBLISHER'S CATALOGING-IN-PUBLICATION DATA
Names: Heilman, Matthew, author. | Henry, Ryan, author.
Title: Lie still the dead / Matthew Heilman and Ryan Henry.
Description: Pittsburgh, PA: Stygian Press, 2022.
Identifiers: LCCN: 2022913656 | ISBN: 978-0-9785591-7-5 (hardcover)
| 978-0-9785591-8-2 (paperback) | 978-0-9785591-9-9 (ebook)
Subjects: LCSH Vampires--Fiction. | Paranormal fiction. | Horror. |
Mystery and detective stories. | BISAC FICTION / Horror | FICTION /
Occult & Supernatural | FICTION / Thrillers / Supernatural | FICTION
/ Noir | FICTION / Mystery & Detective / Police Procedural
Classification: LCC PS3608 .E375 L54 2022 | DDC 813.6--dc23

Paperback Edition
ISBN: 978-0-9785591-8-2

Published by Stygian Press
www.StygianPress.com

25 24 23   LSI   0 9 8 7 6 5 4 3 2

Content Advisory

This novel contains graphic content that may be objectionable to some readers. For more detailed information, please visit the publisher's website.

For James Russell Henry
& James Young Heilman

Amongst the many trials to which the human mind is subjected, that of holding intercourse, real or imaginary, with the world of spirits: of finding itself alone with a being terrific and awful, whose nature and power are unknown, has been justly considered as one of the most severe. The workings of nature in this situation, we all know, have ever been the object of our most eager inquiry.

Joanna Baillie
Plays on the Passions

They laid her where the four roads meet,
Here in this very place.
The earth upon her corpse was press'd,
This post was driven into her breast,
And a stone is on her face.

Robert Southey
"The Crossroads"

How wretched is the man who never mourn'd!
Edward Young
Night Thoughts (IV)

All is not lost; th' unconquerable will,
And study of revenge, immortal hate,
And courage never to submit or yield.

John Milton
Paradise Lost

1

Williamsport, Virginia. October 2016

AN UNMARKED CRUISER PULLED TO A SMOOTH HALT BESIDE the Williamsport Police Forensics Unit step van. Detective Nathan Alderson opened the door in one fluid motion. He ducked out, straightened his long black coat, and smoothed his damp reddish-blond hair. Alderson leaned against the car door, rubbed his cleft chin, and took a moment to adjust the Glock 32 in his shoulder holster.

Although personal tragedy had recently taken a toll on him, Alderson looked much younger than forty-five. He was lean and muscular—in better shape than many of the junior officers on the force. He had only been a detective for two years, but none of his peers treated him like a rookie. With his sharp mind, acute instincts, and keen eye for detail, Nathan Alderson was destined for the higher echelons of police work.

Alderson walked across the muddy soccer field. He weaved through parked vehicles and members of a dispersing search party. As he struggled to don a pair of latex gloves, he noticed a woman in a reflective vest sobbing into the shoulder of a white-haired man. Alderson turned away as the retiree glanced at him with pleading eyes. The detective continued to tug on the gloves and adjust them over his hands.

"Nate!" A familiar voice called out to his right. As Alderson continued toward the periphery of the woods, Frank McCain approached, his features hardened and sour. McCain's hands were shoved into his pockets and the older man shivered in the morning cold. The two detectives stopped and sized each other up in silence. Finally, McCain spoke. "You ever pass through a search party without starin' everybody down?"

"Come on, Frank." Alderson surveyed the thick forest ahead. "Nine times out of ten, the killer's *in* the search party."

"Jesus, Nate." McCain coughed, and pulled his coat tighter to ward off the chill. "You been briefed on what's in those woods yet?" McCain nodded at the sprawling copse of trees before them.

Alderson removed a leather-bound tablet and a ballpoint pen. "Seven-year-old kid named Tyler Marshall. Reported missing by his mother after sundown last night. She made the call from her cell after trying to find him herself, or so she told the 9-1-1 dispatcher. Mitchell and Davis arrived shortly afterwards to scour the woods but couldn't find the boy. Fearing he may have been abducted, backup was called in and an AMBER Alert went out to every cell phone in the Tidewater area."

He continued to comb the tree line with sharp eyes.

"Then Sergeant Perez took charge of the investigation. She made some calls and organized a civilian search party, which didn't ramp up until around nine o'clock. They fanned out through the forest but couldn't find the boy anywhere."

"Yeah, that's exactly what—"

"Perez called in the K-9 units around midnight," Alderson continued, unmindful of McCain's interjection. "The unies with the dogs made a few passes through the woods with the search party. A civilian found the boy's body much further along the trail just before sunrise. That about cover it?"

"Yeah. That's the story." McCain coughed again.

"Fingerprints?"

"Handprints, if you'd believe it. But there are a few oddities. Ash Townsend's in an uproar."

"Oddities?" Alderson adjusted his shoulder holster again as he closed his notepad.

"To start with, Forensics can't match the prints to any registered sex offenders or any other potential suspects in their database."

"Uh-huh. What else?"

"The kid wasn't, uh... *violated.*" McCain grimaced as he corrected himself. "Well, not like that, at least. So we're lookin' at a particularly gruesome murder, but there're no signs of sexual assault."

Alderson acknowledged his partner with a solemn nod of his head. He stepped onto a footpath leading into the forest. "Lead the way."

"Hold on, Nate. I haven't really talked to you since the funeral. Are you and Kelly still seein' that shrink? The grief counselor?"

Alderson's senses were attuned to the swaying trees around him and the moist ground beneath his feet. His voice remained detached and uncaring. "Yeah. I think it's doing her some good."

"How 'bout you, buddy?" McCain rested a hand on Alderson's shoulder.

The detective flinched. "It's a goddamned waste of time, Frank. There's nothing that doctor can say that's gonna bring Cody back." He paused, reflecting on his deceased son, and pointed to a tree with his pen. "Did Forensics turn up evidence of anyone besides the kid or his mother entering the forest from this direction?"

The scanner on McCain's belt warbled. He reached down to mute it. "Just the Marshall kid's shoe-prints." McCain gestured at the ground. "And his mother's. The patrolmen did a good job keepin' everyone off the trail."

"Here's what I don't understand. The initial report from Forensics indicated the kid was murdered off-site, then dragged and dropped in the woods by the perpetrator." Alderson flipped through his notepad to a page of barely legible scribbling.

"Well, they—"

"But that doesn't wash with the story from the kid's mother, who said she brought him to the playground, and he bolted into the woods." Alderson tapped his pen on the paper as droplets of rain slicked the surface. "He outran her, and she got lost. Those were her words. The boy didn't come out of the woods alive. So the killer was lurking in these trees somewhere and entered the forest from another location. Why did Forensics assume the boy was killed elsewhere?"

"You didn't hear?"

"Hear what?" Alderson looked puzzled.

McCain beckoned. "You need to see the body for yourself. It's quite a hike, but we'll get there eventually."

Alderson followed, still searching the surroundings for clues as they walked deeper into the overgrown forest. "You know, I grew up in Williamsport," he reminded his partner. "A few years after I graduated college, a little girl went missing back here. Must've been the summer of '95." Alderson furrowed his brow. "You were on the force then. What was her name? I can't remember it for the life of me."

"It was more than just one little girl. A couple kids disappeared in these woods around the same time," McCain answered. "But the forensics report for *this* case was carefully tailored. D'Amato wants to make sure there's no connection with those missing kids before any public statement's issued. Shit, as far as I know, their faces are still showin' up on milk cartons."

"Did Rudy Pettit work that case?"

"Yeah." McCain droned on as they walked through the underbrush. "It's closed now. I mean, two decades've passed since then. Like I said, he never recovered any bodies. He was pursuin' the usual sex crime and kidnappin' angle. Came up with nothin.'"

"It's too coincidental to have kids disappear in these woods and then have another turn up dead in the same damn place." Alderson ducked under a low-lying tree limb. "I've got a hunch that the perpetrator who abducted those kids also killed the Marshall boy."

"How you figure?"

"The perp got booked on an unrelated offense and did some hard time up at Sussex II." Alderson batted away another branch. "Got out and picked up where he left off. That kinda shit happens all the time."

Frank McCain gestured to a pair of moving figures. A camera flashed through the trees. "If I were you, I'd reserve judgment 'til you get a good look at what happened to this kid. Then you'll get an idea why the chief doesn't want all the particulars of this fiasco gettin' out."

The pair approached the barricade. Yellow crime scene tape was woven loosely between the trees. Alderson scratched his head and picked up his pace.

The younger detective surveyed the parameters of the crime scene. Two forensic specialists, their shoes covered in plastic booties, prowled around the shrunken corpse of Tyler Marshall. The remains had been partially covered by loose branches, mud, and dead leaves.

Ashley Townsend, the senior forensic technician, approached the detectives. She began to ask her usual procedural questions. "Detective Alderson, did you shave this morning? Any open cuts?"

"No on both counts." Alderson spoke before she could continue her lecture on the dangers of decomposing human remains. "Did you call time of death?"

Townsend placed a gloved hand on her hip and blew a strand of bleach-blonde hair away from her face. "We couldn't get a temperature reading. But rigor mortis puts the, uh, *speculated* homicide sometime between five and seven o'clock last night."

"Am I missing something? What about postmortem lividity?" Alderson tapped his pen against his open palm. "What's that tell you about the approximate time he was killed? Two hours is a huge gap, and I need something to corroborate the mother's story."

Townsend's expression sank. She glowered at McCain. "You didn't tell him why there was nothing in the report? No livor mortis?"

The older detective clenched a cigarette between his teeth. "I thought it'd be better if he saw this for himself." McCain flicked the lid of his silver Zippo, lit a cigarette, and took a deep drag. He exhaled the smoke through his nose.

Alderson stepped between his partner and the forensic technician. His eyes were still fixed on the nearby corpse of the boy. "Both of you. Stop fucking around and tell me why postmortem stains aren't present on that body." Alderson pointed at the child's half-buried remains a few yards away.

Townsend held her arm up to her forehead. "Well, uh, he was completely exsanguinated." She looked at the ground in disbelief. "There's no blood left in him."

As if possessed, Alderson charged toward the corpse. McCain and Townsend followed. The forensics tech tried in vain to get his attention.

Townsend gestured around herself. "As you can see, there are bloody handprints on a couple trees here." She waved a finger towards the footpath. "The boy was dragged here off the trail. My guess is the killer was interrupted and only managed to cover the lower portion of the body under those branches. But there's nothing else."

"Is that why your report said the body was deposited here? Even though you knew the kid entered the woods and ended up like this?"

"There was nothing plausible to tell Chief D'Amato," Townsend replied. "And I'll maintain there's no rational explanation for what happened here. But the *forensic* evidence is pretty fucking clear. The child was abducted, murdered somewhere else, and the body was transported to this location and dumped here. In that order." She shook her head. "No other account leaps to mind. At least none that I've ever seen."

Nathan Alderson squatted beside the corpse of Tyler Marshall. "Of course there's an explanation." Using his pen, he shifted the soil piled beneath the boy's pallid arm. There was no postmortem stain. "You said it yourself." He assayed an open wound on the child's throat and looked up at the pair standing around him. "The killer took the kid's blood clean out of him. Drained all of it. And it was probably done right here."

"What, like in a bucket or somethin'?" McCain shrugged. Alderson and Townsend ignored his suggestion.

"But Detective, if that happened, there would've been spillage around the wound. On the ground where the carotid artery was opened. There's nothing. It's as if the perpetrator—"

"Drank the Marshall boy's blood? What do you make of the throat lacerations? Do they look like human teeth marks to you?"

Ashley Townsend nodded in disbelief. "Yeah. That's what they are. But what you're suggesting—that the perpetrator drank this child dry—is impossible from a scientific standpoint."

"You're looking at the empirical data right here." He nodded at the boy's sunken remains. Tyler Marshall's t-shirt was filthy, and his blue jeans were covered in mud. A sneakered foot protruded from the earth. "Can you tell me anything at all about the perpetrator? I was told you ran the fingerprints and came up with nothing."

Townsend confirmed Alderson's question with a strained nod. "That's correct, Detective."

"There was a case two years ago." McCain spoke in a loud voice that got the attention of everyone inside the yellow tape. "Back in town. A girl was attacked by some pervert. Same shit. Guy bit her neck and tried to drink her blood."

"Yeah." Townsend nodded. "Jennifer Stroud. I did her rape kit and tox screen. Pettit was looking for a serial—"

"Whoever attacked her didn't do this," Alderson insisted. "The same perpetrator isn't gonna go from college girls to little boys. There's a world of difference between a serial rapist and a child murderer."

Alderson rose and stepped over the body to examine a nearby tree. A splayed, blood-soaked hand had left a discernible mark. The detective held his hand two inches from the tree trunk, comparing the size of the handprint to his own. Finally, he spun around to face Townsend. "When you ran your query, what did you use for search parameters?"

"The standard stuff for child murders. RSOs in the area were scanned first for print matches. Then we narrowed to Caucasian males. Single or divorced. Typical serial killer profile."

"Maybe the perpetrator doesn't fit the standard child murderer or abductor profiles." Alderson gestured with his pen. "Have one of your techs run the prints again, this time with a general search. No parameters."

"That could take a day. Maybe more."

"I'm not asking here." Alderson took a few steps toward the Marshall boy's corpse. "So is this all you found? Any features nearby I need to know about?" His eyes were riveted to the ground next to his left shoe as he spoke. "Derelict buildings or vehicles? Potential kill-sites? Anything of interest?"

"The power company identified a few abandoned houses in the residential area. We had the unies check those spots first. There are some dirt roads back there." Townsend gestured behind her head. "And an old plantation house pretty far off. We gave it a once-over. Must've burned down over a century ago. Teenagers and other delinquents have been partying up there for sure. Typical signs of vandalism. Graffiti tags, cigarette butts, broken beer bottles. Anyway, it's just a pile of scorched brick now and everything's overgrown. That's it. There's nothing else really."

Alderson raised a curious brow. "You don't sound so certain."

Townsend swallowed hard and chuckled to herself. "Believe it or not, there's an old walk-in mausoleum on the grounds. Eight crypts, four to each wall. Brick construction with oxidized brass fixtures inside and rusted cast iron doors—one of which was unsealed and hanging by a hinge. The second door must've fallen off. But there wasn't anything suspicious about it."

"Anything else?" Alderson asked.

"No," she confirmed. "It was just like the plantation house, only not gutted. Broken glass in and around it. Storm debris. Graffiti tags. Except for one, the brass nameplates are all broken—and the crypt spaces are empty. No sign of any coffins. Morbid fucking kids must've run off with them."

"Christ," McCain muttered.

"Did you notice anything unusual in there?" Alderson asked. "Any signs of struggle? Blood?"

"If you're asking me if I think that's where the Marshall boy was murdered, the answer is no,"

"How 'bout fast food bags or wrappings?" Alderson persisted. "A flashlight? Sleeping bag or blanket? Signs anyone might've been squatting in there recently?"

"No. Nothing. There's nothing in there but dead leaves and spiderwebs. If there *was,* I certainly would've told you."

"Understood."

She sighed. "Right. Well, if it's all the same to you, I've got a job to do *here.*" She nodded at the crime scene. "I'm only one person and Wright's the only assistant field tech the department could spare this morning. So if you wanna go take a look at those ruins, be my guest."

Alderson remained unfazed by the senior forensic technician's defensiveness. "Did you inspect these roads for tire tracks?"

"Of course I did." Townsend crossed her arms and narrowed her eyes. "There weren't any."

"Footprints?"

"Look, we ran a cursory check on the dirt roads closest to the crime scene. We stopped just beyond a small clearing where four of the roads intersect. There were no footprints. There were no tire tracks. Again, since there were only two of us working this morning, we could only do a quick sweep along the edge of the crossroads."

"Crossroads?" McCain pursed his lips. "Ain't there some superstitious mumbo-jumbo about crossroads? Some kinda occult thing?"

"If it were 1986, and we were still in the midst of Satanic Panic, I might be inclined to agree with you," Alderson replied. "But we've learned a lot since then. Besides, if D'Amato even hints that there's any occult significance to this crime, the press is gonna go apeshit." Alderson shook his head. "Don't even suggest it, Frank. WPD'll be dragging in every long-haired kid with a Slayer shirt for questioning, while the real killer's still out there."

"Alright already," McCain sneered. "I get it."

"You ever hear of the West Memphis Three?"

"Of course I have! But this is—"

"The last thing we need is a procedural fuck-up like that in Williamsport," Alderson warned.

"OK, fine. Cult or no cult, this shit's still weird." McCain cast his glance away from the Marshall boy's remains. He pinched the end of his cigarette and pocketed the butt so as not to sully the crime scene. "Whoever did this to that kid ain't right in the head, Nate. So what the hell do you make of the loss of blood? Any ideas in regard to a motive?"

"We really have no idea what—or who—we're dealing with here." Alderson adjusted his coat. "Not yet."

"I'm telling you," McCain responded. "It's the same guy that attacked the college girl. Maybe he travels around, and stopped back in Williamsport for a fresh kill."

"And I'm telling *you* that serial killers usually hunt within a certain age range, gender, and socioeconomic background. They don't just choose victims at random," Alderson said.

"What about the Beltway Snipers?"

"Great, Frank. Pick an outlier."

"Fine. Richard Ramirez. The Night Stalker. He killed women, men, kids. And his victims were all different ages."

Before Alderson could counter, Ash Townsend cleared her throat to interject. "Seriously, if you two gentlemen are done, I still have a job to do."

McCain shifted his weight on a patch of mossy ground. Alderson glared at Townsend before pointing to Tyler Marshall's body with his pen. "We need to get those remains to a lab for a formal autopsy." Alderson dusted off his trouser legs. "In the meantime, we'll question the boy's mother again. You up for that, Frank?"

"If I have to." He sighed and shoved his hands in his coat pockets. "D'Amato's not gonna like us draggin' her in as a suspect, for Christ's sake."

"Then he can fire me." Alderson glanced at the waiting forensics technician. "Townsend, wrap up here and run those prints again. I want this body on the slab and out of the elements by noon."

She beckoned to her assistant, who was taking photographs of clustered handprints on the ground. Townsend drew a plastic sheet over the body of Tyler Marshall. "We'll be back to remove the remains as soon as Wright starts the query."

Hearing his name, Townsend's assistant stood up, and the two forensic technicians began trudging back to the mobile unit beyond the vast tree line. McCain eyed Alderson.

"These are some pretty big assumptions, Nate. You spend ten minutes on the scene and think you got answers?"

"I don't *think* anything. I'm going by what I see. And a bit of a hunch. What I do know is Forensics dropped the ball on this from the get go."

"How? Because they don't believe the killer tore this kid's throat open and drank his blood like Count fuckin' Dracula? Shit, I don't believe that! And I'm pretty goddamn sure you don't either. None of this makes any sense."

"Why does it have to make sense?" Alderson shrugged. "We may never fully understand this crime, or the killer's motive. You've been on the force longer than I have. You shouldn't be asking these kinda questions anymore."

McCain paused and stared down the younger detective.

"You sure you're ready to be out in the field again? Maybe it's too soon—"

"Frank, as a friend and colleague, do me a favor. Go take the boy's mother in for questioning. I don't think she did it, but we need to get her on record. Ask her why she took a seven-year-old to the playground that late in the day, when it was already getting cold and dark. It's odd to me."

"OK. And what're you gonna do?"

"I'll stay on the scene until the techs move the body. I want to walk around a bit. Then, when I get back to the station, I'm re-opening Rudy Pettit's cold case."

Frank McCain gave an uneasy grin. "So you *do* think this is connected to the Stroud attack?"

"It's a starting point." Alderson met his fellow detective's gaze. "Don't read any more into it than that."

"Hell, I'm just thrilled to the fuckin' gills that you're listenin' to me for a change." McCain ducked under the yellow tape between the trees. The older detective began navigating the path out of the woods. "I'll catch up with you later. Call my cell if you need me."

Alderson stood alone by the corpse of Tyler Marshall. When he was satisfied his partner had put a considerable distance between himself and the crime scene, Nathan reached into his coat pocket and removed a plastic evidence bag. He thumbed it open and bent down to the ground.

With his pen, he lifted a torn scrap of black cloth from the wet leaves. He could tell it wasn't fabricated with modern materials—nor was it made of the usual synthetic fibers he had handled in previous investigations. Dried blood and soil encrusted its tattered edge. He slipped it into his evidence bag, sealed it, and placed the bagged scrap into his coat pocket. Forensics hadn't numbered it, so they hadn't seen it.

Alderson slipped under the crime scene tape and maneuvered around the trees. His eyes assayed the ground in search of additional clues that may have been overlooked by Townsend and Wright. After several minutes, he turned his attention back to the trail, where he noticed Sergeant Fernanda Perez was still standing guard over the crime scene. Alderson hadn't interacted with her much since her promotion to Sergeant, but she had always been good police. After glancing at his wristwatch, he ducked under the barricade tape and approached her.

"Would you mind—" He faltered, looking back at the outline of Tyler Marshall's shrouded corpse. "Can you wait here until Forensics comes back to collect the body?"

"Sure, no problem."

"Thank you. I wanna take a look at the plantation house Townsend mentioned earlier."

"Right. Did she tell you there's also some kind of tomb up there?"

"She did."

Perez nodded and pointed toward the path. "It's up that way a bit. Look for the chimneys."

"Great, thank you. I shouldn't be long but ping me on the rover if you need anything."

As Alderson turned to make his way through the underbrush, Sergeant Perez called after him. "Detective, I never got a chance to tell you how sorry I am for the loss of your son."

Nathan froze with his back to the uniformed officer. He turned to face her with an unreadable expression.

"I've prayed to Saint Felicity for Cody." She paused to swallow, choosing her words carefully. "And for you and Kelly."

Alderson looked at the ground, unsure of what to say. A few tense seconds passed before he thanked her, then abruptly changed the subject.

"I should only be a few minutes."

Perez blushed and shrugged her shoulders. "I'll be here 'til you get back."

Alderson started up the trail, hoping it would lead him to the dirt roads Townsend had mentioned. After walking for several minutes, he emerged from the dense forest into a wide clearing. In the distance, over another grove of river birches, the detective saw the chimneys of the demolished plantation house.

Eyes forward and with laboring breath, he hurried through the overgrown crossroads at the center of the clearing. The trees began to thin out and he spied what remained of the plantation house. With a determined gait, he strode across the field, forging his way through weeds and yellow grass. The steady swish of dead leaves beneath his feet was loud and constant.

The large Georgian house was in ruins. The rectangular foundation remained intact, but the grimy rust-brick walls had crumbled into haphazard piles. More weeds shot up from between the debris while small saplings had taken root and forced their way up from the rubble. Hollow squares—formerly windows—still characterized a portion of the left side of the house, but the right side had completely fallen inward. Only the pair of chimneys pierced the skyline, yet both seemed poised to topple to the ground.

Alderson scanned the perimeter of the building, but nothing seemed out of the ordinary. Brown shards of smashed glass and a crumpled box of Swisher Sweets lay at his feet. A faded pentagram had been spray painted in black on the outside wall. He approached the open portal that had once been the front door. A quick glance revealed a veritable jungle of brush, vines, and wildflowers within the interior. The ground cover would have obscured any recent footprints, but the undisturbed nature of the weeds suggested no one had forged a path in or out of the ruin for several months.

As he peered through the doorway, Alderson could see the open field directly behind the house. With nothing obstructing his view, he crept forward and slowly made his way toward the corresponding entryway at the rear of the house. Careful to scan the ground as he walked, his suspicion that neither Tyler Marshall nor his killer had been inside the house was confirmed.

When he emerged behind the plantation, Alderson saw the mausoleum to his left. Its position at the edge of the property left the sides and rear of the building entirely obscured by trees. As he crossed the clearing, he reached under his coat and thumbed open the latch on his holster.

Like the plantation, the four-sided structure was also made of red brick. Enveloped in dry twisting vines, the weathered exterior appeared to be stable despite its apparent age. Just as Townsend said, one of the rusted iron doors hung askew from the topmost hinge. As Alderson inched closer, he could see the second door had fallen to the side of the entrance. It had lain on the ground so long it was almost entirely covered by weeds and had sunk into the earth.

Despite the light of the morning, the interior of the tomb was unusually dark. He fished a pen light from his pocket and poked his head inside. The thin beam danced along the walls of the mausoleum's interior.

After checking the corners, Alderson stepped inside to examine the vaults. Everything was as Townsend had described. The stone floor was littered with dead leaves. Scrawls of indecipherable graffiti tags marred the mildewed walls. The top two vaults at eye-level were empty. He aimed his flashlight downward to illuminate a plaque adorning the crypt in the lower-left corner.

The panel sported a green patina from years of exposure and had become heavily oxidized. Alderson began to pick away at the corrosion until he could read the name on the placard. In plain block letters, it read WILLIAM BRENNEN, BELOVED SON, 1851–1854.

He moved to check the next vault to the right. It was empty, save for thick cobwebs and a few tarnished coffin handles.

Alderson rose and turned on his heel to inspect the other side of the mausoleum. Glass crunched beneath his feet. He glanced at the stone floor but there were no footprints or bloodstains. Lifting his pen light, he scanned the pair of vaults on the upper tier. A few splinters of rotten wood lay near the back wall of the narrow crypt. A strong musty stench wafted from the second vault, which displayed signs of water-damage.

He squatted down to shine the thin beam of his pen light into the bottom left slot. Squinting his eyes, Alderson suddenly cried out and scrabbled backward.

"Fuck!"

The light swept across a pair of gleaming eyes. Instinctually, his free hand went for his pistol, but he steadied himself when he realized it was only a river rat nestled in the corner. The matted rodent scurried out of the vault, dragging its tail along the dirty floor as it sought to escape the intruder.

Calm the fuck down.

Now on his knees, he inspected the last vault in the lower right corner. Satisfied that it too was empty, he rose, dusted off his pants, and lingered at the center of the low-ceilinged room. He glanced up, shining the light at the roof. Through a series of holes, he could see pinpricks of gray sky.

Stepping out from the closeness of the tomb, Alderson inhaled the brisk autumn air. From where he stood, he had a partial view of the James River beyond the dense tree line ahead. He remained fixed for a moment, gazing at the slow-moving waters. He removed the safety gloves from each of his hands with a snap and stuffed them into the pockets of his coat.

As with the ruins of the main house, there was no evidence that the tomb had been recently occupied by any squatters. More importantly, it hadn't served as Tyler Marshall's kill site.

So, if not here, then where? None of this makes any sense. Who was waiting in these woods? Where did they go? And why Tyler Marshall? What's the connection?

The detective's musings were interrupted by his handheld radio and the crackling sound of the lead dispatcher's voice.

"Code-3. All units be advised. Vehicle fleeing scene of accident on Seventh and Main."

Alderson began to make his way back to the crime scene. Once again, his eyes were directed to the looming chimneys of the old plantation house. He paused and turned his back momentarily to look at the mausoleum. The detective reached into his coat pocket and withdrew his pen and tablet. Beneath the notes he made earlier that morning, he quickly scrawled the name he had read from the placard and underlined it twice for emphasis.

BRENNEN.

2

"ARE THERE ANY SPIRITS PRESENT?" DR. VERONICA UPHAM assessed the heavy silence. "We ask you to give us a sign that you are near."

The middle-aged medium and her three associates were assembled around a large circular table. The chandelier above them was turned off. Ivory candles had been positioned around the well-furnished den.

"Give us a sign that you are near," Veronica repeated. Her thin fingers were spread out beside a stack of paper and a row of sharpened pencils.

As she waited for a response, the professor reached up and adjusted the collar of her silk blouse. Her grandmother's pearl necklace lay against her chest, reflecting the light of the candles.

Peter Tully sat to Veronica's right. His dark eyes and thick hair made him look younger than fifty-four. At Veronica's left was Peter's wife Janice. Her delicate frame and bright eyes were inviting. Few would've guessed she spent her weekends dabbling in the occult. Eric Sandoval sat at the foot of the table facing their host. At twenty-six, he was the youngest of the group.

The iridescent light of the candles bathed the room in a luminous golden glow. Several tea lights flickered before each of the four participants and cast long shadows on their stern faces.

Within the smaller ring of glowing flames, an antique handbell had been placed alongside a pair of heavy brass candleholders. Two tapered candles were steadied within the narrow pedestals and towered above the rest. Beside these items, a hand-held digital voice recorder lay face up on the table's polished surface. A tiny red light indicated the device was recording their session.

When Peter arrived earlier that Saturday evening, he had set up a tripod at the far end of the dining room. He adjusted the lens of the digital camera to focus on Veronica. In the event of any anomalies, Peter made sure the dining room and a small portion of the living room were also in frame.

"Are there any spirits who wish to speak to us?"

There was no response to Veronica's query. With an encouraging nod, Peter motioned for her to continue.

The auburn-haired woman forced a quick smile in return and then stared straight ahead. She closed her hazel eyes and listened to the room as it began to settle.

Although the group held eventful circles in the past, their recent sittings had been intense and unpredictable. This was a direct result of Veronica's deepening commitment to the spirit world. What began as an eccentric hobby born from her professional study of Victorian literature was now a serious focus and concern.

As well, a series of terrifying experiences with Edison Raymer—her former colleague and lover—had permanently altered Veronica's perception of the world. She and Raymer witnessed incredible things, but there was still so much more she failed to comprehend. After discovering some of the answers, Veronica was driven to learn all that she could about the mysterious and arcane secrets of the world. And she was now free to do so without having to endure the egotism and condescension of Edison Raymer.

After another moment of silence, the air became heavier. The candle flames burned steady and low, as if frozen on their wicks. The deceptive quiet felt as if it was on the verge of disruption.

"Give us a sign that you are near." Veronica paused and let the stillness envelop her.

Peter Tully's eyes narrowed behind the rims of his spectacles. Eric remained captivated by the candles at the center of the table.

Veronica felt a faint breeze flit across her knuckles. The pair of votive candles before her seemed to flicker. She closed her eyes and made a concerted effort to absorb the energy stirring throughout the room.

Something's definitely happening.

The temperature began to drop. Eric leaned forward with his forearms braced against the table. The shadows seemed to draw closer around them. Janice raised her head and studied the expressions of her husband and the pale-faced medium beside her.

Veronica straightened her rigid posture as the small bell at the center of the table emitted a soft and resonant *ting*.

Janice gasped. Her eyes were riveted to the bell.

Veronica's heart raced and she tilted her head upward to survey the air around them. She spoke with greater command and authority.

"I'm addressing the entity who wishes to speak to us." Veronica's keen eyes searched the perimeter of the dining room. "Did you just ring our bell? Please. Knock on our table. Twice for yes, and once for no."

The table was struck with two sharp raps. Janice flinched as the faint vibrations spread beneath her fingers. Mindful not to break the circle, Eric leaned back in his chair and ducked his head to peek under the table. He cast a suspicious glance in the direction of Peter Tully. The older man shook his head at Eric's implication.

"Thank you." Veronica obliged the unseen presence and took a sharpened pencil in her right hand. She crossed with her left and slid a blank sheet of paper in front of her.

"If I were to write on this paper, will you try to give us a message?"

After a short pause, a single knock erupted from Eric's end of the table. His mouth opened in surprise. "That wasn't me!" His eyes darted from the face of Peter to Janice and then back to Veronica.

"You will not write for us?"

A more violent knock rattled the surface of the table. Veronica glanced at her pencils to discover two of them had been broken in half.

Peter noticed the splintered yellow pencils in front of the professor. He swallowed hard and took a cleansing breath.

"Do you still wish to communicate with us?" Veronica asked in a shaky tone.

Another harsh rap broke the silence, causing each of the adepts to jump in their seats. They glanced at each other in terror and looked to the medium for direction.

Veronica was ill at ease by the immediacy of their results. In the past, it took a fair bit of pleading to receive even the slightest response. This time, it was as if the spirit had been lurking somewhere around them before the séance began.

Something isn't right.

The anxious medium carefully studied the expressions of her colleagues. Each of them appeared to be as perplexed and unsettled as she.

Maybe it's Eric?

He's only been with us for a month or so.

But the reserved bookseller sat with his palms flat against the table. His jaw was taut behind his scruffy beard. When he felt Veronica's inquisitive gaze, he raised his eyes with a pleading look.

"It wasn't me," he whispered. "I swear."

"So what do we do now?" Janice turned to Veronica, then to her husband.

"I don't know," Peter replied. He glanced up and let his eyes sweep along the edges of the ceiling. "Do you think it's still here?"

"You can't feel that?" Eric was incredulous. "It's definitely still here!"

"You're right." Janice nodded. "But *what* is still here?"

Veronica winced and began to tremble.

None of them were prepared for this.

They have no idea what's really out there.

Just like I didn't know. Until Edison showed me.

She cleared her throat and hoped to maintain her outward composure.

This world is haunted by cruel, malicious, and terrible things. Things that are calculated and hide their faces in the dark. Things that we'll never understand.

"Ronnie?" Janice addressed the medium.

Things that can get inside our minds.

"Ronnie, are you listening?"

Things that can transform us into monsters.

Veronica was assailed by memories of a tall man with an angular close-cropped haircut. His face was contorted in rage. His eyes were black with hatred. Edison Raymer bent over him. He raised a heavy hammer above his head and swung it down. The silver stake plunged deep into the vampire's chest.

Stop it, Veronica.

She remembered kneeling on the ground where she and Raymer buried the body of Fenton Luttrell, Jr. Her stomach churned when she recalled the cunning eyes of Laura McCoy.

Concentrate, goddamn it!

"Ronnie!" Janice called out again and finally captured her attention. "Try to channel it. Maybe this time it'll work?"

Veronica shifted in her seat and steeled herself against her memories. "Put your hands back on the table. All of you," she ordered. "Keep the circle unbroken."

The medium nudged the writing utensils away and placed her palms against the table. She closed her eyes and exhaled. Her breast began to swell and recede, until she developed a slow and steady rhythm. The members of the circle watched her. In a matter of minutes, the lulling cadence of their deliberate breathing rose and fell in time with Veronica's respirations.

The cold seeped from every corner of the room. The flames of the taper candles at the center of the table weakened and fluttered. Janice's eyes widened as the color of the flames turned from bright orange to blue. "Something's happening. Look! The candles!"

"Stay focused, Janice!" Eric warned.

Each of the ivory pillar candles around Professor Upham's dining room were snuffed out one after the other. Peter shuddered, and Janice let out a low cry.

A soft wind swept across the face of the table and extinguished the remaining candles. The room was plunged into darkness.

"Keep calm." Veronica's dry voice wafted through the gloom. Peter slid his sweaty fingers forward and clasped the medium's hand. She jumped at the unexpected pressure.

Before their eyes, two distinct blue flames arose from the votive candles in front of the medium.

Black dread crept over Veronica Upham as the room seemed to swarm with moving shadows. Her vision blurred and her face felt numb. She could no longer feel her fingers or the surface of the table.

Just give in to it. You've seen worse. You've faced worse.

They're coming to you now, so you need to listen to them.

Isn't this what you've always wanted?

Veronica bowed her head and surrendered to the energy gathering around her. She began to roll her head in a slow circular motion. Several minutes passed as she let herself drift deeper into the trance. The participants of the séance observed her with curiosity. They could feel an aura of anticipation and unrest in the air.

Within her mind, Veronica improvised a steady yet simple mantra. *Come unto me, Come into me. Come unto me, Come into me. Come unto me...*

Before long, she felt a presence looming close beside her. It yearned to approach her, but hesitated—as if frightened.

Come into me.

"Mommy?"

Janice gasped as Veronica spoke aloud in an unfamiliar tone. After a few seconds of stunned silence, Peter took the lead and addressed the presence.

"What is your name?" he asked.

Veronica refused to look at Peter. She shifted in her chair and shook her head from side to side. She stared straight ahead, her gaze passing through Eric Sandoval.

"Can you please tell us your name?"

Her response was fragmented and delayed.

"Not sup— not ... supposed ... strangers."

The medium spoke with the unmistakable quaver of a young child.

"We're friends." Peter assured the spirit. "Don't be afraid. You can tell us your name."

"Tyler," the voice said.

"And how old are you, Tyler?"

The voice faltered before revealing its age.

"Seven."

"Was that you who rang our bell before?"

"No."

"Did you knock on our table?"

"I don't *think* so?"

"Did you see who did?"

"No."

"Can you see us from where you are, Tyler?"

"Yes."

"Where are you, son?"

"I don't know. I want my mommy."

"Is there anyone with you?"

The voice was silent.

"Besides us, what do you see?"

Veronica opened her eyes. She raised her eyebrows as an expression of confusion spread across her face. "I got lost," the voice finally managed.

"Where did you get lost?"

"In—in—in the woods."

"The woods?"

"Yeah."

"Are you alone in the woods?"

The boy once again hesitated to reply.

"No." Veronica's face took on a ghastly and terrified expression. "The lady!"

"What lady?"

"In the woods!" Tears began to stream down Veronica's cheeks. "There's a lady in the woods!"

"What's the lady doing?"

"Peter," Janice begged. "Please stop."

Eric glanced at the couple, and then back at Veronica. "Keep going."

"What does the lady look like? What is she doing?"

"Damn it, Peter. That's enough!" Janice dug her nails deep into her palms. "Stop it!"

But Peter was enthralled. He watched with wide eyes as Veronica's body began to quake violently in the chair.

22

"What is the lady doing?" Peter demanded. He leaned forward in anticipation of a reply.

"She's—she's—" the voice trembled. "Mommy?"

"What is... what is your mother doing to you, Tyler?"

"*She's not my mommy!*" the voice sobbed, drawing out each of the words in sorrow and fear.

"What does she look like, Tyler? Tell me what you see!"

Without warning, the medium let out a panicked scream. The shrill and woeful cries of the hyperventilating child rebounded against the walls until Veronica shrieked in her own anguished voice.

A cold rush of wind tore through the room and knocked one of the tall candles askew. Peter sank against his chair as his wife stared on in terror. Eric felt the frigid blast of stale air rush past him. He failed to see the flitting shadow sweep across the table, but the unwholesome feeling that accompanied the departing presence was impossible to ignore.

Veronica lay face down on the table. Her breathing was shallow and erratic. Janice moved to rouse the medium from her trance but thought twice about jarring her awake too soon. She had little time to think before she was overcome with nausea.

"Something... something smells damp. Or... or *moldy?*"

"Like dead leaves," Eric confirmed. "You can smell it too?"

Peter sat motionless and stared at the corner of the dining room. His eyes had glazed over, and he spoke not a word.

"Peter?" his wife called out. "Are you alright?"

"Fine," he responded. He turned his head toward Janice, but immediately glanced back at the corner behind Veronica.

"Peter, what is it? What did you see?"

"Nothing. Just... nothing. Forget about it."

A discomfiting silence fell over the bewildered members of the circle. Within a few minutes, the negative energy throughout the room had subsided, and the atmosphere became calm. Veronica's body slumped back into her chair. Her eyes slowly fluttered open. Still short of breath, she raised a trembling hand to swipe the damp strands of auburn hair from her face. The medium looked around the room with a confused and disoriented expression.

The wary participants slid their numb hands toward themselves and leaned back in silence. None of them, however, moved to stand.

"Veronica," Eric spoke up. "You need to close the circle."

At first, she didn't respond. Her expression was blank, and her teeth appeared to be chattering.

"Ronnie, listen to me," Eric commanded. "You cast the circle, so it's best you close it." He looked to Janice as she bit her lower lip. "Otherwise, you might be putting each of us at risk."

Veronica lifted her right hand and placed her palm outward toward the east. She then swept her left hand through the air in a sharp cutting motion. She turned her bloodshot eyes in the direction of Peter. "What the hell just happened here?"

Peter rose from the table without answering her. He walked toward the video camera and switched off the device. He then slammed his palm against the wall and spun the plastic dial to its maximum setting. Veronica flinched as the bright light of the chandelier stung her eyes.

Janice staggered to her feet. Her chair scraped across the hardwood floor and she laid a gentle hand on Veronica's shoulder. The medium was unsure if Janice hoped to comfort her or steady herself.

As if suspended in a dream, Veronica watched the others move around her. She felt drained and couldn't find the will to rise from the chair. She watched Janice extinguish the rest of the candles with a brass snuffer. Her eyes then wandered to Eric, who stood beside Peter. The two were whispering to one another. Peter's arms were crossed as he stole a glimpse in her direction.

Veronica closed her eyes. As she sat slumped in the chair, tuning out the noise created by the others, she could hear the mocking voice of Edison Raymer.

What exactly are you tapping into?

Ironically, a loud knock on the table startled Veronica from her daze. She glanced up at Janice and Peter, who stood crowded around her.

"You OK, Ronnie?" Janice withdrew her fist from the tabletop. "You've been out of it for a while now."

"Should we check and see if she had a seizure or something?" Eric asked.

"Do I look like a doctor to you?" Peter replied. His arms were still crossed, and his face was deathly pale. Veronica noticed he was shaking.

"Well, we can't just leave her like—"

"I'm fine." Veronica used the edge of the table to push herself up from the chair. She glanced at each of them until her eyes stopped on Janice. "How long was I out?"

"I don't know, maybe half an hour?"

"I can't... I can barely remember anything," Veronica admitted. "What happened after—"

"It'll be on the video." Peter nodded. "All of it." He covered his mouth to stifle a sudden cough.

Janice gave her husband a strange look. Eric lowered his eyes and shoved his hands into the pockets of his hoodie.

"Well, I guess it's pretty late," Janice said. "Why don't you give us a call tomorrow afternoon? Maybe we can come by sometime this week and go over the video with you?"

"Sure," Veronica said. "That'd be great."

They're terrified.

What the fuck is going on? They'll barely even look at me.

Peter gave a curt nod to Veronica and led his wife through the living room to gather their coats. The couple departed without another word.

Eric slid on his leather jacket and adjusted the black hoodie underneath. Although clearly rattled, he seemed more concerned with Veronica than himself and continued to linger.

"You sure you're gonna be OK tonight?" he asked. "You, uh, you want me to stay?"

"No, Eric. That's quite alright."

Christ, I'm more than twenty years older than him.

"I'm sorry. I just thought... I mean I wasn't trying—"

"It's OK. There's no need to explain yourself." Veronica hoped to spare the feelings of the shy bachelor without revealing her own loneliness. "I just think I need to, uh, to figure out what the hell happened here."

"You channeled," he confirmed. "But it wasn't anything like the last time. This was much stronger. The knockings were extremely precise, and everything was more coherent."

"I don't remember any of it."

"Peter had a full conversation with it," he said.

"What? But I—"

"Yeah." Eric nodded. "And it was one of the most fucked up things I've ever seen *or* heard."

"Christ," Veronica muttered. "The last thing I remember are the rappings." Her throat was parched, and her voice sounded hoarse. "But yeah, you're right. The rappings never happened so quickly, and the responses are usually delayed."

"There were at least five this time," Eric said. "And I looked under the table. It wasn't Peter or Janice. And it sure as hell wasn't me."

"No..." Veronica drifted off. "Me either."

"But what happened after that is what concerns me," Eric warned. He cleared his throat and rallied his confidence. "When I offered to stay, I wasn't trying to be weird. It's just... you need to be careful tonight. I know you're tired, but if I were you, I'd do a cleansing right away. You may be vulnerable to another attack. Or possibly some kind of... invasion."

That ain't the half of it, kid. I've been waiting for Laura McCoy to come crashing in here for two years. But the vampire we spared hasn't darkened my doorstep yet. Nothing I channeled could be worse than what's already out there waiting for me.

"I'll be fine, Eric. Really. Thanks for looking out for me." Her thoughts returned to Janice and Peter's abrupt departure. "But I don't know what got into *them*. I've known Peter and Janice for years. We've held sittings for as long as I can remember, and they never acted like this."

"I don't think they were expecting something this intense," Eric said. "You'll see what I mean when you review the footage."

"Right..." Veronica trailed off again, her eyes tracing the patterns of a large area rug under her coffee table.

"Listen, don't look at those files tonight. Wait 'til morning," he cautioned. "If things get weird, call me. I can be back in less than an hour."

"OK, thank you." Veronica forced a smile. "Hey, before you go, do you happen to have any cigarettes on you?"

"I didn't know you smoked."

"I don't... usually."

"No, sorry," he chuckled. "I don't either. But I could go pick some up for you if you want? That corner store over on—"

"No, I don't wanna be a bother. It's fine. I'm just gonna turn in."

"OK." The young man gave the professor a reluctant nod and wandered toward the foyer. "But don't forget to bless the house before you go to bed. I'm serious."

"I know. I will. Goodnight, Eric."

"Goodnight," he replied and closed the front door.

When she heard his car backing out of the driveway, she returned to the dining room and switched off the glaring chandelier. Veronica stumbled back into the living room to retrieve a tumbler and a bottle of whiskey from her bar cart. She took a book of matches from the end table, relit a handful of candles, made her way to the couch, and then plopped down with the bottle and glass in hand. Veronica reached for the television remote to fill the deafening silence. She scanned the menu to find the high-definition radio stations and settled on one that played chamber music.

You really don't need to drink.

She frowned at the thought.

Right. I need drinks. Plural.

By the light of a few flickering candles, Veronica poured herself the first of several glasses of Scotch. Within the hour, she passed out as Albinoni's lugubrious *Adagio in G Minor* echoed throughout her house.

3

"KELLY, I'VE GOTTA GO." NATHAN ALDERSON CRADLED the phone between his shoulder and his ear as a barrage of sharp knocks assailed his office door. "Maybe. I'll try but I can't promise—"

"It's McCain." The voice outside his office door was curt and perfunctory.

The detective was about to say goodbye to his wife when he realized she hung up on him. Alderson slammed the receiver back on the hook. "Come in, Frank."

McCain sat down in a chair across from Alderson's desk. He slapped a manila folder down on his partner's blotter, which was covered in departmental forms, paperwork, and a collection of handwritten notes. "That's the second draft report from Forensics."

"I'm guessing the prints didn't match with the mother?" Alderson asked.

"Not even close." McCain sighed. "The fingerprint query came back with nothin' after a long general search."

"No surprises there." Alderson leaned back in his chair. "You learn anything else after talkin' to Ms. Marshall?"

"She didn't do this, Nate." McCain fumbled for a pack of cigarettes, then stopped himself. "She was beside herself in here yesterday. Seems like she really doted on the boy. Maybe a bit overprotective, if that ain't the irony of ironies. I also got the sense he might've been a little behind his peers. You know, like developmentally."

Alderson nodded and waited for McCain to continue.

"Anyway, I asked her why they were at the playground so late in the day and she said she regularly took him there after school so he could have the playground to himself. Guess some of the kids made fun of him at recess or whatever. That particular day they didn't get there until after dinner and were getting ready to leave when he bolted into the woods. She said he never ran off like that before."

"OK." Alderson raised an eyebrow. "So what's the story with the kid's father?"

"Never got hitched. He didn't spend a day raisin' his boy. Just sent child support payments."

"Think he might be the jealous type?"

"If he is, there wouldn't be much he could do about it. Sperm donor's in the Navy. Currently deployed to the Persian Gulf on a guided missile destroyer. I think that rules him out." McCain shuffled his feet. "So, it's back to square one, eh?"

"Looks that way." Alderson rubbed his forehead with his right hand, hoping to stave off a burgeoning headache.

McCain leaned forward and crossed his hands on the surface of Alderson's desk. "So, what are you thinkin'? What exactly *is* square one?"

"Well, one thing is abundantly clear." Alderson glared at his colleague. "I've been looking at Rudy Pettit's notes all morning. There's a lot of gaps here. Sloppy work, as far as I'm concerned."

"Now, Rudy was a decent detective. I worked with the guy for almost thirty years. So don't go—"

"If he was so goddamned good at his job, why'd he leave so many stones unturned?" Alderson gestured at the computer screen. "Like this Stroud case. He had leads, but hardly left any notes."

"Well, that was the last case he worked before his retirement. I'm not gonna deny he was lame-duckin' that one, but..." McCain trailed off. "Wait a sec. I take that back. He investigated an arson in a townhouse row near the college. Suspect skipped town or somethin'. Can't remember the guy's name, but it—"

"Edison Raymer?" Alderson clicked his mouse to scroll through Pettit's notes. "Says here he was a professor at Williamsport. Also considered a person of interest in the Stroud case. They put a BOL on him after Pettit retired. Quite a list of felony charges. Arson, insurance fraud, withholding evidence. It went statewide. Again, no leads or sightings. His picture was on TV, the internet, and in every post office in Virginia. We didn't get a single call about him."

"Weird." Something on Alderson's desk caught McCain's attention. "Hey, what's this doin'..."

The older detective reached forward and righted an overturned picture frame that was face down on the desk. The photograph behind the glass was a close-up of Nathan Alderson and his son Cody holding fishing rods. The James River glistened in the background. WORLD'S GREATEST DAD was painted across the bottom.

"Dammit, Frank." Alderson glared at McCain. "That was like that for a reason."

"Nate, I don't think you're ready to be back here. Especially with a case like this. You need to—"

"Leave it." Alderson tipped the framed picture over so he wouldn't have to see his son's smiling face. "I need to work, Frank. I told you. I'm fine."

"Well, you ain't actin' fine is all I'm tryin' to say."

"Look, this whole thing is a fuckin' mess. Someone needs to clean up all the shit Pettit couldn't handle. I've been looking over his notes from the '90s on those missing kids. They're all in the database."

McCain tightened his fingers around the arms of the chair. "And?"

Alderson leaned in to read the text on the flatscreen monitor. "Emily Ryerson. Parents reported her missing in July of 1993. The family lived at the end of a street bordering those woods. Mother said she went out after supper to catch fireflies. Didn't come home. They went looking for her in the woods, but she disappeared without a trace."

"I vaguely remember that one." McCain nodded. "Just like this case, they called us in with the dogs and a civilian search party. But nobody found a damned thing."

"Sylvia Aptheker. Summer of 1995, just as I remembered." Alderson scrolled through the notes. "She was getting ready to start kindergarten in the fall. Parents let her wander under the bleachers while they watched her older brother play in a Summer League home game. That was the one I was telling you about at the crime scene." He shifted in his seat. "She ran up the same trail as Tyler Marshall and was never seen again."

"Her parents shoulda kept an eye on her." McCain buried his face in his open palms, took a deep breath, then cast a weary stare at the younger detective. "You see why Pettit figured it was an abduction?"

"No, Frank, I don't." Alderson shook his head. "Not after Justin Rooker. He disappeared in those same woods while deer hunting. Just a few months after the Aptheker girl. Rooker was within earshot of his father and some other adults. And he was armed and old enough to fight back. If the perp didn't off him outright, you know a twelve-year-old with a hunting rifle would've raised holy hell—"

"Still coulda been an abduction." McCain shrugged. "Perp coulda been hidin' out with a chloroform-soaked rag. You know, gave the kid a face full of liquid shut-up, then put him over his shoulder and slinked outta there."

"You watch too many movies." Alderson shot McCain a dubious glance.

"Can't deny I've seen my share of slasher flicks. They're a guilty pleasure of mine." The older detective shook his head. "Anyway, can we go back to the Stroud suspect? He was never caught. The method of attack is the same, only this time, he went a little further and—"

"Look, Frank. I'm not ruling out this Matthias Bartsch character. Problem is, I can't find anything on him."

"Same problem we ran into. We had that bastard's name, his place of employment. Hell, we crashed his apartment, but he was gone without a trace. Motherfucker was a pro at coverin' his tracks. Maybe he turned into a bat and flew away?"

"That's not funny, Frank." Alderson leveled an irritated stare at his partner. "We're clearly dealing with someone with a dangerous—if not psychotic—pathology. You saw what the killer did to that boy. It's not something to joke about."

"OK, fine. Sorry." McCain avoided his partner's eyes.

"Anyway, I'm still not convinced it was Bartsch. And if that's the case, then we need to accept the fact that there's *another* suspect on the loose with the same deviant tendencies."

"Which is *very* unlikely in a place like this," McCain fired back. "But, OK, I'll humor you. Did you check with INTERPOL? If you wanna rule out Bartsch as a suspect, then we need to prove he was nowhere near Williamsport on Friday night. Hell, check with the airports in Richmond and Norfolk for passenger manifests. Call a few rental car places. Even fuckin' Amtrak. See if he's already flown the coop or if he's got a hasty retreat planned for some time this week."

"Let's hope he's never heard of the concept of an alias."

McCain exhaled in frustration. "I'm just spit-ballin' here, Nate. We've got options."

"Why don't you follow up on that then? See if you can find anything on him." Alderson returned to the computer monitor. "In the meantime, I'll try to make sense of Pettit's mess. I still don't understand why his trail led from the Stroud girl to a college administrator, and then to this shady professor, who has *also* conveniently fallen off the grid."

"I dunno." McCain unfolded his hands to rub the back of his neck. "Rudy was tight-lipped about the whole thing. But I'm pretty sure he and the Dean were buddies from high school or somethin'. So maybe it was just an excuse to go shoot the shit?"

"There's obviously more to this. Some other connection. But there's nothing in Pettit's notes."

"Shit, if you're so worried about his notes, why don't we just call the guy?" McCain leaned back to dig for his cell phone. He struggled to fish the device from his pocket. "He's down in Florida, collectin' his pension and livin' the dream. I'm sure he'd be *thrilled* to hear from us and how inadequate you find his note takin' skills to be."

"Absolutely not," Alderson replied. "He's the last person I wanna talk to. If he didn't have the foresight to write any of this shit down back then, what makes you think he's gonna remember the details now? No, that's a hard pass from me."

"Well, if you change your mind..." McCain trailed off and chuckled under his breath. "Honestly, I think you need a breather. You're overthinkin' it. I mean, the girl was a college student. So Pettit checked to see if there were any other incidents on campus. That's standard procedure. Or maybe he was lookin' to see if some foreign exchange student was involved?"

"Yeah, but what's the deal with the professor?" Alderson asked. "He wasn't a German teacher, or an ESL instructor. Says here he was in the anthropology department. Something isn't right."

"Well, you've clearly convinced yourself of that." McCain paused to scratch his head. "So now what?"

"I guess I'll go pay a visit to the Dean of Students. It'll probably be a waste of time but I gotta start somewhere." Alderson paused. "The only other thing I've got is a name associated with the old plantation house in those woods. I'm curious if anyone still owns that place or if it's had any other owners. I'd also like to find out when it was last inhabited."

"Shit, it's probably nothin'. There're places like that all over this area."

"Not exactly. Plantation houses along the river are of historical interest. A site like that is a goldmine for attracting tourists. But for whatever reason, that place was left to crumble in the woods. My question is why?"

"Did you check it out yesterday?"

"Yeah, but like Townsend said, there were no signs anyone's been up there recently. My question to you is, do you remember investigating it back when the Ryerson and Aptheker girls went missing?"

"Christ, I don't remember, Nate. That was almost twenty-five years ago! Is there anything in the reports?"

"No, which leads me to believe the house was already abandoned and dismissed as a site of interest. Or that no one bothered to look into it."

"Well, from the sounds of it, it'd be pretty fuckin' hard to miss. In any case, I think you're better off looking for that kraut vampire wannabe and leave the haunted house investigations to one of the rookies."

"Duly noted, Frank."

"Well, I guess that's my cue." McCain rose and stretched. "You oughta go home early. Spend the rest of your Sunday with that wife of yours. This case'll still be here tomorrow."

"Nah, I need to work it now," Alderson muttered as he flipped through the file McCain had brought him. Autopsy photos of the dead boy spilled onto his desk. "Kelly's making dinner tonight and I just told her I'd be working until—"

"I'm serious. This job can wait. Your wife needs your company. It's been barely two months since Cody drowned—"

Alderson raised a hand in protest. "Spare me the sermon, Frank. I know what my responsibilities are. She deals with it her way. I deal with it mine. End of story."

McCain stopped on his way out the door. "You're supposed to deal with this shit *together*. Think about it, pal."

"Believe me, I have." Alderson arranged the photos into a neat pile on his desk. "You take care, Frank."

"I'll follow up on Bartsch and call you tomorrow." McCain's voice echoed back from the hallway. "Go home, Nate."

Alone again, the detective closed Pettit's case notes and brought up the database search screen. He typed in a general query: MISSING CHILDREN. A string of unfamiliar names scrolled down the screen in alphabetical order. He narrowed the search by adding SOUTH WILLIAMSPORT ELEMENTARY SCHOOL.

Five names came back.

...ADAMS, DANIEL T.

...APTHEKER, SYLVIA J.

...BENSON, SALLY

...RYERSON, EMILY

...ROOKER, JUSTIN M.

Two of the names—Adams and Benson—weren't hyperlinked in the database, which meant the entries predated the 1980s. He picked up the phone and dialed the Archives room in the basement.

"Archives and Recordkeeping. This is Carpenter."

"Yeah, Tom. It's Nate Alderson. I need you to pull records on two names."

"Let me get a pen..." The archivist—who was pushing seventy and refused to retire—rummaged around his desk. "OK. Shoot."

"Benson, Sally and—"

34

"No middle initial on that one?"

"That's correct. The second is Adams, Daniel T."

There was a pause on the other end of the line. "You mind me askin' what this is for?"

"I'm doing research on children who went missing around South Williamsport Elementary. A couple of these names aren't in the database, so—"

"I can tell you why," Tom Carpenter said. "Heck, I went to South Williamsport a few years after it was built. That school went up in 1955." Carpenter sighed through the receiver. "Back in those days, we did duck-and-cover drills every Wednesday, and there was—"

"That's great, but I need you to pull these files and have them brought to my office as soon as possible." Alderson tightened his grip in the phone. "I'm trying to corroborate—"

"Would it help your research if I told you I knew Danny Adams?"

Alderson licked his lips. "Go on, Tom."

"Yeah, Danny was a couple grades behind me. Had this bull terrier named Bruno. It was the damndest thing. The kid lived a few blocks down from the school. He walked that dog every night after supper, rain or shine. He wouldn't play ball or army or nothin' like the rest of us—"

"Listen, if it's all the same to—"

"Let me finish." The wizened archivist's voice took on a haughty air. "He went missing one night in '59, out walkin' his dog. I remember it like it was yesterday. The principal called us all into the auditorium the next morning and told us Danny Adams went up in those woods by the school and never came back."

"How soon can you get me that report?"

"Give me half-hour at most. Prob'ly won't take that long as the names are right close together."

"Know anything about the Benson girl?"

"Personally? No, sir."

Alderson exchanged pleasantries and hung up the phone. Immediately, his mind wandered.

He went into those woods and never came back.

1959.

Alderson rubbed his jaw and began to sort through the gruesome autopsy photos of Tyler Marshall. Ash Townsend had penned notes in the margins. He picked up one and scanned it with half-hearted attention.

What the hell does this mean?

Kids have been going into those woods and not coming back for decades.

He flipped open his notes and read them over. On a clean page, he scrawled two words.

CULT KILLINGS?

He narrowed his eyes at the black ink on the page and bit the top of his pen.

There are no satanic cults in Williamsport, Virginia. It has to be something else. Maybe some local family's been...

Wait a minute.

Alderson minimized the database search window and opened a general web browser. In the search bar, he typed the name BRENNEN followed by WILLIAMSPORT and VIRGINIA.

The varied results consisted of nothing more than recent obituaries and social media profiles. He revised his search to BRENNEN PLANTATION. The results included a real-estate agency in Pennsylvania, a history museum in South Carolina, and a car dealership in Richmond.

Nothing.

He clicked his ballpoint pen open and shut. Still fighting the encroaching headache, Alderson dug through his top drawer for a bottle of aspirin and dry swallowed two tablets.

This killer family shit's straight outta one of McCain's slasher movies. Absolutely ridiculous. But I need to look into the history of that property. See if there's a deed on the Surry County Assessment site. Find out who owned that place and how long it's been abandoned.

Or maybe...

Alderson picked up his phone and redialed the archivist. After several rings, the elderly man answered and discreetly tried to catch his breath.

"Archives. Carpenter here."

"Hey Tom, it's Nate again. I have another question for you."

"I was just about to send those files up to you. But first I need to find one of those interdepartmental envelopes we usually use to—"

"Never mind that, Tom. Listen, do you remember if there were any buildings up in those woods? Back where Danny Adams disappeared?"

"Well, the path was just near the elementary school, as I mentioned to you earlier."

"What about further back? Maybe a plantation house?"

"Oh yeah, come to think of it, there was. A big ol' place. All burnt up and fallin' to hell. We used to play cops 'n' robbers up there."

"So it was already abandoned back then?"

"Yes, sir. That place's been up there for as long as I can remember. No idea who it belonged to or how long it was there." Carpenter paused and took a deep breath. "There used to be a mausoleum of some kind back there too. Sometimes we'd dare each other to go inside when we were kids. To be honest with you, I never really liked that place much. Once Richie Stanton's older brother Jim bought his Chevy convertible, we didn't spend much time playin' in the woods."

"Does the name Brennen mean anything to you, Tom?"

"No, sir. I'm afraid that doesn't ring a bell."

"OK, thanks, Tom. Appreciate your help."

"Much obliged, Detective. Your files are on the way. Let me know if you need anything else."

Alderson hung up the phone and sighed.

So that place has been unoccupied for more than seventy years. No one lived there in the 1990s and no one lived there back in the 1950s.

Another dead end.

Alderson's eyes glazed over as he stared out the window. Moments later, a uniformed officer arrived with the archival files he requested. The detective cleared a space on his desk and opened Sally Benson's file.

The paper was old and faded. The staple holding the sheets together had stained the left corner rust red. The missing persons report had been filed in 1965. There was a black and white photo of Sally Benson, who had features consistent with Down's syndrome and wore her hair in two pigtails.

The police notes were limited to an interview with her grandfather. He stated for the record that Sally lived with him and his wife and attended a special education school in town. Roy and Alma Benson lived down the road from the elementary school, but her grandparents kept her away from the regular kids because they teased her.

Just like the Marshall boy.

From what the reporting officer could piece together from the short interview, her grandmother took her to the school playground on Sunday to play. 'When all the Baptists were in church and no other kids were around,' or so Grandpa Benson told the interviewing officer. That time, they'd gone off before sundown but never came back. The grandfather headed over to the playground to find his wife dead on a park bench. The county medical examiner had attached a carbon paper form to the packet. According to his autopsy report, Grandma Benson had a massive coronary while seated on the bench.

Of course, the child had disappeared. Roy was insistent that Sally 'probably thought her Nana was asleep' and 'went off into the woods to collect pinecones or look for bird's nests,' something she'd been scolded for on numerous occasions. The report claimed Grandpa Benson was 'always cleaning out sticks and acorns from the girl's bedroom.'

Armed with that information, the police combed the forest, and found a pile of acorns, wildflowers, and a nest full of smashed eggs scattered across a footpath.

What they didn't find was Sally Benson.

Alderson opened the file on Danny Adams, and an even older and more brittle police report slid out. Everything Carpenter had said on the phone matched the police report. There had also been a witness. A custodian at the school had been outside smoking a cigarette by his car. He saw the boy struggling to reign in his dog on the sidewalk. The dog broke the leash and scurried into the dark woods, so the Adams kid ran after his pet. The custodian tried to chase after the boy but when he couldn't find him, he called the sheriff.

There was a wrinkled photo shoved between the pages, but it wasn't of Danny Adams. It showed the limp body of a bull terrier with a broken neck. Alderson flipped it over and read the note on the back.

DOG KILLED NEAR X-ROADS.

He let the picture slide from his fingers.

Crossroads.

Five missing kids. Maybe more.

One confirmed dead under investigation.

Even a possible animal sacrifice.

Maybe there is an occult angle?

He scanned the file, but, as with the Benson girl, the boy hadn't been found. His sinuses began to throb, and he knew a migraine was on the way.

Now what the fuck do I do?

He locked his computer, staggered to his feet, and made his way into the hall. His entire body was racked with chills, so he leaned against a heat vent.

Easiest thing to do is pare this down. No suspect, no prints, no leads. A record of disappearances that's older than I am.

He let the warm air blow across his face as he fought the nausea rising from his stomach.

I'll pick up where Pettit left off. See if I can find any leads on the German. Talk to the receptionist at the nursing home if she still works there. Find out why Rudy went to see Dean Ritter, and what was so damned important about Professor Edison Raymer.

Suddenly, his train of thought shifted. He swallowed once to ameliorate the oncoming sickness and, with purpose, began walking toward the elevators. Alderson pressed the down arrow and waited for a car. When the doors rattled open, he stepped into the elevator and mashed a button marked B1. When he reached the basement of the police station, the detective sped out of the elevator and down a maze of corridors toward the forensics lab. Just as he turned the corner, he stopped himself from colliding with Ash Townsend.

The lead forensics technician jumped in fright and nearly dropped her belongings. A heavy coat was draped over her arm. She reeked of formaldehyde and surgical alcohol.

"Where're you off to in such a hurry, Townsend?"

"Home." The startled technician caught her breath. "I got two kids and I'd like to see them for at least a few hours this weekend. I mean, I worked all day yesterday and this morning on this—"

"I need to ask you something." He paused to choose his words with care. "A favor, if you will."

"I've already spent a day and a half doing legwork for you and McCain while trying to help the pathologists with the body. You ordered us to run the prints and they came back inconclusive. Not my fault. What else do you want me to do? I've got a dead boy in there and have no—"

"Hear me out," Alderson said. "I've been reviewing Detective Pettit's case notes and other material from the archives. Five kids have disappeared in those woods since 1959. Maybe more that we don't know about."

"I'm sorry to hear that, but so what?" Townsend leveled a cold gaze at the detective.

"What the hell do you mean, *so what?* How can you be so insensitive to—"

"Look, Nate. It's been a long weekend. I'm running on less than four hours of sleep. What do you want?"

"Pettit had three cases involving kids that went missing in that forest in the 1990s. Yet he never entertained the possibility that they were murdered out there, so he never ordered a geophysical survey from your department, did he?"

"I don't know. That was way before my time." Townsend tried to move past him, but Alderson took a step to block her path.

"Wait." Alderson held up a hand. "I know that. But I think there might be at least three or four graves near that crime scene. Maybe more."

"Graves?" Townsend shook her head. "Are you serious? What the hell do you want me to do about this?"

"Conduct a geophysical assessment of that area. There's a possibility we've got a child killer that just went active again after twenty years of down time."

"If you're right, and that much time's elapsed, then methane probes aren't gonna turn up a thing." Townsend raised her voice in protest. "You'd be better off going up there with a shovel and—"

"You're right about the methane probes. But ground penetrating radar would yield better results."

"We don't have that kind of technology." Townsend's thin lips pressed into a wan smile.

"Norfolk does. So does Virginia Beach and Richmond. Now, you can go to D'Amato about this, or I can. But in the end, you know as well as I do that when a detective requests a geophysical survey, it's on your department to make it happen. If I—"

"Alright, dammit. I'll ask him about it. *Tomorrow.*"

Alderson could tell she was dreading the legwork that was about to be foisted on her team. Townsend continued, "I'm gonna need something in writing from you making a formal request. And I want McCain to co-sign it."

"Consider it done."

"Can I offer you a piece of advice, though?"

He gave a curt nod and began to walk with her down the hall to the elevators.

"I wouldn't get your hopes up about D'Amato. He's not gonna rubber-stamp a request based on circumstantial evidence and a vague hunch." She caught herself. "No offense, Detective."

"None taken," Alderson muttered.

"If I were in your shoes, I'd keep looking for the sicko that attacked the college girl." Townsend stopped at the elevator doors. "If you think we're gonna dig up some old bones and you'll somehow solve this boy's murder, you'll drive yourself crazy."

Alderson turned toward the elevator doors.

"One more thing, Nate." Townsend shifted her coat from one arm to the other.

"Yeah?" He looked down at his scuffed shoes.

"This is a really fucked up case. Maybe you ought to let McCain lead this one."

"Why? I'm perfectly capable of—"

"I know you are... capable... or at least you *were*. But after what happened with Cody, maybe it's... Christ, I can't imagine what it would be like to lose one of mine, y'know?"

"Then think about how Tyler Marshall's mother feels right now," Alderson snapped. "Or how those other families felt when their kids went missing out in that goddamned forest. There needs to be closure here."

"Is that what all this is about for you, Nate?" Townsend asked and observed him closely. "Closure?"

Alderson stepped into the waiting elevator and held the door for Townsend. He ignored the implications of the woman's words and added a qualification of his own.

"Just remember everything I said when you see D'Amato tomorrow. I think there's a lot more going on here than anyone realizes."

4

STILL DRESSED IN HER WHITE BLOUSE AND BLACK SLACKS, Veronica Upham awoke to a migraine headache and a quiet house. She raised herself into a sitting position and ran her fingers through her tangled hair. Her mouth was dry. The sour pang of acid reflux caused her to lean forward on the couch. She lifted her head and wearily looked around the living room.

I could've sworn I left the TV on...

She recoiled with a startled cry when she saw the figure of Junior Luttrell sitting in her wingback chair. His head was cocked to the side. Dark blood had congealed on the front of his filthy work shirt. She rubbed her eyes in disbelief as the scowling apparition faded in the late morning sun.

The stunned professor stared at the empty chair. She could hear birds chirping outside her living room window. The tension occasioned by the phantom's appearance soon gave way to a mundane sense of normalcy and calm.

Get your shit together. For Christ's sake.

Veronica rose and stumbled into her kitchen to brew a fresh pot of coffee. She needed something stronger than her usual cup of tea. The professor checked the time and grabbed her cell phone from an end table in the den. After five rings, Janice Tully's voicemail picked up. Veronica left a brief message. As she walked toward the staircase, she cast a wary glance into the living room and was relieved to see the chair remained unoccupied.

43

Her head continued to throb as she made her way up the stairs. The professor's joints ached with the onset of rheumatoid arthritis. Once she stood in the upstairs hallway, she flung open a narrow closet, snatched a towel from an upper shelf, and entered the bathroom. She emerged fifteen minutes later in a gray terrycloth robe and the towel wrapped around her wet hair.

With a hot cup of coffee steaming on the dining room table, Veronica opened her laptop and waited for the computer to boot up. She glanced at her phone to see if Janice had returned her call while she was in the shower, but she hadn't. Instead, a new text message had arrived from Eric Sandoval. Dr. Upham thumbed a quick reply.

"Doing fine, Eric. Thanks again. Talk soon."

"It's better not to encourage him," she said aloud with a wistful smile.

Why the hell not? You haven't been laid in months. That disastrous blind date Professor Coffey set up for you is better left forgotten.

Veronica mused on the absurdity of taking a new lover at her age.

All that awkward fumbling in the dark? It's just not worth it anymore. Besides, the last person Eric slept with was probably some twenty-five-year-old with a perfect body.

Her thoughts returned to Edison Raymer. She hadn't seen him since the morning after their confrontation with Matthias Bartsch and Laura McCoy.

The night Junior died.

No wonder he can't rest. You left him to rot in a shallow grave in the middle of the woods. The two of you rolled him into a hole and never looked back.

After she heard about the fire at his townhouse, she tried Raymer's cell phone for weeks. Before long, the line was disconnected, and he disappeared without a trace. About a year later, she received an email from him. There was no note, just a hyperlink that opened to a digital newspaper article about a suicide on the outskirts of Annapolis. Although the casual reader may have glossed over the clues, the professor knew immediately why her estranged colleague had sent her the link.

The twenty-three-year-old victim's name was Robyn Carter. She had been treated for symptoms of anemia and dehydration for a week prior to her apparent suicide. One morning the girl's mother broke into her apartment and found her daughter dead in an empty bathtub. The girl had bled to death. Her wrists and forearms were severely mutilated. However, the police found very little blood on the scene, 'and presumed most of the deceased's blood had been washed down the drain before detectives arrived.'

The article not only confirmed that Edison was still obsessed with vampires, it was also an invitation. She could hear his insistent voice in her head.

There's still work to be done, Veronica.

You either stand with me, or you stand against me.

But she didn't accept his offer to 'play in the big leagues' as he once threatened her. She wrote a frantic email in response, but he never replied.

Sometimes she wondered if Laura McCoy had gotten him. It was possible the vampire struck him down when he was least prepared. A part of her wondered if in fact Edison had run from Laura, and that the fire was a way to cover his tracks.

But if she did kill him, it's only a matter of time before she'll come after me.

Yet Veronica had known Raymer for more than twenty years. The more probable scenario was that Laura McCoy had somehow perished in that fire.

That would explain why she hasn't shown up here.

The fact that Raymer never confirmed Laura's death was likely deliberate. He probably expected her to beg him for protection.

Not this time. I'm not gonna spend my life as your goddamn puppet. I may be lonely, but I sure as hell don't need you anymore.

Veronica's thoughts returned to the task at hand. She was eager to review the audio and video footage from the séance. Although she still couldn't remember anything after the first few knocks on the table, she knew the previous night's session was different. She never felt so drained after a sitting, nor had she ever blacked out.

Peter and Janice never acted so weird before, either.

The professor gathered the camcorder and hand-held audio device. After connecting the proper cords from the video camera to the rear of her laptop, Veronica took a sip of coffee. She clicked on a prominent shortcut to open the video editing software. While she waited for the data to transfer, she made herself some buttered toast.

She took a deep breath and loaded the video recording. After increasing the volume on her laptop, she clicked the mouse, and the file began to play.

"Dammit," the professor muttered. The screen was marred by the glare of the sun pouring into the dining room. As the first few seconds of the video began to play, she dashed across the room to close the heavy drapes.

Veronica's eyes adjusted to the image on the screen. Despite the dim lighting, the recording had captured the room very well. The dining room was bathed in a warm glow and she could clearly see herself positioned at the head of the table. She heard her voice seeping from the speakers.

"Are there any spirits who wish to speak to us?"

She watched the early portions of the séance with rapt attention—from her initial questions and invitation, through the inexplicable chime of the small handbell at the center of the table. The sight of the dimly lit room preserved on the video file had an uncanny effect on her. Yet so far, the camera hadn't captured anything out of the ordinary besides the faint sound of the bell. But she saw nothing in the video to account for how the sound was made.

As the video neared the sequence of table rappings, Veronica studied the footage very carefully.

"Did you just ring our bell? Please. Knock on our table. Twice for yes, and once for no."

With each successive knock, the participants around the table expressed genuine shock and surprise. Although she couldn't see Eric's face because his back was to the camera, she could clearly see that neither his hands nor his feet had produced any of the raps.

Her voice rang out again on the video. *"You will not write for us?"*

This must be when the pencils were broken.

Veronica paused the video and zoomed in on the row of thick pencils that had been lined up beside her.

She clicked an icon near the top of the screen, which slowed the video to half a frame per second. After adjusting the contrast so the image was sharper, she triggered a loop with the software and watched the short sequence replay several times in a row. But there was no way to account for it—the pencils had just split in half.

How the hell did that happen?

The professor was bewildered. A knot began to form in her stomach. As with the flick of the handbell, there was no visual evidence to account for the physical phenomena.

She froze the video again, zoomed in closer to the tabletop, and boosted the brightness to eighty percent. Once satisfied with the image onscreen, she applied another filter to clean up any noise produced by the exaggerated settings and restarted the loop.

Veronica watched in horror as a shadowy orb collided against the table. *Jesus Christ.*

She swallowed hard and noted the timestamp of the entire loop. She saved the sequence as a separate file simply titled PENCILS.

Before she let the video play further, she backed up and applied the same filter and settings to the portion of the séance when the bell rang. After zooming in on the small knick-knack, she could discern a slight shadow at the side of the bell.

With her heart pounding in her chest, she saved this new file as BELL. Veronica braced herself and allowed the video to proceed to the next sequence.

So this must be before I started to channel, when I was starting to zone out. I remember everything up until this point.

Veronica listened to the anxious whispers between Janice and the others. She kept her eyes locked on her own image, nodding as she watched herself direct the participants to keep their hands on the table and not to break the circle.

Janice's voice rang out from the video. It sounded tinny and hollow. *"Something's happening. Look! The candles!"*

Veronica paused the video and boosted the contrast yet again. She watched spellbound as each of the candles around the room were snuffed out. But even after applying the same filters and slowing the footage down to a few frames per second, the camera failed to pick up what had been responsible for extinguishing the flames.

She let the video continue at its proper speed and watched as the dark room was suddenly lit by the two tea-lights in front of her.

They're blue. The candle flames turned blue, which means a spirit is present.

But I can't even begin to explain how the hell they relit.

The professor watched herself in the video as she began her breathing exercises and opened herself up to receive the spirit. A cold chill spread along her back and shoulders.

I don't remember any of this.

Veronica was not prepared for what she saw and heard next. She watched herself speak aloud on the video with the clear and unmistakable voice of a child.

"Mommy?"

Her eyes wide with terror, Veronica clasped her hand over her mouth and sank back in the dining room chair. The force of her sudden reaction knocked her mug to the floor. The coffee spread across the hardwood, but her attention was riveted to the video.

She watched the entire conversation between herself and Peter in disbelief. The expressions on her face were not her own, and the sound of the boy's high-pitched voice issuing from her lips was almost more than Veronica Upham could bear.

This can't be real. It just cannot possibly be real!

When the spirit speaking through her identified itself, Veronica scrawled the name TYLER on a piece of notebook paper beside her laptop. Her handwriting was barely legible, and the name had no significance to her.

As the footage continued to play, Veronica heard Janice pleading with Peter to stop. The medium watched in horror as her body convulsed in the chair. The frightened voice called for its mother, while Peter continued to press it with additional questions.

Veronica's heart skipped a beat when she heard the scream ring out from the video. She shuddered as the child's bloodcurdling cries blended into her own frantic shriek.

With her arms wrapped around her chest, Veronica paused the video. "There's no way this actually happened!"

She pushed herself away from the table and grabbed her cell phone with a shaking hand. As Veronica tried to thumb through her contacts to find Janice's number, she kept pressing the wrong buttons on the illuminated keypad. She finally managed to place the call and the phone began to ring.

Pick up, goddammit.

As before, Veronica was greeted by Janice's voicemail after only three rings. She immediately redialed the number, but Janice wasn't answering.

"Fuck!" Veronica's voice was hoarse, and her face was flushed from crying.

You need to get a hold of yourself. Calm down right the fuck now. You haven't even finished the video yet.

Unsure if she could stand any more, Veronica slipped back into the dining room chair and stared at the computer screen. After several deep breaths, she allowed the video to advance.

The footage continued as the séance fell to shambles. The commotion made by its participants fell sharp on her ears. She watched in amazement as a shadow emerged from the corner of the room and swept past her in the video. One of the tall candles at the center of the table fell to its side as the dark trail of mist glided by.

Numb with horror, Veronica rewound the video to where she'd just started and slowed it to play frame by frame. With her eyes wide and her jaw clenched, the professor watched as the darkened blur gathered into a wispy stream across the table. But with each stuttering flicker of the screen, the shape seemed to lose a measure of density and mass.

The narrow streak had a bright, almost translucent tail, which inexplicably flipped and shot toward Peter. As the stream of dark light inched past him, Veronica could make out the crude and half-formed shape of a face at the tip of the lengthening object. She squinted and leaned closer to the monitor, but the visage remained indistinct.

Against her better judgment, Veronica applied the contrast and noise filter to better illuminate the image on the screen. There was no mistaking what she saw.

The figure was opaque. Most of its body had been stretched into a stream of gray ectoplasmic light. But the elongated figure terminated in a haggard woman's face. Her long hair was wild and disheveled. Her eyes gleamed with hatred, and her large mouth was twisted in a silent scream.

For several minutes, Veronica sat and stared at the frozen image. The malevolent face chilled her to the bone.

Without uttering a word, she replayed the final sequence of the séance in real time. Whatever shape had been unfurling in the darkness flashed by quickly. All she could make out was a faint ball of gray light, which appeared for less than half a second.

But where did she come from? The spirit that came through was a little boy.

Once again, the trembling professor rewound the video, this time ten seconds prior to the scream she wished she never had to hear or see again.

Oh my God! There she is. Right there!

In the far corner of the room where the shadows were deepest, Veronica could see the faint outline of a tall figure standing behind her. The silhouette was obscured above its torso and was swallowed in shadows. But she could see the folds of what looked to be a tattered black dress. It hung in shreds all the way to the floor.

Veronica stifled the urge to vomit. She sped the video in reverse, her eyes locked on the anomalous figure lurking in the corner. As the video shot backward several frames at a time, the silhouette remained stationary, but then dissolved. She glanced at the time stamp and let the video play again.

Once again, Janice's voice resounded from the speakers. *"Something's happening. Look! The candles!"*

"Stay focused, Janice!"

With Eric's interjection, the shadowy figure materialized in the darkness. It had been there with them—observing them—for most of the séance.

Sick with fear, Veronica marked the video with a placeholder at approximately 9:14 PM and saved a new file entitled HERE.

Who is she?

"Christ," Veronica managed. *"What is she?"*

She replayed the final portion of the séance one more time and watched with deepening dread.

Peter saw her.

"That son of a bitch..."

In a daze, Veronica nodded again, still trying to wrap her mind around all she had seen. But the harried professor's heart sank when she realized she hadn't even begun to review the audio recording of the séance.

Veronica minimized the window display for the video software program and clicked on another shortcut on her desktop. As the audio editor loaded, she donned a pair of thick headphones.

Just one pass. Listen for any EVPs. Focus on the portion when the boy spoke.

She opened the .wav file and pressed play. She watched as the cursor moved past the undulating waves on the computer screen that represented her voice. The cursor swept across a wide gap of silence before the blank space was disrupted by another series of spiking waves. *"We ask that you give us a sign that you are near."*

Veronica noticed a tiny cluster of waves that divided a short period of ensuing silence. When the cursor passed across the visible interruption, Veronica heard a low voice.

"Leave us alone."

A few seconds after the ominous whisper, Veronica heard herself ask the question a second time, *"Give us a sign that you are near."*

"We've n-never... never caught one this clear before."

Of course not. This whole night was completely off the rails. We've had raps before, but it usually took twenty or more minutes just to get one or two. We've got audio of strange mutterings and whispers. We've seen dozens of orbs.

But never anything like this.

She set up an audio loop and saved it as EVP1. She studied the patterns of the sound waves. With twitching eyes, she noted the decibel level.

There's no way that was in a normal range.

While similar in shape to the recorded voices of Peter, Janice, Eric, or herself, the whispered voice was softer. Veronica could rule out anyone sitting at the table as a culprit for the disturbance.

And it was right on cue.

To be certain there was no corresponding visual anomaly, she reopened the video file to review the same sequence. But the camera's speaker didn't pick up the sound of the voice. There were no distortions or visible anomalies of any kind.

Veronica paused to take stock of the situation.

OK, so now you have recorded proof. You already knew what was out there. You were bitten by a vampire, then watched another one burn in the sun. You faced those monsters with nothing but a crucifix in your hands.

So why are you sitting here pissing your pants over these recordings? This is exactly what you were after. And recorded proof of the supernatural is something Edison Raymer failed to obtain two years ago.

Veronica jumped and tore the headphones from her head. Her cell phone was ringing. The vibrations rumbled across the dining room table.

"Janice?"

"Hi Ronnie," she replied with a guarded tone. "I'm sorry we missed your call. We were out on the—"

"That's fine, sure. I understand. Listen, I've been reviewing the video and audio from last night and—"

"Ronnie?"

"And it's absolutely extraordinary. You'll never believe it!" Veronica was breathless. Her words poured out to alleviate the anxiety that had built up throughout the afternoon. "Well, I mean, I guess you *would* believe it since you were there and you saw everything, but Jesus Christ—it's *unreal.*"

There was a pause on the other line.

"Janice? You still there?"

"Listen, Veronica," she hesitated. "Peter and I've been talking and, well, I mean... we think that maybe, you know..."

"What?"

"Maybe things have gotten a little out of hand."

"What the hell are you talking about?"

"Last night, was just... it was too much, Ronnie. After what we heard—"

"Wait a minute," Veronica pleaded. "We've been doing this for years! And now we're actually starting to get some results. I mean, you and Peter *have* to see this footage!"

"I can't." The older woman's response was curt and decisive. "That's all I can say, Ronnie. This is not the kind of thing Peter and I want to be mixed up with."

"Bullshit!" Veronica shouted. "I watched the footage. Peter was enthralled. He kept pressing the spirit that came through. He kept asking it questions. Never mind all that. I mean, Christ. *It came through me!* Do you even realize—"

"I know, but we just think that maybe—"

"Oh, come on! Peter saw it! I know he did. It's on the goddamn video!"

"Veronica..."

"What? He saw it and now he's scared? Well, you know what, Janice? I'm fucking *terrified*. It was in my house, for Christ's sake. It was in my house!"

Veronica shook with fury. Tears came in scalding streams. Nausea overtook her in waves. "Don't do this to me, Janice. I can't deal with this alone. I just can't."

Janice Tully fell silent. Veronica could hear the older woman take a deep breath. "Ronnie, have you seen the news?"

Veronica was caught off guard. She wiped her eyes and rubbed her nose. "No, why?"

"What did the... spirit... say its name was?"

"Um, Tyler, I think?" She picked up the piece of notebook paper. Veronica squinted as she struggled to read her own handwriting. "Yeah, that's it. Tyler."

A heavy sigh erupted from Janice. "How did you know? I mean, how could you have *possibly* known?"

"Known what? What are you talking about?"

"You need to check the local news," Janice said. The trepidation in her friend's voice was unmistakable. "That's all I can say. Goodbye, Ronnie."

"Wait! Janice?"

When she realized Janice had already disconnected, Veronica tossed the phone on the table.

Call Peter. Ask that coward why he won't talk to you himself. After all these years...

"Fuck him," she muttered.

Stop it, Veronica. Think about it.

They weren't ready for this. It's just like Raymer always said. They're bored eccentrics. This is just a hobby for them. You can't fault them for being afraid. They haven't seen the things you have. It's been almost two years and you still haven't come to terms with everything you witnessed.

Veronica took another deep breath and attempted to calm herself down. She returned to the dining room table and rested her elbows against the smooth surface. With her head in her hands, she closed her eyes and counted to ten. When she glanced up, her eyes wandered back to the computer screen.

So what was on the news?

Veronica closed the audio software on her laptop and opened an internet browser window. Her fingers clattered across the keyboard as she called up the website for one of the local news channels. On the homepage was a video link for the day's top story.

LOCAL BOY FOUND DEAD NEAR SOUTH WILLIAMSPORT ELEMENTARY SCHOOL.

You've got to be fucking kidding me.

Veronica clicked the link and a video clip from the Saturday evening news began to play. A sharp-featured blonde correspondent spoke with a sincere yet studied tone.

"Tragedy struck in Williamsport today as the body of seven-year-old Tyler Marshall was discovered early Saturday morning. The boy was reported missing by his mother Friday night after he disappeared in the woods adjacent to South Williamsport Elementary School."

No. This can't be happening...

The video segued to an ominous image of the forest against a gray sky, then cut to a shot of yellow crime scene tape stretched between two river birch trees.

"In the woods! There's a lady in the woods!"

"Richard Baker, a volunteer firefighter and close friend of the Marshall family, made the horrific discovery after participating in a civilian search party led by Williamsport Police Sergeant Fernanda Perez."

The video clip cut to Baker, a bearded man in his early forties. "We found him early Saturday morning in those woods. It's just a nightmare. Things like this ain't supposed to happen in a place like this."

After displaying a shot of two police cruisers parked in the elementary school parking lot, the camera panned out to reveal a younger female newscaster reporting from the scene. "Chief Dominic D'Amato of the Williamsport Police Department has initiated an indeterminate county-wide curfew that begins at five o'clock PM. and warned that the suspect in the boy's murder is still at large."

Veronica watched as the news clip displayed footage of the police chief at a press conference. "We are doing everything we can to bring justice to the Marshall family. The Williamsport community can do its part by reporting any suspicious activity and by adhering to the curfew we have instituted to ensure public safety."

Veronica gripped the arms of the dining room chair as another horrid realization dawned on her.

That thing in the video. That's what killed him. I know it. The cops are never going to find a suspect, because they have no idea what they're dealing with here.

And neither do you.

The video clip concluded with an announcement and final request from the first newscaster. "A memorial service will be held at Long & Fisher Funeral Home on Tuesday. If you have any information concerning the disappearance and death of Tyler Marshall, please contact the Williamsport Police Department Crime Line at the number on your screen."

Veronica leaned back in the dining room chair and folded her arms. She felt exhausted, and her nerves were shot.

So if that thing is the boy's killer, who or what is it? Was it some kind of projection? What the hell was it doing here? And how was I able to channel the boy so well in the first place?

Veronica could still hear the child's voice crying out in the séance footage.

"The lady... there's a lady in the woods!"

Veronica opened the folder where she saved the video files from the séance. She clicked on the .avi file marked HERE. After a few tries, she managed to freeze the frame on the ghostly face.

"So who the hell are you?"

In most cases, spirits aren't violent. With enough energy, the strongest ones can slam doors, bang on walls, move objects. Knock on tables...

But they don't kill little boys in the woods.

Christ, they can't *kill little boys in the woods.*

Veronica was perplexed. She studied the unsettling apparition. Her rational mind refused to accept what couldn't be any plainer for her to see. She shook her head as she stared at the figure's wide mouth and hungry, hateful eyes.

Maybe you're not dealing with a spirit after all?

5

STARING ABSENTMINDEDLY AT THE PLATE OF FOOD BEFORE him, Nathan Alderson adjusted his chair at the dining room table. Kelly Alderson emerged from the kitchen with a tureen of butter sauce for the green beans she had cooked earlier. Wearing more makeup than usual to hide her worn appearance, she rested the bowl on the table and placed a trembling hand on an empty chair. Kelly flinched as Nathan looked up.

"Why'd you do that?"

Kelly looked away, embarrassed, and attempted to change the subject. "Try to enjoy your dinner." She took a seat at the opposite end of the table. "I hope you don't mind I opened the Cabernet from our trip to Charlottesville last fall."

Nathan looked at the half-empty glass of red wine to the right of his plate. "Not at all," he muttered.

Kelly began unfolding a cloth napkin. The silverware clattered against the tabletop.

"I never understood the reason for saving a good bottle of wine anyway," Alderson added, speaking more to himself than his wife.

Kelly ignored his comment as she poured herself a glass. "I'm glad you're home, Nate. We haven't had a meal like this since... well... we haven't had a nice dinner for a long time."

Nathan held a forkful of beef stroganoff inches from his mouth. He slowly put it back on the plate. "Go ahead and say it."

His wife looked across the table at him. "Say what? All I meant was—"

"We haven't had a *nice dinner* like this since Cody died. Why the hell's it so hard for you to say?"

Kelly lowered her head. The dark roots of her dyed blonde hair were showing. "I don't know," she muttered. "Maybe because I'm just not as blunt or callous as you."

She fixed her eyes on the empty chair, realizing that she had set an extra plate and silverware where her son used to sit.

"Yeah?" A pang of cruelty rose in Nathan's heart. The words escaped him before he could silence himself. "I suppose your mother was right when she warned you not to marry a cop. That you were setting yourself up for heartache. These days, I'm thinking she was correct on at least one count. Maybe both."

Kelly remained silent as she took a sip of wine. She looked up at him with a wounded expression.

Nathan picked up his fork again. "Look. That was uncalled for. I'm sorry. I have a lot on my mind with this case. Tomorrow, D'Amato's gonna review my request for a complete forensic investigation of those woods. I have a feeling he's gonna shoot me down."

Kelly returned her attention to her plate. She took a small bite of food and chewed discretely.

"I don't know how just yet, but I'm certain Tyler Marshall's murder is connected with those missing kids Rudy Pettit investigated. You remember back in the '90s when those kids went missing down by the school?"

"No, Nate," she said. "I don't."

"It's strange." Alderson failed to recognize the discomfort in his wife's response. "Three kids in two years, then it stopped. Most predators don't stop once they get a taste for it. But now that we've got a body, we might—."

"Dammit that's enough!" She slammed her fist on the table and nearly overturned her glass of wine. "I don't wanna hear about it anymore."

Her husband clenched his jaw and observed his wife with steely eyes. "Fine. What do *you* wanna talk about?"

Kelly took a deep breath to compose herself. She broke off a piece of toasted bread, and arranged it on her plate. "Well, Dr. Chaykin called this afternoon."

"Ah!" Alderson raised a brow. "Of course. I didn't think therapists worked on Sundays."

"She wanted to know how you're dealing with things. And to remind me you've missed three consecutive sessions."

"What'd you tell her?"

"That you're coping by working. You just couldn't *wait* to get back to work, could you? I told her you were supposed to have the weekend off yet you went in anyway to deal with this... *this* whole thing."

"That's my job, Kelly. Something like this happens and I've gotta be on point. You know this. I couldn't just leave it to Frank."

"I also mentioned that I haven't seen you long enough to speak a coherent sentence to you since yesterday morning."

Nathan grimaced. "And what was her response?"

"Transferrence was the term she used. She thinks it's unhealthy." Kelly took another small forkful of buttered green beans. "You're suppressing your rage and guilt. Channelling it all into your job and this—"

"Is that what you think?"

"What I think is immaterial, isn't it?" Kelly lowered her head but maintained an icy stare at her husband. "Since you came home tonight, you've had nothing to say that didn't involve Tyler Marshall. You never once stopped to think about the kind of bad memories this would stir up!"

"For Christ's sake, you're still setting a place for Cody at our dinner table!" He pointed at his son's empty chair. "And you've got the nerve to lecture me about bad memories?"

"I'm sorry," Kelly responded. Desperate to keep the upperhand in the argument, she held back her tears. "But I want you to stop talking about that little boy! I've heard enough about him in the past hour."

Nathan grew more embittered with the resentment in his wife's voice. He knew her anger was merely the by-product of her sadness. But her sorrow failed to soften him. He took a swig of wine and slid the glass back on the table. A sanguine drop, like diluted blood, splashed out to stain the forest green tablecloth.

"I'm a detective, Kelly. My job puts food on this table. It allows you to work part-time shifts at the hospital."

"First of all, I worked part-time so that I could be home with Cody!"

"OK, fine." Nathan sat back in his chair with his arms crossed. "And where do you think the eight thousand dollars you spent on remodeling the kitchen came from? It sure as hell wasn't from *you* working overtime!"

"Bullshit. You didn't work those hours for the money. You care more about solving cases and being the smartest guy on the force than your salary." Kelly dropped her fork onto her china plate. "And you care more about this dead boy and the sick asshole who killed him than the memory of your own son!"

Nathan snatched his napkin from his lap, wadded it up, and tossed it over his plate of food. "You're way outta line, Kel!" He pointed across the table. "Do *not* bring my son into this!"

"Why not? You're traipsing around in the woods at crime scenes and digging through files at the office when you should be home. *Here.* With me. Figuring out how to cope with this and find a way forward. You know, without *him.*" The diminutive woman shifted uncomfortably in her chair. "I've barely seen you since you went back to work. And when I do, we've been at each other's throats."

She paused to let the gravity of her words sink in. "And may I remind you of something?"

He mumbled an inaudible reply and looked into the far corner of the dining room.

"Cody was *our* son, Nathan. He was my son, too."

Alderson sat in silence, unsure how to answer his wife.

"And if you care about his memory—hell, if you care about how I feel—then you wouldn't be spending all fucking week trying to solve other people's issues when the elephant in the room is in your own home."

Nathan moved to stand. "Are you finished? Because I don't need this shit right now." He held up a hand, not to stop her from interrupting, but to hold back his boiling anger. "I've got a lot on my mind!"

"Oh yeah? Well, so do I." Kelly's eyes glistened and her mouth twisted into a contemptuous sneer. "Where in the hell were you when he jumped off those rocks into that river, Nate? You were supposed to be watching him. Where in the hell *were* you? Knocking back beers with Patrick and Mike? How come it took you so damned long to wade in after him and drag him out?"

Nathan cradled his head, his elbow resting against the table. He couldn't answer. Not right away. He could hear his wife's irregular breathing as she fought back tears, but he was oblivious to her pain. Somewhere, he found his answer.

"Don't you think I ask myself that same question every minute of every day? When I lie awake at night, who do you think I'm cursing for what happened to him? And you sit there and act like I don't feel completely responsible for Cody's death!"

"Do you really?" she asked. "I don't even know you any more. The man I married would never treat me this way. The man I married wasn't such a coward, hiding behind his bitterness and failures."

Nathan bolted out of his chair and swept a hand over his plate. He flung the wine glass across the room to shatter against the wall. A red stain spread on the wallpaper as he tipped his chair over and left the table.

Shaken but not surprised by her husband's outburst, Kelly Alderson listened to his angry footfalls traverse the living room.

"That's right!" she called out. "Walk away. I'll just sit here and play the role of the long-suffering wife of the brave, honorable *detective!*"

She heard the front door slam. With the sound of tires peeling out of the driveway, she could only presume he was going back to the police station.

As she glanced at the stain on the wall and the pile of splintered glass on the floor, Kelly Alderson broke down, silently choking back a flood of tears.

6

VERONICA SPENT THE REMAINDER OF SUNDAY AFTERNOON in a quiet daze. As the hours passed by, she kept thinking of Tyler Marshall and the strange figure in the video footage. She knew the only way to drive the terrifying thoughts from her mind was to occupy herself. But she couldn't find the strength to do anything but lie on her couch and stare at the living room ceiling.

After several glasses of white wine, Veronica managed to calm her nerves enough to review the rest of the audio file. But there weren't any additional EVPs or anomalies that hadn't already been picked up in the video.

As remarkable as the recordings were, she realized she couldn't share them with anyone. She thought of Peter and Janice again but was overcome with frustration as well as sadness. She hoped that after a few days they might change their minds and agree to review the footage with her.

Stop kidding yourself. They don't want anything to do with this. The only time Janice ever sounded this serious was when she asked you to stop bringing Edison to the sittings.

A terrible thought suddenly dawned on her.

What if they think I did it? Jesus Christ. No wonder Janice sounded so upset. But how could they believe I'm capable of killing a child? It's unthinkable!

The professor shook her head and stared at her computer screen. It had been idle long enough to activate the screen saver. Her eyes traced the spiraling patterns.

Well, you've been an accomplice in two deaths already. Three if you count Laura's initial disappearance before she was turned. I'm sure Peter and Janice never would've expected any of that either.

With a sigh, Veronica powered down her laptop. Hoping to keep her intrusive thoughts at bay, she finally decided to clean up the cold coffee she had spilled on the dining room floor. She wandered into the kitchen and grabbed a roll of paper towels.

You could always give Eric a call and see what he thinks about the footage. Maybe he talked to Peter or Janice? You could find out what's really going on with them.

"No, no, and no." She knelt down on the hardwood floor and spread the paper towels over the spill.

So what the hell am I supposed to do with footage like this? I sure as hell don't wanna dump it on the internet. If I took it to the college or the Annandale Institute, they'd just assume it's been doctored or faked.

Once the paper towels had absorbed most of the cold coffee, she crumpled them up, and threw them in the trash.

After all these years, and with all this technology at the average person's fingertips, you'd think that someone would've recorded things even more extraordinary than this séance.

She turned to open a narrow pantry and grabbed a plastic mop from the closet.

Maybe they have? Who's to say all that shit on the internet or some of the footage on those stupid ghost hunter shows isn't real? What would it take to convince the public that these things truly exist?

Gripping the handle of the mop, Veronica pressed the button to activate the nozzle, sprayed the floor with cleaner, and rubbed the sponge over the area of the spill.

Christ, what would happen if people did know the truth? Maybe we were lucky that Edison never managed to preserve the footage of Matthias Bartsch's staking. We'd probably be rotting in jail if we had.

Veronica was jarred from her reverie by the sound of church bells in the distance.

St. Luke's.

The professor's heart sank with dread when she noticed the sky beyond the curtains had darkened. Eric Sandoval's words from the previous night suddenly replayed in her mind.

"If I were you, I'd do a cleansing right away."

But night was already falling, and she'd taken no precautions to protect the house.

Veronica dropped the mop to the floor and hurried through the living room to the foyer. She double-checked the deadbolt to the front door and was annoyed to discover it had been unlocked since Eric left the night before. The professor fastened the bolts and dashed back to her kitchen pantry. She rifled through the shelves in search of a sealed pillar candle and another brass holder.

I can't use anything from last night. It has to be pure.

In her haste, she knocked a box of cake mix and several cans of soup to the floor. One of the heavier cans smashed her toe.

"Goddammit!"

Just leave it. You can clean up your mess later.

Once she found a candle, she took a smudge stick of sage, a fresh pack of matches, and a canister of salt from the top shelf. With the esoteric items spilling out of her arms, Veronica dumped the items on the dining room table. As she spun the dial of the chandelier all the way up, the room was flooded with bright light. The nervous professor jumped at her own shadow as it flickered across the wall. After moving the candle to the center of the table, she fumbled with the matches, quickly lit the virgin wick, and began to pray in a panting whisper.

"Guardians of the East, I call upon thee to preserve me from harm. May your blessed winds confound my enemies.

"Guardians of the North, I call upon thee to preserve me from harm. May your sacred fires consume my enemies."

Outside, the church bells continued to ring, threatening to undermine the professor's concentration.

"Guardians of the West, I call upon thee to preserve me from harm. May your purifying waters submerge my enemies.

"Guardians of the South, I call upon thee to preserve me from harm. May your rich soils imprison my enemies."

Veronica tried to ignore the tolling bells, but the hairs on the back of her neck stood on end.

"With perfect love and trust, I call upon thy aid!"

Veronica held the smudge stick to the flame of the candle. Smoke began to waft from its blackened tip.

You're supposed to open the windows to drive the spirits or negative energy out. But I'll be damned if I'm giving anything out there such an easy opportunity to get in here.

Veronica took a deep breath, cleared her throat, and summoned her waning strength. She turned to stand at the threshold of the kitchen and spoke with authority.

"Bless this room and cleanse it of all evil." She then moved along the perimeter of the dining room. Holding the sage aloft, she moved with purpose toward the dim corner where she had seen the looming figure in the shadows. "You are not welcome here." As the smoke curled upward toward the ceiling, she offered another abjuration. "I revoke my invitation."

Raymer said that wouldn't work. The invitation was already extended to Laura. It doesn't matter if it was before or after she became a vampire.

Anyway, this isn't about Laura, is it?

It's about the thing you called up and let in here last night. That parasitic thing attached to the little boy.

The thing with the screaming mouth.

Veronica maneuvered her way into the living room. She approached the chair where she thought she saw Junior Luttrell's ghost earlier that day. She let the smoke waft around the headrest and arms. When she turned on her heel, she bumped a four-shelved curio cabinet cluttered with Victoriana. With a free hand, she steadied an antique porcelain vase she almost knocked to the floor.

You need to get a hold of yourself or something's going to break through every barrier you try to set up here!

"Bless this house and cleanse it of all evil!" Her voice rose with newfound conviction. She imagined the sinister figure that appeared on the video footage. "You are not welcome here! I revoke my invitation!"

Veronica wafted the sage throughout the rest of the living room, repeated her prayer, and made a loop back to the foyer. With the smudge stick thrust ahead, she flicked on the upstairs hall light and slowly mounted the stairs.

"Bless this house and cleanse it of all evil." The mantra echoed along the high walls of the staircase. Veronica's eyes traced the familiar Waterhouse and Rossetti prints that followed the upward arc of the banister and wall.

When she reached the landing, the professor made her way through each of the upstairs bedrooms and the bathroom. She threw back the ruffled shower curtain and winced as the *fleur-de-lis* hooks scraped along the iron rod. Sage smoke filled the shower, permeating the rest of the small bathroom.

By now every lamp in the house was lit, and Veronica had made her way through each of the rooms. However, she still felt no safer than before she began the cleansing ritual.

You need to believe. It's a matter of willpower, dammit. So dig deep and get your shit together.

You squared off with Laura McCoy. You survived her attack and have the scars to prove it. You watched that German vampire turn to dust at sunrise. You successfully channeled the spirit of that poor little boy from the woods.

Yet feelings of dread continued to wash over her as she tightened her grip on the smudge stick.

And you invited his killer into your house...

"I revoke my invitation," she shouted through clenched teeth. "You are *not* welcome here!"

She decided to make a second pass through the two bedrooms, this time making sure to wave the sage over each of her bookcases and bless the shadowy confined spaces of the closets. When she returned to the hallway, her eyes wandered upward to trace a rectangular outline along the ceiling.

The attic.

I don't want to go up there.

After wiping the sweat from her brow, Veronica stood on her toes to reach the cord to the attic. As she pulled the rope downward, the steps unfolded with a drawn-out creak.

How do you plan to see up there, genius?

Veronica let the ladder slide down to the floor and braced it against the carpet. She went back to her bedroom to retrieve a candle and another packet of matches from her nightstand.

I'm not going all the way back downstairs to grab the damn flashlight.

Veronica relit the smudge stick. Thick smoke billowed forth. With the sage in one hand and the lighted candle in the other, she slowly mounted the wooden stairs into the attic.

The oppressive air almost extinguished the candle. She held out the items in her hands and struggled to stand upright among the network of crossbeams. Veronica ducked and weaved across the plywood flooring, taking care not to tread on any of the exposed insulation. The attic brimmed with shadowed objects. Box after box of decorations, racks of old clothing, an antique sewing machine, and small pieces of furniture blocked her path at every turn.

The agitated professor gasped as she glimpsed the outline of a woman's torso in the corner. Her heart jumped and adrenaline coursed through her as she thrust the candle forward. She sighed in relief as she realized the figure was an old tailor's mannequin, which she picked up at a yard sale ages ago.

After repeating the protective mantra, she turned back toward the trapdoor, guided by the light filtering up from the hallway. She scrambled down the ladder as hot wax from the candle seared her hand.

Veronica descended the stairs and returned to the living room. She carried the sage into the kitchen, filled up a glass of water, and dipped the tip of the smudge stick in the water to extinguish the smoking cinders.

Thankfully this house is so close to the river. It was built on a concrete slab so there's no basement.

She darted back to the dining room, grabbed the canister of salt, and hurried to the first window. When she flung the curtains open, she could see the faded lines from the day before. She poured a fresh line of salt atop the old one.

"Bless this house and fortify it against my enemies!"

She poured another line of salt along the living room windowsill and then entered the foyer. "Laura McCoy, I revoke my invitation!" Veronica bent forward and drew another line of salt along the threshold of the door.

The professor made her way to each window throughout the house. She left all the lights on downstairs, including the garish chandelier.

When she returned upstairs, she continued to administer fresh barriers of salt along the window ledges. Her thoughts wandered back to the first few weeks after Raymer's disappearance, when her fear of Laura was at its highest. She had not only lined the windows and doorways with salt, she rubbed the wooden frames with cloves of raw garlic, hung rosary beads on the windows, and placed crucifixes on the windowsills. She had let her guard down since, but tonight, she wondered if she should reinforce the windows more thoroughly.

Veronica rummaged through her jewelry boxes until she found several rosaries and a few small crucifixes. She placed them on the wooden ledges of the master bedroom.

She was at least partially satisfied that she had done all she could to fortify her home against Laura McCoy. And she hoped she had at least weakened—if not entirely driven out—the mysterious entity that manifested the night before.

Veronica filled a glass of water, brushed her teeth, and changed into a nightgown. Although it was still early, she had to teach in the morning, and she craved the familiar warmth of her bed. She turned down the comforter, adjusted the pillows against the headboard, and got situated. The professor opened the top drawer of the nightstand beside her bed.

Atop a stack of monogrammed stationery sat a snub-nose .38 she'd bought at the local gun shop. Veronica recalled her embarrassment when she presented five silver bullets to the perplexed storeowner. She'd asked for a gun that could shoot the rounds Junior had loaded. The bemused clerk countered by inquiring if she planned to kill a werewolf.

Veronica slunk home with her purchase, loaded the firearm, and shoved it into the drawer. She just wasn't a 'gun person.' The importance of practicing her grip or stance with the weapon had never occurred to her. The trigger hadn't been pulled, and the moving parts weren't oiled. Nonetheless, the untouched weapon emboldened her. She wondered if she could discharge the pistol at her foe 'without thinking or blinking,' as Lord Byron had claimed in a well-known letter.

A handful of worn paperback books were scattered along the top of the nightstand. She had a choice of *Lady Audley's Secret, Our Mutual Friend,* or a collection of Arnold's poetry. Veronica thumbed through the well-worn paperback to find where she'd left off in Braddon's sensation novel. She read for nearly an hour and managed to forget her anxieties in the intricate yet familiar plot of the book. By midnight, she could no longer ignore the house as it mocked her with its ill-timed creaks, cracks, and groans. As she lay in bed, slipping in and out of a restless sleep, Veronica Upham yearned for the light of dawn.

7

NATHAN ALDERSON EASED HIS UNMARKED CRUISER INTO the empty parking lot of South Williamsport Elementary School. He cut the engine, switched off the headlights, and sat behind the wheel in silence.

His son's bright smile—as preserved in the photograph McCain had thoughtlessly turned over on his desk—flashed through his mind.

WORLD'S GREATEST DAD.

Nathan fought the urge to scream.

He drove his fist upward to activate the overhead light and snatched the case file from the passenger seat. The detective began thumbing through the gruesome images within. Once he had immersed himself in the details again, Alderson withdrew a heavy black flashlight from the glove compartment.

The detective wiped the condensation from the windshield with his free hand. He stared intently across the playground and soccer fields. The sodium vapor lamps cast an eerie pall on the trampled grass and mud puddles, which were beginning to collect frost due to the nighttime chill. Beyond the flickering lamps on their imperfect wooden poles, the dark maw of the forest loomed—cavernous and enigmatic.

Alderson unlatched the retaining strap on his shoulder holster. He removed the Glock 32 and thumbed the magazine catch. A fully loaded thirteen round mag fell into his open palm. He felt the comforting weight of the .357 SIG cartridges double-stacked in the magazine, then slid it home and chambered a round.

With the flashlight in one hand and the pistol in the other, Alderson exited the car and kicked the door closed. He began to walk. As the detective crossed the playground and passed under the monkey bars, a gust of wind whipped the tails of his long trench coat against his trousers. He darted around the fence under the vapor lamps, retracing the path Tyler Marshall had followed before his untimely death.

Before crossing into the enveloping darkness of the forest, Nathan stopped to look behind him. He was leaving the well-lit fields, the warmth of the police cruiser, and the faraway lights of inhabited homes in the distance to cross into the domain of a killer. Undeterred, the policeman pushed his way through hanging branches and descended into a low-lying dell. He slogged through a pool of water. The stagnant muck seeped into his shoes to drench his socks. He ignored the discomfort of his soaked feet and flipped on the flashlight. The powerful beam illuminated an endless wall of graying tree trunks surrounded by mounds of wind-swept leaves. Through the overgrowth, the wind howled like the low moan of a child.

Cody.

On the riverbank.

I was too late.

Alderson remembered dragging his son from the muddy river and pressing his fists against the boy's chest.

Thirty compressions and two breaths.

He had failed to force all of the water out of his lungs and push the air back in.

"I'm sorry, sir. It's too late. He's gone."

Nathan stopped in his tracks and winced.

No! Just give me one more minute! One more!

Don't put him on that gurney! Don't cover him!

Don't you fucking do it!

He raised the grip of the .357 and pressed the magazine floor against his right temple. Alderson leaned against a knotty tree. Gritting his teeth, he reminded himself he might not be safe in the woods.

The snap of a twig brought him out of his trance. He began to plow forward, pushing away dead limbs and branches. His feet stumbled on the uneven carpet of moss and leaves, but he kept his eyes—and the flashlight—fixed ever forward.

"Police officer!" he yelled. "Stand where you are and drop your weapon!"

There was no answer as he continued to move ahead through the forest for nearly half a mile. Every shadow was a suspect. Despite the cold, sweat beaded on his brow. Adrenaline flushed through his tense body, accompanied by an uneasy feeling that increased as he made his way deeper into the woods.

Suddenly, something thin yet unyielding wrapped itself around his waist. Alderson looked down. He had run into the yellow tape marking the crime scene. In his haste, he hadn't seen the conspicuous barrier as he'd rushed toward the heart of the forest. After untangling himself and ducking under the barricade, he caught his breath and looked around with the flashlight as his guide. All the tags and forensics equipment had been removed. As he pivoted in a dizzying circle, he could discern the ominous handprints on the trees.

It's all so different in the dark.

Like stepping into a dream world.

After taking a few wide steps, he stood above the disturbed patch of earth where Tyler Marshall had been hastily buried.

Just what do you expect to find out here? The perpetrator digging another grave? You should be somewhere else.

You should go back home and apologize to Kelly.

For a moment, he thought about turning around and forging a path back through the labyrinthine woods to the safety of the car. But he was compelled to forge deeper into the thickets. Nathan Alderson sprung forward on his damp heels and crossed under the tape marking the far end of the crime scene. He used the pistol barrel to edge his way through an endless concatenation of branches in his path. When he slowed his breathing, the only sounds were the trees bending in the wind, the rustling of leaves, and the snapping of dead limbs.

The detective moved forward. In his mad dash, he lost track of time, distance, and direction.

Is this how Tyler felt when he was out here?

Lost and afraid, and unsure which way to go?

Alderson ducked under a particularly tangled mass of deadfall and almost fell to the open ground beneath his feet. He steadied himself and looked up at the sky. Clouds passed across the bright moon, which was no longer hidden by the canopy of the forest. To his left and right, an overgrown road faded into the blackness beyond the reach of his flashlight beam. After he steadied himself, he followed clumps of high grass and weeds that sprouted along the trail.

Before long, Alderson's flashlight fell on a convergence with another road. He negotiated a path through thick brambles toward the center.

The crossroads.

He surveyed the overgrown paths around him with his flashlight.

All those stories about witches and demons are bullshit, because there's nothing more sinister than some guy pretending to lead a normal life while he fills his crawlspace with the bodies of young boys.

Nothing.

Another twig snapped behind him. He spun the flashlight in the direction of the noise and saw a flicker of movement. As the wind was still, he could distinguish the rustle of soft material—reminiscent of a long, trailing skirt—against the forest floor.

"Who's there?" he demanded. "Come out of those woods and show yourself!"

His voice echoed through the husks of dead trees. He trained the flashlight on the surrounding forest. There was no movement. No one was watching him from the opposite side of the road. No one fled from his challenge or materialized to answer him. If there was a presence in the woods, it was indifferent to him.

He moved toward the source of the abrupt sound while expertly wielding his pistol and the flashlight together. To his periphery, the detective saw a dark shadow and a flash of movement to his left.

Alderson spun around to train his pistol on what appeared to be a rapidly departing figure, but it was just a trick of the moonlight. He had been standing on slightly higher ground, and the abrupt maneuver caused his footing to slip. Breathing heavily, he trained his flashlight on the moss-covered ground beneath him. The pale beam traced an irregular depression. A tangle of thorny briars crept out from the center and across the ground.

Roads in disuse usually stay level.

There are no tire tracks, or ruts, or other evidence that a vehicle's been anywhere near this trail in years.

His heart beating faster, he kicked at the roots of the briars to clear the ground. Alderson crouched and ran his fingers across the soil. It was looser than the hard-packed surface to his left and right. The detective sprung to his feet and vaulted clumps of tall grass and briars. The flashlight traced the ground below.

Soon enough, he found another sunken area roughly the same size in the middle of the trail.

Alderson swung the flashlight around again as he returned to a crouch. He pressed his cheek against the soil, so he was eye-level with the ground. The road was covered in growth, which had masked several mounds and depressions.

The detective holstered his pistol and latched the restraint. His apprehension of being followed through the woods by an unseen assailant was now a forgotten memory.

"These are graves!" He staggered to his feet and dusted off his trousers. "In the middle of this road! In plain fucking sight!"

Alderson broke into a sprint across the uneven surface of the wide trail. He passed over the crossing and followed the eastern road toward the schoolyard a mile or more away.

If D'Amato shoots me down, I'll turn up every inch of soil until I find the remains of those children. If I have to operate a backhoe myself, I'll tear these old roads apart.

I know I'm right.

I know it.

8

THE NEXT MORNING, DETECTIVE ALDERSON MADE THE SHORT walk from his parked cruiser to Evelynton Hall, which housed the Williamsport College administrative offices. His expression soured as he crumpled his empty coffee cup and pitched it into a nearby trashcan. He stopped by the brick steps leading to the building's front entrance and leaned on the railing. A group of students on their way to class wandered along the damp brick walkway, chatting in low voices.

Nate had awakened early—but his plans to return to the woods were curtailed by an unexpected call from Chief D'Amato. The chief not only refused the request for a geophysical survey, but he insisted that Alderson follow up on Pettit's leads and have a full report on his desk first thing Tuesday morning.

"I need you to find this boy's killer," the chief had said over the phone. "If there are any connections to the Stroud case, or this Bartsch character, then I need to know. If not, then see if the trail leads you anywhere else. I need something tangible I can present to the press, so don't make me regret assigning you the lead on this case."

Alderson turned around to look up at the Georgian brick building that towered behind him. Bells from a nearby church began to chime. The wind picked up and drove a cluster of leaves across the sidewalk. He climbed the stairs toward the double doors, shoved his hand into his pocket, and withdrew his badge.

Right now, you've got to keep up appearances. Put on a good show for the chief and the department. Get this over with and then you can get back to the real investigation in those woods.

Alderson approached the front desk and laid his badge on the counter. He leaned over to catch the secretary's attention.

A well-coiffed middle-aged woman entering data into a computer spun in her chair to face him. "Can I help you, sir?"

"Detective Nathan Alderson, Williamsport Police." He jabbed a finger against his badge and pushed it toward her. "I'd like to speak to Dean David Ritter."

"Do you have an appointment?"

"I don't, but this is a matter of some urgency."

"Well, I believe he's on a conference call until—"

"I can wait."

With a scowl, Alderson retrieved his badge as the secretary picked up her telephone.

"I'll see if he's available."

"Thank you." The detective turned his back as the administrative assistant spoke softly into the receiver. The secretary cleared her throat to regain his attention. With a steely glance, she waved him in the direction of Ritter's office.

Without bothering to knock, Alderson barged into the office with his badge in hand. David Ritter—bald, broad-shouldered but paunchy—stood behind his teakwood desk. His large fingers fumbled to button the coat of his tailored pinstripe suit. Before the Dean of Students could introduce himself, the detective cut him off.

"I'll bet you're wondering why I'm here, Mr. Ritter."

"Well, the thought did cross my mind," he said as he braced an arm against the shiny surface of his desk. "Is this about one of our students?"

"You could say that." Alderson closed the door behind him. "Although I'm actually investigating the murder of a seven-year-old boy named Tyler Marshall. Have you seen the news recently? Are you aware of what happened over the weekend?"

Ritter's eyes narrowed. "I am." The dean took a deep breath as he continued to prop himself up beside the desk. "Terrible tragedy, no doubt. But I'm not quite sure why you're here to see me about it."

"A couple years back, a Williamsport student was assaulted. My predecessor, Detective Rudy Pettit, came to see you about it." Alderson removed his notepad and clicked his ballpoint pen. "The girl's name was Jennifer Stroud."

"Yes, I remember that rather well. But she withdrew from the college after the attempted rape." Ritter paused to lick his lips. "Which happened off campus, mind you."

"That much I know," Alderson said. "But Pettit left a lot of gaps in his investigation. I'm not sure if he mentioned the suspect's name to you."

"I don't recall..." Ritter trailed off as he watched the younger man pace across the width of his office.

"Try." Alderson glanced over his shoulder at the Dean of Students as he approached a shelf lined with football trophies.

"No." Ritter tapped his fingers on his desk. "No, I don't think he did."

"Does the college have a foreign exchange program, Mr. Ritter?"

"Yes. Of course we do."

Alderson kept his back turned to the dean as he inspected his sports memorabilia. On the center shelf was an old team photograph of the North Williamsport Braves. He scanned the rows of square-jawed athletes until he found the face of a young Rudy Pettit. Satisfied, he spun on his heel to face the dean.

"Do you remember a German exchange student named Matthias Bartsch?"

Ritter shook his head. "No, but you have to understand that I don't meet every student under my charge. Even special cases like participants in the exchange program."

Alderson waved his index finger at the PC and monitor on Ritter's desk. "Think you can look that name up for me? I'm sure you've got access to all the students' files."

"Uh, yes... I do." Ritter took a seat and unlocked the computer. As he began to move the mouse, he glanced up at the detective. "Speaking of names, I didn't catch yours."

"Detective Nathan Alderson. And the name I'm looking for in your records is Bartsch. That's spelled B-A-R-T-S-C-H. First name, Matthias."

Ritter began to type. As the database ran its query, a puzzled look crossed his wrinkled features. "What does this have to do with that murdered boy, if you don't mind me asking?"

"Pettit didn't go over the particulars of the Stroud case with you?"

"I don't remember. Honestly."

"There are certain similarities between the murder of Tyler Marshall and the attack on Jennifer Stroud. In the *method* of the attack, to be specific. It may amount to nothing, but we're trying to cover all the bases here."

"Well, there's nothing in my records about anyone, exchange student or otherwise, named Matthias Bartsch. Are you sure you spelled the name correctly?"

"Yes." Alderson leaned an arm on the shelf behind him.

Ritter raised a hand to stop him, but Alderson continued.

"So what exactly did you and Rudy Pettit talk about?" He nodded to the photo behind him. "Friday nights on the gridiron when you were teenagers?"

"Well, we did reminisce a bit." Ritter massaged his hairless temples. "But he was more interested in chasing down a professor who was teaching here at the time."

"Would that be Edison Raymer?"

"That's him." Ritter leaned forward in his chair to fold his hands on his desk. "There were some problems with Raymer, and Pettit was trying to track him down because Jennifer Stroud happened to be one of his students."

"What kind of problems?" Alderson asked.

Ritter sighed and fidgeted in his seat. "My involvement with Edison Raymer ended shortly after Rudy came to see me. I put him on administrative leave." Ritter sneered before continuing. "The son of a bitch didn't bother to show up for his hearing that November."

"Well, I'm sure you heard why." Alderson studied the dean's reaction.

"There were rumors he burned down his house to get an insurance payoff." Ritter smirked in reflection. "Then he skipped town. Why I didn't get rid of him years before is a mystery to me."

"It's a mystery to me as well, because you still haven't explained what you had against Edison Raymer, Mr. Ritter."

"You saw his files, didn't you? Did you see all the nonsense he was teaching in his anthropology courses? Raymer was possibly the worst educator I've ever had the misfortune of working with."

Alderson glanced up from his notepad. "Well, like I said before. Pettit didn't leave me much to work with, but I don't have to read between the lines to see you held a rather long-standing grudge against the guy. Would that be a fair and accurate assessment?"

"Now wait a minute!" Ritter's round face flushed beet red. "You don't know what you're talking about. Edison Raymer was an arrogant, insubordinate, and irresponsible professor and I have every right to call a spade a spade."

"That's an interesting choice of words, Mr. Ritter." Alderson glanced back to his notes. "Raymer is an African-American man, correct?"

"That's not what I meant, and you know it. He could've been turquoise for all I care. Raymer was a terrible professor and I have dozens of faculty complaints and years of lackluster student assessments to prove it."

The detective ignored the dean and continued to provoke him. "Well, someone hired him. He achieved tenure, didn't he? Let me guess—Affirmative Action?"

"How dare you! I don't have to stand for this. I'm sure Chief D'Amato wouldn't appreciate your methods of interrogation!"

"Call him and find out." Nathan withdrew a personal contact card from his wallet and tossed it onto the dean's meticulously arranged desk. "Here's my information if you wanna file a complaint against me."

Ritter drew the card across the slick surface and placed it next to his telephone.

Alderson stepped backward and resumed his line of questioning. "You ever stop to think that maybe your rush to judge Raymer and all the campus politics might've been what sent him over the edge?"

"Detective, you really have a lot of nerve coming in here and dredging all this up just to drag my reputation through the mud."

"I'm not concerned with your reputation, Mr. Ritter." Alderson met the dean's stare with his own. "I'm not your football buddy from days gone by. My job is to find Tyler Marshall's killer, who may or may not be the same individual that attacked Jennifer Stroud. Edison Raymer was a person of interest in her case. But your buddy Rudy Pettit conveniently omitted any details explaining *why* he was a person of interest in his report. That, coupled with the suspicious activity surrounding Raymer's departure from Williamsport, is why I need to find him and figure out what his connection to all of this really is."

Ritter shifted his considerable bulk in his leather chair but remained silent.

"Now, given your disdain for Dr. Raymer," Alderson held his pen at the ready, "I assume you'd be eager to cooperate with this investigation if it leads to his embarrassment and arrest, no?"

"What do you want to know?"

"Do you think any of Raymer's colleagues might have an idea where he is?"

"As a matter of fact, yes, I do," Ritter answered without hesitation. "Dr. Veronica Upham. In the English department."

"And what, specifically, is her connection to Raymer?"

"They carried on together for quite a few years."

"As a couple?"

"Yes."

Alderson tapped his pen against the edge of his notebook. "Is she available for questioning today?"

"I don't know." Ritter frowned as he picked up the detective's card and studied it. "Maybe. If she teaches a Monday, Wednesday, Friday schedule, she should be here."

"What can you tell me about her?" Alderson paused and gripped his pen as he waited for Ritter's answer.

The dean shrugged his shoulders. "All I can tell you is that she hasn't been herself lately. She's taken a lot of sick days. Been skipping department functions. In fact, she turned down a nomination to serve as chair of the department last semester. I don't believe she's published anything for quite some time. But her students seem to love her, so we've given her the benefit of the doubt. I always thought she was a bit of a flake myself."

Alderson jotted down a short transcript of what the dean had just told him.

"But you never led a campaign to ensure that she was persecuted, shunned, and eventually fired?"

"No, Detective Alderson, I did not." Ritter glared and nodded to his office door. "I'm sure on your way out, if you ask Janine, she'll give you directions to the English department. You can enquire after Dr. Upham's whereabouts there."

Alderson flipped his notebook closed and slid it into his coat's interior pocket. "I appreciate your cooperation, Mr. Ritter. If we're both lucky, I won't have to come back here again."

"I will be speaking with Chief D'Amato. Of that you can be assured."

The detective glanced at the photograph of Ritter in his youth and then back to the flabby, heavily-jowled, balding man behind the teakwood desk. With a shake of his head, he closed the office door behind him.

9

"BEFORE WE WRAP UP FOR TODAY, I'D LIKE TO SPEND A FEW minutes discussing Lockwood's dream sequence." Professor Upham addressed her Victorian Novel class from behind her lectern. "Or more accurately, his encounter with Catherine Earnshaw's ghost."

Detective Alderson eased the lecture hall door closed and slipped into the first available seat in the back of the auditorium. The professor was so engrossed in her lecture that she failed to notice him.

"Lockwood actually has two dreams in Chapter 3." Dr. Upham glanced at a pupil in the first row. "The first dream is a disjointed sequence that revolves around Reverend Branderham's sermon. The whole thing is presented with a dream's feverish logic. It's pure stream-of-conscious writing nearly forty years before Freud. It jumps from one location to another, is characterized foremost by feelings of persecution and paranoia, and ends when Lockwood challenges the preacher and causes a riot to break out."

The professor forced a smile and let her eyes sweep over her students. Alderson reached into his coat pocket for his notepad and pen.

"Now I'm willing to bet most of you just skimmed over this part and thought, 'what the hell is all *this* nonsense?'"

A wave of low laughter rolled through the room. Alderson clicked his pen and flipped to a clean page.

"Well, you aren't alone. Most literary critics gloss over it or make ridiculous leaps of Postmodernist logic hoping to prove Lockwood was masturbating in Heathcliff's closet."

The students laughed again. Despite his foul mood, Alderson couldn't help but smirk as he took notes on Professor Upham's appearance and demeanor.

"Whatever the case, I think this is an important scene, for Brontë catches readers off guard by introducing the supernatural. We don't see it coming, and Lockwood's Enlightenment logic collapses into gothic self-delusion. He convinces *himself* that he's dreaming, and we as readers have been trained to believe him."

Dr. Upham remained rooted at the podium. Alderson continued to study her and make notations in his leather binder.

"But Lockwood's second dream is far more grounded," she explained. "It takes place entirely within the confines of the guest room. Lockwood encounters Cathy's ghost at the window, which is a far more extraordinary and implausible event than the church sermon. But the *description* of this dream is more focused and realistic than the previous one."

Dr. Upham took a breath and raised her index finger for emphasis. Alderson recalled how so many of his own professors had carried themselves in a similar manner.

They always talk with their hands.

"So why should we interpret this second sequence as a dream at all? Just because Lockwood tells us so? My hunch is that Brontë deliberately prefaces Lockwood's encounter with Catherine's ghost with something that cannot be mistaken for anything *but* a dream. By doing so, more careful readers are expected to interpret his encounter with Cathy's ghost as a *real* experience."

Deep in thought, Alderson chewed on the top of his pen.

"OK, so put on your critical thinking caps," Dr. Upham directed. "What other evidence in the book suggests that Lockwood's encounter was a genuine supernatural experience?"

Several students raised their hands.

Dr. Upham called on a girl a few rows from the front. "Crystal?"

"Well, actually, I noticed a few things that suggested these *were* dreams."

The professor nodded with a slight gleam in her eye. "Go ahead."

"So, before he dreams about the sermon, he was reading Cathy's diary and how she hated going to church. So, I assumed Lockwood internalized all this stuff and it influenced his dreams."

"That's a great point," Dr. Upham acknowledged. "That can definitely explain the content of the first dream. But what about the second dream?"

Another student was eager to chime in. "Well didn't Lockwood already have Catherine on his mind? Like Crystal said, he was already thinking about her, so..."

"True," Professor Upham nodded. "But when her ghost appears, Lockwood claims to see a *child's* face, and she tells him she's been wandering the moors for twenty years. Furthermore, the ghost introduces itself as Catherine Linton, but Lockwood says he saw the name 'Catherine Earnshaw' in the diary more times than her married name."

Alderson kept his eye on the professor as she stepped back from the podium. The detective wrote CHILD and GHOST in his notebook. With heavy strokes, Alderson traced the word CHILD numerous times until it stood out from every other word on the page.

"This is an extremely complicated and ambiguous scene." Dr. Upham glanced at her watch. "But let me try to get to the crux of the mystery. Why does Catherine's ghost appear as a child rather than as a grown woman?"

Several hands shot up around the lecture hall as Alderson looked on.

She really does have an impressive command over her classroom. Ritter was right. The students do seem to like her. They respect her. One might say she has the kind of charm and charisma shared by serial killers and cult leaders.

The detective stopped his train of thought.

Yeah, or as a tenured professor, she just knows what the hell she's doing. She's managed to get these kids off their smartphones and interested in boring old books.

"Angela?"

"Because that's when Catherine was happiest? Back when she and Heathcliff were just kids and they could play together. Before everything got all complicated."

"Very good, Angela. That very point is further substantiated when Lockwood hears about Catherine's history from Nelly Dean. In fact, Catherine's appearance to Lockwood is prophesized by Catherine herself. Catherine tells Nelly that she had a dream she died and went to heaven. But she feels unwelcome there, so she says, 'I broke my heart with weeping to come back to earth.' In quite dramatic and Miltonic fashion, Catherine claims the angels threw her out of heaven and she landed in the middle of the heath beside Wuthering Heights, where she awoke 'sobbing with joy.'"

As the professor prattled on, Alderson reflected for a moment before writing down his impressions.

She's spending an awful lot of time on dreams and ghosts. The students are clearly engaged, but what's her angle?

"Therefore, if we reconsider the novel's events in the order they actually happened, Catherine's appearance to Lockwood is foretold. It was destined to occur."

Several students nodded. A few continued to take notes while others appeared to be confused by the professor's emphasis on such a minor scene.

"The strangest aspect of this chapter is of course the description of the ghost itself," Upham suggested. "Lockwood claims he reached out to close the window, but the ghost grabs his hands. In order to free himself, he rubs the ghost's wrists against the broken windowpane. At this point in Lockwood's account, Brontë notes that 'blood ran down and soaked the bedclothes.' Lockwood then piles up some books in front of the broken window, but the ghost knocks them to the floor."

The detective shifted in his seat.

So what? What is she trying to prove with all this? This is a very odd way to apply critical thinking skills.

"Now, how could we substantiate any of these claims?"

A student blurted out her answer. "If the sheets were actually stained with blood when Lockwood wakes up? After Heathcliff comes in to yell at him."

"Exactly. But Brontë never returns to this detail!" Dr. Upham stressed. "She never says that the books were on the floor, or that the sheets were stained with blood at any other point in the scene. This is an example of the frustrating ambiguity that has come to define classic gothic literature. Those of you that have taken Professor Coffey's American lit course have seen this with Hawthorne and Poe, and especially Henry James, who perfected the use of ambiguity in *The Turn of the Screw*. But no matter how ambiguous, ghosts, by nearly all accounts before and after Brontë published her novel in 1847, are not usually described as *corporeal* entities."

Alderson looked up from his notepad when the professor's voice suddenly fell silent. The color had drained from Dr. Upham's face, and she appeared to have lost her train of thought.

"They don't bleed," she said in a faraway voice. Alderson had to strain to make out her words. "They can't feel physical pain, and they don't kill people."

What the hell is she talking about?

After shaking off whatever had distracted her, Dr. Upham resumed her lecture with a more detached tone.

"With these strange and inexplicable details, Brontë manages to give Lockwood's account a sense of verisimilitude. That's what makes this scene so compelling and haunting. And it's precisely this kind of ambiguity that drives Heathcliff mad near the end of the novel. Ironically, he insists that Catherine's haunting him not because he actually *sees* her, but because she *doesn't* manifest. He believes her ghost is real because it would be just like her spiteful personality to torment him by staying hidden from him."

Alderson glanced around at the students. The professor still held their attention. They were taking notes and seemed eager for Dr. Upham to continue.

"According to most accounts of the demonic, that is precisely how malicious and malevolent spirits triumph over their victims. By driving them to question their sanity, and by bending the rules of logic."

Alderson's eyes were riveted to the professor.

To say she's a bit off would be an understatement. But these kids are eating it up. So this is either a brilliant act to engage her students, or she actually believes this shit. Either way, this is going to be an interesting conversation...

"Alright. That's enough metaphysical speculation for today," the professor said. Her students began to gather their belongings and shove them into their unzipped book bags. Dr. Upham raised her voice above the shuffling noises of her students. "For Wednesday, make sure you've read through the rest of volume one and be ready to discuss the chapters up to and including Catherine's death."

"Umm, spoiler alert!" A boy a few rows from the front groaned.

"Really, Connor? Catherine's ghost appears in Chapter 3!" Veronica quipped. "We're reading classic Victorian novels here. Of course the heroine's gonna die. That shouldn't surprise you."

The students began to exit the auditorium. Several of them passed by Dr. Upham's desk, but one of them stopped to speak with her. Alderson couldn't make out the conversation, but he watched as the professor nodded her head, forced a smile, and waved the student off.

She's playing nice, but she wants to get out of here. Ritter said she hasn't been as involved in campus events, but that doesn't seem to have hurt enrollment for this class. This is a huge turnout for a course on stuffy Victorian novels.

A dark-haired girl glanced at Alderson as she passed but didn't say a word. After the last few students made their way to the exits, Alderson rose from his seat and walked down the angled ramp to approach the professor. Her head was lowered as she gathered up her notes and dog-eared copy of *Wuthering Heights*.

"Dr. Upham?" he called out, reaching into his pocket for his badge. "Detective Nathan Alderson. I'd like to ask you a few questions."

The professor looked up from her briefcase and froze when she saw his badge. Up close, Alderson was taken aback by her appearance. Although well-dressed in a black pencil skirt and olive cashmere sweater, the professor looked exhausted. She had heavy bags under her bloodshot eyes and wore very little make-up.

All she could manage to say after a few seconds was, "In regard to what?"

You need to loosen her up. You caught her off guard. And you were right. Her mind is clearly elsewhere. That must have been the twentieth time she's delivered that lecture. Otherwise, she's a fucking mess.

"So, *Wuthering Heights*," Alderson began and glanced down at his notes. "Charlotte Brontë, right?"

Veronica continued to stare at the detective. His mistake, however, snapped her back to reality.

"Uh, no. Emily. Charlotte wrote *Jane Eyre*. And their sister Anne wrote *Agnes Grey* and *The Tenant of*—"

"Yeah, that's right," Alderson interjected. "There were three Brontë sisters. It's been years since I read *Wuthering Heights*. My wife was watching the Laurence Olivier version on PBS a few months ago."

When the detective mentioned his wife, the professor's eyes darted from his left hand and then back to his face. Alderson detected a hint of disappointment in her weary eyes.

"But I don't remember the scene you were lecturing on being so crucial," Alderson noted. "In the book, or the movie."

"Most people overlook it," Dr. Upham replied. She eyed the detective with apprehension.

"And all this stuff about ghosts? When I think of this novel—"

"You think of Heathcliff and Catherine on the moors," Veronica speculated. She continued to ramble nervously. "Their ghosts gliding side by side in the moonlight. Yeah. That's kind of a cultural cliché. So, you know, I try to give the kids what they want even though—"

"I was going to say I usually think of this novel as a love story," Alderson corrected her. "I don't remember there being many supernatural elements. Are you a believer in the supernatural, Professor Upham?"

She narrowed her eyes at the question. "I am. I'm sorry, what did you say your name was again, Detective? And what exactly can I do for you?"

"Nathan Alderson," he repeated. "I'm investigating the death of Tyler Marshall. I'm assuming you've heard about the case on the news?"

The professor nodded without responding. Her eyes were wide, but she refused to meet the detective's glance.

"I, um... yeah." She swallowed, still staring at the edge of the podium. "I did hear about it."

"Well, I had a couple questions for you," he said. "First of all, where's Edison Raymer?"

"Raymer?" The professor's jaw dropped open when Alderson mentioned her former colleague's name. "I... I don't know. What does he... I don't understand?"

"Were you involved romantically with Edison Raymer?"

"I suppose you could call it that," she replied with a hint of malice. "Look, I don't understand what this has to do with... with Tyler Marshall. I told the last guy that came down here all I knew about Raymer."

"Last guy?" Alderson was taken aback. "You mean a detective? Like me?"

"Uh-huh."

"Do you remember the name of the man that came to see you?"

"No," she replied. "He was a bit older. Heavy-set. Kind of a curmudgeon."

"Pettit?" Alderson asked. "Was his name Rudy Pettit?"

"Yeah, that sounds familiar. Why?"

"No reason."

That asshole already talked to her. But he never noted a goddamn thing. What else did he leave out of his reports?

"So when was the last time you spoke with Raymer?"

"I haven't seen him since the fire."

"The fire?" Alderson studied her reaction carefully.

Typical. Play her like a spurned ex-lover. Get her all pissed off about this Raymer character. Just like Ritter.

"Yeah. His house went up in flames and he skipped town. That other detective made it pretty clear he thought Edison burned down his house. You know, for the insurance money."

"Do you think that's what happened?"

"No." The professor folded her arms across her chest. Her anxious expression became a look of disdain. "Edison Raymer was stubborn, but he'd never resort to something so pedestrian or vulgar. Things weren't going well for him here. We'd broken up, though that seemed to bother me more than it affected him. Also, he was pretty much fired from the college, but he hated teaching. So, the fire was probably the last straw. For one guy to have so much bad luck in so short a time, it's no wonder he left town. Mid-life crisis. Who knows?"

"You rehearse all that as much as your lecture on Brontë?"

Veronica pursed her lips, then spoke. "I don't know what you're talking about. Like I said, I already told Detective Petty about all this a while ago."

"Pettit," Alderson corrected. "That had to have been almost two years ago."

"Right," she said. "And nothing's changed since then."

"May I ask why you and Edison broke up?"

"May I ask how that's relevant to your current investigation?"

"That's what I'm trying to find out," Alderson said with undisguised frustration. "I'll level with you, Professor Upham. Detective Pettit never said a damn thing about meeting with you. I'm retracing his steps from a case a few years ago. A student at your college was attacked and maimed. Jennifer Stroud. Apparently, she was one of Raymer's students. Do you remember that?"

"I can't say I do," she lied.

Alderson noted her eyes beginning to wander. A look of fear soon reclaimed her features.

She's full of shit.

"Well, there are similarities between that case and the Marshall boy."

"What kind of similarities?"

"I'm not at liberty to divulge that information."

"Well, I mean, what kind of similarities could they have? Wasn't that girl raped?"

"I thought you didn't remember Jennifer Stroud's attack?"

Veronica stumbled over her words. "I don't know. I didn't remember her name. But I remember the, uh, the incident. Some European guy, right? He tried to attack her."

"He bit her," Alderson confirmed. "Which was the same method of attack on Tyler Marshall. But this time, the killer succeeded. The boy's body was entirely drained of its blood."

Alderson watched unmoved as Veronica Upham grasped the edge of the podium to steady herself. She dropped her briefcase to the floor.

"Dr. Upham, I'm gonna be straight with you. Your behavior right now is extremely suspicious. I don't want to cause a scene here at the college, so I'll ask you this once, and only once. Are you willing to cooperate with me?"

She nodded in silence.

"Good. Can you take half a day? Who do you need to report to?"

"I'm done for the day," she managed. "I've got office hours but it's fine."

"OK. Even better. No one here has to know anything, but I'm going to escort you to the parking lot—"

"Am I under arrest?"

"No, but—"

"I think I can help you," she whispered. Her eyes were filling with fresh tears. She balled her hands into tight fists and nodded over and over. "I promise. I can help you. But I don't want to talk about it here."

"I understand that, Professor Upham, which is why I'd like us to head down to the station so I can get a statement from you."

"No."

"No?" Alderson raised his eyebrows in surprise. "I don't think you meant that, so I'll give you a chance to rephrase your answer."

"No, I mean, not there. I don't want to talk about any of this there either. They'll think... they'll think I'm crazy. I'll only talk to you. At my house."

"That's not how things work, Professor."

"I have evidence." She swallowed hard and struggled to meet his gaze. "I can't explain it here. But I can show you. And... and you can judge for yourself. I swear I'll cooperate with you. I'll do anything you say. But you have to believe me."

Alderson stared at the anxious professor as a whirlwind of thoughts spun through his mind.

She's terrified. But what's she so afraid of? Maybe she's trying to lead me into some kind of trap and the killer's at her house? Christ, Raymer or possibly this Bartsch guy could be squatting back at her place.

"Fine." Alderson responded and threw open his coat. "You see my duty weapon, Professor Upham? It's loaded, and I've got a keen eye. If you've got someone lying in wait at your house, I won't hesitate, you understand?"

Tears streamed down the professor's face.

"There's no one at the house," she said. "Just me." She wiped her nose on the arm of her sweater and laughed awkwardly. "I'm so sorry, Detective Alderson. I'm a mess. But you'll see why soon enough. I just hope to Christ you believe me."

10

THE PROFESSOR'S AGING VOLVO MADE AN ABRUPT TURN INTO a smoothly paved driveway. Detective Alderson, following behind in his unmarked cruiser, slammed his foot on the brake pedal. He shifted into park. Before Veronica could ease out of her car and approach the front door, Alderson was across the lawn and standing at the driver's side window.

Her pale face glanced up at him, surprised by his sudden appearance. She stopped and put the window down.

"Turn off the ignition." Alderson leaned over and pressed his palms against his knees. "Put the car in park and walk with me to the front door."

"But I—"

"No argument," Alderson stated. "Just do as I say."

Perplexed, Veronica collected her belongings, cut the engine, and stepped out next to the edgy detective. She noticed him part his long coat, so his duty weapon was in full view. "There's no need for any of this, Detective. There's no one else here but me. I swear. I'm not stupid."

"I understand, but this is how we're gonna do things. You don't leave my sight until we're finished."

Veronica led him up the sidewalk to the front door as she fumbled for her keys.

Alderson stood by as she fought with the lock and managed to wrench the door open. "You should fix that deadbolt."

"Yeah," she answered, then entered the foyer. "Please excuse the mess. I haven't done much housekeeping since Saturday."

Alderson followed her into the living room. His right hand rested on the butt of his duty weapon. He scanned the room and listened for movement, but there weren't any unpleasant surprises waiting for him.

As Veronica tossed her briefcase on a chair, he glanced around the cluttered room. He noticed a half-empty bottle of blended whiskey on the coffee table. After maneuvering around the furniture, Alderson approached the picture window and parted the heavy drapes. A line of white powder along the windowsill caught his eye. The detective licked a finger, pressed it against the white line, and smelled the crystalline powder.

"Table salt?" He glanced back at Veronica, who was returning the bottle to its proper place alongside a decanter set. "Put that whiskey down and have a seat."

She nodded as a trembling hand reached up to straighten her reddish-brown hair. Still watching the detective, she settled into a tall wingback chair. Alderson took out his pen and notebook. He flipped it open and paused. "So what's with the salt on the windowsill? Is that to keep out bugs or something?"

"It's to keep out evil."

Alderson glanced down at the blank page in an attempt to contain himself. "Don't you think an alarm system would be more effective?" He tapped his pen against the edge of the small leather binder. "Or perhaps a firearm?"

"I've got a pistol upstairs," Veronica said as she crossed her legs and folded her hands. "But I don't take any chances. Not when—"

Alderson looked up as the professor stopped herself. "You were saying?"

"Never mind." She glanced with longing at the decanter set. Alderson remained by the window.

"You have a drinking problem, Dr. Upham?"

"Yeah, the *problem* is I've got a detective in my house grilling me, and I sure could use a drink."

Alderson disregarded the professor's response.

She's definitely an alcoholic. I bet the first thing she does when she gets home is get completely loaded. She's trying to numb herself.

The detective pursed his lips, still deep in thought.

But this business with the salt is odd. There's another line of it along the threshold of the door. Probably around the whole damn house. What's she trying to protect herself from?

He stood behind a long sectional sofa that faced a mantle and fireplace. "Let's cut to the chase. I'm here because you said you could help me with this case. You said you had evidence to show me. So where is it?"

"Can I ask you a few questions first, Detective?" Her tone indicated fear, but her nervous demeanor seemed to have little to do with Alderson's presence in her home.

"You'd best not be wasting my time," Alderson warned.

"Do you believe in... in ghosts?"

"No, I don't." Alderson felt his blood boil. His vision blurred with anger. "Now I have a question for you," he said. "Did you kill Tyler Marshall?"

"Christ, no!" Veronica nearly bolted out of her chair. "I'd die before I'd ever hurt a child! I'm not a killer! I can't believe you'd even—"

"Where were you on Friday night? Between the hours of five and ten o'clock?"

"Here," she replied. Alderson noticed her hands were trembling. "In my house."

"And what were you doing here in your house?"

"I was reading. Then I graded a few papers. Although it doesn't look like it now, I spent part of the night and most of Saturday cleaning."

"So, you've got no alibi for Friday night?" Alderson spoke as he wrote.

"No. Unfortunately, I don't."

"Hold up your hands."

"What?"

"Hold up your hands. Palms outward and spread your fingers."

With a puzzled look on her face, the professor did as she was told.

Alderson took a few quick steps across the living room and paused in front of her chair. He examined her quaking hands and nodded to himself.

They looked to be far too small to match the handprints at the Marshall boy's crime scene.

"What the hell was that for?" she asked.

"You ever been arrested, Dr. Upham?"

"Absolutely not!"

"Would you be willing to submit your fingerprints and a mold of your teeth for forensic analysis?"

"Wait, what? Teeth?" The professor furrowed her brow. "I mean, if you insist. But I'm telling you, I didn't kill that boy."

Alderson nodded, finally took a seat on the sectional, and turned to face Veronica.

"Yet there's no one to vouch for your whereabouts on Friday night," he reminded her. "Did you make any phone calls? Run any errands? Go to the store?"

"I told you, I was here at home." Veronica's face conveyed a range of emotions. She was at once embarrassed, indignant, and frightened. Her voice quavered as she spoke. "I left campus around two or three o'clock that afternoon. Is it a crime to have no social life? To spend your Friday nights alone with a bunch of books... and a bottle?"

Alderson continued to scrutinize the middle-aged woman. She failed to disarm him with her pleading eyes.

"Is that when you put the salt on the windowsills?"

Veronica was thrown off by the sudden shift in his interrogation.

"No," she replied. "I did that on Sunday night."

"Why?"

"Uh, because I was... I was afraid."

"Afraid of what?"

"Alright, look. I'm just gonna spill it, OK? 'Cause there's no other way to do this. On Saturday night, I held a séance. I've been doing this with a few of my colleagues for several years. Maybe once or twice a month. I'm what you'd call a medium, although up until recently—"

"Colleagues?" Alderson interrupted, his pen at the ready. His mind was reeling with the absurdity of the professor's confession. He could only imagine how much more ridiculous the conversation was about to become. "OK. First of all, who else was here with you for this séance or whatever it was? I need first and last names."

"Uh... Peter Tully and his wife Janice..." Veronica uncrossed her legs as she trailed off.

"They from around here?"

"Sort of. Peter's an editor for an academic press. Janice owns an art gallery closer to Richmond. I've known them for over fifteen years."

"But *they* can't vouch for your whereabouts on Friday night?"

"No, our sitting was on Saturday."

"Sitting?" Alderson wrinkled his brow at the unfamiliar term. "Is that what you call these... rituals?"

"Well, no. I mean..." Veronica sighed and attempted to gather her thoughts. "It's not necessarily a 'ritual' in the strict sense of the term. The word 'séance' in French roughly translates to a sitting or session."

"OK. Was there anyone else at your sitting beside the Tullys?"

"Yes. A friend of theirs named Eric Sandoval."

"And who is he?"

"He's also from Richmond. Eric works at a bookstore up there. He's about twenty-five... maybe twenty-six."

"Kind of odd for him to be hanging out with a bunch of middle-age academics, isn't it?" Alderson clicked his pen and searched her expression. "Was Edison Raymer here, too?"

"No, like I said before, I haven't heard from him in almost two years." The professor's tone grew agitated at the mention of Raymer. The detective decided to push her further, hoping her emotions would get the best of her and he'd catch her in a lie.

"Earlier today I spoke with Dean Ritter. He implied that before Professor Raymer was dismissed from the college, some of his students complained about what he was teaching. From what I understand, Dr. Raymer was an anthropologist. Do you know what was so unusual about his lectures?"

"Ritter never liked Raymer. He was constantly trying to find a reason to fire him."

"You didn't answer my question, Dr. Upham. So, let me rephrase it for you. What reasons did Edison Raymer give to Dean Ritter to cause him to question his competence in front of a classroom?"

"Raymer was interested in various aspects of American and European folklore." She hesitated and glanced away from the detective. "His research skewed toward the esoteric and obscure. He was a brilliant man, but not everyone shared his preoccupations. He was hard on his students, but he maintained high standards and expected a lot from them."

"OK, but every department in every university has cranky or eccentric professors. Why was Ritter so frustrated with him? You said not everyone shared his preoccupations. What do you mean by that?"

She sighed. "Over the years, he developed a fascination with the occult. And that fascination began to influence the direction of his research, as well as the content of his courses."

"And I gather that you *also* share a similar fascination with the occult and the supernatural with Dr. Raymer?"

"Yes, you could say that."

"OK, so you and he were both into this whole occult thing. Ghosts. Séances."

"Look." Veronica scowled at Alderson. "We shared a general interest in the paranormal, but we had significant differences of opinion on the most basic and fundamental things, and could never see—"

"What kind of differences?"

"I suppose I tend to gravitate more toward the lighter side of things. White magic. You know, like—"

"Are you insinuating that Raymer was drawn to the darker side?" He furrowed his brow. "Like Satanism?"

"No. What we... I mean, what *he* was interested in has nothing to do with the Christian devil. The term 'occult' isn't synonymous with devil worship. It's an umbrella term, encompassing the unknown or unseen."

"Believe it or not, I'm aware of that." Alderson scratched his cleft chin as he studied her body language. "So you had a séance with Peter and Janice Tully?"

"Yes, that's what I've been trying to—"

"And Eric Sandoval?"

"That's correct. Now—"

"What about Matthias Bartsch? Was he here?"

"Alright, stop it!" Veronica had reached her breaking point. "You know damn well Matthias Bartsch wasn't here."

"No, actually I don't know that," Alderson replied. "But there's some connection between him and Raymer. And possibly you. So, you need to start telling me the truth."

"Matthias Bartsch didn't kill Tyler Marshall."

"How do you know that?"

"If you'd quit playing the role of bad cop and listen to me, I'll tell you."

"Calm down, Dr. Upham. I'm just—"

"You're just trying to get me to crack," she interrupted. "There's no need. I've already fucking cracked. You have no idea what I've been dealing with the past forty-eight hours. You want me to stop wasting your time? Fine. Then you need to listen to me and stop scribbling in that goddamn notebook."

"You're out of line!" Alderson pointed a finger at the professor. "I've been more than patient with you when I should've hauled you into the station. I came here out of courtesy, and you've—"

"On Saturday night, I channeled the spirit of Tyler Marshall."

"What?" Alderson slapped his notebook shut and glared at her.

Veronica sat up straight and collected herself. "At the séance. At that table." She pointed a thumb into the dining room. "And I have it all on video. That's what I brought you here to see."

"That's what you brought me here to see," Alderson repeated, nodding his head. He rose to tower over the professor and locked his hands on his hips.

"Yeah." She looked up to meet his incredulous gaze. "I've got audio and video to prove that his... his spirit *spoke* through me."

"And his spirit spoke through you." Alderson turned his back on the professor and began to pace around her living room.

"And there's more. You see, in that footage, something else came through."

Alderson spun on his heel. He ground his teeth together in anticipation of the professor's next outrageous claim.

"I think I... uh, we... brought something into this house besides the spirit of that little boy. Something malevolent." Tears welled in her eyes. She could barely catch her breath as she spoke. "And..."

"Go on."

"I think it might be responsible for Tyler Marshall's death."

Alderson rubbed his temples and leaned over the back of Veronica's chair. He had no words for the professor as she rose to her feet. She motioned for him to follow her into the dining room.

"Just take a seat." She gestured to the table. "All I can do is show you what happened. You can decide for yourself."

"Fine." Alderson threw his hands up and stormed toward the dining room table. He grasped the back of a wooden chair, tossed his notebook on the table, and sat down.

As Veronica booted up her laptop, she gave him a weary glance. Alderson avoided her gaze and stared at a half-melted candle resting at the center of the table.

What the fuck are you doing here? Wasting time with this attention-starved professor when you should be out in those woods. What are you gonna tell D'Amato? That your only lead is some crazy woman's found-footage horror movie? This whole day's been shot. You best get your shit together before tomorrow.

Alderson glanced up as Veronica closed the curtains.

"For the glare," she explained. "It needs to be dark in here so you can see."

Alderson nodded and folded his arms across his chest. He had never removed his coat and had only now realized how warm it was in the professor's house. She seemed to have noticed and offered to take his coat.

"Just show me the video," he snapped.

Veronica flinched at the detective's curt response. She clicked her mouse, turned up the volume, and angled the laptop toward him. Alderson reached across the table and adjusted the screen to enhance his view.

The detective watched in silence as the footage of the séance began. When the tiny bell rang on the table, Nathan's expression remained unfazed. Standing beside him, Veronica kept her eyes on the detective rather than the screen. After the first rap struck the table, he glanced at Veronica and sighed.

"That one actually broke my pencils," she noted a few minutes later. "I could show you. I saved a file where I enhanced the lighting and slowed it down. You can see a distinct shadow across—"

"That won't be necessary," Alderson said. He kept his eyes locked on the screen.

Veronica took a deep breath as the video reached the sequence where the boy's spirit began to speak through her. When the light airy voice identified itself as Tyler, Alderson clenched his fist.

"Where did you get lost?" Peter Tully asked the spirit.

"In—in—in the woods."

The hair on the back of Alderson's neck bristled. He leaned forward and folded his hands under his chin.

"There's a lady in the woods!" the boy's voice cried out.

Despite his better judgment, Alderson felt uneasy.

"Watch closely, Detective."

He held up his hand to silence the professor as he focused on the video footage. Peter continued to ask the frightened boy questions.

"What does the lady look like? What is she doing?"

Alderson was taken aback when the child began to sob.

"She's not my mommy!"

"Jesus Christ," Alderson muttered. His skin began to crawl.

These are just parlor tricks.

But how the hell did she know? That can't be her voice.

Don't be a fool. You're not gonna be duped by some crackpot professor. There's only one way any of them could have known. The suspect was in that room.

Was it Tully? His wife?

The speakers on Veronica's laptop crackled as the child's voice cried out. Alderson watched as one of the candles in the video was knocked on its side.

"Right there," Veronica whispered.

"Huh?"

"Did you see that streak of light?"

"No." Alderson's mouth was dry as he attempted to speak. "I didn't see a damn thing."

"Hold on." Veronica leaned forward and reached for the mouse. She paused the video and with a few clicks of her index finger, she opened the .avi file she had saved as HERE.

"There she is, Detective." Veronica pointed at the screen and addressed Alderson in a low whisper. "I think that's your killer."

Alderson was dumbfounded as he stared at the image frozen on the screen. He could clearly see the outline of a woman's face. Her expression was contorted with rage. Her mouth hung open in a terrifying scream.

"Can you play it again?" he asked. "In slow motion?"

The professor complied with his request. Alderson watched as the streak of dim light slowly swept across the tabletop and veered away from the camera. He could see the furniture and decorations of Veronica's living room in the background as the strange anomaly floated out of frame.

"You altered it," he said aloud, indifferent to whether he offended the woman at his side.

"All I did was slow it down and boost the contrast. That's it."

"Then someone else did." Alderson's tone was flat and without emotion.

"No one's been here since Saturday night," she insisted. "And besides, when I told Peter and Janice about this, they refused to talk to me. You're the only person I've shown this to."

"You had all weekend to edit this footage." Alderson continued to reach for a rational explanation. "Or more likely, you could've made the video on Sunday night, after you heard about the boy's murder."

"First of all, I don't know the first thing about that kind of detailed editing," Veronica admitted. "I just know how to do basic stuff on here. In regard to the timing, I can assure you this happened on Saturday night. You can look at the specs on the files themselves. They tell you when the files were created."

"So there's some kind of time stamp on this footage?"

"Yes," Veronica confirmed. "It can be activated during playback. See? Like this." She replayed a small portion of the video. Alderson noted the pale-yellow digits in the bottom right-hand corner of the screen. The counter indicated the footage had been recorded at 9:14 PM.

"Is that all of it?"

"No."

"No?"

"That thing was here the entire time. I guess it just got angry when Peter kept asking questions. Here. Look."

Veronica pointed to the screen where a shadowy figure stood in the background.

"Watch carefully, and you'll see the point when she first appears."

As she suggested, Alderson noticed the silhouette suddenly appear. To reiterate her point, Veronica forwarded and rewound the footage one more time.

"Like I said, she was there all along. Watching us."

"Pause that," Alderson commanded. "Can you zoom in? Right there?"

"Yes."

Alderson squinted his eyes as he examined what appeared to be a black dress hanging from the figure. He remembered the piece of cloth he'd taken from the crime scene.

That can't be possible. There's no fucking way.

"Is there anything else?"

"Not really," she replied. "There was an EVP on the audio that occurred earlier."

"EVP?" Alderson turned to the professor with hollow eyes.

"Electronic Voice Phenomena," she explained. "It's when you're able to record a spirit voice that's inaudible in real time."

"What did it say?"

"'Leave us alone.' Here, listen."

Veronica pulled up the EVP file and played it for the bewildered detective. His reaction was stoic and cold. He simply nodded.

"Do you have audio of the, uh... boy's voice?"

"Yes."

"Pull it up."

Veronica did as Alderson requested. The detective leaned forward and watched as the cursor moved across the irregular sound waves.

"Tell me something," Alderson asked. "Do the patterns of those waves match your voice? Or are they different?"

"It doesn't work like that. The spirit used my body as a vessel. It spoke with my voice. So, if you're thinking the waves of his voice are going to look different than my own, then you'll be disappointed. It's not like a fingerprint where—"

"What about the EVP? You said that voice was... how'd you put it? 'Inaudible in real time?'"

"The wave patterns are weaker, yes. They are several decibels lower than Peter's voice, or my voice. But unfortunately, none of this can really prove anything. At least scientifically speaking. It's just a matter of my word. And I swear to Christ I didn't fake any of this."

Alderson didn't reply. After a moment of awkward silence, Veronica ventured to ask the detective's opinion of what she had just shown him.

Instead of replying, Alderson pushed the chair back and stood. His abrupt movement startled Veronica and she watched him pace with apprehension.

"One of you had to have known," he said with a furious glare. "Either you or that Tully woman threw your voice. I'll admit it. You spooked me out. But I'm not gullible enough to believe any of this horseshit."

"Detective, I swear to—"

"How did you know?" Alderson slammed his palm against the table. He leaned forward and stared into Veronica's bloodshot eyes.

"I'm not a ventriloquist if that's what you're trying to imply!" Veronica snapped. "And this... this whole thing has ruined my relationship with my only friends!"

"Well, I'm really sorry to hear that," Alderson replied with no trace of sympathy. "But that boy is *dead*. I saw his body in those woods. And there's no way you could've known those things unless one of you put him there!"

"Listen, it wasn't me, and it sure as hell wasn't one of my friends. There's no way they would've done this."

"I'm through with all this bullshit, Dr. Upham. You're coming with me. Now."

"Hold on a minute!" She raised her hands in protest. "I showed you this in confidence. I showed you because I'm afraid. And goddamn it, you're afraid too! Why else would you start puffing up and playing alpha dog?

You're afraid. This is exactly what people do when they're faced with things they can't explain."

"Save it for your students, Professor. I don't need a lecture. I've had it with all of this. Now are you gonna cooperate like you promised, or do I have to drag you away in handcuffs? It's your choice."

"I've got nothing to hide," Veronica responded. "I just thought you were going to be different. I thought you'd understand. There are things out there you can't just catch and put in a jail cell. And if you don't listen to me, you'll never find that boy's killer."

"So what the hell am I supposed to do, huh? Tell the chief of police that his suspect is a ghost? You just sold yourself out, Upham. Every bit of so-called evidence you showed me suggests that one of you are the suspect, or at best, this is some sick joke. You claim this happened Saturday night? This story hit the news by noon, so one of you decided this would be a great way to add a little drama to your experiment!"

"I don't watch the news!" Veronica shot back. "And you don't know Janice. If she or Peter knew about this ahead of time, she would've said something about it. She would've asked if I'd heard the news and—"

"An AMBER Alert went out to all cellular phones in the area Friday night when the Marshall boy went missing," Alderson countered.

"I don't answer the phone unless it's a number I recognize."

"It would have been a text message, Professor."

"Wait a minute." Her eyes lit up with recognition. "Do you mean one of those loud random warning things? A few months ago, one of those went off in my classroom. Half the students' phones started to buzz all at once and derailed our entire discussion. I probably spent an hour messing with the settings on my phone and finally figured out how to disable the damned thing. So, I'm sorry, but I never received it."

"You have an answer for everything, don't you? Wanna know what I think?"

"Look, I'm not trying to—"

"I think you faked it. All of it. So you'd look like a credible... psychic or medium or whatever the hell you call yourself."

"No, I didn't," Veronica insisted. "I blacked out. I don't remember most of what I showed you. All I have is the footage itself. I'm seeing the same things you saw, and they don't make sense to me either."

"What was the purpose of this séance, anyway?" Alderson asked. His emotions had gotten the better of him, and he spoke with open disgust. "What the hell were you people even *doing*? You think there's an afterlife? You think there's a heaven or hell?"

"You better believe there's a heaven. And a hell." Veronica's eyes gleamed with fury. "Maybe not in those specific terms, but I assure you. This world isn't everything. I only wish it was."

"You're wrong." Alderson was unyielding.

"I'm not gonna argue with you, Detective. I'm telling you the truth. I don't know what else I can do."

"I want contact information for everyone involved in that séance. Now."

"You can have it. But they're just as clueless as I am. They're harmless people. Review the footage. You'll see that Peter was just as taken aback by all this as I was. His wife was a nervous wreck, and that sure as fuck wasn't Eric Sandoval playing ventriloquist."

Alderson could barely see straight. He had no idea how to react to what the professor had shown him. His instincts revolted, for he knew none of it could be real. Yet it made more sense than he'd ever admit to Veronica Upham, Chief D'Amato, or even himself.

You gonna go tell Tyler Marshall's mother her son was murdered by a ghost? How do you think that one's gonna go over?

"Detective Alderson?" Veronica asked with a timid frown. "I know what you're thinking. You can't believe any of this. But I'll come with you to the station. You can run my prints. Take blood and hair samples. Take a cast of my mouth or whatever. I don't care. I'll take a polygraph if you want. It's fine. I'll do whatever I can to help you."

"That won't be necessary." His tone was matter of fact. "Just give me those phone numbers and don't make any plans to leave town."

"Where am I gonna go?"

"Nowhere," he said. "If there's even the slightest credence to anything you said... I might need your help."

Veronica nodded as the detective snatched his notebook from the dining room table and adjusted the collar of his coat. After double-checking her cell phone, she provided Alderson with contact information for the Tullys as well as Eric Sandoval. Veronica caught the detective's eye as he slipped his notebook and pen into his coat pocket.

"I know you think I'm a lunatic," she said with sincerity. "But I appreciate the fact you at least came here. A lot of people wouldn't have done that. I can tell you're a good person. And if there's anything else I can do, I will help you."

For a moment, Alderson was moved by her candor. With a nod he moved toward the professor's foyer. Veronica trailed behind him with a look of disappointment in her eyes.

"As far as the particulars of the Marshall case, don't discuss them with anyone," he advised. "And for your sake, as well as that boy's family, don't mention anything about ghosts or séances or any of that paranormal shit."

"I understand."

As Alderson swung open the heavy door, he glanced down at the line of salt along the threshold and then back at Veronica.

"And if you're so concerned for your safety, I'd suggest you throw the salt away and fix your deadbolt."

11

NATHAN WOKE WITH A START. HIS CELL PHONE CONTINUED to vibrate on the nightstand until he reached to silence the alarm. Although it was still dark, his wife had already vacated her place beside him. He could hear her scrambling about the kitchen as she prepared to leave for her morning shift at the hospital. The smell of fresh coffee and burnt toast had made its way to the bedroom.

Alderson kicked away the covers, slipped out of bed, and padded down the hall to the bathroom. After a quick shower, he dressed and descended the stairs. Kelly had gone, but she left half a pot of coffee brewing for him. She also scrawled a message on the dry erase board affixed to the refrigerator.

I still miss you.

Nathan paused and then wiped it clear with his hand.

Forgoing breakfast, Alderson poured himself a cup of coffee and took a seat at his dining room table. With an irritated sigh, he tossed his ledger and cell phone onto the smooth surface. The digital screen temporarily lit to display the time.

6:37.

As the sky began to lighten outside the kitchen window, Alderson thumbed through his notes from the previous day and frowned. His stomach churned as he mentally rehearsed the finer points of the discussion he was about to have with his superior.

Just get it over with. You don't have time to waste another day chasing dead-end leads or bullshit claims of paranormal activity.

Alderson snatched up his phone, selected Dominic D'Amato from his 'Favorite' contacts, and placed the call. Only two short rings sounded before the chief of police answered.

"You're up bright and early this morning, Nate."

"Yeah, well, I was eager to talk to you, sir. Although—"

"I had the distinct privilege of speaking to David Ritter yesterday," he interrupted. "You left quite a first impression."

"Oh? And what'd he have to say about me?"

"The pompous prick had his secretary phone me first before she connected the call. Fucker thinks he's the head of MI6 or somethin'. Anyway, after Moneypenny formally announced his arrival, I let him air his grievances and promised I'd have your badge polished if you behave like that again. Nice touch with the Affirmative Action angle, by the way."

"Uh, thanks," Alderson replied.

"So, let's get down to brass tacks, Detective. I'm looking around my desk here, but I don't see your report anywhere."

"Well, sir, I've gotta be honest with you. Yesterday didn't go very well at all. You don't have a report because I don't have anything *to* report."

Alderson hesitated, bracing himself for his supervisor's reaction. D'Amato simply waited for him to fill the awkward silence.

"As you've already gathered, my chat with Ritter was a complete waste of time. The girl attacked in 2014 withdrew from the college. Her alleged attacker, Matthias Bartsch, was not a registered student, nor was he part of the foreign exchange program. He has no affiliation with the school whatsoever."

"OK," D'Amato acknowledged. "What about the girl's professor?"

"He's been a thorn in Ritter's side for years. The dean was trying to find a reason to fire him. He probably persuaded Detective Pettit to intimidate Raymer and shake him down after the Stroud girl was attacked. She was one of Raymer's students."

"And this Raymer guy is also the one who split after supposedly burning down his house?"

"That's correct. But if you remember, the BOL for Stroud's assailant was for a blond-haired German Caucasian in his late twenties. Edison Raymer is a black man in his fifties. The bad blood between him and Ritter isn't pertinent to this case. Simply put, Chief, he's not our guy."

"So what happened to the German?"

"Yesterday I asked McCain to track down Bartsch's current whereabouts. Frank said he ran down all the original contacts we had for him. His last known employer was Serenity Springs Elder Care. Unfortunately, they're under new management. The receptionist and supervisor we pulled in for questioning back in 2014 no longer work there. It's unlikely they'd have any new information to share."

"Couldn't hurt to try," D'Amato advised. "Maybe one of them heard something through the grapevine after the fact?"

"Possibly. But my guess is that if Bartsch is still in Williamsport, he's laying low. Or he's operating under an alias and got himself fixed up with new paperwork and a false ID. Just to be sure, Frank contacted all the local airports, train stations, car rentals, and bus terminals to see if he skipped town recently. And I don't know if he's talked to you yet, but he didn't find anything. He tried INTERPOL but again. Nothing. There's simply no trace of him."

"Unless you count the body he left in the woods on Friday night," D'Amato reminded him. "That would suggest to me he's still somewhere in or near Williamsport."

"With all due respect, sir, I don't think Bartsch killed Tyler Marshall. As I noted in my initial report, even though the MOs are similar, I find it odd that he'd switch from assaulting a college girl to murdering a child. The profile just doesn't add up."

"Of course it does. First of all, this freak bit that girl on the neck. The only reason he didn't finish whatever sick Dracula bullshit he was trying to pull was because he got interrupted, and the girl got away. So the creep went after someone who couldn't fight back. Someone isolated. And this time, he finished the job."

"And it took him more than two years to try again? In my opinion, that just doesn't wash."

"Like I said, he had to wait for the right opportunity."

"The forensic evidence doesn't support the notion that he was squatting out in those woods." Alderson took a cleansing breath before continuing. "There were no signs anyone was holed up or camping out there. We canvassed the entire area. I don't think he was just biding his time waiting for Tyler Marshall. Why didn't he attack any other kids near the elementary school?"

"I don't know, Nate. But it's your job to find out."

Alderson paused. He couldn't afford to lose his temper. Blood rushed to his ears. His stomach was in knots. He considered his response carefully.

"This isn't the first time kids have disappeared in those woods. There are three other missing persons cases that went unsolved on Rudy Pettit's watch. It was *Pettit's* job to find out what happened back then, but the trail went cold."

"That was all the way back in the 1990s! That's got nothing to do with this case."

"I think it does. It's too much of a coincidence for those kids to disappear in the same place. Which is why—"

"That's precisely what it is—a coincidence. Now before you ask me about arranging a geophysical survey out there, I'm going to tell you the same thing I told Ash Townsend. The answer is no."

"Again, with all due respect, sir, that's not good enough."

"Pardon me?"

"Please, Chief. Hear me out. I don't think it was Bartsch because he would've been too young to kill anyone in the early 1990s. And he certainly wasn't alive in 1959."

"Wait, what? What the hell are you talking about?"

"There are two more unsolved cases involving missing kids near those woods. One in 1959 and another in 1965. I pulled the reports and talked to Tom Carpenter from Archives. He verified that a boy named Danny Adams ran after his dog and was never seen again. Then, a little girl, Sally Benson, wandered away from her—"

"Alright, stop," D'Amato warned. "Kids go missing all the time. This is nothing new. They run away. Or they get *abducted* and—"

"No. With one exception, these kids were too young to run away from home."

"OK, so where are you going with this, Detective? You think we need to look for a seventy-five-year-old retiree with a penchant for kidnapping? Does Tom Carpenter have an alibi for Friday night? Listen to yourself, Alderson. None of this makes any sense."

"You're right, sir. It doesn't make any sense. Which is why I haven't written my report yet."

D'Amato sighed and muttered an indecipherable obscenity. "Let's back up. What do you think is going on here? Do you even have a working theory?"

"Well, the only thing that comes to mind is that it's some kind of cult. Or a family with some pretty disturbing traditions. But that doesn't sit right with me either."

"Good, because that's the last thing I want to tell the goddamn press. You're really putting my balls in a vice here, Alderson."

"Then reconsider my request for the geophysical survey," he replied. "Think about it. It's the only lead we have. If we can prove there are more bodies up there, we can blow this whole thing wide open!"

"That's the last thing I wanna do! Have you thought about the optics on this? How the hell am I gonna—"

"Forget the optics! The parents of those missing kids deserve to know what happened. *We* need to know what we're dealing with so we can prevent this from happening *again.*"

D'Amato fell silent. As his supervisor continued to mull things over, Alderson pushed him further.

"If I'm wrong, then so be it. We tear up an ugly patch of forest and are spared from having to confirm those parents' worst fears. Fine. I'll take full responsibility. We've got nothing to lose."

"Just our reputation. We'll look like a bunch of incompetent fools. Not only that, but this shit costs money. The department's gonna have to pay an astronomical sum for your wild conspiracy theories."

"It's all we've got, Chief," Alderson said. He shifted the phone to his other ear and waited for D'Amato to reply.

"Christ, even if we *could* get a more advanced forensics crew up there, it's going to be *days* from now, if not a week or more," D'Amato said. "And the longer this shit drags out, the more likely some of the facts about this case are gonna start to leak. Those NDAs won't mean jack-shit if someone from the search party throws back a few cold ones and tells his buddy the killer drank that kid's blood."

"I understand, but that'll happen whether we find this boy's killer tonight or three months from now. Williamsport's a Southern town, sir. People talk."

"Well then, you and McCain need to get your ears to the ground. Start branching out. Even if we do find more bodies up there, we still need *a* suspect. If it isn't Bartsch, then you need to find out who it is!"

Dr. Veronica Upham has an idea who killed Tyler Marshall. But I don't think you're gonna like the so-called optics of what she has to say either, Chief.

"I'll see if I can pull some strings up in Richmond," D'Amato continued. "But I can't promise you anything. If I don't have any luck there, I'll try Norfolk. Just don't ask me for any more favors. You and McCain better sort this out."

"Thank you, Chief. We'll do our best."

"What was it you said?" D'Amato paused. "Oh, yeah. *That's not good enough.*"

Before Alderson could reply, the call went dead. He tossed his phone on the table and hunched forward. He ran his fingers through his hair and slapped his palm against the table. His coffee mug sat cold and untouched beside him. His adrenaline was starting to slow, but his stomach still churned, and his jaw ached. Alderson continued to stare ahead, replaying the conversation in his mind.

He's going to fuck me over. The same excuse as before. It'll be some bu-reaucratic formality. More red tape. Paperwork. LOAs. Lack of funding. The wrong optics.

"Fuck it." Alderson grabbed the coffee mug, drained its contents, and slammed it back on the table. He forced the dining room chair backward with a loud scrape across the floor and rose to his feet. He raced back upstairs to the master bedroom, where he quickly exchanged his black slacks for a pair of worn bootcut jeans. He slipped a dark-red flannel work shirt over a charcoal Henley and returned to the downstairs foyer.

The closet doors swung open with a clatter. He rummaged through a pile of mismatched shoes and sandals until he found a pair of worn hiking boots. He bent down, wrenched them onto his feet, and returned to the kitchen.

Alderson pocketed his phone and took his ledger. He rifled through his work satchel until he found a folded topographic map. It smelled musty, just like the back room of the police station's archives where he picked it up. He curled it into a scroll as he darted through the kitchen. Finally, Nathan walked into the garage and opened the door of his pickup truck. He pitched the map inside and left the door ajar.

One by one, he threw a shovel and a pick-mattock into the truck bed. As he lingered by his vehicle, Alderson decided to bring along some insurance. He ducked back into the house, unlocked his gun cabinet, and removed one of his hunting rifles. It was a .243 with a telescopic sight mounted on the receiver. Why he picked that rifle over one of his shotguns, he had no idea. The detective wasn't thinking clearly, but he knew enough to shove the correct box of ammunition into his jacket pocket.

Before he got into the driver's seat of his truck, he locked the .243 onto the gun rack. The rifle was already loaded. Alderson threw the box of ammunition into the glove compartment as he slid behind the wheel.

After turning the ignition, he untangled his phone charger, plugged the narrow end of the cord into his cell, and connected the other end to a cigarette lighter in the center console. He tapped the button above his visor and watched the garage door rise in the rear-view mirror.

When it was clear, he backed down the driveway and onto the street. He swung the wheel in the opposite direction he usually took to the police station. Another quick jab to the garage door opener and Alderson was on his way to South Williamsport Elementary School.

✝

By way of the old map, he found a discreet entrance to the forest in the form of a fire trail. The trip got rougher as he plowed through a creek bed, so he shifted into four low. He spent a good fifteen minutes slow-crawling over rocks and deadfall. When he thrust the 4x4 shifter back to high, he glanced at the map, then back through the windshield. Above the tree line, he could see the tall chimneys of the gutted plantation house.

As he drove on, he placed his finger on a convergence of roads in the center of the map and corroborated his destination.

The crossroads.

His head shook from side to side as the truck rumbled across the uneven turf. Tree branches scratched and scraped against the windshield of his pickup. He reached up to shield his eyes as the sun began to cut through the trees, momentarily blinding him.

Alderson stopped the truck and killed the engine. As he exited the cab, he shoved his keys and the fully charged cell phone into his pockets. He reached in to withdraw the rifle from the rack, then propped it against the rear tire. Finally, he removed the pick-mattock and shovel from the truck bed.

With the tools in hand, he walked down a slight grade and made his way toward the area of depressions he had noticed on Sunday night. He cursed himself for not bringing a machete to clear the waist-high brambles and weeds.

Once he reached a small clearing, the detective tossed the pickaxe to the ground and used the shovel to balance himself. Alderson took a few minutes to assay the land in the bright light of the clear morning sky.

In the middle of the crossroads—barely visible due to the tall clumps of grass—was a large sunken area.

Nathan picked up the mattock and moved into the center of the crossroads with his tools. He pitched the shovel aside and surveyed the ground at his feet. As he raised the pickaxe to break the soil, he hesitated.

Do it, Nathan.

No one else will.

The burden of proof lies with you.

He brought the pickaxe down. The soil—bound together with roots from brambles and briars—was rough and stony. The detective cursed himself again. He'd forgotten to bring work gloves, so his hands would be a bloody mess by the time he finished.

He raised the mattock and brought it down repeatedly until the soil was loose, turning the earth so the shoveling would be easier.

Satisfied with his handiwork, Alderson stepped back and dropped the pickaxe. Although it was chilly in the barren forest, he was soaked in sweat. He paused to wipe his brow on the back of his sleeve. He then bent his knees and used the shovel to unearth layer after layer of soil from the suspected grave.

When you hit the top of that skull, or see that first little finger, you keep your shit together.

You will not lose it.

Not here. Not now.

The pile of dirt beside the rough-hewn ground increased while the shovelhead probed deeper.

This is it. Barely three feet beneath the ground, you careless fuck. I've got you.

A manic grin tugged at his lips as he hauled up another shovelful of soil. "I've fucking got you."

But the sight of a discolored bone protruding from the earth sent Nathan Alderson spinning on his heels. He regained his footing, steeling himself upright with the long-handled shovel.

Keep going. You can't stop now.

Alderson fell to his knees and used his bare hands to sift through the dirt. An earthworm twined itself around his fingers. With a cry of disgust, Nathan shuddered and flung it away from his hand. He cleared enough soil and sediment to expose the skeletal remains of a small child. The flesh and tissue had rotted away long ago. A greenish mold clung to the stained bones. Alderson fought a wave of nausea as he surveyed the features of the half-exposed corpse.

The distal phalanges of the left hand were curled into a tight fist. A handful of baby teeth protruded from the jaw line. The crown of the skull bore a long fracture. The small ribcage was shattered in several places. Encrusted against the dead child's sternum was a gummy, viscous piece of yellow material. Alderson could trace a faint floral pattern on the rotten fabric.

It's Sylvie Aptheker.

Alderson recalled Pettit's old case file—specifically, Deborah Aptheker's statement. *She said her daughter was wearing a printed sundress when she disappeared.*

Alderson felt compelled to uproot the entire forest until he found the missing bodies of Emily Ryerson, Justin Rooker, and the others. Yet the father in him balked at the gruesome discovery. He pushed himself backwards on unsteady hands. His eyes never left the grotesque cluster of Sylvie Aptheker's bones.

He rose to his knees and doubled over, clenching his teeth in a futile attempt to prevent sickness from overtaking him. Vomit spewed past his lips and seeped between his filthy, lacerated fingers. The dark brown fluid splattered on the weedy ground beside him. The smell of coffee forced him to retch again.

Goddamn it. Get it together.

Alderson smeared his lips against the flannel sleeve of his shirt and fumbled a trembling hand into his pocket to retrieve his cell phone. He slid his finger to unlock the main screen and tapped the camera application. Once he could see the grisly sight of the child's corpse within the frame, he snapped a succession of photos.

He managed to take a half-dozen more shots of Sylvie Aptheker's remains from various angles. Seized with a fit of blind fury, Alderson slid the phone into his shirt pocket and grabbed the shovel. He thrust the head into another sunken rut in the ground.

Let's get this over with. There are more of them buried here. You've only just begun, and you fucking know it.

The nauseous, sweat-soaked detective dug like a man possessed. He didn't bother to break up the soil first, and his shoulders began to ache as he threw large clumps of rocky clay from the shovel. This time, he left no neat pile beside the would-be grave. He simply flung the dirt clods off into the nearby brambles.

The blade of the shovelhead struck something soft and yielding. Alderson stopped digging. He noticed something protruding from the hole before him. It wasn't moving. As Nathan lifted the shovel, the shadow cast by the steel head disappeared. A faint, inexplicable hiss began to issue from the ground. The detective crouched and pushed away the loose soil around the object and saw another resting close by.

Is that a...

No, it can't be.

It looks like...

Nathan tore at the ground with his blistered hands, and uncovered part of a thin shriveled arm. His heart pounded in his chest as the strange hiss grew louder.

It couldn't have been in the ground long. Decomp isn't too far along, but something isn't right.

Alderson continued to push away the soil until he unearthed the desiccated limb and shoulder of a dead infant. He flinched as wisps of fetid smoke curled up from the baby's shrunken flesh.

"What the hell?"

He watched in confused terror as the edges of the leathery skin darkened. As Alderson uncovered the worm-eaten material of a rotten undershirt, the hand and arm burst into flames. He gasped as the erupting flames scorched his fingers. He continued to pull away clumps of soil as the newborn's corpse smoldered in the light of the morning sun.

Alderson removed another clump of dirt and found himself gazing at the withered face of the buried infant. But as the sun beat down overhead, the baby's face experienced a terrifying transformation.

The child's eyes were obscured by milky cataracts. Its fibrous jaw slipped open and produced an unmistakable groan.

Jesus Christ, it's alive. It's still alive!

Incredulous, he watched as the infant's wrinkled countenance changed. Its mouth puckered and seemed to curl inward. The lids of its white eyes suddenly closed, and then fluttered opened again.

Your phone! Get your fucking phone!

The mummified corpse continued to twitch. Its small fingers dug into the earth as Alderson fumbled with the phone, smearing his dirty thumb across the screen. He tapped the red button on the video app and began to record the incomprehensible phenomena transpiring in front of him.

The infant's lips began to sear. Its jaw fell agape. A thin line of smoke issued upward and began to pour from its nose.

Alderson slid his thumb and forefinger across the smudged screen. He zoomed in as the infant's face crumpled inward, consumed by sparks of discolored flames. The pungent stench of burning flesh assailed the detective's nostrils.

Nathan kept his grip on the phone and continued to document the flames rising from the makeshift grave. It wasn't long before the small inferno died out, leaving nothing but a silhouette of ash and a dark-boned skeleton.

Alderson stood frozen in horror. His eyes swept along the ground as he noticed other depressions in the earth around him. He slid the phone into his pocket, retrieved the shovel, and staggered to his feet.

He took a few short steps toward another brush-covered depression in the ground. With his mind blank, the detective cleared away the growth and hollowed out the earth with methodical precision.

Before long, he unearthed another petrified child. Wisps of dark hair still clung to its head. As with its predecessor, its white eyes lay open, staring upward at the sky. Her lips were pursed in a tight frown. Her small hands were resting on her chest, crossed over her heart. The detective groaned as the dead girl's arm began to inch upward. The bony fingers twitched, as if rediscovering their dexterity. It struggled to raise its hand higher—a futile attempt to shield its blank eyes from the sun. Smoke began to drift from her fingertips.

Alderson shuddered as the thing in the ground cried out. Its parched voice was weak, but maddeningly audible. Bright flames flared up to devour the disinterred body. The detective steadied his hand to ensure he captured the horrific transformation on video. He recoiled from the putrid stink as the unburied corpse was reduced to cinders and bone by the daylight.

Nathan stared at the smoking gash in the earth. His first instinct was to call D'Amato and beg him to send Townsend and her team as soon as possible.

Yet in the back of his mind, the detective imagined Townsend babbling about spontaneous combustion from putrescine gas or some other desperate scientific theory.

"Fuck that," he rasped.

Alderson struggled to process the situation he suddenly found himself in. His reason had all but threatened to desert him. There was only one person who would believe his story and the bizarre evidence he had managed to gather.

After a few minutes of stunned silence, the detective reached a decision. He wouldn't call Forensics. Not yet. Not until he knew exactly what they would be dealing with.

His eyes swept the crossroads. He scanned the edges of the path that led to the plantation house. His gaze lingered on the clumps spread out on the road winding in the direction of the river.

There were sunken pits and depressions everywhere.

The evidence has been here the whole time. Right under my feet. I walked right over these graves twice the day I went up to the plantation. How the hell could I have missed them?

Alderson felt light-headed. His vision blurred and he struggled to maintain his balance. He reached up and clutched the back of his sweaty neck. Everywhere he looked he spied an unmarked grave.

A guttural yell—half-pleading, half-enraged—sprung up from deep within. He ground his teeth together and turned back to face where the bones of Sylvia Aptheker lay.

I need to cover my tracks. In case the killer comes back. Or on the off chance someone else comes out here. I can't leave her like that.

Gripping the shovel, he returned to the moldering skeleton. For a moment he stood before the yawning grave, studying its gruesome occupant.

Why was she different? Why didn't the same thing happen to her?

Against his waning judgment, he bent forward with the shovel and commenced to cover the remains. One by one, he refilled each of the three graves he'd hollowed out. All the while, he struggled with the awful implications of what he had just witnessed.

Those bodies went up in flames after they were exposed to light, not just the air. It was the light of the sun.

"Like a... like a fucking vampire," he muttered aloud to no one. The sour taste of bile fouled his breath. A sharp breeze whipped up the path and rustled through the piles of dead leaves. The trees swayed slightly in the wind. The Virginia forest enveloped him on all sides—silent and dense. Indifferent.

He shook his head as tears burned his eyes. He felt the urge to vomit again. In his dehydrated state, he only managed to gag. He recalled the words of Veronica Upham, which he'd been so quick to dismiss.

"There she is, Detective. I think that's your killer."

Alderson's calloused hands tightened around the wooden handle of the shovel. In a rage he kicked a stray clod of dirt at his feet. Although he couldn't account for the dreadful conviction welling up inside him, the detective's instinct returned to permit a moment of clarity.

Those things were placed here. Deliberately. Like some perverse collection.

Alderson began to chuckle under his breath. Silent tears streamed down his face as he bent forward, his hands clutching his knees.

"Vampires," he said aloud again. Still bent double, he glanced to his left and then to his right. Another wave of laughter erupted from the detective. "A fucking vampire!"

That explains why the killings go back so far.

Goddamn things live forever, don't they?

Who knows how long this has been going on?

The detective retched once again. The cramping in his stomach was severe but nothing but acid reflux filled his mouth. He spat a wad of dark phlegm on the ground and staggered forward. He dragged his muddy boots through the tall grass along the path and fell breathless against the side of his truck.

With his back against the passenger door, Alderson took out his phone and began to review the footage. He frantically thumbed through the photos and watched the videos at least three times before he closed the application.

It had all been real.

He glanced down to see the rifle propped against the rear tire. Taking it in his unsteady hands, he considered turning it on himself, as he had been tempted to do at least once or twice since Cody's death.

Man up, motherfucker.

Find another way.

Nathan returned the long gun to its designated place at the rear of the cab. Next, he pitched the muddy pickaxe and shovel into the bed of the truck. He crawled into the driver's seat, turned the ignition, and shifted the truck into four high to get moving.

Alderson sped through the underbrush, careless of the low-lying limbs that blocked his path. As he made his way from the mouth of the forest, he emerged into the open and overgrown field near the ruins of the burned plantation. The brick chimneys loomed in his rear-view mirror.

The detective thrust a booted foot down on the accelerator pedal and drove down the path. Eventually, he was out of the forest and back on State Route 619 with only one destination in mind.

12

WITH HER BODY SLUMPED ON A WEATHER-BEATEN PORCH swing, Veronica Upham took a drag from a cigarette. The morning sun was warm, but the air retained a seasonal chill. She had just returned from purchasing two packs of Marlboro Lights at the corner store a few blocks from her house. The professor hadn't bothered to shower or apply any make-up. Instead, she grabbed a rumpled sweater from a drawer and threw on a pair of loose-fitting jeans. Her foray into civilization was brief, and she had been sitting on the swing for half an hour. The lesson-plans for her Wednesday morning class remained unfinished and nagged at the back of her mind.

Fuck it. You know that book inside and out. Just point out the sadomasochism of Catherine and Heathcliff's doomed love affair and be done with it. That's all they're gonna write about anyway.

Today, you're going to sit on this porch and do nothing.

A half-dozen cigarette butts had already been smashed in a rectangular ashtray on the patio table at her side. Although she questioned her unhealthy impulse purchase, her fingers were spinning the tiny metal wheel of the plastic lighter in anticipation of her next cigarette. The craving for nicotine was accompanied by an even greater thirst for liquor.

A new vice helps to balance another.

Is that Oscar Wilde?

Probably not, but it should be.

122

Indifferent to the filmy ashtray, Veronica flicked her ashes into the air and let them drift to her feet. Each chirping bird reminded her how out of synch she had become with the world around her. The occasional car whizzed past her house, but the professor remained lost in her thoughts, which drifted back to the previous day's visit from Detective Nathan Alderson.

You should've never shown him those videos.

You put your already tenuous reputation on the line. If word of this gets around campus, you're through. End of story.

Veronica had already dodged a bullet two years before. Rumors swirled around the college campus after Raymer disappeared. She did everything in her power to reassure Dean Ritter that her relationship with Edison was finished and that her dedication to teaching remained intact. But Veronica knew that her tenured status as full-professor and the prior years of service to the department were the only reasons she still had a job. She could sense that Ritter barely knew what to do with himself now that Raymer was gone, and she worried she could be his next target.

The professor also knew that her attitude wasn't helping matters. She had become complacent. Distracted. The joy that once accompanied teaching had slipped away long ago. The names and faces of her students were indistinguishable from one another. She hadn't written anything for months and had no intention of publishing another article if she could help it. The novels she once loved, the penny dreadfuls and poems that once thrilled her, all paled in comparison to the cold hard facts of the world she inhabited.

We're all doomed. Everything. Everyone.

It's only a matter of time.

"This is the way the world ends," she muttered to herself. The rusty chains of the porch swing creaked above her. She bit the filter of the cigarette between her teeth, took another drag, and exhaled. Veronica watched as the smoke drifted upward. Her thoughts became preoccupied with the case of Tyler Marshall.

The details she learned from Detective Alderson confirmed one of the professor's worst fears—that another vampire was active in Williamsport.

But this one is different, she reminded herself and reflected on the spectral figure in the video footage.

Either way, it's not human. If it's not like Matthias or Laura, it's just something else lurking out there that we weren't meant to discover.

The wind picked up and rattled the wind chimes above her head. Veronica snubbed the spent cigarette in the ashtray, its successor already between her lips awaiting the flame of her lighter. The one she had just finished continued to smolder as she wondered how much the boy's family had discovered. Did Alderson tell them how he died? Did they see his corpse? Do they actually expect justice? Closure?

They'll never catch the killer because the police have no idea what they're dealing with. Even if they do find it, they'll have no idea how to stop it.

Veronica was overtaken by a sudden coughing fit. Her lungs were unaccustomed to such heavy smoking, but she continued to savor the deceptive comfort of her cigarette.

So why don't you just tell them?

The professor had worked up enough courage to tell Alderson about the séance. But confiding the whole truth, as it were, was a risk she couldn't afford to take.

He didn't believe you anyway. You're lucky you're not in a padded cell right now telling your life story to a therapist.

"No cops," she reflected aloud with bitterness. "Isn't that right, Edison?"

Raymer is no longer running your life. You make your own decisions, remember? If you can save a few lives, who the fuck cares about your reputation? What happens when this thing kills again? You wanna carry that around on your shoulders too?

Veronica was startled by the sound of a loud engine and the screech of tires in front of her house. The professor glanced up to see a dusty gray pick-up truck pull into her driveway. Squinting her eyes, she could see the face of Detective Alderson through the soiled windshield.

"Speak of the devil," Veronica marveled under her breath. A knot was already forming in the pit of her stomach. She rose from the swing, the half-smoked cigarette still between her fingers. She watched with apprehension as Alderson leapt out of his truck and slammed the heavy door with a loud bang.

When the detective emerged around the side of the truck, Veronica noticed he was wearing civilian clothes. His jeans were covered in mud and his flannel shirt was soaked with perspiration. He charged toward the professor's front door without a greeting or acknowledgement.

"Detective Alderson?" Veronica asked in surprise. Her eyes lingered on his face, which was drained of color.

"We need to talk. Now."

Alderson shouldered his way past the professor and snatched the handle of the Plexiglas storm door. Dumbfounded, Veronica flicked her cigarette into the yard and followed him inside. The distraught police officer made a beeline to the bar cart near the back of her living room.

"Help yourself," she said as he snatched a bottle of single malt scotch. Veronica noticed he overturned two glasses to receive the alcohol, which he poured with an unsteady and filthy hand.

The detective held up the beveled glass. "You're gonna need one of these after I tell you what I saw today."

"Mr. Alderson," Veronica began, taking a tentative step into the room. "Pardon me for saying so, but you look like shit." She reached out to retrieve the drink he had poured for her. "What the hell happened to you?"

"I was just in the woods." He swallowed a mouthful of scotch and winced as the liquor burned his throat. "Where they found Tyler Marshall. Not too far away, there are some overgrown crossroads. You know, like old fire trails or something. And I had a little... uhh... a little *excavation.*"

"What are you talking about?"

"I dug up three bodies," he revealed. "But I'm certain there are more, still in the ground. I'm also pretty sure the first one was a little girl named Sylvie Aptheker. She went missing almost twenty-five years ago." His eyes were glassy and vacant.

"I'm... I'm sorry," was all she could manage. She lowered her eyes to stare at the glass of scotch in her hand. Veronica lifted the tumbler and drained its contents. The awkward silence remained.

"So what are you doing here?" As soon as she spoke, she regretted the abruptness of her words. She quickly attempted to recover her visitor's unexpected confidence. "I mean, how can I help you, Detective?"

"The second one was a baby." Alderson's voice briefly cracked. "Probably no more than six months old."

"Jesus Christ, that's horrible!"

She stood frozen as Alderson prepared a second shot of whiskey. His hand continued to tremble, which caused him to spill a portion of the amber liquid over the rim of the glass.

"When the sun hit its body, it burst into flames." Alderson fought to maintain control of his emotions. "Right in front of my eyes."

Veronica nearly dropped her drink to the floor. "What did you say?"

"The damn thing looked at me." The detective's unexpected laugh made Veronica's flesh crawl. "It looked me square in the eyes, then its face shriveled up and the rest of it caught on fire."

"Oh my God," she whispered. The edges of the room started to fade. Veronica steadied herself against her wingback chair. She sank down into its cushions as Alderson finished off his second shot. He glanced at the bottle but resisted the temptation to pour a third.

Leaving his empty glass behind, Alderson made his way toward Veronica. He reached into his pocket and withdrew his cell phone. The detective sat down on Veronica's sofa and placed the phone on the coffee table.

"That phone contains both photographic and video evidence of what I've just described to you. Proof of..." Alderson trailed off, then cleared his throat to regain his composure. "Now it's your turn. You're going to look at *my* evidence, and then you're gonna tell me *exactly* what the fuck is going on."

"Look, I don't know what you—"

"Cut the bullshit, Upham." The detective's eyes bore a hole through the professor. "I need you to level with me, because I think you know a lot more about what happened to Tyler Marshall than you told me yesterday."

"But I—"

"And I think you know damn well what I found buried up in those woods today."

Veronica took a deep breath. She placed her empty glass on a ceramic coaster and reached for Alderson's phone. Her pulse was pounding in her ears as she scanned the interface in search of the photo app. She tapped on the icon and a grid comprised of several small thumbnails appeared on the screen. Without her reading glasses, the images were hazy and indistinct.

She used her thumb to scroll upward and tapped on the first photo that appeared to be in focus.

The picture was of Detective Alderson smiling and hugging a fair-haired boy against his bare chest. Both father and son were smiling and clad in matching navy-blue swimming trunks. Veronica could see the sun shimmering off the surface of a river or lake behind them. She scrolled her thumb to the left to reveal a more candid photo, likely taken a few seconds later. Alderson was looking down at his son and was pointing a finger at the camera. The bright-eyed child—who must've been around the same age as Tyler Marshall—was looking up at his father and laughing.

"This must be your son," Veronica said. "He looks just like you."

Alderson blinked. His face darkened as if from an unforgivable insult. Veronica flinched as she observed his expression shift from confusion to rage, and then from disgust to sorrow. When he finally spoke, it was as if his face had turned to stone.

"He's dead," Alderson replied. "He drowned this past summer. You must have scrolled up too far. Those pictures... are the last of him."

"I'm so sorry. I didn't know."

The detective continued to stare her down. His expression was cold and unreadable.

Veronica scrolled past more pictures of Cody Alderson and the river where he died. She felt a deepening pity for the detective, which soon gave way to dread, as she braced herself for whatever disturbing images she was about to see.

The first picture was blurred. She could barely discern the loosened ground and weeds. The second photo, to her dismay, was far sharper, and revealed a perfectly centered shot of a small skeletal ribcage. Clumps of muddy soil were still wedged in the narrow gaps between the child's bones. Veronica closed her eyes and thumbed to the next photo. Alderson had turned the phone vertically to better frame the child's exposed torso and to provide scope for the shallow grave where it had been unearthed. It appeared that he had repeatedly mashed the button, for several nearly identical photos followed in succession. Veronica paused when she reached the next sequence of pictures. Alderson had zoomed in on the child's skull, which appeared intolerably small and fragile.

"My God," she whispered.

Despite all that she had experienced with Raymer two years before, nothing could have prepared her for the series of images that followed. It was exactly as Alderson had described. A shriveled infant lay screaming in a muddy depression in the earth. The first few shots were unclear on account of the photographer's unstable hand. Veronica clenched her eyes shut but the images were forever burned into her memory. One photo in particular stood out. The unsteady motion of the camera—coupled with the curling flames and rising smoke—had caused a grotesque distortion akin to a double-exposed negative.

Veronica felt sick to her stomach. Her thoughts raced with the implications that began to take shape in her mind. Yet with each successive image, she felt herself growing numb to the atrocities preserved in the detective's photographs. She wondered if the ability to develop a tolerance to horror was one of humanity's most vital traits, and if such a defense mechanism suggested a potential for mercy within the grand design of the universe. She knew the desperate lack of feeling creeping through her was something she shared with Detective Alderson, and that it was the only thing keeping each of them from coming apart at the seams.

The next photo in the sequence was blurred and indistinct. Then she noticed the small white timestamp in the bottom right corner of the square.

It's a video.

With a flinch, Veronica tapped the screen. She gasped as the video began. The volume had been maximized and the hiss of the flames and Alderson's heavy breathing startled her almost as much as the confusing visuals. The flames had already begun to consume the mummified infant's body. She squinted as the lens was mercifully obscured by the rising smoke. Before long, it cleared again and the charred remains of the child lay smoldering in the ground.

"Jesus Christ."

Alderson's shaky camera work lingered on the blackened skeleton for another five seconds until the video suddenly stopped. Veronica braced herself and started the next video. Another small, shriveled body lay in the ground. At first, its demeanor seemed peaceful. But it looked as though its wrinkled skin was already smoldering when Alderson began recording.

Veronica nearly dropped the phone when the girl's hand slowly reached upward.

"Oh, God!" The professor looked on in horror as black smoke floated upward and out of frame. Tiny yellow flames spread across the corpse's exposed limbs.

It's just like Matthias.

Suddenly the professor jumped and tossed the phone onto her coffee table. The device had perfectly captured the undead infant's shrill yet feeble scream. Veronica clenched her eyes tight as the video continued to play. She fumbled blindly until she managed to minimize the app and stop the video.

She sat mute as Nathan studied her blanched expression. Careful to avoid his searching glance, she leaned forward and pushed the phone as far across the table as she could reach. As she slumped back into her chair, she eyed her empty glass with longing, and fought the urge to weep.

Veronica was startled when Alderson's voice cut through the silence.

"On my way over here, I racked my brain trying to come up with an explanation for what happened to those bodies." His tone was clipped and defiant, but the quaver of anxiety had yet to fade. "I'm not sure if you know anything about the process of human decomposition, but those... those two bodies displayed minimal signs of putrefaction. If anything, they looked to have been unnaturally preserved somehow. Petrified. The soil around them was untouched. There were fuckin' weeds growing on top of them!"

The professor stared forward with a pained expression. She could think of nothing to say that would reassure him. She simply listened as he failed to rationalize the shocking phenomenon he had witnessed.

"We can rule out the possibility of spontaneous combustion, because there wasn't enough time for gas to build up. Like I said, those bodies hadn't fully decayed. But there's no way they could've been preserved to that degree in this climate or in that kind of soil. It sure as hell looked like Sylvie Aptheker's body had rotted away right the fuck on schedule!"

Veronica glanced away in repugnance as the child's discolored bones flashed through her mind.

"So," Alderson concluded with a grimace, "there must be *another* explanation. One I can't tell my partner, my superiors, or my forensics team. I sure as *fuck* can't share this with the Aptheker family, even though they've been wondering what happened to their daughter for more than twenty years!"

The incensed policeman recognized he was shouting. He closed his eyes and bit his lower lip.

"So, I came here to ask *you* something, Dr. Upham." He leaned forward and slid his hands across the worn knees of his jeans. Before he spoke, he chose his words carefully. "Those things up in the woods... are they what I think they are?"

"Yes," Veronica confirmed. Tears began to stream down her face. "They are."

The policeman abruptly rose and began to pace behind the sofa. Veronica watched with indifference as he tracked mud from one end of her living room to the other. "How is that even possible?" he shouted. "How could... No!" He spun on his heel. His voice boomed throughout Veronica's house. Alderson paced like a rat in a cage, and the professor was certain he yearned to tear the room apart. "How could something like that even *exist?*"

Veronica sensed the detective couldn't bring himself to say the word aloud. She watched as the rational man before her questioned his reality. She saw the fear and doubt driving the hardened certainty from his eyes as he struggled to come to terms with the truth.

"Vampires?" Veronica finished for him. "Is that the word you're trying to say? The same thing happened to me. When Edison Raymer first proposed the idea. As you'd expect, I thought he was batshit crazy."

"It's not possible," he said. "It's just not possible."

"I assure you, Detective. It is."

"I don't understand," Alderson said. He continued to shake his head in disbelief. His pacing came to a sudden halt and he turned a suspicious glance on Veronica. "Wait a minute. Back up. What does Raymer have to do with this?" Alderson rubbed his hands through his hair and darted back toward Veronica and the sofa. "You need to start at the beginning. And don't bullshit me. I want to know *everything* you know about whatever is going on in this town."

"Alright look," Veronica began. "I'll tell you everything. But you have to promise you won't turn into a complete asshole and haul me off to jail!"

"I can't promise you anything, Dr. Upham."

"Matthias Bartsch is dead. Raymer drove a silver stake into his chest, and we watched him burn when the sun came up the next morning. It was just like in your video. His body was completely consumed as soon as the sun hit his skin."

Before Alderson could interrupt her, she forged ahead with her story. "Bartsch was over ninety years old. But he hadn't aged a day since he had been a German soldier in World War II. We found photos of him that dated back to the '30s and '40s. Then, our theories were corroborated by a man named Fenton Luttrell Jr., from Poquoson."

Veronica paused as she remembered the ill-fated veteran who had come to them for help. Alderson struggled to recall the name, but he hadn't seen it mentioned in Detective Pettit's files. He had the presence of mind to make a mental note of the unfamiliar name as she continued.

"Luttrell's father was murdered by Matthias in 1957. Junior and his older brother witnessed the whole thing. After the attack on the Stroud girl, Bartsch's sketch was all over the news and Junior recognized him." Veronica cast Alderson an irritable glance. "He came up here and said he tried to tell the police, but of course, no one believed him."

"Do you know who he talked to?" Alderson asked. "Was it Rudy Pettit? The same guy you said came to see you?"

"I have no idea. Whoever it was must've gotten fed up with him and sent Junior to talk to Raymer."

"It had to have been Pettit," Alderson mumbled. "Pettit talked to Raymer, but he never reported anything about this Luttrell character."

Veronica proceeded with her story. "We figured the attack on Jennifer Stroud was some kind of mistake. Bartsch slipped up and left her alive. So, Raymer got the bright idea to set a trap for him."

Veronica hesitated once again, as she reflected on how far-fetched her account was about to become.

"What kind of trap?" Alderson prodded her.

"One of Raymer's former students. There's really no other way to put this. We used her as bait."

"What was her name?"

"Laura McCoy."

"And how old was she?"

"She was in graduate school. Northern Virginia. Late twenties. She was a willing... participant."

"So then what happened?"

Veronica sighed. "Our plan totally backfired. Bartsch kidnapped her. Before long, we realized he turned her into one of those things."

Alderson clenched his jaw. He wished he had remembered to bring his notebook from the truck. "OK, so you said Raymer killed Matthias Bartsch. What happened to Laura?" He furrowed his brow in confusion. "You think she's the one out in the woods?"

"No," Veronica replied. "I highly doubt that. I don't know what happened to Laura. For all I know, she's still out there," the professor admitted with anxiety. "But I don't think she's been killing kids. Plus, like you said, the first body you found out there was from over twenty years ago. Laura probably wasn't even in grade school then."

"But Tyler Marshall was found on Friday. Drained of blood. So how do you know she isn't—"

"Look, call it a hunch. Whatever," Veronica said. "These things... they retain the personality traits of whoever they were before. When we saw Laura, she was still herself. She was just... angry. And very strong."

The professor tried to suppress the memory of the fledgling vampire's face buried in her neck.

"So what? She was *assisting* Bartsch?"

"It appeared that way," Veronica recalled. "In fact, she seemed pretty goddamn content to become a fucking monster."

"OK, hold on a second." Alderson rubbed his chin. "Did they come after you? How'd you find out Laura was... turned?"

"After she disappeared, we tracked them down. They were hiding out in a cabin. Basically, we got lucky."

"When you say 'we,' you mean you, Raymer, and Luttrell?"

"Yes."

"So, what happened to *him?*"

"He's dead," Veronica explained. "Laura broke his neck. But not before he fired off a few rounds of silver into Bartsch. That's how Raymer was able to take him down."

"Silver?" Alderson's head was spinning. "So, where's Luttrell's body?"

"We buried him," Veronica confessed. "Laura ran off. We had Bartsch pinned to the ground with the stake. And like I said. The sun came up, and that was the end of him."

"So neither one of you reported his death?" Alderson eyed her coldly. He shifted his weight on the sofa.

"Of course not," she admitted. "Who would've believed us?"

"And you just left him there?"

"Yes, we did, and I feel more shame and guilt than you could possibly imagine. But I didn't kill him, and neither did Raymer. There was nothing we could do. And I'll be damned if I was gonna take the fall for what Laura did to him!"

"What about Laura?" Alderson wondered. "Didn't her family report her missing? Did they come looking for her?"

"I have no idea," Veronica responded. "She was a bit of a loner. I certainly wasn't in a position to file a missing person's report."

"You know I could have you arrested for withholding evidence, right? Not to mention coercion, attempted homicide..." Alderson began to count off the charges on his fingers. "And you were an accomplice in the murder of Matthias Bartsch."

"Yeah, well, I'd like to see you try, Detective," Veronica shot back with unusual vehemence. "There's no trace of Matthias' body. He wasn't human. We did the world a favor when we erased him from existence."

"Did you record Bartsch's death?" Alderson asked. "Like you did with your séance?"

"We did. But Laura destroyed the camera."

"And Laura's still on the run," Alderson reiterated.

"I guess so. Thankfully, I haven't seen her or Raymer since that night. God knows I've been expecting her to show up for her pound of flesh. But she never came."

After a moment's reflection, Alderson nodded. "So that's why you have the salt around the windows. To protect yourself from her."

"Yes." Veronica felt foolish and crossed her arms over her chest.

"And you said this was the last time you saw Raymer?"

"It was the last time I saw or spoke to him directly, yes. After all that happened, we had a bit of a falling out to say the least." Veronica sighed. "But that was it. A couple months back, he sent me an email out of the blue. I think he's been... hunting these things. There was a link to a news story about a girl's suicide. Or at least, the police had declared it a suicide. But there were signs it was actually a vampire attack."

"Where did this take place?"

"In Maryland." She tilted her head to recall the specifics. "Annapolis, I think."

"OK." Alderson drew in a deep breath. "Do you still have that email address?"

"Yes."

"Good. Anything else I need to know?"

"No, I'd say that about covers it, Detective," Veronica said with bemusement. "You mind if we have another drink? I also think I'm about to break my house rules and smoke a dozen cigarettes."

"I'll pass," Alderson replied. "But you go ahead and knock yourself out."

Alderson pored over the information the professor had just shared with him while Veronica went outside to fetch her cigarettes, lighter, and ashtray. The screen door slammed behind her when she returned from the porch. She dashed to the bureau, poured herself a drink, and returned to her chair. Veronica studied the detective as he sat on the edge of her sofa. His eyes were miles away, tracing the patterns of the oriental rug beneath his mud-caked boots.

"So if Bartsch is dead," he finally said, "and you're sure the killer isn't Laura, then who do you *really* think murdered Tyler Marshall?"

"Well…" Veronica sipped her drink. "My hunch is that it was the thing in the video I showed you yesterday."

Alderson nodded without any sign of protest. Veronica felt encouraged by his lack of objections.

"So who is she?"

"I don't know."

"What is she? Is she a vampire? Or some kind of ghost?"

"Honestly, I don't know. She must be a vampire. Given what happened to Tyler Marshall and… and those kids up there." Veronica swallowed with the unpleasant reminder of the unburied infants. "But there's something different about her. She's not like Matthias or Laura. I'm afraid she's much older and unfortunately, much more powerful."

"How many of these things are out there?"

"Once again, I don't know." The cigarette steeled her nerves, making her feel jaded and resigned. "But there's probably a handful of them in every city or county. Christ, there's been at least three in Williamsport. Just think about Richmond. Or New York. London. L.A."

"Maybe they just stick to rural areas?" Alderson suggested. "So they don't expose themselves?"

A momentary hush fell across the room. The detective reached up and rubbed his eyes.

"I've seen and heard a lot of crazy shit today."

"It's a lot to take in." Veronica exhaled wearily.

Alderson gestured to the professor's crumpled pack of cigarettes. "You mind?"

"Go for it." She leaned forward and slid the ashtray closer to her guest.

"I haven't smoked since I was in college."

"I'd say today's a fine day to start again."

Alderson lit the cigarette and took a tentative drag. He coughed and tossed the pack and lighter on the coffee table. The detective leaned back on the sofa and continued to sort his racing thoughts.

"How could they have still been alive?" Alderson asked, breaking the lull in their conversation. "Or conscious. Whatever they were. It doesn't make sense."

After a moment's hesitation, Veronica offered a disturbing reply. "Because something must've made them that way."

The pieces of the puzzle were starting to fit together in her mind, but she could hardly bear to admit what the evidence suggested. As she gathered her thoughts, she spoke aloud in a quiet and reserved tone.

"It's not like the old movies. That is, vampirism is not transferred through a bite alone. If that were the case," she paused, reflecting to when she was bitten by Laura, and immediately stopped herself. "They'd be everywhere. Instead, it's passed on through the vampire's blood. In most legends, the victims are drained and brought to the brink of death. Then, they're forced to drink the vampire's blood, which restores them to life."

Veronica shook her head in bewilderment as she continued to test her knowledge of vampirism. "But I've never come across anything like this in the classic stories, myths, or folklore."

"You mean... children?" Alderson asked. The cigarette burned between his fingers, but he hadn't taken more than two drags since he first lit it.

"Infants," Veronica clarified reluctantly. "There've been a few very young or adolescent vampires in fiction. Le Fanu's Carmilla and Rice's Claudia are probably the most famous. More recently there was that Swedish novel by Lindqvist. But never any *that* young. It's abominable."

"So what are you saying?"

"I'm saying," Veronica swallowed hard, "that their transformation must've been *deliberate*. Some kind of cruel and terrible punishment." Her eyes gleamed with a raw and incredulous sorrow. "Can you imagine it? They were buried alive, Detective. They were turned, but they were too weak to fight their way out of the ground. So they lay there languishing. Starving. For God knows how long. I mean, they're practically immortal. The only thing that can kill them is sunlight, and I assume fire. Dismemberment, specifically severing the head. The stake through the heart just paralyzes them. It keeps them in place until the job is finished."

Alderson was dumbfounded. "You mentioned silver earlier? Silver bullets. I thought—"

"Yes, and before you say anything about werewolves, just trust me. Pure silver has occult properties, so it works on vampires too. But it just slows them down. It won't kill them."

"Crosses? Holy water?"

"Just slows 'em down," she repeated.

The pair sat in silence as Veronica continued to piece things together. Alderson spoke up after his thoughts returned to the ghostly presence at Veronica's séance.

"When we found the Marshall boy's body, there were handprints on the trees. Of course, we haven't been able to match them with any known suspects in the database."

"You're not going to, either," Veronica declared. "If what you said is true about the first body you found, she's been doing this for decades. Possibly even centuries."

"So how do we catch her?"

"That I don't know. But I assure you, it won't be easy."

Alderson began to speak with greater confidence and authority. "So she preys on children. She killed Tyler Marshall, but she didn't try to *turn* him. Or Sylvie Aptheker. Why?"

"Maybe she was interrupted?" Veronica suggested.

Alderson nodded. "It's possible. When we found the body, it looked as though someone had dragged it off the main path. He was covered in loose branches and leaves, as if she tried to hide him in hurry."

Veronica's back went rigid. "You said you found the bodies today at a crossroads, right?"

"Yeah, that mean something to you?"

"Well, in various myths and legends," Veronica explained, "people at risk of becoming vampires were often buried at crossroads. Usually criminals, suicides, or some unfortunate outcast. The idea was if the person returned from the dead, they'd be confused and not know which way to go. Then they couldn't find their way back to their families or raise hell in the villages."

"Yeah," Alderson recalled McCain's comments at the crime scene. "My partner actually alluded to something along those lines. At least, he seemed to know there was some kind of significance about crossroads."

Alderson considered the facts and then posed another question to the professor.

"Do you think someone buried those kids up there because they thought they were vampires? Who the hell would do something like that?"

"Well, two of them *were* vampires," she reminded him. "Any way you try to rationalize it, that's an irrefutable fact."

"OK, here's another thing." Alderson seemed more at ease and eager to consult the professor's opinions. "There used to be a plantation up there, but it's in ruins now. There's also a mausoleum at the edge of the property. I can't believe I'm even about to say this, but—"

"That's probably where she rests during the day," Veronica concluded with a fearful gleam in her eye.

"When I went out there the tomb was empty," he explained. "But one of the vaults was still intact. It had a name on it. Does the name 'Brennen' have any significance to you?"

"I can't say it does."

"Well, maybe your academic expertise will come in handy. I need you to find out all you can about that place. The full name on the vault was William Brennen. It was… a kid." Alderson froze as the significance crept over him. "I can't remember the exact dates, but they were only a few years apart. He had to have died very young."

Veronica felt a chill ripple over her flesh. "I can look into it. I'm a member of the local Historical Society. I also have access to a variety of research databases through the college. I'm sure I could find something."

"On the other hand," Alderson said, snuffing the malodorous cigarette in Veronica's ashtray. "We could just go up there and tear that tomb to the ground."

"I don't think that's a good idea."

"Why not?"

"Because we have no idea what we're dealing with. If this thing's as old as we think, and if she has the ability to… *astral project* or whatever the hell she did at the séance, we could be in serious danger."

"So, what do we do? I'm sorry but I don't know if I can buy into all this. I mean," he paused to correct himself. "If these things are really… *vampires,* and all this shit with Bartsch went down like you said it did, let's just find her and kill her! Isn't that what you and Raymer did?"

"Yes, but we got lucky. I hate to admit this, but I think we need to find Raymer."

"We don't have time!" Alderson cried. "She could attack again. Tonight, for all we know. We need do something now."

"Do you have any silver stakes lying around? Holy water? Your gun isn't gonna do shit against her. We're not prepared. But Raymer will know what to do."

"OK, but you said you don't know where he is. Or he's in Maryland or somewhere. How are we gonna find him?"

Veronica's shoulders slumped and she shook her head in defeat. After a few minutes' reflection, she gripped the arms of the parlor chair.

"The Aston house!"

"The *what?*"

"When Raymer was a grad student, he was a teaching assistant for Dr. Jerry Critchlow at the Annandale Institute."

"Never heard of it," Alderson said.

"It's a small school dedicated to parapsychology. That's where Laura was studying before Raymer coaxed her down here. Anyway, this house was where he had his first encounter with one of these things. It pretty much messed him up for life and set him on this path."

For a terrifying moment, Veronica wondered if the vampire they were searching for had been the same one that attacked Jeffrey Aston.

"It couldn't be..." she whispered to herself.

"What?" Alderson demanded.

Veronica's mind continued to retrace the arguments she had with Raymer about the strange circumstances involving the Aston boy. She had been convinced it was some kind of telekinetic or poltergeist phenomenon, but Raymer insisted otherwise. He had seen the vampire himself... reflected in a mirror.

In spirit form.

"Dr. Upham?" Alderson pressed her. "You wanna clue me in here?"

"It's nothing," she assured him. "But we definitely need to find Raymer."

139

"So how are we gonna do that?"

"When I last saw him, he told me if I wanted to find him, I'd know where he'd be. The last thing I wanted to do was track down that son of a bitch, so I never gave it any thought. I just figured it was his usual condescending bullshit. But that's where he went. I'm almost positive. He went back to the Aston house."

"So where is it?"

"I'm not sure. I've never been there, but it's somewhere outside of Richmond." Veronica remembered that she still owned a copy of Critchlow's book. "Hold on! I'll be right back."

The professor darted from her chair and sprinted upstairs to her home library. When she returned to the living room, she was scanning through a battered paperback in search of a glossy page of black and white photos. When she found it, she handed the open book to Alderson.

"There's the house itself. For the sake of privacy, there are no pictures of the family. Their names were also changed for the book, but Raymer always referred to them by their real name, which was Aston." Veronica racked her memory to recall the names of Jeffrey Aston's parents. "I can't remember the mother's name. But the father's name was Arnold... or... no! Oliver! Oliver Aston."

"How long ago did all this take place?" Alderson asked.

"In the mid-eighties. 1986 to be exact."

"OK, I've got a contact in Richmond. I'm sure he can trace the Aston's records and pull an address. We can narrow it down. I just need to give him a call."

Alderson suddenly rose but seemed unsteady on his feet. He turned slowly and began moving toward the door.

"Wait, where are you going?"

"Just outside to get my notebook. I'll be right back."

Veronica breathed a sigh of relief. She turned and went into the kitchen to fetch the detective a glass of ice water. When she returned to the living room, she placed the glass on the coffee table, snatched up her pack of Marlboros and decided to break her 'no smoking in the house' rule a second time.

Alderson returned as the screen door clasped shut behind him.

"I'm sorry about the carpets," he muttered. He paused at the entry way and slipped off the muddy hiking boots.

"It's no bother," she replied. She was careful to blow her smoke upward and away from her bleary-eyed guest. "Listen, don't take this the wrong way, but you don't look so hot. And after everything that's happened today, that's completely understandable. You're welcome to hang out here as long as you want, and I'll try to answer as many questions as I can. In the meantime, have you eaten anything today? I could make you a sandwich or something. I'd be happy to—"

"Honestly... I don't think I could eat right now," he replied. He opened his ledger and clicked his pen to write. "If you don't mind, I'd like you to repeat some of those names you mentioned a few minutes ago."

"Sure, Detective. But I'm not going anywhere." Veronica nodded to the glass of ice water. "At least drink some water."

"Please, call me Nathan," he corrected her and reached for the glass. "I guess since we're in this shit together now, we might as well be on a first name basis."

Veronica forced a smile and nodded.

13

ALDERSON AND VERONICA SPENT THE EARLY AFTERNOON together in occupied silence. After further coaxing, she managed to convince him to eat two slices of buttered toast and drink a can of ginger ale. She forced herself to do the same—with the addition of a ripe banana—but felt too unsettled to enjoy it. Alderson had slipped back into work mode, with Veronica's sectional serving as an impromptu workstation. She found an extra charger for his phone and after struggling to remember the password, he was able to gain access to her private wi-fi. His ledger lay open on the couch cushion, while he leaned forward and scrolled through the web browser on his phone. He occasionally paused to take notes.

Veronica phoned the secretary of the Williamsport Historical Society and tasked the elderly volunteer to search for any online or physical archival materials pertaining to the name 'Brennen.' She also mentioned the plantation house and asked the archivist to pull any holdings related to it as well. The woman promised to call back with any information she could uncover but cautioned that "it might take a day or two."

Meanwhile, the detective made two phone calls of his own. The first was to Detective Timothy Parnell of the Richmond Police Department. Alderson provided the information on Oliver Aston he received from Veronica and asked Parnell to obtain any addresses, public records, or phone numbers associated with him.

His second call was to the Poquoson Police Department. After mentioning the name Fenton Luttrell Jr., Alderson learned that he was reported missing by a foreman at the Newport News shipyard two years ago. No next of kin. The officer he spoke to noted that a pickup truck registered to Luttrell was discovered by the Williamsport police. The vehicle had been ditched on a side street near the site of a townhouse fire—also two years prior. The officer from Poquoson asked if Luttrell was a suspect since the fire was flagged as an arson, but Nathan simply said he was cleaning up some old records from the impound yard. The officer seemed to buy the story, so Alderson thanked him and ended the call.

While they waited to hear from Detective Parnell, Veronica took a seat on the opposite sofa. She clasped her hands together between her knees and observed her guest. Alderson looked pale. Dark circles shadowed his eyes and he seemed to be staring not at her but through her. His posture was rigid against the back of the armchair. His pen pointed out from between his fingers.

"So, how're you holding up?" she asked.

"Honestly? I don't know," he replied after some hesitation. He shook his head slightly. "I'm think I'm still trying to wrap my head around all this."

"Well, whatever it's worth, I understand," she assured him. "None of this is easy."

"No, it isn't." He exhaled and tossed his pen and phone on the coffee table. Alderson leaned forward, his palm resting against his stubbled chin. His bright eyes had dimmed to a filmy gray. "It doesn't even seem real. But then... I can still see those things." His voice quavered. "I can still taste the smoke that came up out of the ground. I still see their eyes and that smell. That stink. It's all over me and... *fuck!*"

The agitated detective shot to his feet and turned his back to Veronica. His hand rose up and clutched the back of his neck. He dug his filthy nails into the sunburnt flesh.

"Hey. Hey... it's OK. I'm sorry. I didn't mean to upset you. You can talk to me, remember? I get it. I know what you saw up there was real. And I believe you."

He spun back to face her. His face was red with anger as another thought dawned on him. "There are still more of those things up there. Dozens. Maybe more. The whole place is littered with corpses. It's a fucking *graveyard*. Full of *kids!*"

"I know," she replied. She continued to wring her hands in her lap and looked on helplessly as Alderson stared at her. She struggled to formulate a response—anything to try to calm or pacify him. "Eventually, we'll find a way to make this right. Ensure they receive a... a proper burial and rest."

"Look, I don't want to talk about this anymore." He stood stock still, his fists clenched at his sides. "I've seen a lot of fucked up shit in my line of work. Teenagers with needles stuck in their arms. Crippled veterans driven to spray their brains all over their living room walls. Christ, I watched my son die right in front of me. I pulled his body out of the water. But I've never seen anything like this!"

Veronica flinched. A pained expression darkened her features. She looked on as Nathan stormed across the living room. The incensed detective stopped short of her bar cart, glanced at the assorted bottles of scotch, and then turned away in disgust.

"I'm so sorry," she said softly. "I wish there was something I could say but—"

"Just don't." He raised his hand and then let it fall to his side. He lingered a moment to collect his composure, then slowly made his way back to the sectional. With his elbows on his knees, he cradled his head and ran his fingers through his hair. With a frustrated sigh, he leaned back and let his eyes trace the textured spirals along the ceiling.

"I'm scared too, Nathan. That thing was in my *house* for Christ's sakes." She lifted an unsteady hand and pointed to the dining room. "Right over there. I don't know how much longer I can even stay here without feeling sick to my stomach. I'm fucking *terrified!*"

Alderson met her eyes and nodded silently.

"But," she added, "we're gonna figure this out. If there's anything I've learned over the past few years, it's how to compartmentalize. There's no other way to rationalize it or come to terms with it. It just is."

Veronica sank back into the sofa and folded her arms. She pushed a stray lock of hair behind her ear. Alderson reached for the glass of water, lifted it to his lips and finished the contents. He placed the empty glass on the coffee table, his thumb leaving a ghostly impression in the condensation.

The weary detective snapped to attention when his cell finally began to ring. With a quick glance to Veronica, he placed his index finger over his lips, leaned forward, and tapped the screen to place the call on speaker phone.

"Nathan Alderson."

"Hey Nate, it's Tim. So, here's the deal. I only found one residence for Oliver Aston in the area, but he hasn't lived there in decades. The place is in Dutch Gap Trace, an old subdivision off East Hundred Road. About a half-mile from the 295 interchange—Exit 15, if you're splitting hairs. Technically, that's Chesterfield County, so it's not my jurisdiction. But it's the metro area, so we work with them all the time. Anyway, I had a buddy in the department out there run the name."

"That's great." Alderson quickly jotted down the details relayed by Detective Parnell. "What did he find?"

"The location of the house is 1596 Orkney Springs Court. This Aston guy bought the place in May of 1977. It went into foreclosure in 1987 and was abandoned. It was off the market for a couple years before, and this is kinda weird, it was purchased from the bank by the Roman Catholic Archdiocese of Richmond. Then about a year and a half ago, the deed was sold to a man by the name of Ray Edwards."

Alderson lifted his eyes to Veronica. "You said 'Ray Edwards?'"

The professor shook her head in disbelief.

"That's correct, Detective. Clean record, barring a traffic violation about a year ago. Name's come up in connection with a local carpenter's union."

"Anything else?" Alderson asked. "No chance you have a picture of him, do you?"

"Unfortunately, no mug shot. Poor bastard just failed to signal through a busy intersection. That's all."

"How about a phone number?"

"Unlisted, but the Chesterfield officer and I managed to dig a little deeper. We've got three potential numbers."

As Parnell rattled off the numbers, Alderson scribbled them down in his ledger.

"Thank you, Parn. I owe you one."

"No problem, Nate. And listen, I don't want to step out of line here, but I heard about what happened to Cody, and I just wanted to offer my condolences."

The reference to his son rekindled his anxiety. Alderson's cold eyes went blank and his jaw tightened.

"OK, Tim. I'll be in touch."

Alderson reached forward and disconnected the call. With his head down, he sat poised on the edge of the sectional and continued to write in his notebook.

Veronica leaned forward and arched a reddish eyebrow. "Ray Edwards? That's so typical of Edison. He's so arrogant he can't even come up with a respectable alias."

"Uh-huh." Alderson finished writing with a sudden flourish, punctuating the final line with a tap of his pen against the notebook. He rose from the couch and extended his arms over the coffee table toward Veronica. When she reached up to receive the ledger, he had already spun it around so the numbers on the pages were upright and facing her.

"You try first," Alderson suggested.

"Sure," she said with some apprehension. She picked up her cell from the coffee table. "He might still recognize my number. Not sure if that's a good thing or a bad thing."

Veronica dialed the first number. After several rings, there was no answer, nor any voicemail box to leave a reply. She placed the second call, which immediately triggered a series of beeps and a pre-recorded message from a robotic operator: "We're sorry, the number you have dialed is not in service. Please check the number and try your call again."

"Strike two," Veronica noted with a frown. Alderson continued to pace the perimeter of her living room.

She dialed the third number and held her breath. After four rings, a generic voicemail box delivered a bland greeting. The disappointed professor ignored the request to leave a message after the tone.

"Damn." Veronica placed her phone on the arm of the sofa. "So now what?"

"Let's just go up there," Nathan replied.

"Wait? What? *Now?*"

"Yes, now."

"Hold on a minute..." Veronica shifted uncomfortably. "Maybe we should wait and see if—"

"Look, I've gotta do something," Alderson insisted. "I can't sit around this house anymore today." He glanced away from Veronica awkwardly. "I need to be on the move. We need to find Raymer."

"I understand that, but let's be rational, Nathan. It's nearly an hours' drive up there. He may not be home. Like I said, that last email from him was about some dead girl in Annapolis. He may not be at the Aston house."

"You said that's where he'd be!" Alderson raised his voice in frustration.

"I know, I mean, I'm sure that's where he's *living*. That it's his—fuck, I don't know—his *headquarters* or whatever. But he could be out of town, hunting one of these things. Hell, he could be at work. In the shower. At the grocery store. Why don't we wait awhile and try the numbers again later?"

"We can call from the truck," Alderson replied. He leveled a beseeching look at her. "Please."

"OK, fine. Would you give me a few minutes? I'd like to... I'd like to freshen up."

"Fine," Alderson glanced at his watch as Veronica sped past him and up the staircase. He grabbed his work shirt from a coat rack in the hallway, which was still damp with perspiration. As he buttoned up the shirt, he returned to the living room and gathered his belongings from the couch.

Veronica returned moments later. Her auburn hair was freshly brushed and released from the casual bun she had arranged earlier that morning. A heavy pullover black sweater, the same worn jeans, and a pair of low-heeled boots made her feel a few inches taller. In her right hand, she held the .38.

"Listen, I don't know what I'm doing with this." She held out her cupped hand and placed the loose ammunition onto Alderson's palm, then handed him the gun.

"Watch where you point that thing!" He flipped open the cylinder. Before sliding in a cartridge, he inspected the hand-loaded hollow point.

"Silver?"

Veronica nodded as Nathan loaded each round into the .38. Once he was satisfied, he locked the cylinder back into place. "Let's go."

☦

The unlikely pair of sleuths rode together in silence. Alderson's hands gripped the steering wheel as he leaned slightly forward. Veronica stared out the windshield at the passing cars on Route 10. Dusk was slowly beginning to claim the late afternoon sky, an inevitability that further unsettled both of them. Dry heat seeped from the vents as the rhythm of the road hypnotized the driver and lulled his passenger into a nervous stupor.

A low buzz issued from Alderson's phone, which he had placed in the cupholder between them. He glanced down to see a text from Kelly.

"Will you be home tonight for dinner?"

With one hand still on the steering wheel, he picked up the phone and thumbed a curt reply. Almost immediately a second text came through—this time a longer wall of words the detective could not fully read without distraction.

"Would you do me a favor?" he gestured to Veronica.

"Sure?"

"Please text her back and write 'Driving.'"

Veronica smiled faintly and did as he requested. She took it upon herself to add 'I'll call you later.'

"Have you told her anything about this?"

"About the case? Yeah, I uh..." Alderson recalled the disastrous dinner he spent with Kelly—and her discomfort when he discussed the Marshall case. "I mentioned a few things."

"I meant about my video," Veronica corrected. "And what you found in those woods."

"Fuck no!" Alderson glanced at his passenger with an incredulous look.

"Well, I'm just saying. It may not be right to keep her in the dark. We could all be in danger."

"No, she doesn't need to know," he said decisively. "I came directly to you. I haven't told her anything. Nor have I told my partner, who is working this case with me."

The conversation fell into another temporary lull. Alderson glanced up as they passed a green sign with mileages for Hopewell, Enon, and I-295. They were getting closer.

Despite the recent tension between them, Alderson felt a creeping sadness at the thought of his wife. As he reflected on Veronica's suggestion of danger, a long dormant feeling of protectiveness arose inside him.

"You ever been married?" Nathan asked the woman riding shotgun beside him.

"I was," she responded. "A long time ago. It didn't last very long. We were in grad school together. He was a Romanticist. Studied Blake, Shelley, Byron. He was a little too taken with Shelley's ideas of free love, to put it mildly."

"Ah," Alderson replied.

"I didn't really mind his wandering eye. What did us in was my infertility," she admitted. "He constantly talked of having a son or daughter. And when that dream proved impossible with me, he found a fruitful blonde Modernist in one of his seminar courses. His very own Lady Chatterley. They're married now with three kids, living somewhere in Connecticut."

"I'm sorry to hear that," Nathan said.

"Eh, we all lived happily ever after," she replied with a wave of her delicate wrist. "Not long after the divorce, I took up with Edison Raymer, which if I'm honest, was more like being single after the first month or two."

Veronica crossed and uncrossed her legs, and then shifted in her seat. She reached into her purse, withdrew her pack of Marlboros, and held a single cigarette and lighter aloft.

"Do you mind?"

"No, just crack the window."

"You want one?"

"I'm good."

Assured the cigarette was fully lit, she thumbed the power window backward. A rush of crackling wind flooded the cab. After a few minor adjustments she positioned the window so her hair was no longer whipping into her eyes and the ashes weren't at risk of sullying the pickup's interior.

"You're worried about seeing him again, aren't you?"

Veronica side-eyed her companion and took a deep drag on her cigarette. "What gave you the first clue?"

The detective offered no response. Veronica exhaled, careful to blow the smoke through the gap between the window and the side-view mirror.

"We were on the rocks for a long time before all the stuff with Bartsch and Laura went down. That was just the straw that broke the camel's back."

"Is that why you didn't leave town with him?"

"No. It's hard to explain. There are a lot of reasons." Veronica tapped her ash out the window. She watched the scenery speed past before she continued. "To put it bluntly, he was an asshole. He was cruel, conceited, callous. He didn't respect me. I was barely even his sidekick. And also, the way he... the way he handled everything. He was so unmoved by it. Just... totally obsessed but... cold. There was no awe there."

"What do you mean by 'awe?'"

"Like, he expressed no reverence or humility once he learned about Bartsch. And what he really was."

"I don't blame him."

"No, I don't think you understand. You weren't there." She shook her head and glanced over at Alderson. "He became the worst kind of zealot. When he caught up with Bartsch, it was something else entirely. He had already beaten him but that wasn't enough for Raymer. He had to make sure he suffered, and he relished every sadistic second of it."

"Yeah well, if he can figure out what to do about this thing we're dealing with, that's all that matters to me. I'm sorry if this unexpected reunion is dredging up bad memories, but you need to get past that."

Alderson immediately regretted his tone. Out of the corner of his eyes, he noticed the professor purse her lips. She flicked her cigarette out the window and had another cupped and ready for her lighter.

"Well, my life doesn't revolve around Edison Raymer anymore," she replied. An angry puff of smoke issued past her lips. "We have a lot of history. Like you, I'm more concerned about the present and the future. But we need to get something straight here, Nathan."

"And that is?"

"Having to visit my conceited ex-boyfriend and colleague is an inconvenience. Knowing that we're going to have to eventually confront one of these dead-alive monsters is why I'm so fucking rattled right now."

"Fair enough." Alderson turned his attention back to the road. The burnt orange sky continued to fade along the horizon. Nathan estimated they had less than an hour before nightfall. Glancing at the speedometer, he lowered his speed as they approached a boxy nondescript school to their left. Ahead was a Burger King, and beyond that, a weather-beaten sign marked the entrance to Dutch Gap Trace.

Nathan slowed down, signaled, and eased the truck from Route 10 into the subdivision. The pavement of the winding street was in serious disrepair. Potholes and cracks marred the faded surface. Alderson scanned the houses on both sides of the narrow street as the truck crept along. Lawns grew untended and driveways sat empty. Most of the dusty windows of the nearly identical houses were dark. Other windows were smashed or boarded up. A few faded FOR SALE signs rusted along the broken sidewalks.

As he drove through the derelict neighborhood, Veronica scanned the passing street signs until they found Orkney Springs Court.

"Turn right here."

Alderson turned onto the side street. When they reached the cul-de-sac, Veronica identified the house and pointed a finger past Alderson's face and out the driver's side window.

"That's it. It has to be. It looks just like the photo."

Alderson spun the truck around slowly and found a parking spot along the curb. He cut the engine, turned off the lights, and withdrew Veronica's .38 from his glove compartment. Nathan gripped the gun properly with his trigger finger resting against the frame, opened the door, and stepped onto the street.

Veronica exited the truck. The slam of her door reverberated through the chill air of the abandoned neighborhood. She glanced up at the sky. It was getting darker than she'd realized. Tiny white stars were beginning to emerge against the fading purple firmament. The smell of woodsmoke and burning leaves was pervasive.

With the .38 lowered at his side, Alderson beckoned to Veronica as she rounded the front of the truck. "Stay close and follow my lead."

They cautiously approached the sidewalk leading to their destination. The condition of the Aston house stood in stark contrast to the other neglected buildings surrounding it. The white-washed siding appeared to have been recently painted. The gray slanted roof was freshly shingled and displayed no signs of wear or discoloration. Not far behind the home was a thicket of trees. The front lawn was neatly trimmed, the grass a vibrant shade of green despite the lateness of the season. Yet the clapboard split-level home cast an aura of palpable dread. Its defiant ordinariness failed to fully mask its true face.

Alderson noticed there was no vehicle in the driveway. He turned for a moment and surveyed the other homes on the dead-end street. In one driveway, he saw something peculiar—a rusty, navy blue International Harvester Scout. He could see a white Virginia plate on the bumper and a state inspection sticker on the windshield.

He motioned to Veronica. "Does that look like his vehicle over there? In that driveway?"

She shook her head. "Raymer wouldn't be caught dead driving something like that. No way in hell."

They made their way onto the walkway of the Aston house and slowly mounted the steps. Veronica reached out with a trembling hand to ring the doorbell. Alderson stood at the ready by the front door with one hand still gripping the .38.

There was no sound from inside to indicate the doorbell was working. Veronica began to mash the button compulsively.

"Stop," Nate said.

He rapped on the door sharply, then stepped back.

Alderson angled his head to look inside the nearby window to his left, but the curtains were tightly closed.

Chkk-clack.

The unmistakable sound of someone racking a pump action shotgun echoed along the empty street. A low, commanding voice rang out from behind them.

"Put your hands up and turn around slowly."

14

EDISON RAYMER TIGHTENED HIS CALLOUSED GRIP ON A pump-action 12-gauge shotgun. With the barrel pointed at his former colleague and the square-jawed stranger she had led to his doorstep, he narrowed his eyes and spoke to Veronica.

"I guess you've finally decided to play in the big leagues." He spoke with careful deliberation. "It took you long enough."

Veronica Upham was stunned by the physical transformation of her estranged partner. He had completely shaved his head and graying beard. His wire-framed spectacles had been exchanged for a pair of less conspicuous contact lenses. A black slim-fit sweater clung to his chest, accentuating his physique. Beneath the sleeves, massive biceps and forearms rippled. Scars covered the dark skin of his hands. A muscular neck emerged above his collar and broad shoulders. Black cargo pants were tucked into a pair of steel-toed work boots, buffed to a polished sheen. Grim-faced and poised with almost military precision, he appeared younger yet paradoxically more hardened and world-weary.

Raymer nodded his head toward Alderson and then returned his gaze to Veronica. "Who's your friend?"

Before she could speak, her companion broke the silence. "Detective Nathan Alderson. Williamsport PD."

"You brought a *cop* here?" He shot an incensed look to Veronica and lifted the barrel higher. "To *my* house?"

"It's not like that," she managed. Still distracted by Raymer's altered appearance, she hesitated before continuing. "We need your help."

"Listen, I know *everything*," Alderson interjected. "If I wanted to haul your ass in for what happened to Junior Luttrell or for burning down your house, you'd already be in handcuffs. So lower that shotgun and let's talk inside."

"Not until you hand me that .38," Raymer insisted. "I don't know you from Adam, and I'll be damned if you think you're going into my house holding that weapon."

Alderson stared into the face of the dark-eyed man standing before him. After a moment's hesitation, he passed the short-barreled pistol to Raymer. With his left hand, Raymer lowered the shotgun and collected the detective's firearm with his right. Now brandishing both weapons, Raymer gestured toward the house.

"The door's open, Veronica. Go inside and I'll meet you in the living room."

The professor slowly turned and did as she was told. Alderson followed her as Raymer trailed behind. Still carrying the shotgun, he now pointed the .38 ahead as he closed the front door behind him. The two uninvited guests crept to the middle of the sparsely furnished living room and turned to face their host. Raymer paused in the archway and flipped a switch to illuminate the shadowy room. He leaned the shotgun against the wall, opened the cylinder of the .38, and dumped the cartridges into his palm.

"Silver?" Edison enquired as he pocketed the rounds. "This was Junior's ammunition."

"Yes," Veronica confirmed. "It was."

Raymer continued to eye the pair suspiciously. He took a few steps forward and placed the pistol on an end table beside a blue accent chair. "So, what exactly are you doing here?" Raymer crossed his thick arms over his chest.

Alderson cleared his throat to ensure he spoke before Veronica. "I'm investigating a homicide that took place near South Williamsport Elementary School last Friday night."

"You mean the boy they found in the woods?" Raymer asked with nonchalance.

Disarmed by Raymer's unexpected knowledge of the case, Alderson momentarily faltered.

"Wait... what?" Veronica placed a hand on her hip. "How did you—"

"I keep my ear to the ground," he explained. "It's been a top story on all the local news channels since Saturday."

Alderson continued, "The boy's name was Tyler Marshall. What you *don't* know is that he was completely drained of blood, with his throat torn out."

"The following night," Veronica added, "I held a séance with Janice and Peter Tully. Somehow, I managed to channel that boy's spirit. But someone, or rather some*thing*, came through with him. I've got the whole thing on video. There was something standing in the corner of the room. Watching us."

"Well." Raymer arched an eyebrow. "It certainly sounds like your skills as a medium have improved."

"You've got a lot of nerve after—"

Alderson raised a hand to silence Veronica. He took a tentative step forward, maintaining eye contact with Raymer. "Children have been disappearing in or near those woods since the 1950s. I haven't had any luck convincing my superiors that these crimes are related. So, this morning I went out there with a shovel and a pickaxe to see for myself. Now, I'm going to reach into my front pocket for my cell phone so I can show you what I found buried up there."

Raymer nodded as Nathan withdrew his cell phone. The detective tapped on the interface to access the photo app and cued its contents before handing over the device.

Edison held the phone in his hands, occasionally turning it to account for the various angles of the photos. With a wrinkled brow he silently thumbed past each still image and examined the video footage. His expression remained stoic and unreadable.

Veronica flinched at the dissonant sounds emanating from the tiny speaker. The horrific images of the disinterred infants replayed in her mind. Alderson eyed Raymer with anticipation, his hands balled into fists at his sides.

Unfazed, Edison returned the phone to Alderson and began to pace with his hands behind his back. He hung his head as if momentarily lost in thought. Impatient with his show of superiority, Veronica spoke up.

"Obviously, Nathan and I believe that whatever put those things in the ground is also responsible for killing Tyler Marshall. In the video footage from the séance, it appears to be a woman. It's definitely not Laura, because this has obviously been going on for much longer than—"

"Of course it's not Laura," Raymer replied. "She's been dead for two years. I shot her point blank and then staked her to my living room floor. Why the hell do you think I burned down that house?"

The blood rushed to Veronica's face. "You son of a bitch." Her eyes glistened with fury. "I've spent the last two years absolutely fucking *terrified*, thinking she was still out there somewhere! I was pouring salt along my doors and windows every night, praying it would keep her out! Why didn't you tell me?"

"Well, first of all," Raymer replied, "salt is ineffectual against vampires. That's just a myth."

Veronica wrinkled her brow. "What?"

"Think about it. Blood contains a significant amount of sodium. If vampires were repelled by salt, they couldn't drink blood."

The professor's face turned red. "Well, you still should have told me that you killed Laura!"

Raymer shrugged. "I guess it didn't seem pertinent at the time."

"Oh, but you apparently thought it *pertinent* to send me that email about the girl in Maryland!"

"Alright, stop!" Alderson yelled. "We don't have time for this shit." He looked away from Veronica and caught Raymer's eye. "We came here because we need your help finding and stopping this thing before it kills someone else. Are you willing to help us or not?"

Edison withheld his reply. His gaze lingered on the beige curtains drawn across the living room window. He placed his elbow on a mantle affixed to the wall above a screened-in fireplace. Upon the otherwise empty shelf, a faded photo of Oliver, Maggie, and Jeffrey Aston was propped up in the center. The Aston family sat back-to-front with their heads tilted to smile at the camera. An orange tint had given the image a soft, almost hazy hue.

"What is that?" Veronica pointed a finger at the picture frame. "Why do you have a picture of them here?"

"It's a reminder," Raymer said curtly before turning his attention back to Alderson. "I presume that whatever we discuss here, or whatever we may have to *do,* is going to remain off the record. Is that right, Detective?"

"Yes," Alderson replied. "I can't go to my partner or the chief of police with *any* of this."

Raymer carefully considered Nathan's response before he continued. "Over the past two years, I've dispatched nearly a dozen of these things—and that's in *addition* to Matthias Bartsch and Laura McCoy. If your plan is to hunt this thing down and destroy it, then you've come to the right place."

"I still think you should've told me about Laura." Veronica folded her arms over her breasts. "I had a right to know."

Nathan shook his head and cast an irritated glance at Veronica. "Save it for later."

Raymer sprung into a quick stride and turned to make his way through the adjacent dining room. "Pick up your weapon and follow me."

Veronica followed Raymer through the dining room and into the kitchen. With the empty .38 at his side, Alderson caught up to her. Edison gestured toward an open door. "This way," he said as he flipped another light switch.

They descended a flight of rickety wooden stairs into a spacious yet musty basement. In the far-right corner was a bench press. Weights were stacked on the floor and lined up on a short metal rack. A heavy bag was suspended from the ceiling. A water-stained concrete floor with a spotted drain cover separated the two ends of the basement. On the wall opposite the stairs was a massive workbench. The doors to two large cabinets were closed underneath.

With his back to Alderson and Veronica, Raymer bent down, opened one of the cabinets, and began to rummage through the contents. The sound of metal clattering against metal echoed through the cellar. Veronica noticed that he had procured two oversized gym bags from one of the lower shelves. He began to shovel items into the black heavy-duty bags.

Along the wall above the workstation was a large-scale map of the Mid-Atlantic area, with the state of Virginia dead-center. A series of red and white pushpins dotted the multi-colored landscape. Veronica squinted to discern what looked like a handful of headshots pinned to the map. Several black and white newspaper clippings were tacked within and beside the borders.

As Veronica stepped closer, she was startled to see a veritable arsenal of heavy-duty weapons fixed to a black pegboard along the wall to the right of the workbench. Several dense rubber-headed mallets and sharp metal-claw hammers hung from the glimmering pegs. What appeared to be a pair of sleek black crossbows were suspended in the top corner. Dozens of silver-tipped bolts clung to the space between the weapons—as if magnetized and held firmly in place. An inestimable number of rosary beads, crosses, and ornate crucifixes of various sizes hung from small chains.

When Raymer bent down to grab another item from the lower cabinet, she noticed several silver stakes laid out across the tabletop. Alderson remained quiet as he craned his neck and turned his head from left to right, taking in the cache of unconventional weapons and religious paraphernalia.

Veronica was the first to speak up. "Where are all of your books? I thought you would've tried to salvage at least a few of them."

"I sold them to pay for weapons and other necessities," Raymer said. "Everything I need to know is up here." He pointed a finger to his temple as he turned to face them at last.

The former professor reached into his pocket and withdrew the five silver bullets he had emptied from the .38. He extended his closed fist and returned them to Alderson.

"Reload these," he said, then turned back to obtain another item from the work bench. "As an experienced policeman, I'm sure you recognize that weapon's good for backup. But you're going to need something with more firepower and better range for what we're about to do."

"I have a hunting rifle in my truck," Alderson said.

"What caliber?" Edison asked as he continued to load items into the bag.

".243."

Edison stopped and turned for a moment to gaze at the detective. "I only have silver-tipped rounds in 7.62 by 54R, .303, .30-06, and .338 Lapua." He gestured to an array of bolt-action sniper rifles mounted on the left wall. "But I have something with enough stopping power to slow that thing down, and it's relatively concealable, too."

Veronica was thrown by Raymer's newfound expertise on firearms and ammunition. Her stomach churned, and she attempted to speak up, but found herself mute.

Raymer turned around and dug into the other cabinet. He stood up and handed Alderson a narrow leather shoulder holster with a chromed .44 magnum revolver. "That firearm you're holding is already locked and loaded with 180 grain anti-personnel silver hollow points. No lead, just silver through-and-through. I tool and hand-load each cartridge myself. The muzzle energy on those rounds is about 899 FPE. You hit a vampire with that, it's gonna drop and stay down."

Alderson nodded and accepted the weapon. He slipped the holster over his shoulder and fastened it tightly against his chest with a quick tug.

As the detective finished slipping the .44 into place, Veronica glanced in desperation at the two men gearing up before her. "Wait a minute. Seriously... hold on a second." She reached up and massaged the bridge of her nose. "You two aren't planning to go out there and try to find this thing tonight, are you?" Her face blanched and she swallowed nervously. "For Christ's sake, I have a class to teach tomorrow morning!"

Raymer suddenly paused and lifted his head to cast an incredulous glance at Veronica. He clutched a small glass ampule in his hand and resumed wrapping it in cloth before carefully placing it in his bag. "What the hell did you think we were gonna do?"

"I don't know!" Veronica responded. "I just didn't think we were gonna rush out all half-cocked tonight. This is happening way too fast." She turned to Alderson. "And *you!* Are you just gonna start strapping on these more than likely *illegal* weapons without asking any questions?"

Alderson looked away and clenched his jaw.

"Uh-huh," Veronica responded with a hand on her hip. "I thought so. We need to formulate some kind of plan before we go anywhere."

Raymer frowned as he zipped up the first gym bag and then turned his attention to the second. He looked up and caught Alderson's eye. "From everything you've seen, you believe this thing has been hiding somewhere out in those woods, right?"

"Yes," Alderson replied. He raised a hand to quiet Veronica and prevent Raymer from speaking as well. "Not far from where I found those graves is an old plantation house. It's in ruins, but there's a private family tomb on the grounds."

"A tomb?" Raymer asked. He turned and reached up to remove one of the crossbows from the pegboard and gently placed it in a fitted case.

"Yeah, there are several slotted vaults but all of them were empty. Only one of them is still sealed. I figure it's probably hiding out in there."

"Possibly." Edison carefully slid the case and several of the silver-tipped bolts into the second bag. He glanced at his wristwatch and shook his head. "Now that it's after nightfall, it's not going to be in there any way. Our best bet is to enter the forest and wait for it to come to us."

"Hold on!" Veronica shouted. "That's your plan?" She glared at Raymer. "You wanna march into the woods and sit there all night hoping this thing appears? Then what?"

"We kill it." Edison narrowed his eyes. "End of story."

"What if it doesn't show up?"

"It will."

"And what makes you so goddamn certain? This thing appeared at my house like some kind of shadow or ghost. How do you explain that?"

"I don't need to," Raymer fired back. "It's a vampire, so we just have to take it down."

"What if we *can't* take it down?" Veronica pressed. "Unless you have another surprise up your sleeve, you never killed the Aston house vampire, did you? You still don't know how she was able to appear and disappear from Jeffrey Aston's bedroom, do you?"

"Will you two *stop* with the bickering?" Alderson held out his arms between them. "I am *not* going to listen to this shit all night."

"Some things never change, do they, Edison?" Veronica ignored the detective and stared her ex-partner down. She then turned her glance to Alderson with an admonishment of her own.

"Have some sense, Nathan. Don't let him pressure you into doing something stupid. You've been awake for hours. You've barely eaten. We need to come up with a better plan!"

"I'm going to stop you right there," Alderson said. "I want that thing dead. This isn't a matter of me taking sides in whatever petty arguments you two are going to have. We have a job to do, and I'm not going to rest until it's finished."

"Well, hopefully your impatience won't get us killed!"

"It won't." Raymer's deep voice rang out, effectively silencing his squabbling companions. "I managed to stake Bartsch despite you and Junior nearly bungling the entire affair. Since then, I've been taking vampires down by myself. Sometimes two at a time. You both came to me because you obviously weren't up to the job on your own. Now, you either follow me into those woods and do as I say or go back to your séances, class preparations, and cheap scotch. Whatever you decide to do, just stay the fuck out of my way."

"How dare you!" Veronica clenched her fists and dug her fingernails into her palms.

Nathan stepped in front of her, obstructing her view of Raymer. He clasped her by the shoulders. The shock of contact and the pressure of his grip sent a bolt of adrenaline through her. She lifted her red-rimmed eyes to meet his equally bloodshot gaze.

"Compartmentalize, remember?" He spoke in a low, yet tender tone. He gestured to Raymer over his shoulder. "Fuck him. Don't let him bait you anymore. We came here for a reason. Let's finish this and then you never have to listen to him again. You hear me?"

"Well played, Detective." Raymer said from behind them. "You've got her on a tight leash I see."

Alderson ignored the former professor's barb and kept his eyes locked on Veronica. "He's a means to an end. We do this for Tyler Marshall. We do this for those kids buried up there."

Veronica nodded as a tear streamed down her cheek. She reached up and angrily wiped it away. The professor turned her back on both men and made her way to the stairs.

Alderson spun to face Raymer, who glared back in anticipation. "Those woods are overgrown and filled with weeds and thorn bushes. If we're going to bed down out there for any period of time, we need tools to clear the area."

"Not a problem," Raymer replied. "I've got a kaiser blade and machete out back in the tool shed."

"Good. What about flashlights?"

"This isn't my first rodeo. I packed three and there's one in my truck." Raymer handed Alderson one of the gym bags and fastened his grip on the handle of his own. As he attempted to maneuver past the detective, Alderson extended his arm to halt Raymer's progress.

"Lay off her," he warned. "She obviously respects you or we wouldn't be here. But I think you're smart enough to recognize this shit goes way beyond your issues with Veronica Upham."

Raymer smirked and shifted the weight of the bag. He pushed Alderson's arm down until it no longer obstructed his path. "You said you wanted to take this thing out, right, Detective?"

"I think I made myself clear on that matter."

"And to make *myself* clear, I'm calling the shots here. Do as I say, and I won't be the only one that gets out of this mess alive." He turned and began to ascend the stairs, his tread slow and his boots heavy on the bowing wooden steps.

15

NATHAN ALDERSON GLANCED INTO HIS REAR-VIEW MIRROR, making sure the pair of headlights continued to trail close behind them. Satisfied that Raymer still followed in the Harvester Scout, Alderson accelerated as they drove through Williamsport toward Route 619. They were nearing their destination.

Veronica said little during the drive. She hadn't even bothered to smoke any cigarettes. The professor was brooding over her encounter with Raymer, the stress of which was only further compounded by the tasks awaiting them in the forest. Nonetheless, Veronica's relative silence surprised and unsettled Alderson.

"I guess the Scout was Raymer's after all." He gripped the steering wheel, hoping his passenger would reply. Veronica's pale face was briefly lit as the truck passed under a yellow streetlamp.

"Yeah," she answered. "Didn't see that one coming. Nor the black skinhead look. Not to mention the fact he sounded like a spokesman for the NRA." She slumped back into the passenger seat. "Yet in other ways, he's still the same stubborn son of a bitch."

"Well, like I said, he's just a means to an end."

"Listen, I'm sorry for the way I acted back there." She shifted in the seat and turned to face Alderson. "He brings out the worst in me. And this whole scenario reminds me of when we went after Bartsch. The same smug, know-it-all attitude. It just puts me on edge."

"Then don't take the bait," Alderson replied. "He knows exactly how to push your buttons. So don't let him."

"Easier said than done," she reflected. "I just want this whole nightmare to be over with."

"I think all three of us can agree on that."

Veronica hesitated before adding, "All of this freaks me out, but I have to admit, both of you were right."

"About what?" Nathan asked.

"Going out there tonight. We can't fuck around while this thing is on the loose." She drew in a sharp breath. "I'm just scared, to put it mildly."

Alderson nodded. The glaring beams of an oncoming car caused the detective to flinch. As the truck sank back into the dark again, he stared at the road ahead. "I'm not exactly looking forward to any of this either."

They neared a stoplight, and a reflective sign indicated a right-hand turn to access 619. The light was red, so Nathan eased his foot off the gas as the truck approached the intersection. He checked the rear-view mirror to make sure Raymer was still in tow.

Glancing both ways, he made a quick turn onto 619, hoping that Raymer would follow before a line of oncoming vehicles blocked him. Raymer spun right and followed Alderson's pickup. Veronica pointed out a distant glow ahead.

"Do you see that?"

The detective leaned forward to peer through his filmy windshield. The area around the elementary school seemed brighter than usual for this time of night.

"What the hell..." he trailed off as they approached South Williamsport Elementary School.

The parking lot was filled with vehicles. Two large local news vans idled with their antennas spiraling up to the night sky. The bright halogen lights above the baseball field were lit up, and the meadow leading to the path was teeming with people. They were gathered at the mouth of the forest. Each member of the crowd held a tiny white candle.

"It must be some kind of vigil," Veronica realized, craning her neck as the truck crept past the busy congregation. "For Tyler Marshall." She strained to make out a large poster board surrounded by balloons, stuffed animals, and wreaths of flowers. The makeshift monument was the only thing separating the crowd from the potential danger lurking in the forest.

"Dammit," Alderson cursed as he recognized the familiar outline of police cruisers in the parking lot. He accelerated and progressed another half-mile along the road. Raymer continued to follow behind them. When he reached the alternative access point leading into the forest, Alderson signaled and turned onto the fire road. He only drove his truck a few hundred yards up the trail before he powered down his window and used his hand to signal Raymer to stop. He shifted the truck into park, cut the lights, removed his seatbelt, and exited the cab.

Alderson jogged back to the Scout. Raymer had already turned off his lights, but the engine continued to idle. As the detective approached the vehicle, Edison rolled down the window with a manual handle.

"OK, unforeseen turn of events." Alderson stood before the driver's side door and addressed the man inside. "We need to wait this out until that crowd disperses. I don't wanna take any chances and risk anyone seeing or hearing us. The last thing we need is someone getting the bright idea to wander up there."

Raymer nodded but offered no reply. His elbow poked over the side of the open window.

"Furthermore," Alderson added, "you're still a wanted man around here, and there's heat all over that gathering. I saw at least a half dozen cruisers back there. So, you need to stay put. Don't get out of this truck."

"Understood," Raymer agreed. "How long do you think this little ceremony is going to last?"

Alderson shrugged his shoulders. "I don't know. But sit tight. I can't imagine they'll be here too much longer."

Raymer nodded and began rolling up his window. He cut the engine as Alderson returned to his truck.

Veronica eyed Nathan with anticipation.

"So now what?"

Alderson adjusted himself in the driver's seat, slammed the door, and turned off the engine. "Now, we wait."

✝

Nearly an hour passed before Alderson's cell phone began to ring. He slipped his fingers into his pocket, struggled to withdraw the slimline device, and turned it over in his hand. The display revealed the caller to be none other than Frank McCain.

"Shit," Alderson muttered. He silenced the ringer and let the call go to voicemail. Veronica sat quietly beside him in the passenger seat. She had just lit her second cigarette. Smoke was drifting out of the cab.

After a few minutes, Alderson lifted the phone to his ear to replay McCain's voicemail.

"Hey Nate, it's me. I know it's gettin' late, but I figured you would've made an appearance at the Marshall boy's vigil tonight. D'Amato just asked if you were gonna show up. Anyway, give me a call tomorrow. We need to touch base. I might have somethin' on Bartsch. It's nothin' to get too excited about, but it's a possible lead. Alright? Call me."

I've got a few leads on Bartsch myself, Frank.

Alderson deleted the message and noticed he had two unread texts from his wife. The first simply read: *"Dinner for one again?"* The second, which had just been sent, read: *"This has to stop. You could have at least called me like you said you would. I guess you're with McCain at that memorial thing so I'm not waiting up for you."*

Alderson scrolled up to see the text Veronica had sent on his behalf when they were driving to Raymer's. She had told Kelly he'd call her. The detective was momentarily irritated with the professor's presumptuous act but thought better than to confront her about it.

You ought to follow her lead and show your wife some respect. None of this is Kelly's fault.

And that includes Cody.

"So, who was calling?" Veronica asked.

Alderson exhaled heavily. "That was my partner. I haven't talked to him since yesterday. He was here tonight. At the vigil."

"Oh?" She extended her small hand and flicked an ash out the window. "Honestly, I'm glad he was there. Those people are so close to..." Veronica stopped herself. "I just hope they leave soon."

Alderson nodded and consulted his watch. He lifted his eyes to check on Raymer in the rear-view mirror. The detective could see the man's round-headed silhouette behind the rusty Scout's dim windshield.

"Maybe I'm overthinking shit and getting paranoid," Alderson said, "but I don't think I should go down there either. If McCain is still hanging around, he might see my truck. But someone needs to do a quick drive-by and see if things are wrapping up over there."

"Right," Veronica agreed. "I guess I could climb behind the wheel of that monstrosity behind us. Then again, like I said earlier, no one's going to recognize him in that pile of junk. Christ, I barely recognize him." She exhaled another puff of smoke. "At least until he opens his mouth."

"I'll be right back," he said, flinging open the door. Once again, Raymer rolled down his window and waited for instructions from the detective.

"Here's the deal," Alderson explained. "My partner and the chief of police are at that vigil. By now, I'd imagine the crowd is thinning out. But on the off chance any of them are still there, I can't be seen. One of them would definitely recognize my truck."

"So, you want me to check it out." Raymer nodded. "I can do that." Without a moment's hesitation he turned the engine over and the Scout roared to life. Edison's dark eyes lingered on Alderson, as if awaiting further direction.

"Listen, be careful." Nathan pointed a finger at Raymer. "Watch your speed. Make sure you don't blow through any stop signs. You don't wanna draw *any* attention to yourself."

"Once again, slipping past men like you and your colleagues is kind of my specialty, Detective. I'll be right back."

With a series of cranks on the handle, Edison rolled up the window and began inching his truck backward down the fire trail. He paused, swung the vehicle to the side, and reoriented the truck to drive headfirst down the path toward Route 619.

Alderson leaned against the rear of his truck bed and waited for Raymer to return. The night was already cold. The moon cast some light, but the fast-moving clouds and treetops prevented it from fully illuminating the forest. Alderson carefully combed the clusters of trees and underbrush surrounding him, but nothing seemed out of the ordinary.

In a matter of minutes, Raymer's truck returned and made its way up the wide path.

"We're clear," he reported. "All the police cars and press vans are gone. The ballfield lights are off. The parking lot isn't completely empty, but the remaining vehicles could belong to janitors or night crew working at the school. There may be a few civilian stragglers, but I imagine we'll be far enough away that no one's gonna notice us."

Alderson nodded in agreement. "OK, follow me in four-low. The terrain starts to get rough a little bit ahead. We should get there in about fifteen minutes. The roads converge and then beyond that a short way is where we can park the trucks."

Raymer began rolling up his window when Alderson issued another command. "Kill your lights. I'll do the same. Give it a minute or so and your eyes will adjust."

Nathan turned his back and returned to the truck cab. Veronica waited inside, her eyes wide with expectation. He turned the ignition and began to creep forward up the path.

Before long, they reached the clearing where Alderson had spent the morning. He spun the wheel of his pickup and parked near the tree line facing the direction of the school. Raymer pulled up beside him. The Scout sputtered into silence.

The trio emerged from their respective vehicles and began to unload their gear. Veronica scanned the overgrown clearing. "Where do these two roads meet? I don't even see—"

Without speaking, Alderson tapped her shoulder, handed her a flashlight, and pointed to an area close by.

"Is that it?" Raymer startled them as he approached with his flashlight in hand. The beam danced across the freshly turned earth concealing the graves. "I think I can see the crossroads."

"Yeah," Alderson confirmed. "This is the area we need to clear."

Raymer turned his attention to Veronica. "And what are you planning to do while the detective and I cut down this brush?"

"I'll unpack your bags. Get things set up and organized. Then we can regroup and see how much of what you lugged up here we'll actually need."

The experienced vampire hunter scrutinized his ex-colleague for a moment. He tossed his keys to her, but she fumbled the catch. As she bent to pick them up, Raymer's heavy boots inched toward her and stopped. She straightened up and lifted her face to meet him eye to eye.

"Inside that gym bag," Raymer explained as he pointed, "there are two smaller military surplus bags, each with a shoulder strap. Put as many crossbow bolts in one of them as you can. Then fill the other one with crucifixes and wafers."

"Sure." Veronica followed him to the Scout as Raymer opened the rear of the aging vehicle. Alderson leaned against his mud-covered pickup truck and studied their surroundings.

After giving Veronica further instructions in a low voice, Raymer removed the fitted leather case from one of the gym bags and withdrew the menacing crossbow. He prepared one of the silver-tipped bolts and slung the weapon over his shoulder. Finally, he grabbed the brush-clearing tools from the rear of his truck and beckoned to Alderson.

The two men made their way through the tall grass toward the center of the crossroads. Raymer handed the kaiser blade to Alderson and they began to cleave a path through the briars and weeds. When Nathan reached the area where he had been digging earlier, he froze—the curved blade in one hand, his flashlight trembling in the other.

When I woke up, all I had was a hunch.

And now less than twenty-four hours later, everything has changed.

He set the heavy-duty flashlight on the ground and angled it to illuminate the area where he would be working. Much of what was in his path he had already stamped down that morning. To silence his unquiet mind, he began to methodically swing the kaiser blade in a semi-circle.

Behind him, he could hear Veronica laying out heavy objects on the metal tailgate of Raymer's Scout. By now, his vision had adjusted to the stifling darkness. It was only when he stopped to toss some of the underbrush aside that he realized he couldn't see far into the forest surrounding them.

Despite the moonlit sky, his surroundings seemed more oppressive and foreboding than when he had first investigated the area on Sunday night. A chill ran down his spine, and he turned to see Raymer, still swinging the machete, not far behind him.

"Hey!" he called out in a half-whisper.

Raymer kept on swinging his machete. "What?"

"You feel that? Something's not right. It's like the shadows are—"

"Pick up that blade and keep working," Raymer answered. "The vampire prowling these woods is somewhere close. It's watching us."

Alderson took the warning to heart. The blood pulsed in his ears. His shoulder began to ache as he mowed his way forward. The underbrush he missed in his labor with the kaiser blade was expertly cleared by Raymer. Alderson stopped and returned to gather the flashlight. He picked it up and scanned the tree line to his left and right.

Nothing out of the ordinary was there.

He breathed a sigh of relief and directed the light onto the area where they had been working. Between the two of them, they had managed to etch out a crude but wide circle. Almost nothing but the sandy soil remained. Raymer continued to tidy up—chopping at brambles and clumps of grass on the periphery to widen the circle's radius.

Alderson picked up the flashlight and walked back to the Scout, where he tossed the kaiser blade into the bed. It clattered loudly. Veronica was still sorting the contents of Raymer's gear. He saw her pull out a pair of long boxes, which piqued his curiosity.

"What the hell are those?"

"Communion wafers," she answered and opened one of the containers. She held up a sleeve of the edible disks wrapped in plastic.

"Why would we need—"

"As much as I hate to admit it, Edison really covered his bases here. These can be crumbled up and blown into a vampire's face to blind them. We had them when we took down Bartsch, even though we didn't wind up using them."

"Hold on a second," Alderson said loudly so that Raymer could overhear him. "Don't these things need to be consecrated by a priest or something to be effective?"

"Who's to say they weren't?" Raymer shouted back.

Alderson stood perplexed for a moment, but his keen intuition kicked in. "Are you working with someone else, Raymer? A priest or some kinda clergyman? Who else knows about these things?"

"Look." Edison stopped swinging the machete and stood still for a moment. "All *you* need to know is that vampires hate them. The wafers can be ground to a powder and used to make a protective circle, which they won't try to cross."

Alderson stood with his hand on his waist. He turned and opened the cab of his pickup to retrieve the .38. The detective held it up so they could see, then tapped the .44 magnum in its holster. "Whatever you say, but I'm putting my faith in superior firepower."

"I hope you don't come to regret that," Raymer muttered.

"What's that supposed to mean?"

"Nathan, remember what I told you back at my house," Veronica interjected. "Silver bullets only slow them down. We have to stake them to the ground to finish them off." She placed the wafers into one of the musette bags and turned to her former colleague for support. "At least that's how it was with Bartsch."

"Yeah?" Alderson scoffed. "We'll see about that."

"Stay focused," she warned him. She reached up to adjust her loose hair. "Even though some of this may seem like bullshit to you or whatever, you need to trust us." Veronica pulled her thick hair through an elastic band and into a tight bun.

Alderson turned his back to her and resumed his habit of pacing, this time along the rear of the truck bed back to the freshly shorn clearing.

Veronica slipped a silver cross around her neck. It hung between her breasts, shining in the moonlight. The professor picked up one of the large crucifixes and slung the musette bag holding the communion wafers over her shoulder. She approached Alderson's truck and scooted herself onto the tailgate, her legs dangling over the side.

172

"Nathan," she called out. "Come over here a second."

Still clutching the .38, he directed his steps back to the rear of the truck bed. "What is it?"

"Put this on." Veronica extended her small fist and placed one of the silver crosses into Alderson's hand. The long heavy chain curled like a coiling serpent into his open palm.

"You're kidding me, right?"

"No, I'm not." She met his eyes with a pleading glance. "Just humor me."

Nathan sighed and slipped the awkward pendant over his neck and adjusted it so it wouldn't get caught in the shoulder holster.

"Don't lose sight of what we're doing here," she reminded him. "And forgive me for bringing this up, but it's for your own good. Remember what you found up here today."

"Fine." Alderson avoided her gaze.

She's right and you know it.

This isn't some pissing match between you and that Wesley Snipes wannabe over there. You're in unknown territory. Get your goddamn head in the game.

Nathan continued to wrestle with his thoughts as Veronica dug into her pocket for a cigarette and lit up. Raymer joined them, tossing the now dulled machete into his truck. As he unslung his crossbow, he studied the professor's impassive face. "You put everything you could into those musette bags?"

"Yeah." She blew smoke in Raymer's direction, avoiding his gaze.

"And you were careful with the holy water vials?" The meticulous hunter draped the army surplus bag filled with silver-tipped bolts over his shoulder.

"Of course." Veronica shook her head. She steeled herself and turned to Edison, handing him another silver cross on a slender chain. "You think you brought enough holy water? There're only two vials. We probably could've used more."

"Is that your expert opinion?"

"Yes, it is." She took another drag on the nearly spent cigarette and blew a cloud of smoke out of the corner of her mouth.

"So, when did you take up this filthy habit?" Raymer slipped the cross over his smooth head and let it rest against his solid chest.

"When my other vices proved to be ineffectual," she replied. Fighting to maintain her composure, she turned to Alderson. "You OK?"

With his eyes fixed on Raymer, Nathan nodded.

"Good," she replied and flicked the cigarette on the ground. She hopped down from the truck bed to stamp out the smoldering butt under her boot. As she ground her curving toe into the dirt, she muttered, "I'm starting to feel like a den mother to a bunch of Cub Scouts here."

When the cigarette was fully extinguished, Veronica spun around to Edison. "What now?"

Alderson raised his hand to curtail any further discussion. "Do you feel that?"

Raymer said nothing, but Veronica felt a sudden shiver ripple across her arms and neck. Her breath condensed in the air around her. She looked back to Nathan nervously and stood perfectly still.

"Our mark is coming back," Raymer observed. He nodded toward the area they had cleared out. "We need to take up our positions. Get ready."

He nodded for Nathan to follow and the two men each took up one of the large gym bags. The trio made their way into the circle of barren earth. Raymer dropped his bag at his feet. Alderson followed suit. The detective could discern the clink of the glass vials and the rattle of silver stakes.

"Leave the stakes and hammers in the bags," Raymer directed. He squatted down and removed one of the ampules of holy water. He tossed the cloth back into the bag and rose, carefully slipping the glass bottle into his left pocket.

Mounted to the underside of the stock on Raymer's crossbow was a three-bolt side quiver. He reached into his shoulder bag and rapidly filled each of the open slots with bolts.

Veronica stepped forward to stand behind the two men, both hands clutching her crucifix.

Raymer activated the night-vision scope mounted atop the crossbow and began sweeping the tree line. The light stock pressed into the hollow of his shoulder. "Just keep watching the woods around us," he commanded. "Veronica, cover our six with your cross. It's only a matter of time now."

174

"Edison," her voice quavered. "Everything happened so fast with Bartsch and Laura. How will we know when it's... you know... about to strike?"

Raymer kept his grip on the crossbow, and dropped the tone of his voice, as if he sensed something the others had not. "First, you're gonna feel the air pull around you. Then, the woods will get even darker than they already are."

Alderson shuddered at Raymer's comment.

"You'll feel that cold again, like you did back at the trucks," the hardened vampire killer continued. "And right before it shows itself, you'll feel something trace the blood pumping through your veins."

Alderson tightened his right-handed grip on the .38. He glanced down to ensure the silver cross still dangled freely from his neck. "Probably a bit late to ask you this now, Edison, but is there anything else we need to know? Anything else we can do to protect ourselves?"

"No."

16

WITH HIS SENSES ATTUNED FOR ANY MINOR ANOMALY, Edison Raymer listened as the woods settled around them. Cold winds rose and fell, driving dead leaves in every direction. The tall trees bent their limbs slowly, creaking as they swayed from side to side. Hypnotized by the forest awakening to life around them, the three hunters stood with their backs pressed to one another, searching the seemingly endless and hostile terrain for the first sign of attack.

A twig snapped sharply in the distance. Alderson spun to face the direction from which the sound had issued. Veronica's heart pounded in her chest as she clung to the crucifix—her knuckles white, her arms tense. Raymer narrowed his eyes and tightened his grip on the crossbow. Another twig cracked beneath an unseen foot—this time from the opposite direction.

"What the fuck was that?" Alderson whispered.

"Get ready," Raymer commanded. "It's coming."

"Where?" The detective asked. "It sounds like it's moving all around us."

"It is," Raymer confirmed. With his eyes still trained on the gloomy thickets before him, he spoke in a careful, measured tone to Veronica. "I need you to reach into your bag and get the communion wafers. Crush 'em up and use them to cast a circle around us."

"But what about—"

"Make it wide enough so we can move within it." He maintained an even keel. "And make sure you keep some distance between us and whatever's about to come out of those woods. Stay calm but move quickly."

Veronica knelt and withdrew the wafers from her musette bag. She gathered several of the thin discs and crushed them in her fist. On her hands and knees, she began to crawl along the ground, sprinkling the white powder onto the earth. She whispered a rhythmic mantra to herself, the words too low for either of her partners to hear. Alderson looked on in mute fascination.

"Nathan." Raymer jabbed an elbow into the detective's side. "Stay sharp and keep your eyes locked on that tree line."

In the distance, a low *swish* cut through the heavy silence. Another similar sound immediately followed.

Swish.

Swish. Swish.

Veronica continued to craft the circle but only managed to form a partial barrier around them. She reached into the shoulder bag and frantically withdrew another handful of wafers.

Swish. Swish.

Something was creeping its way through the forest, its feet parting the dry sea of desiccated leaves.

Swish. Swish. Swish.

Veronica ground the hosts to dust, letting the chalky grains of consecrated powder slip through her fists. She glanced over her shoulder to ensure nothing was approaching from the trees and then returned to the task at hand. Three-quarters of the circle was cast.

Swish. Swish.

The encroaching enemy was inching closer, its steady gait the lugubrious tempo of a funeral march.

"Hurry, Veronica." Raymer's voice was clipped and betrayed more than a hint of unease.

She rapidly brushed the line of white powder with the tips of her fingers, edging closer to where Nathan stood poised to her left.

"What is that *smell?*" Alderson covered his mouth. "It's like something... *rotten.*"

Swish. Swish.

The putrid stench was carried by the cresting breeze. Raymer clenched his eye and strained to see through the mounted scope of his crossbow.

Veronica gagged as the foul smell reached her. She fumbled with another load of wafers. Alderson stepped aside so the professor could crawl in front of him. Now smashing the hosts in both fists, she slammed down her hands to spread the holy dust, tracing a curving line around herself and toward Edison Raymer. She was only inches away from closing the gap. With a desperate lunge to her left, the professor crumbled four more wafers in her trembling hands and finally reached the point where she had begun only moments ago. The protective circle had been cast.

Swish.

"Good. Now stand up," Raymer directed his colleague. "Keep your cross raised."

The blood rushing to her head, Veronica stumbled to her feet, her knees caked with mud and faded white powder. She dusted herself off, took a breath, and thrust her cross forward.

The mouth of the trail leading into the forest beyond was steeped in black shadows. Their eyes were drawn directly ahead. Raymer stood with his feet apart, his finger curled around the trigger of his crossbow. Alderson's gaze swept the tree line. Veronica's arm trembled as she held her crucifix. The suffocating woodland unfolded its arms, and a tall, silent figure began to emerge.

The silhouette of a woman seeped out of the darkness. A filthy black gown clung to her body. Swathes of shredded fabric hung from her limbs. Through the threadbare and splitting seams of her rotten garments, snatches of gray flesh were exposed. She bore the face of a long-dead corpse. Her sunken cheeks and wrinkled forehead were begrimed with layers of filth and age.

Black eyes gleamed with palpable hatred—ancient, knowing, and malevolent. A disheveled mane of tangled, white-blonde hair fell over her shoulders and down her back. The matted locks were strewn with twigs, leaves, and debris. Two large, gnarled hands emerged from the frayed cuffs of her dress. She glided forward with unnatural momentum—her bare feet caked with mud. As the vampire appeared in the moonlit clearing, a marbled hardness defined her.

"Oh my God." Veronica's arms fell limply to her sides as she looked on in disbelief.

The vampire crept closer to their circle.

"What the fuck *is* that thing?" Alderson whispered.

"Wait until she's within range and then drop her," Raymer commanded. He observed the monster through the lens of his scope, counting each step she took against his own steady pulse.

The vampire stood before her prey—imposing and grand. Her eyes drank in their fear. Misshapen lips opened to expose stained and jagged teeth. Her hideous face twisted with rage as she inched closer to the center of the crossroads. She stared down her enemies—those who had defiled her private domain. With a guttural snarl, she rushed forward.

"Now!" Raymer shouted. His finger pulled the trigger on the crossbow. The silver-tipped bolt whizzed past her. Alderson took two steps to the edge of the circle, swung his left hand to steady his grip, and rapidly fired the .38.

Five quick blasts succeeded one after the other. Nathan was momentarily blinded by the searing flashes from the short barrel. Two of his shots had missed his mark, but the other three hit the target center mass. The creature stumbled backward, but then charged forward, unfazed by the impact of the projectiles.

Wide-eyed, Alderson dropped the .38 and quickly withdrew the .44 magnum from its holster. He took aim and extended it outward. The undead woman cupped her left hand over the barrel of the massive pistol. Alderson bellowed in rage and pulled the trigger. The kickback sent him reeling and he dropped the gun to the ground. The marauding creature's hand disintegrated into a loathsome shower of blood and bone. Steaming black ichor drenched Alderson's face, hands, and clothes. The sleeve of his work shirt dripped with black blood. Alderson frantically wiped the fetid gore away from his eyes.

The crippled vampire howled in fury and bent over, clutching her shattered arm against her chest. Dead blood spilled onto her stiff gown. The stump where her hand once was glistened in the moonlight. Her eyes fell on the gun Alderson had dropped beyond the confines of the circle. She kicked it into the overgrowth and the weapon disappeared from view.

Thunk.

She spun as one of Raymer's silver-tipped bolts pierced her back, entering just below her right shoulder. Before he could reload the crossbow, the vampire charged forward, moving so fast neither he nor his companions were able to anticipate her movements. She stopped short of breaching the circle and attempted to wrench the crossbow from his hands. Raymer dug his heels into the earth and clung to the weapon with all his might. But the vampire's grip was unyielding.

As Raymer continued to pull on his crossbow, his vision blurred. Adrenaline rushed through his temples. He could feel his grasp loosening. He grit his teeth as the vampire tore the crossbow away. She hurled it to the ground, kicking it behind her with the back of her filthy heel.

Raymer cursed to himself and then cried out in unexpected pain. With a quick snap of her neck, the vampire had locked her jaws around Raymer's wrist. She drove her teeth into his flesh, clutching his forearm in an unbreakable grip. With his left hand, Raymer swung his fist into the monster's back, but the fiend refused to let go.

Nathan sprang forward and grabbed Raymer under the arms. He was blinded by a searing blast of pain as Alderson yanked him backward. The vampire continued to gnaw upon Raymer's wrist. Low bestial sounds came from her throat. She opened her black eyes and looked up at him in triumph.

Raymer grimaced though the pain as he met the gaze of his attacker, shoved his free hand into his pocket, and withdrew the vial of holy water. Clutching it tightly, he swung his hand upward and smashed the bottle against the vampire's skull.

The ampule exploded against her head, driving shards of glass into Raymer's hand. The powerful stench of burning flesh comingled with rot as the holy water ate like acid into the side of her face. Wisps of stinking hair shriveled up as if devoured by an open flame. The vampire staggered backward, mewling in pain.

With his arm free at last, Raymer fell backward onto the ground. Veronica rushed to his aid and knelt beside him. He panted and stared forward, reluctant to survey the damage to his wrist.

Alderson watched the hag in spellbound horror. She lifted her head and roared at the night sky. Raymer's blood stained her mouth and soaked her chin. Dark red rivulets ran down her filthy neck. The flesh on the side of her face began to blister from the holy water. The feral creature tore away clumps of burnt hair from its scalp.

"Nathan!" Veronica shrieked. "Give me your shirt!"

Alderson snapped to attention and quickly unfastened the buttons of his work shirt. He glared at the retreating vampire as she fell to her knees several yards from the protective circle. Kneeling low to the ground, she continued to watch him but remained preoccupied with her own wounds.

Unbuckling and jettisoning the shoulder holster, he tore off his shirt and tossed it to Veronica. Trying to keep the stained portion away from Raymer's open wound, she wrapped it around his forearm until it was tight and then knotted it.

Breathing heavily, Raymer's eyes glazed with shock. Veronica held her arm against his back to support him.

"Can you stand up, Edison?"

"Yes," he said after a moment's hesitation.

Veronica and Alderson lifted him to his feet. He wavered for a moment but regained his footing and asked Veronica to hand him the second—and last—vial of holy water. She did as he asked, and withdrew a second large crucifix, which she handed to Alderson. The unarmed detective took the weapon with an uncertain glance.

"We need to get ready for another attack," Raymer said as he caught his breath. He winced in pain and gestured to the vampire. She was on her feet, pacing along the edge of the clearing. Her disfigured face studied them as they tried to regroup.

"She's been weakened, but she won't stop." Raymer beckoned his compatriots to huddle closer. "Stand your ground and be ready for anything."

181

A sudden flurry of violent sounds startled them. They turned to observe the vampire repeatedly stomping on the crossbow with her bare feet. Over and over she lifted her mud-spattered legs and brought them down, crushing it into a pile of splintered shards. Bloody footprints trailed behind her with each step she took. When there was little left of the weapon, she raised her head and locked her eyes on Raymer with a spiteful, menacing glare.

"What the fuck are we gonna do now?" Alderson asked. His dark gray undershirt was drenched in sweat. The detective awaited Raymer's reply in dread.

"We're out of long-range weapons, but—"

"I've still got a rifle in my truck."

"That won't be enough." Raymer shook his head. "Besides, the minute you step out of this circle she'll take you down. No. We have to be patient. She'll slip up... eventually."

"Try to make contact with the cross," Veronica advised Nathan. "When she gets close, press it against her. It should have the same effect as the holy water. But be quick, and whatever you do, do *not* step out of the circle!"

"Everybody stand guard!" Raymer suddenly cried out. Alderson glanced up but the vampire was gone. She had vanished right before their eyes.

"Where the fuck did she go?" Alderson yelled.

"Edison?" Veronica whimpered. The professor spun on her heel and shrieked. The vampire appeared behind them. She began to stalk the perimeter of the circle. Careful not to step over the line, the hag extended her arm over the protective barrier, clawing through the air to catch her prey. Raymer and Veronica retreated as Alderson brandished the heavy crucifix.

"Back off!" He lunged forward with his arm thrust outward. At the sight of the cross, the vampire grew incensed. She hissed and leapt forward, swiping at him with savage ferocity. Alderson managed to dodge her attacks, carefully maneuvering beyond her reach. From behind, Raymer splashed her with a stream of holy water.

The vampire faltered, but the sight of the crosses spurred her forward. She ran around the outer edge of the circle, forcing Raymer and Veronica to shift positions. The unpredictable creature began to dig her feet into the earth, kicking up clumps of soil, which she directed toward them.

"She's trying to cover the circle!" Veronica thrust her crucifix outward. The prowling monster clawed at its chest.

With his thumb covering the small stopper, Raymer clutched the ampule tightly. He flung his good arm forward, eliciting a long vertical splash of holy water. He immediately repeated the gesture but cut his arm from left to right to complete the sign of the cross. The creature backed away and bared her rotten teeth. Alderson heard the vampire's flesh sizzle and watched a thin line of smoke curl above her head. A stream of black saliva dribbled over her chin. Raymer's blood was starting to congeal around her mouth in a deep red crust.

"The crosses are just pissing her off," Veronica shouted.

"We need her to come closer," Raymer said. "Then you two can burn her with them. I'll try to douse her with the rest of the holy water."

"No!" Veronica grasped Raymer's shoulder. "We need to save it. What the hell are we going to do if you run out?"

"This better work!" Alderson warned. He glanced down and noticed the empty .38 laying near the edge of the circle. He kicked the gun away in frustration. "Why the hell didn't we bring more ammo?"

Raymer bristled as the vampire made another run at the circle. She continued to kick up loose soil, hoping to cover the protective barrier. Once again, Veronica and Nathan provoked her with the crosses. As expected, she charged forward. From behind, Raymer sprayed another thick stream of holy water into her face. Half-blinded, she rushed to the other side of the circle. Alderson shoved past him, causing Raymer to drop the vial.

"Dammit!" The water was steadily flowing into the ground. Raymer clenched his jaw as pain flared up in his arm. He reached down, righted the overturned bottle, and clutched it close to his chest. Less than half of it remained.

Alderson's sudden dash forward had caught the vampire off guard. He managed to force the heavy crucifix against the crone's forehead and drag it down the side of her face. As he withdrew the sacred weapon, strips of the vampire's flesh came with it and left a blackened scorch on her cheek.

Veronica appeared at Alderson's side—her crucifix held aloft. The vampire spun and swung its arm, knocking the cross out of Veronica's hand.

It landed just beyond the confines of the circle, where the vampire angrily trampled it with the heel of her foot. The empty-handed professor scurried backward into Raymer's chest. With another flick of his wrist, he drove the vampire back with the last few drops of holy water.

Alderson made another attempt to ward her off with his crucifix, but she reached forward and grabbed it. With a snarl, she wrenched it from the detective's grasp and hurled it into the woods. She spun away from the hunters and stared at her open palm, which had blistered at the touch of the cross.

Nathan panted in frustration. He bent down in search of another crucifix from the gym bag. To his relief, he found one and held it close to his side. Raymer and Veronica stepped forward to stand beside him. Huddled close together, they retreated until they stood at the center of the consecrated circle.

As the vampire paced toward the edge of the clearing, she came to a sudden stop. Her body went rigid, and she turned to look at Alderson. She took a few tentative steps forward, careful to maintain her gaze on him. Now only a few yards away, she froze and slowly knelt down. She began to crouch in an obscene yet inviting posture—her thick legs parting as she sank down to the earth. Despite her unnatural movements, she never dropped her eyes from Alderson.

"What the fuck is she doing?" he yelled. "Why is she staring at *me?*"

"I don't know," Veronica whispered. "But be ready for anything."

Raymer observed the vampire carefully. Her eyes were glassing over, and milky cataracts were beginning to form. Black veins branched along her throat and under her skin. Through the rips in her moldy dress, he struggled to see if the vampire's flesh exhibited any further signs of discoloration.

"I think the silver's taking effect," he called out. She continued to stare at Alderson, following him with empty eyes while he stood at the edge of the circle. Raymer spoke up again, hoping to keep the detective engaged in conversation. "Those bullets are lodged in her chest, spreading poison through her bloodstream. I also hit her with one of the crossbow bolts."

"How long will it take to kill her?"

"Days," Raymer answered. "And that's a liberal estimation. That's also assuming she doesn't feed in the meantime. Fresh blood will heal her and counteract the effect of the silver."

"Great," Alderson responded and turned his attention back to their enemy.

Still kneeling low to the ground, the vampire tilted her head sideways, as if searching for something. Her face was charred. Streams of yellow pus ran from her wounds. Yet her eyes remained fixed upon Alderson.

"Why the fuck is she *still* looking at me?" Alderson turned in a defensive posture. He clenched his jaw and watched as she bent her head forward. Her bloodstained lips curled into a wolfish grin. She quickly rose to her feet, causing Raymer and Veronica to withdraw further into the circle.

She walked until she was less than twenty feet from Alderson. Her scorched face seemed to slacken, and the unsettling smile disappeared. The vampire stared at him—cold, calculating, brutal.

"I can see your boy," she said.

Raymer's skin crawled when he heard the creature speak. Veronica covered her mouth in terror.

"What did you say to me?" Alderson addressed the undead woman, his eyes narrowing with disbelief.

"I can see him." She spoke again, nodding slowly. Her voice a maddening yet lilting tenor. "I see him right there beside you. But you can't see him, can you? Nooooo." The words oozed over her lips. "But he's *right there.*"

"What are you talking about?" Alderson's eyes were wide with fear. He turned to look behind himself in confusion. He shot a pleading glance to Edison Raymer. "What is she saying? What is she talking about?" He turned back to the hag standing motionless before him. *"How did you know?"*

"I can take you to him," she promised. "Do you want to see him again?"

"Don't listen to her, Nate." Veronica stood close beside him.

Raymer moved to stand between Alderson and the vampire beyond the circle. He pressed his uninjured hand against Nathan's chest and stood eye to eye with the trembling detective. But Alderson craned his head to look past Raymer—back to the woman in black.

"How do you know about him? What do you know about my boy?" Tears burned the grieving father's eyes. He pushed against Raymer to move forward, but the vampire hunter stood his ground.

"Alderson, she's lying," Raymer said. "Don't listen to her."

"How do you know?"

Veronica wrapped her hands around his arm. She pulled him tight against her. "Nathan, look away from her! It's a trick! She's trying to draw you to her!"

"Come out of that circle," the vampire beckoned. She lifted her arms and sweetly called to him. "I can take you to him. Come on out. I know you want to. I know you want to see *Cody* again." His name dripped like sour honey from her tongue. "I'll take you to see your boy, just come out of that circle."

Alderson shrugged and tore his arm away from Veronica. Raymer wrapped his arms around him and shoved him back. Veronica quickly grasped him by the shirtsleeve and tightly held on.

"Come out, Nathaniel!" The vampire stepped backward, continuing to motion to him. She chuckled softly and retreated, sinking into the shadows.

Suddenly the spell was broken. Alderson blinked his eyes and looked at Raymer. Confused, he turned to face Veronica and was puzzled by her sorrowful expression. He turned back to Raymer and his eyes fell on the woman in the distance. His jaw tightened as he remembered what had just taken place. Alderson's eyes flooded with rage, and he lunged forward.

"Let me go! Let me after her!" He raved and forced himself against Raymer. "I'll kill her! I'll *fucking* kill her! I'll put a goddamn bullet between—"

"Nathan! Stop!" Raymer ordered. He struggled to restrain the detective. "Snap out of it. She'll kill you. She'll kill all of us! You have to calm down!"

"No!" Nathan fought against his companions. "You keep my son's name out of your mouth." His voice cracked. "Out of your stinking, filthy mouth. Do you hear me? You keep him out of—"

Nathan doubled over and began to sob. He clutched his knees and turned away from the vampire that taunted him. Veronica slid her arms around his shoulders and pulled him against her.

"What the hell are we going to do?" she whispered to Raymer. He spun around to face the vampire. She met his gaze in defiance but kept her distance.

Still clutching the nearly empty bottle of holy water, he corked the lid and turned to face Veronica. "Take this," he instructed. "Stay behind me and keep Alderson at bay. Don't let him leave the circle."

Edison Raymer grabbed the musette bag in the center of the circle and withdrew a silver-tipped bolt, clutching it in his hand like a dagger.

"Raymer, what are you doing?" Veronica asked.

The single-minded man ignored her.

"Come on," Raymer muttered. He adjusted the plain silver cross hanging around his neck and continued to stare the vampire down, certain that his scrutiny would provoke her into action.

The vampire uncurled her lips as Raymer braced for attack. She hissed and took several rapid steps toward him. With his arms outstretched, Raymer sprung forward—the bolt gripped tightly in his left hand.

"Raymer!" Veronica screamed.

The two enemies collided with a crash. The cross around Raymer's neck pressed deep into the vampire's chest. He wrapped his wounded arm around her back and angled his left hand inward. He repeatedly drove the silver-tipped shiv into the fleshy side of the vampire's torso. He delivered a relentless series of quick jabs, puncturing her dead organs.

The vampire groaned as Raymer lifted his left arm and curved the weapon downward to reign blow after blow into her back. Before she could retaliate, he plunged the bolt deep into her shoulder and shoved her away. The wounded hag bent forward, clutching her side. Greasy blood seeped from between her fingers. Smoke wafted from where the cross had scorched her chest. She tried to pull the bolt protruding from her shoulder but could not reach it.

Blind with fury, the vampire sped after Raymer. Veronica raced to his side—her crucifix thrust forward.

"Get back!" the professor commanded. The monster crept backward, eyeing its prey with the promise of vengeance.

With her eyes still trained on the crouching vampire, Veronica scolded Raymer. "What the fuck were you thinking?"

In a frenzy of adrenaline and rage, Raymer snatched the vial of holy water from her and threw it at their enemy. The bottle crashed in front of the vampire. The few remaining droplets burned her feet.

"We broke the circle," Veronica panted, trying to catch her breath. "There's nowhere for us to go. We're dead. She's going to kill us. All three of us!"

His hands still dripping with the vampire's dead blood, Raymer returned to the circle. He bent down and snatched up one of the heavy black bags. His expression unreadable, he overturned it. Silver stakes and several hammers clattered to the ground. After tossing the empty bag aside, he bent forward and selected one of the large metal hammers. He turned and handed it to Veronica. She took it from him after switching her crucifix to her left hand.

"Keep an eye on that thing." Raymer pointed his thumb over his shoulder. "If she comes forward, drive her back with the cross."

"But that hasn't been—"

Raymer lifted his hand to silence her. He glanced at his watch and frowned. "Just buy us a little more time."

He turned his attention to Alderson, who stood in a daze along the outer edge of the circle. Raymer placed both hands on Nathan's shoulders. The exhausted detective glanced up and Raymer looked him square in the eyes. "Nathan, we only have one more chance at this or all three of us are gonna die out here. Do you understand me?"

Alderson nodded his head.

"We've got more than an hour before we're anywhere near sunrise," Raymer continued. "I need you to stand up and give it one more go. Do you think you can do that?"

"Yeah." His voice was raw. "Just promise me we're going to kill her."

"Believe me, we'll kill her." Raymer cast a hateful glance at the vampire over his shoulder and then beckoned Veronica to come closer. He spoke in a low voice first to Alderson. "We need to flank her. I'll go right, you spin left. She's going to fight like hell, but we just need to hold her down." Raymer nodded to Veronica. "That's where you come in. Pick up one of those stakes, bring the hammer, and drive it home while we hold her down."

"Are you crazy?" Veronica replied. "I can't."

"You have to!" Raymer insisted. "There's no other way. We're out of weapons, and we're out of options! Pretty soon, we're going to be out of time!"

Alderson spoke up. "Let's do this. I want her dead."

"You can do it, Veronica," Raymer encouraged her. "Just don't hold back. You've got to drive it through and pin her down or we're dead."

She nodded in silence. Her eyes were blank with terror. They all turned to observe the vampire, who was watching them closely.

"One more thing." Raymer gestured to Alderson. He tore his silver cross from its chain and directed him to follow suit. "Keep the cross inside your palm. Like this," he demonstrated. "Push it against her as you hold her down."

Alderson nodded and tugged the symbol from its chain. The weary detective clenched the cross in his right hand and turned to face the vampire. He shuddered as she began to glide toward them. Raymer stood unfazed and began to count.

"One... Two... *Three!*"

The two men charged across the clearing. Nathan lowered his head and rammed into the vampire's side. Raymer threw his good arm over her left shoulder, and they drove her to the ground.

In an absolute frenzy, the vampire writhed beneath them. She strained her arms and dug her calloused feet into the soil. Low threatening growls—punctuated by higher-pitched screams of desperation—rang in the hunters' ears.

Alderson pinned her right arm and shoulder under his body weight. He slid his leg across hers to prevent her from kicking, but she bucked and thrashed against him. Nathan drove his cross hard against her wrist and dug his fingernails into the loose, sloughing flesh of her upper arm.

With his left hand, Raymer pushed his cross against the vampire's clavicle and angled his body to pin her to the ground. He ignored the pain as the makeshift tourniquet slid from his arm. Blood gushed from the wound as it scraped against the vampire's stiff clothing and the coarse patches of earth beneath her. He curved his fingers around her shoulder and strained to keep her down.

The vampire arched her back and pushed against her captors. She gnashed her teeth, snapping her head from side to side. The men matched her brute strength, which had been tempered by the silver coursing through her veins. They managed to avoid her jaws and keep her pinioned to the earth. But Raymer knew they only had a matter of minutes before she would overpower them.

"Veronica!" Nathan yelled. He could already feel his strength ebbing away. "Hurry!"

Still inside the broken circle, Veronica clutched the mallet in her dominant hand. She had traded the crucifix for a silver stake. Her hand trembled as she wiped a tear against her sleeve. After a deep breath, the professor stepped forward, crossing the thin line of crumbled host.

As she crept closer, she was almost felled by the noxious stench emanating from the vampire's body. Veronica froze. The mallet hung heavy in one hand. The stake threatened to slip from her sweaty fingers. She steeled herself and took another step forward, her eyes fixed on the squirming creature sprawled out before her.

"Now, Veronica!" Raymer yelled. "Do it now!"

She leapt backwards to avoid the vampire's flailing legs. "Hold her goddamn feet down!"

Alderson drove his right knee into the earth and wrapped his legs around her. Raymer pressed his shin over the vampire's ankle and dug the toe of his heavy boot into the ground. She continued to fight but was momentarily restrained.

"Don't look in her eyes!" Raymer commanded. "The heart! Drive it through her heart and into the ground! Like I did to Bartsch!"

Veronica stepped forward, careful to avoid her partners as they struggled to keep their enemy restrained. She stood with her feet apart, straddling the vampire's torso. With a quaking hand, she placed the tip of the stake against the vampire's breast. She raised the mallet above her head. The silver seemed to burn through the torn dress and ignite the flesh above the dead thing's heart.

"Fucking do it!" Alderson screamed.

Raymer shifted his position to reorient his grip on the vampire's arm, which caused his foot to slip. The vampire struck out and leveled a hard kick into Veronica's groin. Another flurry of kicks hit the professor in the stomach. The impact knocked the wind out of her, and she dropped the hammer to the ground. The stake, in turn, slipped from her fingers and rolled out of reach.

As Veronica doubled over to catch her breath, Alderson's hand slipped. Immediately, the vampire broke free. Raymer's arm buckled and he fell face first onto the gore-soaked ground. The vampire rolled on top of Alderson, craned her neck, and tried to bite his throat. He managed to escape the first attack, but when she struck a second time, the vampire sank her teeth into his shoulder. The detective howled in pain.

Now on his feet, Raymer quickly scanned the ground in search of his cross, which he had lost during the skirmish.

"Get her the fuck off of me!" Alderson roared. He pummeled his fists into the creature's back. But she held fast, sinking her fangs deeper into his flesh.

Raymer snatched the cross from the ground, placed it in the palm of his right hand, and dashed toward Alderson. He wrapped his injured arm around the vampire's neck and shoved the cross against her forehead, forcing her to relinquish her prey. Alderson rolled to the side and heard something crack in his pocket. Gripping his shoulder, the stunned detective staggered to his feet and wandered back to the circle.

With the vampire in a chokehold, Raymer pulled her backward, her heels dragging in the mud. Before he could cry out for help, Raymer felt an explosion of pain as the vampire drove her elbow into his ribs. With his last bit of strength, he spun her around and flung her into the overgrowth. She stumbled and fell to the ground, but quickly righted herself into a low, crouching position.

Panting for breath, Raymer took up a fighting stance. He fumbled with the musette bag and withdrew another silver-tipped bolt and stood at the ready. With her arm thrust forward and her fingers splayed wide in the dirt, the vampire stared up at him with filmy, blood-rimmed eyes. Her ruined dress clung to her limbs in tatters. Her rank body was covered in sores and charred impressions from their crosses.

As Raymer continued to catch his breath, the woman simply remained poised like a malformed statue. She betrayed no signs of respiration. No perspiration dripped from her pores. If she felt pain, she did not yield to it. The sight unnerved him, but he took a step forward, wielding the bolt. The vampire held her ground and did not flinch.

"Stay in the circle!" He called to his allies over his shoulder. "Do not move!"

Veronica watched in terror as Raymer stood face-to-face with their enemy. She feared the vampire would strike again and their ruined sanctuary could no longer protect them.

Raymer made another step forward, still clutching the bolt. Resigned to meet his fate, he swung his tired arm, slashing through the air. His rival made no move against him.

"Come on!" he bellowed. "Let's finish this!"

With a flash of her bloodstained teeth, she slid backward, melding into the deep shadows of the woods.

"No!" Raymer cried out and charged after her.

With a rush of cold musty air, the vampire was gone.

Raymer spun and looked behind him, but there was no sign of her. He quickly turned, letting his eyes sweep over each of the divergent paths but she was nowhere to be found. The shadows had swallowed up the thing that lurked in the woods.

Cursing to himself, he hurried to rejoin the others. "Do we have any more wafers left?"

"I... I think so," Veronica stammered. Her eyes were wide as she tried to maintain focus.

"Good." He continued to comb the tree line. "We need to reinforce the circle in case she comes back."

"Shouldn't we just get the fuck out of here?"

"We can't." Raymer shook his head, still nervously scanning the forest. "We're too far from the trucks and she's still here. I can feel her."

"How much longer until sunrise?" Alderson asked in a faraway voice. His breath was strained, and he was drenched in sweat.

Raymer consulted his watch and winced. "At least forty-five minutes. Maybe an hour."

"Jesus Christ," Veronica muttered. She quickly reached into her bag for the rest of the wafers. Dropping to her knees, she hurriedly began to consecrate another circle.

Alderson stood motionless at the edge of the clearing. He scoured the ground in search of another crucifix. Raymer was already kneeling where he had emptied the gym bag earlier. As Alderson approached, Raymer had a crucifix waiting for him. The detective accepted the weapon and studied the older man as he rose to his feet.

"I thought you killed dozens of these things," Alderson said. "So what the hell happened?"

Raymer met Nathan's disappointed gaze with tired eyes. "I failed."

Veronica paused and glanced up at Raymer. She wiped a loose strand of sweaty hair from her brow and observed her ex-partner. His eyes glistened with determination. A moment later, she finished casting the protective circle and rose to her feet.

The professor's knees almost buckled. Her joints ached from the constant tension. She brushed the powder from her hands and joined Raymer at the threshold of the circle. With the crucifix lowered at his side, Raymer stood guard and watched the woods with unease.

The forest was quiet—its darkness impenetrable and at its deepest. Raymer couldn't help but think of the clichéd expression—*it's always darkest before the dawn.* He yearned for the phrase to be rendered trite and meaningless once again. Staring at his blood-drenched hands, he wished they had remembered to bring bottled water. He rubbed his palms against his cargo pants, but gore still sullied his fingers. Raymer was startled from his reverie when Alderson began to cough heavily behind him.

"You OK?" Raymer asked.

Nathan nodded without a response. His hand was pressed tightly against his shoulder. His face and hands were also caked with dried blood.

"You need to tend to that wound, Nate."

"As soon as we get out of here," he finally spoke up. "My wife's a nurse so—"

"You can't show her that!"

193

"Obviously!" He took a breath and closed his eyes for a moment before continuing. "I'm sorry. That's not what I meant. We've got bandages and other supplies. Painkillers. I'll be fine."

"You need to use disinfectant," Raymer cautioned. "And a whole lot of it."

"Why?" His voice betrayed a flash of panic. "Jesus Christ, I'm not going to turn into one of these things, am I?"

"No," Raymer stated. "No, it's OK. Calm down. That's not how it works. Nevertheless, you're still at risk for a general bacterial infection."

Alderson breathed a sigh of relief. After a moment he pointed to Raymer's arm. "What about you? Are you OK?"

"I'll patch myself up later," he replied.

"Edison," Veronica interjected. "You need to see a doctor." The professor shot a worried glance to Alderson. "Both of you. I can drive us to the ER."

"And tell them what?" Raymer shrugged. "Anyway, I'm a wanted man, remember? I can't be seen here. I've got lidocaine, sutures, and everything I need back at my house."

"That's a long drive back to Richmond," Alderson said.

"I've done it many times before," he replied. "This time's no different." He turned his attention to Veronica. "How are you feeling?"

"Fine, I guess." She frowned. "Although I totally fucked up back there. I'm so sorry! I should have—"

"Hey, you had her." Alderson took a step forward. "This was my fault. I slipped and she got free."

Raymer looked away and made sure the vampire wasn't lurking along the tree lines behind them. He craned his neck to see further into the woods and then studied the thickets to his left.

"Listen, Edison, I really don't think we should stay here anymore," Veronica said. "If she was gonna attack us, don't you think she would've come back by now? We should make a break for it."

"Seriously, Raymer. She's right. We need to try."

"Listen to me, because this is the last time I'm gonna say it." He pointed his crucifix to the dark sky. "Until you see the sun rise above those motherfucking trees to our east, we will remain on guard and within the confines of this circle."

194

Alderson's jaw tightened. He was about to challenge Raymer's command.

"She's still out there, and she's angry." Raymer gestured back to the woods. "We have to stay put."

Nathan stepped aside so that Raymer could observe a different portion of the forest. Edison froze when there was an unexpected rustle in the trees. He raised his crucifix and kept his eyes locked on the footpath ahead. Veronica stiffened and pulled up beside him. Alderson remained at the rear of the circle. Still lost in thought, the weary detective was alarmed by his companions' sudden movements. He lifted his cross and drew up on them from behind.

The three of them stood perfectly still—poised and ready for attack. After a few minutes passed, it became clear that nothing was going to emerge from the woods. Veronica breathed a sigh of relief and rubbed the back of her neck.

Nathan was still uneasy. He turned to Raymer with a perplexed and haunted expression. "I just have one question," he asked. "All those things she said about my son. How did she know?"

Raymer considered his words carefully before replying. "Honestly, Nathan, I don't know. Sometimes these things—"

"What do you mean, you don't know? I thought you were a goddamn expert?"

"Look, sometimes they get inside your head," Raymer explained. "But what's even worse is she's tasted our blood. Yours as well as mine. We're both marked, and we need to be on our guard."

"Raymer's right," Veronica said gently. "She seemed to fixate on you, Nate."

"But why?" Alderson was incredulous. "And what do you mean marked? I don't understand. Why the hell was she focused on me? And how did she know my son's name? I never said it!"

"You didn't have to say it." Raymer shook his head. "She just knew."

"Wait a minute." Alderson held up a tremulous hand. "Are you saying she read my mind? Or... that she... that she was telling the truth? That she *could* see him?"

Neither Veronica nor Raymer spoke. Alderson grew agitated. "Alright, I swear to Christ I'm going to bury her. I'm going to ram a fucking—"

"Nate, calm down." Veronica reached out to him. But the irate and frightened detective shrugged her away.

"There's a lot we still don't know about these things," Raymer admitted. "When I hunt them, I take them down. Sometimes it's messy, but I don't give these parasites time to fuck with my head." He turned to Veronica. "You said she appeared at your séance, right?"

"Yeah," she confirmed. "But we didn't know she was there. I only noticed when I played back the video. She was just a shadow in the corner, watching us almost the whole time."

"I presume you remember the girl at the Aston house?" Raymer asked with a grim expression. "And how she was able to manifest in spirit form?"

Veronica swallowed hard and nodded.

"Then we need to be ready." Raymer turned back to Alderson. "We have no idea what she's capable of doing. And we absolutely *have* to kill her."

"How?" Alderson demanded. A wild, haggard look possessed him. "What the hell are we going to do now?"

"We'll come back." Raymer exhaled heavily. "But not tonight. We need to rest. When we come back here, we have to be on our A-game."

"No, we need to come back here fucking *strapped!*" Alderson shouted. "Christ, we almost had her! I'm not saying it was easy, but we had her down. We just need more firepower."

"Not necessarily," Raymer said. "You buried three rounds of silver in her. And you blew her hand off. But she kept coming."

"Alright, then why don't we just set her on fire? Instead of dousing her with holy water, how about some gasoline?"

"Fire will destroy her." Raymer sighed. "Not to mention all the dry brush in these woods."

"Fuck that. This whole place is..." The detective glanced down at the ground and trailed off. He recognized more unnatural depressions in the earth, just a few steps from where they stood. "I mean, this whole place should be destroyed."

Raymer reached over and clasped his hand on Nathan's good shoulder. "I promised you back there we'd kill her. And we will. I've got more than enough weapons and ammunition back at the house. We'll take her down. I promise you."

Alderson glanced up and noticed the sky was beginning to lighten. Raymer followed the detective's eyes and turned to look over his shoulder.

"Not much longer now," Edison nodded. "But stay on guard. She could try for one last attack."

Exhausted but determined, Raymer stood firm. Veronica inched closer to him. Her damp clothes were heavy and uncomfortable. She shivered and clutched her arms close to her chest. Alderson stepped in front of her, to shield her from the wind. His head pounded and his shoulder burned. With his head hung low, he turned the crucifix over in his hands and mourned for his absent son.

Almost at once, the sense of oppression lifted. The sky above had faded from dark purple to a pinkish gray. Birdsong filled the air. The breeze coming up from the James River was fresh and clean, bearing no trace of death or decay. Incongruous with the nightmare they had just endured, the morning disoriented rather than relieved them. The three hunters felt as though they awoke to a world that no longer belonged to any of them.

Raymer cleared his throat and motioned for them to begin gathering their belongings. Alderson placed his crucifix into one of the unzipped bags. He bent to retrieve the empty .38 and made a quick pass near the overgrowth in hopes of recovering the .44, but the heavy pistol was nowhere to be found.

"We need to find that .44," Alderson said as he approached Raymer and handed him the .38. "It's got my fingerprints all over it."

"We will," Raymer assured him. "We're coming back, and it'll be easier to spot in the daytime."

They collected whatever scant items remained and tossed them into the open bags. After a few minutes, they gathered around the tailgate of Raymer's Scout. He hefted both bags into the utility vehicle, slammed the hatch shut, and turned to face his companions.

"I'll drive home and load up my truck," he explained. "Then, I need to pay a visit to someone in Richmond who may be able to help us with this situation."

"Wait a second." Alderson eyed Raymer with suspicion. "Who are you going to see?"

"We can discuss it later. Let's meet at Veronica's place later this afternoon and we'll make our plans."

"OK, but lay low," Alderson reminded him. "The last thing we need is for you to get yourself arrested."

"Understood. Now, you two get some rest," Raymer advised. "I'm going to need both of you, because I can't do this alone."

Veronica nodded. For the second time in twenty-four hours, Edison Raymer had managed to surprise her. His expression of need and the hint of humility was sincere.

"This battle is far from over," he added. "I promise our next trip into these woods will not be a repeat performance of this one."

17

THE MORNING FULLY BROKE, COLD AND GRAY. NATHAN AL-derson slowed his truck as he approached his empty driveway. He activated the garage door opener and breathed a sigh of relief to see that Kelly's car was gone. His wife had already left for work.

After exiting the cab, he slapped the lighted panel on the concrete wall and the heavy garage door began to close. He opened the door leading into the kitchen and glanced inside to ensure that he was alone. No lights had been left on and the atmosphere was perfectly still.

Before stepping across the threshold, he slipped off his muddy boots and began to peel off his soiled clothing. Now in his boxers and bare feet, he reached into the pocket of his discarded jeans and withdrew his cell phone. Splinters of thin plastic fell to the floor. The entire illuminated face of the phone was smashed. The screen was frozen in place on the weather app. It was going to remain partly cloudy and thirty-eight degrees until the half-drained battery of the dysfunctional device finally died.

With the broken phone clutched in his hand, Nathan bent to retrieve his rank garments and stuffed them into an oversized garbage bag along with his ruined pair of boots. The grease-stained concrete floor was cold beneath his feet. He crept to the rear of the truck and tossed the bag into the flatbed to dispose of it later.

Finally making his way into the kitchen, he retrieved a glass from one of the overhead cabinets, filled it with cold tap water and downed it in one long swallow. He left the empty glass in the sink and turned toward the dining room. As he passed the dry erase board on the refrigerator, he noticed there were no new messages from his wife.

At the top of the stairs, Alderson ransacked the hallway closet for medical supplies. He grabbed a large adhesive bandage and a tube of Bacitracin to treat the wound. When he didn't see any rubbing alcohol, Kelly's voice played in his head. *The solution for pollution is dilution.* Alderson remembered that she had told him it was now common practice to disinfect a wound with soap and water.

Nathan grabbed a fresh towel and a few washcloths and carried them to the bathroom. He placed the items beside the sink and turned on the shower. Hot water spilled from the showerhead. Staring into the mirror, Alderson watched as his haggard reflection was erased by the enveloping steam.

With the washcloths and a bar of soap in hand, he slipped out of his boxers and stepped into the tub. He yanked the green shower curtain closed behind him. Within the dark steam-filled space, Alderson began to feel safe and warm for the first time in several hours.

He pressed his forehead against the smooth tile and let the water run over his head and shoulders, then down his aching back. The hot water drove away the chill—but not the memories of what had just taken place in the woods.

The vampire's black eyes were foremost in his mind. The awful smell that clung to her body still lingered. The painful sensation of her teeth tearing into his flesh continued to smart.

But worst of all was the sound of her voice when she spoke to him of his son.

I know you want to see Cody again.

He slapped his open palm against the tile and opened his eyes. Dense, murky water swirled around the open drain. Several minutes passed before the water running off his body had gone from brown to clear. He grimaced as the water burned the wound in his shoulder.

Nathan retreated to the back of the tub, letting the spray douse his lower body. He lathered the washcloth with soap until it was coated in thick foam. For several minutes, he dabbed at the bite, which had already begun to bruise around the edges. The sting caused him to clench his teeth.

His mind suddenly came alive with images that made him want to retch. The hag's filthy body writhing beneath him. Her twisted fingers clawing at his face and arms. The shower of gore that had exploded from her hand.

He fought to shake the visions away and kept working on the wound with the cloth. The soapy water ran down his body and flowed into the drain. He moved on to scrub his arms, chest, and legs where other minor nicks and bruises had recently formed.

Nearly twenty minutes passed before Nathan Alderson had felt anything remotely comparable to clean. He stepped out of the tub onto a soft floormat and toweled himself dry, gently dabbing the wound. He smeared his hand across the fogged mirror to inspect it and was relieved to see the wound was not as deep as he feared. With the blood cleared away, it appeared far less intimidating and troublesome.

Alderson fumbled for the tube of Bacitracin. He squeezed a generous measure onto his fingers and massaged the topical antibiotic directly onto his wound.

After carefully affixing a clean bandage to his shoulder, the exhausted detective padded to the master bedroom, fished a pair of boxers from his dresser drawer, and then crawled into bed. He pulled the soft down blanket over him and immediately maneuvered into a comfortable position. Face down into his pillow, Nathan Alderson fell into a deep yet restless sleep.

✝

The corpse of Cody Andrew Alderson lay stiff and white beneath the waters of the James River. River rock provided him a pillow. The muddy depths and deadfall the bed upon which he slept. His father's strong hands broke through the ice-cold waters and lifted him into his arms. Cradled against his chest, the boy's head lulled backward. Brackish water ran from his open mouth—his chest hollow and motionless. His tiny fingers were pruned and caked with mud. The boy hung like limp seaweed over Alderson's arms as he carried him to rest along the riverbank.

The boy's eyes fluttered open. There were no pupils. No irises. No colors and no window opened to his soul. White. Like the underside of the fish he caught and released hours before his lungs filled with water and he sank beneath the river's surface.

"I wanna go back into the water."

Nathan shook his head and caressed the side of his son's smooth white face. He stared down at him and watched as the blond-haired boy wrinkled his brow with a pout.

"You need to rest for a while, buddy."

"No." The boy shook his head. "Put me back in the water, daddy."

"Why, son?" his father asked. "Why do you wanna go back to the water?"

"Because I'm dead there."

Alderson scooped his son into his arms and lowered him back into his riverbed grave. He gently pressed his hand against his son's bare chest and pushed him downward. Nathan watched as Cody sank to the bottom of the river, until there was nothing but his own reflection on the rippling surface.

Thunder boomed overhead. A fork of lighting flashed above the river as it wound its course toward him. Another crash of thunder shook the woods and caused the ground to momentarily tremble.

Alderson spun to find himself standing further along the desolate riverbank. The choppy waters splashed along the edge of the mud, advancing and retreating in silence. The sky above rolled with dense, fast-moving clouds. It stretched above and beyond him, a dark blanket of roiling indigo—touched with a turbulent purple hue. At the threshold of night, the trees loomed dark against the bleak horizon. The foggy marshland ran along his left side. To his right rolled the fast-moving currents of the James.

Ahead he spied a diminutive figure. A small silhouette against the yawning blue darkness that stretched out before him. From behind, he could see his son's light blond hair as the boy walked forward. He wore his favorite red t-shirt and a pair of tan cargo shorts. "The ones with the big pockets," he'd say. The boy used to fill them with Matchbox trucks and race around the house from the front yard to the back and then around again.

202

Nathan called out to his son, but the boy did not hear him. Thunder rolled again and seemed to overpower the whole earth. Only the sound of the churning rapids of the James could rival it.

After another flash of lightning, the forest grew dark again. But a second figure now appeared along the riverbank. Like his son, the silhouette faced away from him. The train of a long black gown trailed behind it, sweeping through the lapping waves of the river. Cascades of rich golden hair spilled down the tall and stately woman's back.

A tattered black veil spun out, flapping wildly in the breeze. A white hand reached up to hold the mournful coronet in place, while the other hand extended outward, stretching toward the small boy.

Cody strolled alongside the strange woman. He lifted his tiny arm and clasped the hand of the lady in black who continued to glide beside him.

"No! Wait!"

The boy remained deaf to his father's pleas.

Alderson raced forward to catch up to the trailing pair of shadows. No matter how fast he ran, or how hard he pushed himself, the distance between father and son only seemed to increase. His legs were heavy and the wind seemed adversarial, blowing in direct opposition to him.

Nathan continued to cry out his son's name. But the boy never turned to look at his father. Instead, he craned his small neck upward and smiled at the lady that towered above him. Alderson could discern the curves of the unnatural woman set against the darkness. He shuddered when he realized she was humming softly to his son—a simple, funereal air that felt both familiar and repulsive to him.

Suddenly Nathan found himself face down at the mouth of the forest path that led to the graves of Tyler Marshall. Sylvia Aptheker. Sally Benson. And scores of other children who had lost their way in the forest. His ears adjusted to an unnerving absence of sound.

The raging of the storm and the roaring of the river had fallen silent. Now he was beset by the indiscernible whispers of children. A chorus of hushed voices harmonized among the swaying trees. He could not see them, but he felt their eyes watching him, staring from the shadows at the mouth of the woods.

He staggered to his feet with his trench coat wrapped tightly around him. The detective adjusted his tie, angled his flashlight beam, and pressed forward along the winding path, which had grown steeper and climbed upward into the forest. The whispers turned to crickets and the crickets rose and fell as he angled the beam along the clustered rows of trees. Sometimes Alderson caught a flash of a lost or scowling face. In the distance one of them was weeping.

As he pressed forward, a freckled girl with an ornate braid over her shoulder pointed with a rigid finger. The sad-eyed girl directed Alderson to take a different path diverging from the one he had followed. She placed her finger over her lips to stress that he stay quiet. Alderson nodded and reached into his pocket for the snub-nose .38.

Far ahead on the path, the detective could discern the pair of crooked silhouettes he was pursuing. Again, the anxious father cried out to his son. His words felt slow and heavy, for there was so little breath to give them strength. The detective gasped as he felt himself suffocating—as if the air of the forest now flowed with the smothering waters of the James.

The woman in black continued to lead the boy through the forest. Together they passed between the trees and knotted thorn bushes. Sometimes the moonlight would spill through the canopy of leaves above. Alderson raced forward—his eyes riveted to the fast-moving figures ahead.

"Run, Cody! Run away! Run!"

Suddenly the boy broke free and darted away from the mysterious woman beside him. She remained still, as if watching him flee. She gently pinched the sides of her full skirts—lifting them above her ankles—and began to chase after him.

"Run! Get away from her! Hide, Cody! Find a place to hide!"

Alderson raised his gun to fire at the ghostly woman. He pulled the trigger but was met with a series of impotent clicks.

The chamber was empty.

Nathan dashed forward, dodging low-hanging tree limbs and rogue branches, desperate to catch up to the two figures in the distance. He could no longer see them, but he could hear his son's panicked footfalls and low panting breaths. The woman sped forward, moving with certainty and assurance.

204

A tightness pervaded his limbs. A stitch began to unfurl in his side. But the frantic detective charged onward. The path seemed to raise and drop, forcing him to climb upward against the grip of gravity, only to topple over a sudden, sprawling precipice. Spinning out of control, his limbs flailing, Alderson failed to orient himself as the amorphous paths transformed before him.

At last, he came to a clearing and saw his son's sneakered foot clip a half-buried root, which sent him crashing to the ground. The boy spun onto his back. Winded and unable to push himself to his feet, he retreated as the black-clad woman's shadow fell over him. Wide-eyed, Alderson watched as the woman bent over his son. She lifted her tattered veil, and the boy began to scream.

Alderson raced forward but his limbs were ensnared by the invisible web permeating the vampire's domain. Mired and leaden, he could do nothing as his son's final moments played out in front him, a new and unthinkable coda to the tragedy he had already once endured.

Still hunched over the terrified child, the cruel woman bent forward and scolded him in a deafening voice.

"You will not run from me!" she roared. "Because I will find you. No matter where you try to hide, I will find you!"

The enraged woman turned to reach above her head and snapped a heavy branch from the arm of an oak tree. She broke the limb over her knee and then drove the sharpened end through Cody Alderson's torso, pinning him to the earth.

Through her clenched teeth, the vampire issued a final admonition to the motionless child at her feet.

"You... will... lie... still!"

✝

Nathan Alderson awoke with a devastated scream. He rolled to his left and felt his stomach sink as he fell out of bed. His head struck the nightstand as he crashed to the floor.

"Sometimes they get inside your head." Edison Raymer's voice rang out in his troubled mind. *"We're both marked, and we need to be on our guard."*

Nathan drew his knees inward and cradled his throbbing head in his hands. He began to sob heavily, rocking his body backward and forward, his breathing short and labored. Before long, he curled into a fetal position and fell into a dreamless sleep on his bedroom floor.

18

VERONICA WAS AWAKENED BY THE SOUND OF A TELEPHONE ringing in the distance. Determined not to open her eyes and fully resurface to consciousness, she blindly reached out in search of her cell to silence the clamorous sounds. She squeezed the buttons on the side of the plastic case and dropped it back on her nightstand. The phone continued to ring.

The landline?

Who the fuck is calling me on the landline?

The aggravated professor threw off her covers, hurried down the hall, and descended the stairs into her living room. By the time she reached the telephone, whoever was calling had already hung up.

She adjusted the damp towel on her head and turned to go back upstairs, hoping it wasn't too late for her to resume the sleep she desperately craved. However, she feared the mystery of the caller's identity would gnaw at her until the anxiety forced her to stay awake.

The phone began to ring again. This time she was quick to snatch up the receiver.

"Hello?"

"Dr. Upham?"

"This is she." The voice was familiar, but she failed to identify it.

"Oh, you had me worried there," the man continued. "I was just calling to make sure everything was OK."

Dean Ritter.

"I'm fine, Dr. Ritter. Sorry, I just woke up and was a little confused why someone was calling on this line when—"

"Oh, believe me, I tried your cell numerous times," he explained. "I was concerned when I heard you hadn't shown up for your class this morning and thought—"

"I wasn't supposed to teach this morning," Veronica corrected him with a furrowed brow. "My class is on Wednesdays."

"It is Wednesday, Dr. Upham."

The dean was silent as he awaited her explanation.

"Oh, wow. I'm sorry, I totally mixed up my days." The professor scrambled to think of an excuse. "The truth is something's come up. A minor family emergency. I may have to go up north for a bit."

"This wouldn't have anything to do with the detective that came to see me on Monday, would it?"

"Huh?" She tightened her grip on the phone. "What detective?"

"Some hotshot cop came around asking about Edison Raymer." The voice on the other end sighed. "As is customary, when police officers come knocking on my door asking questions about Raymer, I send them directly to you."

"Well, like I told you before. And the time before that. I haven't seen or spoken to him since he skipped town two years ago."

"OK, Veronica. There's no need to get defensive. I just wondered if there was any trouble I should know about." He paused. "Did the detective come to speak to you?"

Fuck.

"Yeah, come to think of it, he did," she said irritably. "Damn near disrupted my lecture but thankfully I was almost through. I didn't think much of it at the time and haven't given it a second thought with all that's going on with my family. Funny thing though that all these cops can't track down a petty arsonist. I guess Raymer had the last laugh after all."

"Do you know where Raymer is, Dr. Upham?"

"For the last time, no, I don't!" Veronica raised her voice. "What the hell is this? Why the third degree?"

"You tell me, Dr. Upham. I just called to make sure nothing was amiss. But you've been rather... *antagonistic* this entire call."

"Oh, come on, Ritter. You don't make courtesy calls. First of all, why are *you* calling me instead of Sue? If I need to cancel a class or make alternate arrangements, that's something between me and the chair of the English department."

"True," Ritter replied. "But don't forget who Sue reports to. And besides, Sue is the one who brought it to my attention that you missed your class. A few of your students checked with the department secretary since they never received an email from you, and nothing was posted outside the classroom. I'm sure some of them were disappointed to have driven all the way to campus only to learn there'd be no lecture on *Jane Eyre* or whatever dusty old book you're teaching this semester."

"Well, as I said, that was my mistake. And I apologize." Veronica attempted to temper her tone. However much of a prick Dean Ritter may be, he was still technically her superior. He could see that her tenure was reviewed or possibly even revoked. "I'll make arrangements with Sue to have one of the adjuncts teach my next few classes. Like I said earlier, I need to take some personal time. And Christ knows the adjuncts would welcome the chance to teach something other than a freshman writing course."

Ritter sighed again. "Well, let's just hope one of those adjuncts isn't asked to take over your classroom permanently."

"Is that a threat? I've been at Williamsport College longer than *you* have. I've put more of my time and energy into the English department than anyone. I've arranged colloquia, organized conferences, made cookies for bake sales, donated materials for book sales, not to mention I've had *numerous* publications on—"

"You've missed office hours, you skipped the last three fundraisers, and you turned down the position of chair two years in a row. Yeah, I've been keeping score. So, if you want to discuss your CV with me, Dr. Upham, you need to understand that what concerns me is the *present* and the future. And today, I've got 28 students on this campus whose professor was a no-show. In the interest of ensuring that something of this nature doesn't happen again, you can consider this a formal warning."

"You know what, David?" The blood rushed to Veronica's temples. Her hand trembled as she pressed the phone tight against her ear. "Just admit it. This isn't about me. It's about Edison Raymer, right? Your crusade to kick him out on his ass finally came to fruition and now you've—"

"I suggest you mind your tone, Veronica."

"And now you've set your sights on *me* because you've got nothing better to do!" Veronica's voice quaked with adrenaline. "So, I have a suggestion for you. Instead of worrying about me and my personal life, do something constructive. Improve campus housing. Look into getting healthier food options in the dorms. Update the campus wi-fi. Seek out grants to expand the library's holdings so my students don't have to use Interlibrary loan every time they have to write a research paper. But, with all due respect, leave me alone!"

She slammed the phone back onto its cradle and caught her breath. Her eyes swimming with rage, she stormed into her kitchen. After igniting the stovetop, she filled her tea kettle, and spent the next few minutes waiting for the water to boil.

I guess I'm up for the day.

As she stood beside the gaslit stove top, her hands continued to shake. The adrenaline failed, however, to mask the physical toll the previous evening had taken on her aging body. Despite the hot shower she took earlier that morning, her lower back still ached. The taut muscles in her arms were sore, and her legs were stiff and bruised.

Inevitably, the pompous, ruddy face of David Ritter began to fade in her mind. In its place rose the charred visage of the ghastly creature from the woods. Her decaying teeth and furious eyes. Her abominable stench and ragged claws.

The Nightmare Life-in-Death was she,
Who thicks man's blood with cold.

Veronica jumped as the tea kettle began to scream. Her heart raced as she removed it from the burner. With an unsteady hand, she poured the steaming water over the sachet of green tea leaves in her china cup. After administering several liberal spoonfuls of sugar, she placed the cup on a small saucer and wandered back into her living room.

Enough with the goddamn poetry. Coleridge's opium-drenched visions mean nothing when things like that monster are out there. This nightmare is real.

Still lost in thought, Veronica absent-mindedly began to ascend the soft carpeted stairs. A small splash of hot tea spilled over the side of her cup and onto the saucer. The spoon awkwardly spun and threatened to fall out.

Who the hell is she? Bartsch and Laura were still themselves. This fucking thing was like an animal. Feral. Driven. Why? How long has she been here? Why did she kill Tyler Marshall?

As Veronica entered the bedroom to return to her bed, her troubled heart suddenly sank.

Nate.

Why was she so focused on him? Was it because he found those things buried up there? More importantly how did she know about his son?

As she gently placed the cup and saucer down on the small ornate nightstand by her bed, the face of her cell lit up but then faded to black again. Taking up the phone, she sighed upon discovering a flurry of missed activity and sat heavily on the edge of her bed.

In all, the professor had five missed calls and nearly twice as many text messages.

"Jesus Christ," she muttered and tapped the voicemail box. She lifted the device to replay the first message.

"Hey, Veronica. It's Eric. I've been trying to reach you for a few days now. But umm... yeah, this whole Tyler Marshall thing is fucked up. Are you OK? We need to talk about this. I tried calling Janice, but she isn't calling me back. Do you think we should tell somebody? What are we going to do? Please. Call me back. I'm worried about you."

"Goddamn it, Eric. Just let it go!"

The less he knows, the better off he'll be. I need to—

Once again, Veronica's train of thought was interrupted when the second message began to play. As soon as she heard the reedy voice of Dean Ritter, she lowered the phone from her ear and poked her finger against the screen to delete his message. When another message from Ritter began, she groaned and repeated the same impatient gesture.

The next message was from Susan Watkins, the chair of the English department.

"Hey Ronnie, it's Sue. Not sure what happened today but I just wanted to check in and see if everything was OK. And listen, I also wanted to give you a heads up that Ritter caught wind of your absence. Apparently, the nosy bastard was talking to Fred in the lobby when he overhead one of your students asking Nora if your class was cancelled. Nora hadn't heard from you, so she never posted a cancellation notice on the door. So of course, Ritter butts in and... anyway, I tried to play it off, but the whole thing's a mess. Would you please give me a call as soon as you can? Let me know if you'll be in on Friday. If not, I need to make arrangements with one of the adjuncts ASAP. OK, talk soon. Bye."

"What a clusterfuck..." Veronica mumbled. She would indeed have to make arrangements. But her pulse began to pick up again when another thought crossed her mind.

How am I supposed to wake up Friday morning, throw on a cardigan, and teach Wuthering Heights?

Struck by the absurdity of her current situation, the professor stiffened with an even more disturbing thought.

I could be dead by then.

Before long, the fifth and most recent voicemail message began to play.

"Dr. Upham? Hello, yes. This is Joyce Lambeth from the Williamsport Historical Society. I hope you're doing well. I just called to let you know that I've followed up on your request for information concerning the name Brennen and that old plantation house near the elementary school and I think you're going to love this. The whole thing is pretty spooky and right up your alley. Just in time for Halloween! Give me a call and let me know when you'll be in. There's a good bit of material here that you're welcome to sort through. I can set everything up for you if you just let me know when you'll be in. OK. Alright. Thank you and we'll see you soon."

The robotic voice of Siri announced she had reached the end of her new messages. With her cup of tea growing cold beside her, Veronica immediately redialed the Historical Society. After three consecutive rings, the call was connected.

"Williamsport Historical Society, this is Joyce speaking. How may I help you?"

"Joyce? Hi, it's Veronica Upham. I just listened to your voicemail. Thank you for getting back to me so quickly. So, what exactly did you—"

"Oh, you're welcome, dear. You know we appreciate your help and generosity as a member. We're always happy to help you with your research."

"Right, of course," Veronica replied, struggling to keep her patience. "So, what did you find, Joyce?"

"Well, it's quite a story," the elderly woman hesitated and then laughed nervously before she continued. "Like I said, just in time for Halloween, and all."

"Yes, you know I love a good ghost story. So why don't you go ahead and tell me all about it?"

"OK, well, the name Brennen as you might guess is indeed connected to that abandoned house up in those woods," she stated. "The house was owned by a Mr. Henry Brennen and his wife Charlotte. Now this was back in the 1850s, just before the War Between the States, when Williamsport was just that, an *actual* port. Our small city used to be the central hub for all inland tobacco farmers to get their crops sent further down river. They could pay a fee to—"

"That's very interesting," Veronica interjected. "But what else can you tell me about the family that owned this plantation?"

"Well, it seems they ran into some tragedy. They lost a few children over a relatively short period of time."

Children.

Veronica's skin crawled.

Oh Christ...

"Yeah, it seems the poor woman lost three or four babies right in a row. Can you imagine? Drove her completely mad with grief. Now back then as you know, childbirth was more dangerous, and many mothers and infants didn't survive. But to lose them one after the other like that? Why, it's just unthinkable!"

Her heart racing, Veronica pressed the curator further. "Do you know what happened to this woman, Joyce?"

"Well, that's the mystery, I'm afraid. She disappeared in the winter of 1858 or '59. It was just a couple years before the War broke out. But here's the spooky part," the woman said. "Henry Brennen was found dead not long thereafter with his throat torn out."

Veronica reeled and felt herself losing her grip on her cell phone. The elderly historian continued.

"My guess is one of the slaves went and pulled another Nat Turner and rose up to murder their master. I'd rather not think about what they probably did to that poor woman. The slave patrols tracked down most of the runaways, but none confessed to killing Mr. Brennen, much less rebellion..." The old woman prattled on, but Veronica only heard half of what she said as her own thoughts threatened to overwhelm her.

Charlotte.

That filthy rotting thing in the woods once had a name.

Charlotte Brennen. And she lost several children.

Jesus Christ, the Civil War.

The Nightmare Life-in-Death.

Mrs. Lambeth's inane chatter suddenly ceased. "Dr. Upham? Are you still there?"

"Uh yes, Joyce." She struggled to swallow as her mouth had gone unbearably dry. "What was that you said? I was just, uh, jotting down a few notes. Please continue."

"I said a few years later, during McClellan's Peninsula Campaign, the abandoned plantation house was used as a Confederate field hospital. In May of 1862, it was hit by a Yankee gunboat patrolling the James. And as far as I was able to tell, it's sat abandoned up there ever since, which as you know, is somewhat puzzling considering the historical significance and value of a place like that so close to the river. But I must say, after reading over these papers, I do seem to vaguely recollect hearing some odd stories about that place when I was just a girl."

"What kind of stories?"

"Well, I'm sorry to say it's been so long that I daren't remember any specifics," she admitted. "It's just... well, it's just an impression, I guess. No one ever seems to want to talk about that place. Those woods are mostly owned by the city, but don't you think it's odd that after all these years no one's tried to buy that land from the planning and development commission? It would be prime real estate for waterfront condos and what not. And it's not too far from the school, either. Well, in any case, I can't blame them if all those terrible things happened out there. And..."

The talkative woman suddenly trailed off, which prompted Veronica to ask if she was still on the line.

"Oh, yes, I'm still here." The jovial tone that had characterized her banter had cooled. She continued with a measured and unsettled voice. "You know I guess it just sort of struck me that they found that poor little boy not far away from those very woods."

Veronica clenched her eyes tight and fought to maintain her composure. She failed.

"Joyce, I need to know. Where did you get all this information? I mean, what's the source for all the things you've been telling me?"

"Oh, why, I'm sorry, I thought I mentioned that," she apologized. "Most of this information I read in a diary we have here from a Mrs. Jane Westcott. Jane was the sister of James Stuckley, a lawyer and respected delegate in the state legislature. So, her papers were among the things that were preserved after the War. She was also the wife of Dr. Richard Westcott, the family physician that tended to Mrs. Brennen. And it appears she was also one of the only friends that poor Mrs. Brennen had. Anyway, we have Mrs. Westcott's memoirs, as well as some miscellaneous papers, several letters." There was a pause on the other end, and Veronica could hear the archivist rummaging through what could have been a filing cabinet. "Let's see, oh! There are also a few very well-preserved daguerreotypes of Mrs. Brennen and her deceased children. Now that's a very sad and dare I say, morbid custom best left to the past."

"Daguerreotypes?" Veronica's voice was quaking. "You're kidding, right?"

"Oh no, they're quite impressive. Some of the cases are a little worn and they must be handled with absolute care, but they're quite astounding. I sure hope you'll be in soon so that you can see them for yourself."

"Oh, you can count on that, Mrs. Lambeth," Veronica said, her voice shaking. "I'll be there within the hour."

19

W ITH HIS RIGHT ARM SUTURED AND FRESHLY BANDAGED, Edison Raymer stood at the metal door marked APT 3C and knocked. He stepped away for a moment to look at the set of similar doors surrounding him on all sides. The inner-city apartment complex was old—built sometime after the Second World War—and poorly maintained. Behind the door, he heard the shuffle of feet, and then a brief pause. An old brass tumbler clicked from inside and Raymer heard the rattle of a security chain.

Father Bill McCallum opened the door and took a moment to study his visitor. The former army chaplain was tall, broad-shouldered, and his gray hair was clipped into a military-style flat top. He wore a tight undershirt and a pair of loose-fitting black sweatpants. McCallum cut an imposing figure for a man in his mid-seventies.

"Dr. Raymer," he spoke in a gruff yet inviting tone. "No need to stand on ceremony. Come on in." Raymer nodded and stepped into the living room of the small apartment as Father McCallum shut the door and locked them inside.

Aside from a worn recliner, an old sofa, two small tables, and a roll cart for his modest flatscreen television, most of the living room wall space was packed tightly with dark wooden bookcases.

Above the couch was a folded flag in a presentation box with service medals. A gold oak leaf signified his rank upon discharge as a major. There

216

were numerous framed photos taken during his deployments in Vietnam, as well as pictures of him sparring in trunks and boxing gloves. A large unit insignia plaque presented by the Chaplain Corps with his name and years of service hung above the presentation box.

McCallum glanced over at the television, which was tuned to a boxing match in progress. He retrieved a remote from the seat of his chair, and then turned off the TV. The priest returned his full attention to Raymer and pointed to the bandage. "Looks like you just went a few extra rounds with someone yourself."

"You could say that." Raymer folded his arms.

"Can I get you anything?"

"I could use a glass of water, Father."

"Water for you, Johnnie Walker neat for me." The priest clasped his large, calloused hands together. "Be right back." McCallum stepped out of the cramped living room and into a short, dark hallway. The Roman Catholic priest turned right and disappeared from view.

Edison wandered over to one of the bookcases. On the topmost shelf were books and treatises by Aquinas, St. Augustine, Swedenborg, and Merton. Raymer traced the edge of the bookcase to the second shelf, which housed works by Alighieri, Milton, Cervantes, and Thoreau—as well as a collection of catechisms.

The third shelf down was packed with occult tomes, grimoires, and books of ceremonial magic. *The Abramelin. The Key of Solomon the King.* Frazier's *Golden Bough.* Various works by Waite and Crowley caught his eye. The fourth and final shelf contained books preoccupied with a singular subject—the vampire. Many of these books Raymer himself had owned only a few years ago.

Father McCallum returned with a glass of ice water for Edison, and a tumbler of scotch for himself. He took a sip and nodded for his guest to sit down. Raymer knew better than to sit in the priest's recliner, so he took a seat on the edge of the couch as McCallum returned to his customary position.

"So, this is the point where I'm supposed to say, 'unburden your soul, my son.'" McCallum smiled bitterly. "I presume you went hunting last night."

"That's correct. I attempted to stake one of them." Raymer paused and gulped down half the water in the glass before adding, "I failed."

McCallum placed his tumbler on a side table cluttered with periodicals. He leaned forward and studied Raymer's reaction. "What do you mean you failed?"

"A situation was brought to my attention yesterday by a former colleague of mine," Raymer began. "Dr. Veronica Upham."

"The literature professor." The priest nodded. "Wasn't she the one who assisted you in the staking of Matthias Bartsch?"

"Yes, that's correct." The normally unshakable Edison Raymer braced himself and continued. "You're not gonna like this, but she was accompanied by a Williamsport police detective by the name of Nathan Alderson."

"We discussed this, Doctor." McCallum glowered at Raymer. "Under no circumstances were you to involve the police. For any reason."

"I realize that," Raymer said clutching his glass with an unsteady hand. The ice cubes clinked against the side. "But he didn't come to me as a policeman. For all intents and purposes, he's gone rogue. He assured me everything was off the record and that he'd never show his superiors the evidence he uncovered."

"Do you trust this man?" McCallum asked.

"I do," Raymer said without hesitation. "He's a good man. Still coming to terms with the things he's witnessed, and he's got a bit of a temper. But he wants the same thing we do."

McCallum finally leaned back into his chair. "Go on."

"So, Detective Alderson was investigating the murder of a boy named Tyler Marshall who was found dead in the woods near a local elementary school. The body was drained of blood."

"Yes, I heard about it on the news," McCallum remarked. "But I wasn't aware of that particular detail."

"Right, the police department has been able to keep it out of the press. At least so far." Raymer continued to brief him on the remaining details of the case. "One thing led to another, and the detective found his way to the college. Likely trying to connect things to the Stroud case, which was what led me to Bartsch."

McCallum nodded—his eyes attentive as Raymer spoke.

"At the college, he spoke to Veronica, and then she had the foresight to get back in touch with me." Raymer took a deep breath. "Veronica claims to have channeled the spirit of this child during a séance she held the night after the boy's murder."

"Wait a second." McCallum lifted his hand. "Was she deliberately trying to communicate with the boy? What the hell is she doing messing around with this stuff?"

"No, it wasn't deliberate," Raymer assured him. "Veronica considers herself to be a medium. It goes back several generations in her mother's family. Her great-grandmother was a medium up in Boston at the turn of the last century. What concerns me more about this séance is that something *else* has apparently attached itself to the boy. And that's what worries me."

McCallum leaned forward and folded his hands.

"Did you attend this séance?"

"No, but Veronica recorded it and has it on video. When she played it back, she could see a shadowy presence. It was the vampire who murdered the little boy... in spirit form."

The square-jawed priest scratched his chin. "Have you seen the footage?"

"No, I haven't. But I saw the thing in the flesh last night."

"Where?"

"In the forest next to the school," Raymer explained. "I need to back up a bit to make sure you're entirely brought up to speed."

McCallum patiently listened to his protégé speak.

"The detective discovered that kids have been disappearing around this area for years. All the way back to the 1950s. So, a few days after the Marshall boy was found, he returned to the crime scene. Near a natural crossroads in the middle of the forest, he dug up the skeletal remains of a girl who had been missing since the 1990s, along with two infants that had been turned into vampires and left in the ground."

McCallum shifted uneasily in his recliner. He stared ahead, lost in his own private thoughts, and waited for Raymer to continue.

"Alderson showed me some video he took with his phone," Raymer confirmed. "It's genuine. I've never seen nor heard of anything like this before. At least not—"

"See to it that the video footage is destroyed," McCallum commanded. "No exceptions. I understand that you trust this man, but this is something we can't afford him showing to the wrong people. Same goes for the footage of the professor's séance. Destroy it."

"Understood."

"So what happened last night? Were there any casualties or anything else unpleasant we need to clean up?"

"No," Raymer said. "We went out to those woods and threw everything we had at her. Alderson shot her with three rounds of silver bullets. He blew her hand off with a .44. I sank a few silver-tipped bolts from my crossbow in her, but none of this stopped her. It barely slowed her down. The holy water worked as usual, and we managed to cast a protective circle around us with consecrated hosts. But the crosses only pissed her off."

"So she got away?"

"Yes," Raymer admitted. "Once we were out of long-range weapons, I basically wound up in a street fight with her. I managed to shank her repeatedly with one of the bolts. Then Alderson and I rushed her and held her down for Veronica to stake her." He shook his head as his lips curved up in a half smirk. "To my surprise, Veronica almost went through with it. But the vampire overpowered us before Veronica could bring the hammer down. Both Alderson and I were wounded. Unfortunately, she's tasted our blood."

McCallum breathed heavily and cast a disapproving glance at his protégé. "So, who the hell is she?"

"I don't know," Raymer said. "All we know is she's attached to this particular area in the woods. You know how territorial these things are."

"Anything up there of interest? Where she may be hiding?"

"Yes," Raymer nodded. "Alderson says there's an old burned-out plantation house and a family tomb on the property. I did not, however, inspect these areas myself. We arrived at night, and I figured the thing would have already left the tomb if that was her resting place. But my plan is to go back out there by day and scour every inch of those woods."

"Good. Check under the foundations of the house," McCallum advised. "The tomb is probably too obvious but be sure to check the ground around it closely. Are these woods near the river?"

"Yes, they are."

"Check the riverbanks. Remember, they don't need to breathe, Edison. The riverbanks are soft and easy ground for them to burrow under and rest undisturbed."

"There are miles of riverbank along the James," Raymer lamented.

"And therefore miles, on both sides of the river, where she could possibly hide."

Raymer's shoulders sank as he thought of the insurmountable tasks ahead.

"Well, look, Dr. Raymer, you've got a few options here." McCallum leaned back into his recliner and tapped a thick finger into his open palm. "One, you go back out there by day, and with luck on your side, hopefully one of you will find her resting place. You expose her to the sun and boom." He smacked his powerful hands together. "She's history."

Raymer moved his head in agreement.

"Two, and the more likely scenario, she'll elude you by day, but return to finish the job at night. This time, you must be fully prepared and heavily armed. Take your biggest and baddest sniper rifle and blow that thing into oblivion. Do you have enough weapons and ammunition?"

"Yes, I've already loaded the truck," Raymer explained. "I've got a McMillan TAC-338 sniper rifle, as well as a .303 Short-Magazine Lee-Enfield."

"Good, but be mindful, weapons are only half the battle," the veteran reminded him. "You need to be strategic. And think tactically."

"Understood," Raymer said. "After we finish here, I'm going directly to Williamsport. The three of us will return to the woods early tomorrow morning and begin the hunt by day."

McCallum gripped the arms of his recliner. "Do you think you'll need me to call in reinforcements? I'd rather not have to—given my current standing with the Archdiocese. I've exposed three pedophile shitbags wearing the collar and ensured the bureaucrats covering up for them were thrown in jail alongside them."

"That won't be necessary, Father." Raymer leaned forward on the sofa. "But you said we had a *few* options. What else did you have in mind?"

"Well, clearly, this thing is an anomaly," Father McCallum stated. "And considering all that business about it appearing at your friend's séance, I'm sure the similarities to the Aston house vampire haven't alluded you."

"No, that's the reason I'm here," Raymer said. "You were there in '86. You saw how it had toyed with Jeffrey. And we told you how it moved through the mirrors. How it came and went like a shadow. Jerry and I took all precautions against it, but she still got to him. No matter how much we tried to protect him."

"It still rattles you, doesn't it?"

"Of course it does," Raymer said. "I realize I'll probably never find her. But that won't stop me from trying."

"Your tenacity is admirable, Dr. Raymer." McCallum eyed him carefully. "You're gonna need it. You've been fortunate so far in that you haven't run into any of the more... *difficult* vampires out there. The ones I've sent you after are like drones. Worker bees. But there are other ones that are much older. Stronger."

"I wouldn't call that nest of fiends I destroyed in the Pine Barrens a cakewalk." Raymer pursed his lips and finished the glass of water.

"No, of course," the priest replied. "But what I'm saying is there are other ones—like this one you've encountered—that would pose a problem to even the most experienced hunters among us. So, you need to set aside your hubris and listen to me carefully. Otherwise, this thing's gonna kill you and both of your friends."

Raymer swallowed hard and listened to his mentor.

"First of all, these things are rare, thank God." McCallum quickly made the sign of the cross, tapping his fingers from his forehead to his stomach and then to each of his shoulders. "But they're out there. They are driven by malice. Pure unadulterated spite. Their will power is *strong*, sometimes so strong that traditional holy relics have little to no effect on them."

Raymer nodded, thinking of the crosses and how they seemed only to infuriate and provoke the vampire.

"Furthermore, and perhaps most important of all considering what you said about this thing tasting your blood, their attacks are not limited to the realms of the physical. They can enter dreams. They've demonstrated mild forms of telepathy, telekinesis, mesmerism."

"Yes," Raymer interjected. "She managed to cast the detective into a mild trance. For whatever reason, she seemed to be focused on Alderson and tried to lure him out of the circle. She only spoke directly to him."

"What did she say?"

"She said she could see his son. Apparently, the detective's son recently died."

"How?" McCallum's shoulders tensed. He awaited Raymer's response with anticipation.

"Honestly, I'm not sure. He didn't tell me. I'm assuming it was some kind of accident. But she picked up on it. Tried to use his grief against him."

"Well, you need to get the full story from him. Then you need to use it against *her.*" McCallum leveled his finger at Raymer. "If she's singled him out, take advantage of that. Lord forgive me," he glanced up in mock reverence, "but use him as bait. Isn't that what you did with the girl that Bartsch turned? I'm sorry, what was her name?"

"Laura McCoy."

"Yes, Laura," McCallum remembered. "Like I said, be strategic. Hell, put him front and center while you hang back with that sniper rifle. Presuming the lit professor's not a crack shot, give her a pair of night vision goggles so she can be your spotter. In all directions."

Raymer nodded as his busy mind began to formulate a plan of attack.

"But be careful," the priest warned. "The last thing we need is a dead cop on our hands, so be sure your aim is true."

As Raymer carefully reflected on his mentor's advice, Father McCallum eased himself forward and rose from his seat. He slowly made his way to one of the bookshelves and scanned the spines for a particular volume. He turned around and handed Raymer a thin, worn book bound in dark red vellum.

"It's a reprint, so don't get too excited," the priest explained. "But that's a fascinating read. It's a direct first-person confession from a sixteenth-century Italian priest by the name of Giovanni Apuzzo."

Raymer wrinkled his brow and turned the book over in his hands. He thumbed through its scant pages and then glanced searchingly back to McCallum.

"With all due respect, Father. I no longer bury my nose in books. I'm a man of action and—"

"Don't be a fool, Edison. Put aside your grudge against academia and listen to me." McCallum's blue eyes swept over the hundreds of books lining the perimeter of his living room. "That book painstakingly documents his transformation from a mortal to vampire. He was the epitome of a multi-disciplined Renaissance-era scholar. His interests and expertise ran the gamut of medicine, alchemy, physiology, biology, poetry, necromancy, and anatomy. His rigid attempts to understand what had happened to him gave birth to many of the legends concerning vampires that appeared in his wake. His studies form the basis of the Church's understanding and awareness of these creatures."

"Why didn't you tell me about this before?"

"Because you're a man of action," McCallum chided. "I'm telling you now, so listen to me. The most significant take away from Apuzzo's experiments is simply this: these creatures we call vampires are in essence spirits inhabiting or rather *animating* a human form. A corpse with a soul. Now some philosophers have said that description applies to all of us—a soul carrying around a body just waiting to die. But Apuzzo meant it in the most literal sense.

"Now, what this means to you and how it pertains to this particular case," McCallum continued, "is that, like demons, spirits are subject to the laws of metaphysics—whether it be the holy rite of exorcism, or the meticulous rituals of advanced ceremonial magic. Either way, when wielded with the appropriate amount of willpower and intent, a spirit—in other words, the conscious, animating, personal force inhabiting a vampire's corpse—can be manipulated and *bound* to obey a powerful and experienced magician."

Raymer hesitated before responding to the priest. "Again, with all due respect, this is interesting and something I've already, in a roundabout way, considered for a number of years." He met the eyes of McCallum with intensity. "But I don't have that kind of time. This thing is already responsible for a very public murder. She has to be destroyed."

"I'm not questioning that," McCallum responded. "Nor do I doubt the urgency of your situation. But you may not have a choice. If you fail to find her resting place, and she manages to elude or repel any further physical attacks, this may be your only option. And as you know, ceremonial binding requires an incredible amount of preparation and focus. In your haste, you may have to forego some of the steps in the ritual. You can't wait for a new moon, fast for days, or steep mandrake roots in the secretions of a dead widow for thirteen nights or whatever other arcane bullshit these texts sometimes require."

"So what's the point? Why bother with this if I can't execute it properly?"

"Because all you need to do is find out where she rests by day. Then you expose her to the sun and kill her." McCallum reminded him. "You only need to solicit that key piece of information from this spirit. Subject it to an exhausting series of questions and enquiries. Wear it out until it gives in. But, above all, before you begin, you need to obtain *the name* of this vampire. And discover as much personal and background information about her as you can. Obviously, personal objects can be used to forge a psychical connection between yourself and its spirit."

Raymer exhaled heavily. He rose and began to pace. "Let's just hope that we either find her in that tomb or hiding out somewhere else in the forest. And if not, we take her down tomorrow night."

"Indeed, let's hope," McCallum echoed. "I'll pray for you and your friends. But I'm afraid this thing is smarter than that. And I think you have your work cut out for you."

Raymer turned to eye the priest with disappointment. The older man recognized his pupil's discontent and offered him a bit of encouragement. "If there's anyone who *can* take this thing down, it's you, Edison. I have faith in that. But you need to be cautious, tactical, and careful. Try to find her. But if that doesn't work, you know what to do. That stubborn streak of yours might finally be employed to your advantage. Your will must be strong enough to eclipse hers. Now," McCallum asked, "what else do you need from me?"

"Wafers. Loads of 'em," Raymer requested. "And I want to be armed with several ampules of holy water. Can you consecrate and bless them for me today? Before I go?"

"Of course I can." Father McCallum moved across the living room and clasped both of his hands onto Edison Raymer's tense shoulders. "You've been my best soldier. My strong arm against our sworn enemies. I'll assist you in any way that I can."

"I promise I won't let you down," Raymer swore an oath to his mentor.

"I know you won't." McCallum nodded with an acerbic grin. "Now, enough with all this pep talk shit. Why don't you go pour me another scotch while I sanctify your weapons?"

20

MRS. JOYCE LAMBETH LED VERONICA TO THE SPECIAL collections room of the Williamsport Historical Society. The walls of the dimly lit room were lined with metal shelves, dresser drawers, and filing cabinets of various sizes. The professor took a seat at a polished rectangular table and donned a white pair of gloves. The historian carefully arranged clusters of items in a loose semicircle in front of her, and then yanked the beaded pull chain of a small lamp at the head of the table.

Veronica was shocked by the sheer volume of archival material relating to the Westcott family. It would take several days to thoroughly review all of its contents.

Fortunately, Joyce had already set out a handful of artifacts she believed would be most pertinent to Veronica's interest in the Brennen family's history. To the professor's left was the small leather-bound journal that had belonged to Mrs. Jane Westcott. Joyce promised that the diary would provide the most detailed account of the Brennen's history.

"I've placed several bookmarks in there for you so you can easily find the entries that pertain to the Brennens," she said. "Most of them occur between 1854 and 1859. There are many non-related entries throughout this period as well. Apparently, Mrs. Westcott was an aspiring journalist and had a few articles published in her time. She's a very competent writer and her memoirs are an enthralling read."

To Veronica's right was a stack of ledgers. Joyce noted that these were the financial records of the plantation. Beside the ledgers were three piles of bundled letters. Each packet was bound by a string.

Joyce explained that Mrs. Westcott's letters were generally concerned with fashions, recipes, and local gossip, as well as her more famous brother, Delegate James Stuckley. The letters only made a few passing references to the Brennens.

Mrs. Lambeth drew Veronica's attention to the letters belonging to Richard Westcott, which included a few letters from Henry Brennen regarding his wife Charlotte. "Unfortunately, they provide a rather sad record of Mrs. Brennen's troubles and decline." She gently tapped the stack of letters with her gloved finger. "I placed those on the top of this pile for you."

According to Joyce, the final bundle of letters belonged to Henry Brennen. "Most of his correspondence I found to be dull and business-oriented," she said, "but I did set aside one of them for you to see."

This was a letter Henry had written to his mother from Scotland in September of 1844. The young man had gone abroad to collect on an inheritance left to him by a deceased uncle. While overseas, Henry visited a cousin who lived just outside of Glasgow. It was there, according to the letter, that Henry first met and courted a farmer's daughter by the name of Charlotte Gordon. Mrs. Lambeth noted that despite the air of tragedy and mystery that characterized the latter portions of Mrs. Westcott's diaries, the Brennen's story began with a passionate love affair "right out of one of those Romantic novels you teach at the college."

Veronica was not so sure.

My God, there's so much here.

There has to be something in this mess that can help us.

What was conspicuously absent from the collection of letters was the correspondence of Charlotte Brennen herself. Mrs. Lambeth suggested that either her letters had been lost, destroyed, or were possibly misplaced among the other papers.

Again, Veronica had a sneaking suspicion that there was another reason none of Charlotte's letters had survived.

"One thing you *definitely* won't find is Mrs. Brennen's personal diary," she said in a more detached tone. "You'll see in Mrs. Westcott's memoir that she thought it best that Mrs. Brennen's journal was destroyed."

Veronica's heart sank. "Why?"

"You'll see when you read it," was her curt reply. "It's one of the final entries I've marked for you. Early 1859."

Mrs. Lambeth ran her finger across the spine of the old journal. "When you reach the final entries, you'll learn how Mrs. Westcott wound up with all of these things," she said. "But they never found either of their wills. Henry's death certificate, of course, appears and is signed by Dr. Westcott himself. Not surprisingly, however, there were no birth records."

Joyce leaned over the table. "While you're back here, I'll run a search to see if I can trace their ancestry. It may be a bit more difficult since their line came to a premature end. Much like that story penned by Mr. Poe about the Usher house." The eccentric old lady chuckled to herself. "But I've been meaning to find that information for you, and I'll do my best to get it today."

Veronica looked at Joyce and nodded as if she was paying full attention to her. In truth, she was slowly counting to herself to curtail the onset of a panic attack.

"There is one more thing." Mrs. Lambeth carefully placed an ornate jewelry box in front of Veronica. "These are the daguerreotypes I mentioned to you on the telephone." The otherwise talkative and cheerful historian seemed to be uncomfortable handling the box. "I have to be honest with you. I'm no stranger to postmortem photography from this period. But there's something about these images, my dear, that I just do not like. And if I never have to look at them again, I will be grateful."

Veronica stared at the jewelry box with surmounting dread.

"I'll leave you to it then." Joyce weakly grasped Veronica's shoulder. "Take as long as you like, dear, and don't hesitate to fetch me if you need anything."

"You're a lifesaver, Joyce." Veronica forced a smile. "I can't thank you enough for helping me get a head start on all of this."

"Oh, it was no trouble," she replied. With that, Joyce left the room and firmly closed the door behind her.

Veronica took a deep breath and slipped her reading glasses over the bridge of her nose. She steeled herself, reached out, and opened the lavish jewelry box.

Inside were a half-dozen slim rectangular cases sitting upright front to back. The cases were of differing sizes and materials and had thin pieces of tissue paper between them. Veronica removed the daguerreotype cases one at a time and arranged them side by side on the table. Most were comprised of soft worn leather and wooden frames, with tarnished bronze hinges and minute clasps on the front. Two others—which Veronica inferred were the most recent—were a pair of Union cases. These were marked by intricate textured patterns on their outer shells.

Holding the first small leather-bound object in the palm of her gloved hand, Veronica carefully opened the case to behold the image of a handsome dark-haired man.

Henry Brennen.

His dark penetrating eyes had stared directly at the camera when the portrait was taken. He sat with his right arm resting on a small tabletop. Dressed predominantly in black, he wore a form-fitting waistcoat and double-breasted vest with a thin silver watch chain running from a pocket to one of the lower buttons. The pointed tips of a white collar were turned up on each side of his neck. Thick, heavy sideburns covered a strong jawline. Beneath his thin lips was a smooth, freshly shaved chin with a prominent divot in the middle.

As Veronica tilted the case in her hands, the highly polished surface of the print briefly acquired a negative effect. The image itself was incredibly sharp and clear for its age.

After she placed the portrait of Henry face up on the table, Veronica lifted the second case and used her gloved thumb to open it. The left panel was lined with padded black velvet to protect the image housed on the right. The oval-framed portrait was of a young blond-haired boy—about the age of three—lying on a white-sheeted bed. His head rested on a pillow and his small hands were clasped over his chest. A sprig of wildflowers had been placed between his folded fingers. The boy was clad entirely in white. The lids of his eyes were closed, which suggested he was merely sleeping.

The image was so sharp that Veronica could discern small scars marring his otherwise placid face.

Once again, Veronica gently placed the open case face-up on the table, next to the portrait of the boy's father. She reached for a third case, housed in another embossed, black leather exterior. As she delicately opened it, the brass hinges gave some resistance. The portrait within was practically identical to the previous image of the blond-haired boy but for one significant detail—the boy's mother was now sitting next to her deceased child.

Veronica gasped as her eyes swept over the portrait. Clad in heavy black weeds, the woman sat beside her son with her white hands folded tightly in her lap. A stern yet sorrowful expression was fixed on her face. Large, light eyes stared forward in a daze. Thick blonde hair was swept back from her brow, resting beneath a gauzy black veil. It had been cast backward over the crown of her head and framed her shoulders. Whereas Henry's gaze pierced the viewer, his wife appeared to be fixated on something that only she could see.

It's her. Oh my God, there's absolutely no doubt about it.

That's the woman from the woods.

Charlotte Brennen.

Veronica drew in a sharp breath. She could feel her chest tightening. Her eyes watered, and her heart raced. She exhaled and attempted to regulate her breathing, a feat that grew more difficult with each instant she spent looking at the portrait. Yet she could not look away.

Get ahold of yourself, Upham.

For Christ's sake. It's just a picture.

And there are three more of them.

She placed the portrait of Charlotte and her son at the center of the table, the cases now forming the first half of an arch across the smooth surface. She opened the fourth case. The tarnished hinges creaked ever so slightly to reveal a baby girl lying in a black wooden cradle. The infant had been placed on a white pillow. The weight of its body caused the cushion to curl upward and envelop the child's fragile form. Its head seemed large in comparison to its body. Its eyes were closed above a pair of swollen gray cheeks. Its full lips and nose appeared somewhat large. A few very fine hairs were brushed over its forehead. Its plump arm and spindly fingers clutched an embroidered blanket, which had been lain atop the child's torso and filled the bottom of the cradle.

Overcome with a sudden wave of sadness, the professor stared at the mournful portrait of the lifeless child and fought the urge to weep.

Veronica braced herself and slid the first of the harder and textured Union Cases toward her. As she pried its panels apart, a dry, fully pressed lily slid out and drifted to the table below. Its flaking yellowed petals had been preserved between the soft velvet pad and smooth polished glass.

Something suddenly broke within Veronica Upham. Whether it was the fragile keepsake or the sight of yet another infant already laid out in its coffin, she was uncertain. But her vision blurred with tears and she could no longer bear to confront the sight of the baby sinking into the padded cushion beneath it—its hands clasped over its stomach, the fresh lily across its chest.

Veronica removed her glasses and cast them aside. She rubbed her damp eyes as two quick shaking sobs bent her forward. She leaned back in the hard, uncomfortable chair and once again attempted to control her breathing.

There's only one more. Just one more and you're done. You can go home. You can lock your doors and draw your blinds and hide from it all. You can turn your back on this threat and forget about it all and you can run and hide and give up and—

She snatched the final case and unclasped it with a knotted stomach. The same coffin was displayed at the lower edge of the portrait. But its previous occupant was now in the foreground, cradled in the arms of its black-clad mother. The face of the infant was rigid. Its eyes had been pried open and were cast upward. Sitting on the edge of an ornate chair, Charlotte bent forward, the child wrapped in a dark tartan blanket. Her movements had interfered with the rendering of the photograph, causing an eerie blur to obscure her face. Her blonde hair was down and spilling in unkempt waves over her shoulders. A long black veil was tangled within her wild locks. The fingernails clutching the infant were long, broken, and ragged. At Charlotte's feet was the cast aside lily. Splotches of mud had dried along the frayed edges of her floor-length skirt.

Veronica set the case down, rose to her feet, and took out her cell phone. She snapped close ups of each daguerreotype for Raymer and Alderson to see. Once her task was completed, she closed the cases, tossed her phone to the side, and sat back down in the chair.

With her arms crossed, she spent several minutes letting her eyes sweep over the contents of the table. She then leaned forward, took up her reading glasses, and reached for Mrs. Westcott's journal. Palms sweating within the white cotton gloves, the professor picked up the diary and carefully opened the stiff pages to where Joyce had placed the first marker. Veronica adjusted her wire-framed spectacles and began to read:

March 28, 1854

Richard has received a most distressing call. The Brennen boy has taken a turn for the worse. A messenger arrived this morning and demanded R. return to the estate. Perhaps his fever will break. Will pray for all.

March 29, 1854

The boy has succumbed. R. to help with arrangements. Funeral to be private. Henry says Mrs. B. in great distress. But R. says she's a strong, able woman. Yet how could he understand? I think I should visit her...

Veronica thumbed ahead to the next marker Joyce had left in the diary. A longer entry spread across two pages. Careful not to crease the delicate binding, she continued to read:

April 2, 1854

Today I paid a visit to Mrs. Brennen. I woke early and accompanied Richard to town. I returned with the most beautiful bouquet of white roses and forget-me-nots, which I wrapped carefully. A heavy rain fell and threatened to postpone our journey, but we pressed on for Mrs. B.'s sake. R. anxious to see how she recovers.

When we arrived, a heavy gloom presided over the main house. The curtains were pulled tight. Black crepe covered every mirror. Henry waited for R. in the study, so I let myself upstairs, hoping not to disturb or further distress Mrs. B.

She was sitting up in her bed with a pillow behind her. Despite her disheveled state, she proved to be an incredibly striking woman. So tall and grand with milk-white skin and wild yellow hair—in want of a brushing, I confess, but breathtaking all the same.

I introduced myself, offered her my condolences, and placed the flowers beside her bed. She turned her head to them and looked upon me with such sorrow. My heart broke for her. Fearing myself presumptuous to think the poor woman was ready to receive guests so soon, I turned to take my leave. But then she called out to me in a soft voice and asked me not to go.

At once I returned, taking up a small chair beside her. We spoke for hours, and I was entranced by her strange, exotic brogue. I knew she came from Scotland, but I was not prepared for that voice! So rich and expressive. She spoke of her home and confided that she had missed its hills and glens. But she spoke most of her boy. Even in the depths of her grief her eyes continued to shine. She dotes upon him still. I told R. and I would declare it

234

before all the world. Never has a mother loved a son as deeply as Charlotte loved her poor William.

As I rose to leave, Mrs. B. begged me to come again the following day, claiming it a relief to have met so kind a companion. I clasped her soft hand in mine and promised her I would indeed return.

As we journeyed home, Richard said Mr. B. is to have a mausoleum built behind the main house. I believe it will do her well to be able to visit her William. Nothing can soften so heavy a blow. But to know that he rests nearby will surely bring her some comfort.

Veronica lifted her eyes from Mrs. Westcott's neat and elegant script. She had not expected to be so moved by the woman's melancholy account. She skimmed over a few more passages that summarized the early days of Jane's friendship with Charlotte. During a short period when Charlotte was in better health, Mrs. Westcott compared the captivating woman to "one of Mr. Scott's or Mrs. Porter's Highland heroines." In early 1855, Charlotte learned that she was pregnant again. But the cause for celebration was short-lived:

August 12, 1855

My dear friend has suffered yet another great loss. In recent months she has expressed nothing but happiness, believing herself to be blessed. She spent the last several days knitting a new blanket. I hoped the arrival of another child would have worked in some way to temper her previous grief.

She teased me with claims of the second sight, and how she knew in her very bones that it would be a baby girl. But who could have prophesized so cruel a turn? What reason is there

for her to suffer so? I have sinned in my heart, wondering how
the Lord could be so unjust as to visit such pain upon so noble
a soul. Instead, our hopes have been blasted. I fear she may not
recover. Richard plans to watch closely. Henry braces himself
and remains strong. She christened the poor girl Joanna after
a poet from her home country. The baby breathed but one day.
She now lies at peace in the vault beside her brother.

Veronica looked up from the journal. Remembering the images in the daguerreotypes, she presumed this was the child that had been laid out in the cradle.

"A poet from her home country."

Probably Joanna Baillie.

She folded her arms across her chest and glared at the various objects spread out in front of her.

You know what? To hell with this bitch.

Who cares if she read poetry or her best friend thought she was the Bride of fucking Lammermoor? Enough already.

You're sitting here getting all caught up in this sentimental bullshit when that thing tried to kill you. Not to mention Raymer and Alderson. So, if she possessed such admirable fortitude, it's beside the goddamn point.

Veronica's thoughts rapidly darkened.

She recognized that Charlotte's resilience in life had persisted in death. So much so that her fury enabled her to resist the weapons she, Raymer, and Alderson had wielded against her. That very same unconquerable will now resided within their opponent—an enemy they had to destroy.

So how did she get this way? How did she transform into the monster we confronted less than twelve hours ago?

Hoping to find the answers to her questions, Veronica returned to the diary. Picking up where she left off, she read a passage from March of 1856:

More awful news concerning Mrs. B. Thank God Richard
was able to save her. He said she lost much blood, which was
only further exacerbated by her frenzied state. Molly had gone

with him to assist as midwife. The poor girl said that Charlotte suffered a myriad of delusions—that she would succumb to fits of weeping and rave about wanting to go to the forest. She'd then lapse into snatches of lullabies from the old country, as if she were singing to William or Joanna. I daresay that Molly was frightened. I don't know what to think, but I fear the worst.

With a gloved finger keeping her place in the journal, Veronica muttered to herself, "Why did she want to go into the woods?" She skimmed over a few entries until she came to the next reference to the Brennens. Joyce had folded a piece of acid-free paper to mark the page, along with a short personal message: *I think you will find this entry particularly interesting.*

May 11, 1856

A most unpleasant night. Charlotte arranged to host a séance. It was only a matter of time before all the recent talk of those Fox Sisters up north would make its way to my unhappy friend. She learned of one of these so-called mediums holding sittings in Norfolk. After much resistance from Henry, she had her way. I do not deny that Mrs. B. possesses a streak of stubbornness. But it is her nature. Given all that she has endured, I had believed there was no harm in humoring her whims. This night has proven the contrary.

I must confess that I was curious to experience one of these séances myself. Molly too was beside herself with anticipation. We arrived at the estate shortly before dark and Mrs. B. had arranged a most glorious vigil. I've never seen so many candles in my life!

The medium introduced herself as Miss Florence Brown and directed Charlotte to sit across from her. Molly and I were to her left. Two other women and a young man accompanied the medium and rounded out our party of seven.

We gathered beside the fireplace and joined our hands around the table. Henry and Richard refused to participate and sulked with their brandy and cigars in Mr. B.'s study.

Miss Brown told us to concentrate and keep our hands clasped while she worked herself into a trance. For some time, it was silent. But there was a queer tension in the air. I kept an eye on Charlotte, who of course yearned for an opportunity to make contact with her dear departed William. A great restlessness had possessed her, and she sat leaning forward in her chair.

Much time passed and there was nothing. The medium complained of interference and cautioned that sometimes, the spirits do not wish to communicate.

At this, Charlotte became incensed. She suddenly rose, knocking the chair to the floor. She accused the woman of lying and insisted that William wished to speak to her. She knew, for he had just told her so himself. With this unexpected confession, I turned to her and was disturbed by the transformation I saw.

Such a mask of malice had distorted her fair features. Her mouth had turned ugly and savage. Hateful words slipped past her lips as she demanded the medium and her entourage depart the house at once. She flew into a rage and swept candle after candle to the floor. I feared she would burn the entire estate to the ground in her carelessness.

Henry and Richard rushed in from the study and led the frightened guests away. Molly and I approached Charlotte and tried to calm her, but she turned her anger on us. Never did I think she would have treated me so, and her cruelty to Molly was unwarranted. The poor girl simply said that perhaps William was hiding, at which Mrs. B. lunged at her from across the room. I feared she was about to raise her hand against my girl, and it may have been better had she done so. Instead, she told Molly that she knew nothing of her William, and then warned her never to sully his name with her spinster's tongue.

When I moved to defend her against so cruel a charge, she turned to me with eyes ablaze. I will never forget the pang her words left in my heart when she told me I was no longer welcome in her home.

With that, she turned, mounted the staircase, retreated to her bedroom, and slammed the heavy door. We left with heavier hearts. Still I sit awake and wonder what awful influence has come over my friend.

Veronica was taken aback by the sudden turn in Charlotte's demeanor. She skimmed over the journal's next few pages to learn more. Several entries were preoccupied with Mrs. Westcott's falling out with Charlotte. For months, Jane went to the estate, but was repeatedly denied entry by its mistress. Mrs. Westcott learned from her husband—who still made frequent calls to the house—that Charlotte continued to host séances, although she was disappointed by their results. Henry still objected to them but found it easier to keep the peace by turning a blind eye on his wife's eccentricities.

In February of 1857, Jane also learned from her husband that Charlotte was with child again, which prompted a sharp critique of Henry Brennen:

Cannot that blasted man keep his hands to himself and resist laying with her? Perhaps he was fool enough to believe that after the death of William, another child could possibly make things right for her. But after the death of that baby girl? And the miscarriage? If the delivery itself does not kill her, another

stillborn will drive her mad. God knows her mind... oh, but
I dare not admit it.

Veronica momentarily pushed the journal aside as her thoughts began to drift. In the mid-nineteenth century, regardless of wealth or status, she knew that a married woman's purpose was to bear her husband a male heir. But in this case, Veronica had the distinct impression that it was *Charlotte* rather than Henry who was so insistent on conceiving a child.

Even if it killed her.

Veronica wondered why Dr. Westcott hadn't intervened to reprimand Henry for being so careless on account of Charlotte's previous complications. But then she considered the way Jane described Charlotte's behavior at the séance—and how she continued to hold sittings despite Henry's opposition. It was possible that the beleaguered man wasn't given a choice in the matter.

If that was the case, Charlotte's purposeful seduction of her husband was an act of vile desperation. Suddenly, it wasn't so difficult to imagine Charlotte Brennen as the hateful creature that taunted Nathan Alderson and tried to lure him out of their protective circle.

I can see your boy.

A sinking feeling overcame her. She suddenly felt sick to her stomach but pressed on to the next bookmarked entry. It was dated November of 1857:

R. has returned home exhausted. Another baby has died. Mrs.
B. inconsolable. He says she named it Lillian and fought to keep
her an extra day to have her likeness captured. How sad that
these photographs are all that she has to remember them by. She
has her memories of William. But what good are these images,
within which are frozen two tiny seeds that can never flower?

Inevitably, Jane's somber reflections prompted Veronica to recall the final set of daguerreotypes and the withered flower that Charlotte must have pressed within it. To dispel the black dread creeping over her, she took a breath and quickly turned to the next marked entry:

June 4, 1858

Mrs. B. is with child again. This will never end. Richard has done all that he can for her. Clearly, her maladies are beyond his expertise. I told him that last year when the fits of somnambulism worsened. There was some talk of placing her in the public hospital, but Henry remains conflicted. He worries the talk will tarnish his reputation. Stupid, prideful man! Even Richard foolishly believes her delusions will become worse if she is taken from the estate. To which I say, how could they get any worse? She wanders to that horrid tomb and walks those dreary woods by night looking for her dead children. This has gone far enough! God forgive me, but I have prayed more than once for her death, so that she would finally be at peace.

Gooseflesh erupted on Veronica's arms as the puzzle pieces began to fall into place.

She was fixated on the woods. So, what was drawing her out there? Was she meeting someone? Who or what was she meeting? And why did she think her children were out there?

Is that what draws her out there to this day?

Veronica rubbed her temples to fend off a headache that was beginning to form from the constant strain on her eyes. She pushed the diary forward, closer to the table lamp, and continued to read:

January 24, 1859

I always fear when R. must ride this time of night. But it is a journey he has made so many times it no longer begs counting. Mrs. B.'s latest burden now to arrive earlier than expected. Does not bode well. Molly leaves in the morning to aid as midwife. Despite how cruelly Mrs. B. once treated her, she insists on helping in any way she can. Again, I considered accompanying

*her. But would she even recognize me? Would she even know
if I was there?*

Her eyes darted to the next entry. Veronica's pulse pounded in her ears. She clutched her neck—in the exact spot where Laura McCoy had bitten her two years ago.

January 25, 1859

The baby is dead. Messenger says Mrs. B. hangs by a thread. Richard and Molly to remain at the estate. Molly to keep watch. R. staying in case of complications. Perhaps this will be the final blow...

January 27, 1859

Mrs. B. is determined to bring about her own destruction.

Richard writes to relay that she has gone out in the night and taken the child with her. She was found nearly frozen to death by those d---- crossroads. What is her fascination with those accursed woods? What superstitions have infected her? For the life of me I do not know. One could say it is a miracle that she lives. But heaven has naught to do with any of this. Enough!—I await further news...

A sudden *clang* caused Veronica to jerk her head up and frantically scan her surroundings. A low hum, which rattled the ceiling tiles allowed her to sink back into the chair. It was just the furnace kicking on in the basement. Although the oppressive stillness of the room threatened to push her over the edge, she fumbled for the next bookmark, and read the short entry:

February 5, 1859

Mrs. B. has been missing for several days. There is no hope of finding her alive. Molly deeply upset. The poor girl blames herself for falling asleep on her charge. The snow continues to fall.

⊙•————•⊙

February 7, 1859

Henry is dead. Richard found him this morning—in the nursery—with his throat torn out. Charlotte still missing. Her body yet to be recovered. Considering her weakened state and this weather, she could not have survived unless she made a pact with the devil himself.

Veronica struggled to make sense of the facts before her. First, she was surprised to discover that a fourth child had died. There were only three in the daguerreotypes, indicating that by this point, Charlotte had become so disconnected from reality that she hadn't even bothered to have it photographed. Instead, she went out into the woods in the middle of winter and took the stillborn child with her.

But why? To bury it? To offer it to something?

How was she physically able to go out there in such a state of frailty? Not once but twice? How the hell did she get past Henry and Westcott? What was she trying to accomplish?

Jane clearly recognized her fixation on the woods and specifically mentioned the crossroads. Christ, did she make a deal with the devil? What was she bargaining for? To become a vampire?

Veronica tried to remember the mythological and occult significances of crossroads. She recalled the stories she had recently told Alderson concerning suicides being buried at crossroads. It was believed that if they rose from the dead as vampires, they would forget which path led them back to their homes or loved ones.

243

But Jane said Charlotte was looking for her children there. She would have wanted them to return to her, not lose their way. It doesn't make sense.

She continued to try her memory for other variations on the myths. In America, particularly in New England as well as the Deep South, she knew that villagers believed the devil could be called and bargained with at or near a crossroads. But beyond that, she was uncertain.

However, there was no doubt in Veronica's mind that Charlotte murdered Henry. She concluded that Charlotte must have been turned into a vampire at some point when she disappeared in the woods.

So what happened to the thing that made her? Where is it now? Again, how many of these fucking things are out there?

The fact that Mrs. Westcott also specified that Henry was found dead in the nursery had not escaped Veronica. Obviously, she found the circumstances of Henry's death odd enough to emphasize it in her journal.

Did she know?

Veronica remembered that Joyce had said the entries concerning the Brennens ended in early 1859. With these latest entries dating from February, the professor guessed there were only a few more passages left. She anxiously continued to read:

February 10, 1859

> *I can barely muster up the courage to write these words. I have seen something... something that simply cannot be. It must have been a dream. There can be no other explanation. Otherwise, I can no longer trust or rely upon my own senses. I pray that the morning comes soon. So tired...*

With the journal now gripped tightly in her gloved hands, the professor grit her teeth and read the cryptic entry a second time.

"What the hell did you see, Jane?"

Chilled to the marrow, Veronica raced through the final passages Joyce had marked for her to read:

February 16, 1859

The locals continue to spread rumors of revolt. The Brennen's negroes have long fled or have been caught by the patrols. The few that remain don't say a word. Richard says some are still missing. Many of them seem frightened. When I asked of what, R. simply said, whatever got to Henry. Do I dare share with him my suspicions?

⊙⸻⊙

February 17, 1859

R. and I have discussed what must be done. With the plantation unoccupied, we must act fast. They've likely already ransacked the silver. But perhaps we can still preserve their papers and other personal belongings. God knows what else might be hidden in that house...

After reading this pair of entries, Veronica was certain the Westcotts suspected something unnatural was taking place. Why else would they be so concerned with taking things from the estate? What did Richard mean when he said, "whatever got to Henry?" And what exactly were Jane's suspicions? Did she believe that Charlotte had simply gone mad and murdered her husband? Or did Jane witness something supernatural that she couldn't bring herself to confess in her diary? What happened that night and why did she try to convince herself that it was only a dream?

And what of the slaves that Richard said were unaccounted for—did Charlotte kill them? Were they her first victims after Henry? Is that why the slaves were so afraid? Did they know what happened to her too?

Veronica tried to think of any instances concerning crossroads pertaining to slave history or African folklore, but she couldn't think of anything. She would have to research it when she got home or see if Raymer was aware of anything from his research.

Her hands still shaking, Veronica flipped to the next bookmark, trying not to damage the fragile pages in the process:

February 18, 1859

We have returned from the estate with many of our lost friends' personal belongings. Among the things we were able to rescue was a jewelry box that belonged to Mrs. B. Inside she kept the photographs of her children. I can't help but shudder when I look on them.

Yet there is more.

While going through her things, I came upon her diary. Hoping to call to mind the essence of my friend before her troubles began, I sat down before the fire to read it. It was not long before I could bear to read no more. Not another sentence. For it was a record of the most abominable... awful... godless things. Unspeakable. Ill is too feeble a word to describe her. The ravings of not just a madwoman, but something worse. Something evil.

Without a second thought, I tossed the journal into the fire and watched until there was nothing left of it but ashes.

What did Henry Brennen bring to these shores? What has God turned His back upon in His distraction that He has allowed her to walk free?

I no longer wish to speak of it, nor think of it. No more!

Veronica slammed her fist against the cluttered desk. "Goddamn it, Jane! What was in that diary?"

The frustrated professor clenched her teeth in defeat.

It had all been recorded. In Charlotte's own hand! But now we'll never know what she was thinking, or exactly what she was trying to do. What the hell could have disturbed Jane so deeply that she destroyed the whole diary?

Glancing back to the journal, she realized that she had reached the final entry that Joyce had marked for her to read:

May 2, 1862

The war rages on. Today we learned that one of the patrol boats has hit and destroyed the field hospital at the B. estate. Many patients lost. Richard and Molly safe thank God. I can't help but feel that if that house were razed to the ground and sown with salt, that land—and those woods—and that place will be forever spoiled. Oblivion isn't enough.

"That's it?" Veronica panicked. "Wait a minute!"

She frantically skimmed over the remaining pages and happened on an entry from July of 1862. Richard Westcott accepted a commission as a regimental surgeon for the Confederate Army. Jane wrote, "With what is unfolding before us now, the unpleasantness regarding Mrs. B. and that estate seems like a distant dream." Veronica continued to page ahead but could find no other entries that referenced Charlotte, the Brennens, or "Mrs. B."

That can't be all there is. I still have so many questions!

The professor's eyes swept over the other stacks of letters. She remembered that Joyce told her that some of Henry's correspondence with Dr. Westcott had survived.

Maybe there are additional clues in them?

She tapped the screen on her cell phone to discover it was nearly 3:00 PM. She was supposed to meet Raymer and Alderson at her house this afternoon.

"Dammit," she cursed to herself.

She took a moment to decompress and reassess her situation. Even though there were some gaps and ambiguities in what she was able to learn from Mrs. Westcott's journal, she was infinitely wiser than she had been earlier that morning.

You're lucky to have discovered this much. We may never know the full story, but one thing is abundantly clear.

Charlotte must be destroyed.

Veronica rose, removed the gloves, and began to gather her things. She made a genuine effort to tidy up the artifacts resting on the table but knew the archivist would see to everything after she had gone. With her purse strap over her shoulder, she took a deep breath, lifted a hand to fix her hair, and made her way to the front desk of the Historical Society.

Joyce was on the telephone and gestured for her to wait until she finished. Veronica glanced up at a clock on the wall and shifted her weight from one foot to the other. Mrs. Lambeth hung up the phone and turned to greet Veronica.

"Well, dear, how did you make out? I'm surprised to see you're wrapping up already."

"Uh, well," Veronica stammered, "I actually have another appointment this afternoon. But I hope to come back tomorrow."

"Oh! Of course, of course," Joyce said with a smile. "You're welcome anytime. Speaking of which, I haven't forgotten about those birth dates. But I haven't had much—"

"Listen, Joyce. I have a question," Veronica interjected. "How long would it take to scan the entirety of Mrs. Westcott's journal? Or get someone to prepare a typed transcript of the whole diary?"

"Well, I'd imagine the scanning would take much longer as we'd have to be incredibly careful with the pages," Joyce said. "But someone that doesn't hunt-and-peck at the keyboard could probably transcribe the journal relatively quickly."

"I could send someone over from the college," Veronica offered. "The adjuncts and grad students are always in need of research projects."

"Let me see if Barbara's available," Joyce said. "She'll likely have it ready for you by the end of the week."

"That would be wonderful," Veronica said. "And thank you so much for helping mark those pages. You've saved me hours just by doing that."

Joyce's response caught Veronica off guard.

"If I may ask, Dr. Upham. Why exactly are you so interested in the Brennen family?"

"Uh, one of my students is researching local plantation houses. I was asking on her behalf since I'm a member. And when you called me back and said it was spooky, well, you know me! I couldn't resist!"

"I see." Joyce nodded. "Well, you can always send your students to us. They, too, are welcome. That's what we're here for."

"Can I ask you something else, Joyce? What do you think happened? To the Brennens?"

"Oh, like I said..." She waved a hand as if to swat away the threat of nonsense. "I'd chalk the whole thing up to a slave uprising."

"But what about Charlotte Brennen?" Veronica pushed back. "What do you think happened to 'Mrs. B.?' Really?"

Mrs. Lambeth laughed again, eyeing Veronica through the frames of her horn-rimmed glasses. "Just superstition, my dear. Poor Mrs. Westcott had a very romantic and overactive imagination. I'm sure she missed her friend and thought she saw her everywhere. As for Mrs. Brennen, well, people really didn't understand how the mind worked back then. I'd say she went mad." Joyce adjusted her glasses. "But it sure makes a great story. Just in time for—"

"Just in time for Halloween," Veronica finished for her. "Yes, indeed it does."

21

As Veronica struggled to unlock her front door, she sensed movement behind her. The professor turned to see Nathan Alderson approaching her driveway from across the street. With his hands thrust into his coat pockets, he looked to his left and right and then jogged across the narrow road. The cold October wind blew through his hair. His gray eyes were fixed ahead.

"Sorry, I was just getting home," Veronica called to him, short of breath. "Hope you weren't waiting long."

"It's no problem. I was just sitting over there." He gestured absently over his shoulder, pointing to his truck, which was parked along the curb.

Veronica led him into her unlit house. Alderson closed and locked the door behind them. Hurrying into the living room, she switched on a small table lamp. Veronica tossed her keys into a marble dish, set her purse beside them, and spun to face the detective. He removed his coat, hung it on the rack, and then politely extended a hand to take her jacket.

"I just got back from the Historical Society," Veronica said, handing him her coat. Still short of breath, her auburn hair was tousled, and her eyes possessed a haunted sheen. Her thoughts raced as a torrent of disconnected and fragmented information came pouring out of her mouth.

"Whoa, hey! Slow down." Alderson raised his hand. "What the hell are you talking about?"

Veronica blinked and tightened her fists. She took another deep breath and started again.

"That thing in the woods has a name."

The muscles of Nathan's jaw tightened. Course reddish hairs bristled on his unshaved chin. Dark circles curved under his eyes.

"Her name is Charlotte Brennen," Veronica said. "The same surname you saw on that tomb in the woods. That was her son in the vault, and those ruins were once her family's home."

The professor quickly summarized the information she learned from Mrs. Westcott's journal. Alderson stood in rapt attention with an uneasy look on his face.

"But there are still some things I wasn't able to find out," Veronica admitted. "Like exactly how she became a vampire. Or how she managed to—"

"None of that matters," Alderson interrupted. "As I've said a thousand times, all I wanna know is how to kill her."

"Well, yes, I agree, but we still don't know exactly what we're dealing with, particularly the nature or *source* of her powers. The entries in Westcott's journal verify her obsession with the woods and those crossroads. But I don't fully understand what she was trying to *do* when she was still alive. Obviously, the journal implies—"

"Did *she* have a journal that survived?" Alderson rubbed his forehead. Several cuts and scratches marred the back of his hand. "Wait, whose journal were you reading again?"

"Jane Westcott!" Veronica paused to catch her breath. "She was the wife of the doctor who delivered Charlotte's children."

Nathan flinched slightly at Veronica's use of the vampire's name.

The professor hurriedly continued. "In one of Jane's last entries, she said she burnt Charlotte's diary. She was completely horrified by what she read in it."

"Stop saying her name."

Veronica hesitated. She narrowed her eyes to study the expression and defensive posture of her guest.

"Are you OK, Nathan?"

"I'm fine." The detective avoided her gaze. He pushed up the sleeves of his dark green thermal shirt to reveal bruised forearms and wrists. "Considering the circumstances."

"Look." She lifted a hand to reorient herself. "Why don't you take a seat. Fix yourself a drink. Whatever you need. There's some stuff I wanna do before Raymer gets here. On the drive home, I was thinking about a few old books I have upstairs. I remember reading some weird stories about this area, but I never thought anything of it. Just the usual urban legend stuff. But now I'm not so sure."

Alderson nodded and turned his back on her. Veronica watched as he walked across the living room and sat down in her chair.

Something's up with him. I should hold off on showing him those pictures until Raymer gets here.

"I'll be right back," Veronica said. Alderson sat motionless—his eyes cast downward to the floor.

She ascended the stairs, entered the bedroom at the end of the hallway, and flipped on a switch to illuminate her personal library. Veronica approached one of the tall bookcases and squatted down to scan the spines of several well-worn paperbacks. Having forgotten her glasses in her purse, the professor squinted to discern the following titles:

Ghost Stories of Eastern Virginia.
Terror in Tidewater: True Stories of Ghosts & Hauntings.
Virginia's Haunted Battlefields.
Civil War Ghosts.

After grabbing each of the books, she moved to review another bookcase, in search of any general studies pertaining to American folklore, witchcraft, or voodoo. As these topics were outside of her primary focus on British literature and customs, her offerings on these subjects were scarce.

Raymer will know. He taught that stuff in his anthropology courses for years.

She pulled one thick tome on American folklore and slapped it on top of the other books she had gathered in her arms. After turning off the light, she closed the door behind her and returned to the living room.

Alderson watched as she raced to the sofa and dropped the contents from her arms onto the padded cushions. She then fetched her reading glasses from her purse, and briefly disappeared into the dining room, returning moments later with her laptop, the tangled cord trailing behind her.

Not meaning to ignore her guest, the professor turned her attention to Alderson while the laptop began to boot.

"Do you need anything?"

"I could use a drink," Alderson replied.

"Help yourself." She nodded toward the bar cart. "Might as well pour me one, too."

Alderson seemed confused for a moment, his cold eyes swimming back to reality. "No, I meant a glass of water or something with caffeine. Maybe a Coke…" He trailed off.

"Oh," she said, somewhat embarrassed. "There's filtered water in the fridge. Maybe a few more cans of ginger ale. Or, I can brew us some coffee if you want."

"That'd be good." Nathan rose from the chair. "I'll handle the coffee. It's fine."

"You sure?" She sank back into the couch cushions.

"Do your research," he said and made his way through the dining room. "I've got this."

The expected sounds of cabinets opening and closing, tap water running, and clattering silverware came from the kitchen. Veronica picked up the first book and began to skim over its table of contents.

"When do you think Raymer will be getting here?" Alderson called out.

She glanced at the fading light beyond her living room window and then tapped her cell phone to check the time.

"Soon, I'm sure," she replied. "Depends on the traffic coming into town on Route 10."

As she turned over the pages in search of a particular passage, Alderson returned to the living room. He placed a cup of coffee on the table in front of her and then took his customary seat in the chair.

"It's black," he said suddenly. "Hope that's OK."

"Yeah, that's fine. Thank you."

Alderson leaned forward on the edge of the chair, his elbows on his knees. Instead of jeans, he wore a pair of black cotton chinos and a pair of basic dress shoes. She assumed he had dressed for work, but doubted if he actually went in.

Still unsettled by his detached demeanor, Veronica attempted to engage him in conversation.

"Have you been to the station today?"

"No."

A few moments later, she tried again. "How's your shoulder?"

"It's OK," he said. "Took care of it this morning. Looked worse than it was."

"Did you get enough sleep?"

He hesitated before answering. "Not really. I took a shower when I got home and then..." He ran his fingers through his hair. "Well, I kinda slept for a bit but then woke up after lunch. I got dressed and came here."

He must have been outside in his truck for a few hours.

"Did something happen, Nate?"

The detective exhaled and cast an irritated glance at her. Behind his eyes, however, the professor recognized a poorly guarded fear.

"Did you forget about our little stakeout in the woods last night?" He scowled at her. The anger faded almost at once and he continued. "After these last few days... I mean, how can you just sit there looking through a bunch of books?"

"I'm keeping my mind busy," she replied. "As soon as I stop thinking, it all comes back."

"That hasn't worked for me." Alderson shook his head. "All I've been doing is thinking. Because, honestly, there's nothing else I can do 'til we get back out there and kill that thing. I can't stand sitting around here waiting."

"Nate, believe me, I understand," she insisted, and folded the book over her knee. "But we can't go back there tonight. We need to regroup. If I know Raymer, I'm sure he'll wanna go out there tomorrow." She felt her stomach beginning to churn again. "And we will."

Alderson nodded and then lapsed back into silence. Veronica adjusted her glasses and resumed her perusal of *Virginia's Haunted Battlefields*. After scanning over several alleged accounts of paranormal incidents that took place outside of Williamsport, her eyes widened, and her heart began to race. She cleared her throat to address Nathan.

"OK, so stories about black-clad women or ghosts on the battlefield are a dime a dozen during the Civil War," she explained. "But listen to this. A handful of Confederate soldiers were separated from their company when a Yankee gunboat began to fire on their position. Now, this was right along our side of the James River. It says here, 'Forced to take refuge within a family mausoleum, four exhausted cavalrymen, bereft of their horses, decided to bed down until the shelling ceased. They were armed with carbines, pistols, and sabers.'" Veronica paused for effect, her finger tracing the words on the page. "'Just after dark, the horsemen were horrified when a pale woman in a black dress slithered out of an open vault. They opened fire and forced her to retreat into the forest. Corporal Robert Pembroke swore on his mother's grave that he had never been so frightened in his life.'"

Alderson stared at her with anxious eyes. "Is there more?"

"The tomb," she continued, "was behind a ruined plantation house overlooking the James River."

Alderson swallowed and kept his eyes forward. His hands were steepled in front of his mouth, his elbows resting on his knees.

The pair once again fell silent as Veronica read to herself. A few minutes later, she exchanged the first book for *Terror in Tidewater* and leafed through its pages. About a third of the way through, she spoke up again. "OK, so, throughout the mid to late nineteenth century, there were a number of ghostly sightings as well as *disappearances* reported around this area," she emphasized.

Her voice trembled as she skimmed over the words on the page. "In one instance, a pair of fishermen claimed to have come across a quote 'blonde woman kneeling along the riverbank, shortly before sunrise.' They said her back was to them, but she wore—and I quote—'a long black veil' and her face was buried in her hands. That was in 1882."

Alderson cradled his cup of coffee but didn't respond. His right foot seemed to be involuntarily tapping on the floor.

"There's no way to be sure that these sightings were *definitely* her," she offered nervously, "but it's a hell of a coincidence."

After skimming over the rest of the book, which documented strange stories in regions further north of Williamsport, she snapped the book shut and took up *Ghost Stories of Eastern Virginia*. Veronica began to pore over its contents.

Alderson set his empty mug on the table and rose to his feet. He stood next to the living room window, parted the sheer curtains, and peeked outside. He wandered back to get his coffee cup and went to refill it in the kitchen.

"More coffee?" he called out.

"No." Veronica shouted back in return. She had just begun reading a disturbing account, which took place in 1901. Her eyes raced along the description as she muttered the words beneath her breath. She jumped a few moments later when Nathan placed his refilled cup on the coffee table.

"You're never going to believe this, but I found something that happened here in Williamsport just after the turn of the last century," she said. Veronica's grip on the book was unsteady. As she began to read the full account to Alderson aloud, the slim paperback trembled in her hands:

> "...*One night, Mrs. Rebecca Headley had a terrible dream. She said she woke to the sound of someone singing outside her window. The sleepy woman rose from her bed to investigate the odd and unexpected sounds. Her six-month old daughter, Abigail, began to cry in her cradle. Mrs. Headley claimed a sinister chill suddenly rippled through her body. She bent to lift her baby into her arms, but the unhappy child continued to cry. Her husband was fast asleep, oblivious to any of the sounds or disturbances. Mrs. Headley was then overcome by an irresistible urge to go out into the night. Still carrying her daughter, the bewitched mother descended the staircase and unlocked the door that led to a narrow street. Mrs. Headley saw a tall woman dressed in black standing beside a gas lamp. She was drawn forward to meet the veiled stranger, who lifted her arms to receive the child. Mrs. Headley handed her baby over to the mysterious woman, who then turned and glided down*

256

the cobblestone street. Convinced she was only dreaming, Mrs. Headley returned to her home, climbed into bed, and awoke to find an empty cradle the following morning."

"Jesus Christ, Nate." Veronica shuddered and let the book slip from her quaking hand. "There's no question about that one. It was her."

Nathan glowered. "I wonder if Abigail Headley was one of the infants I dug up yesterday morning?" He gripped the arms of the wingback chair.

"Well," Veronica leaned forward with her head in her hands. "Now we know at least *one* of the ways she managed to get a hold of her prey."

22

NIGHT HAD FALLEN OUTSIDE OF VERONICA'S HOUSE, AND the bells of St. Luke's had just chimed the hour. The professor stopped reading for a moment to listen to them. For the first time in two years, the familiar sound had not immediately sparked feelings of dread within her. Laura was dead, and Veronica no longer had to fear that she would return.

But now there's another threat.

And she's already been in this house.

Veronica shuddered and glanced over to Alderson, who remained absorbed within his own nervous reflections. Despite his relative silence, she felt grateful for his company and had the impression the feeling was mutual. The detective at least appeared to be comfortable in her chair.

A few hours from this time tomorrow night, all three of us could be dead.

Hoping to drive her intrusive thoughts away, Veronica returned to her work. She had spent the last twenty minutes bookmarking any other potential references to the Brennen vampire in *Civil War Ghosts*. Having exhausted the resources from her home library, she set aside her books to consult her laptop. She had just begun to sift through the initial search results for the word "crossroads" coupled with the terms "American" and "folklore," when a pair of headlight beams swept across the ceiling of her living room. Nathan was on his feet before he heard the muffled *thump* of a door from the driveway.

"It's him," he confirmed after a quick glance out the window. The detective rushed to unlock and open the door before Raymer had a chance to knock. The stern-faced man entered the familiar foyer with a nod to Alderson. He removed a brown knit cap, unzipped an oxblood flight jacket, and hung both items on the coat rack.

"Sorry I'm late," he said to Veronica. "Ran into some traffic on Route 10."

"Good to see you, Edison." A wan smile tugged at her lips. Her face was bathed in the glow of her laptop. She slid the device aside and swung her legs over the edge of the sofa.

After securing the front door, Nathan followed Raymer into the living room. "There's coffee in the kitchen," he said, then returned to his seat in the wingback chair.

With another cursory nod, Raymer turned to Veronica with an eager gleam in his eye. "We've much to discuss."

"Agreed." She leaned forward to place her spectacles on the coffee table. "But if you don't mind, I'd like to start."

"Sure." Raymer sat down on the opposite side of the sectional. He carried a nylon duffle bag, which he set next to his feet.

"So, I spent the afternoon at the Historical Society."

Veronica provided a methodical and detailed summary of the contents of Mrs. Westcott's journal. Raymer listened carefully, nodding at times and wrinkling his brow at other details. He seemed particularly interested in the vampire's fixation on the crossroads.

Alderson crossed his legs and listened as Veronica concluded her story with the destruction of the diary and the mystery of how Charlotte had been transformed into a vampire.

Raymer leaned backward and began to drum his fingers on the armrest.

"This is all very valuable information." Veronica could see his shrewd mind working behind his dark eyes. "Most importantly, we have her full name. Her maiden name, married name. The names of her children. It's exactly what we need."

"I've got something else," she piped up with a hesitant glance at Nathan. "I've got the photographs."

Alderson gave her a puzzled glance. "What do you mean photographs? You didn't mention that earlier?"

She held a hand up to him and glanced back to Raymer.

"The daguerreotypes that Jane mentioned in the diary," she clarified. "They were saved along with all the papers. I couldn't believe it when the archivist set the goddamned jewelry box in front of me." Veronica dropped her eyes to pick up her cell phone. "Now obviously, I couldn't walk out of there with the originals, but I took a picture of each of them. Here." She rose and leaned over the coffee table to pass her phone to Raymer. Alderson remained seated, a disconcerted look still troubling his face.

Raymer pulled up Veronica's photo app and spent a few minutes studying the images. He used his thumb to zoom in on one of the hi-res photos. With a nod, he passed the phone to Alderson. "It's her," he said. "There's no doubt about it."

With unsteady hands, Nathan took the device and began to examine the pictures. Veronica kept a close watch on him as he scrolled from image to image. At one point, he scowled and narrowed his eyes—never for a second looking away from the screen. His grasp on the cell phone had tightened.

"So," Raymer spoke up, drawing Veronica's attention back to him. "Do you remember Father Bill McCallum?"

"Of course," she answered. She returned to the couch, pushed a few books aside, and settled in. "He was the priest who performed the exorcism on Jeffrey Aston, right?"

"Yes, but that barely scratches the surface," he replied. "Bill McCallum was, and is, much more than that."

"OK?" Veronica knitted her brow. "What's this about, Edison?"

Raymer cleared his throat. He looked to Alderson and then back to Veronica. "I suppose you both deserve full disclosure, so bear with me."

Alderson glanced up from the images on Veronica's phone. He shot a bewildered look to her and then directed his tired eyes to Raymer.

"When I left Williamsport two years ago, I already decided I wanted to relocate to the Aston house. That's where this all began, so it only made sense. But when I looked into buying the house, I ran into a complication."

"The property was owned by the Catholic Archdiocese of Richmond," Alderson interjected.

"That's right." Raymer turned to the detective in surprise. "How'd you know?"

"It's how we found you," Nathan explained. "Veronica figured that's where you were, but she didn't know where the house was. So, I had a buddy of mine in Richmond track down information on Oliver Aston. He found the deed and ownership records. I remember thinking it was odd."

"Not as odd as discovering it had then been sold to 'Ray Edwards.'" Veronica chimed in. "That wasn't a very good alias, Edison."

"Well, I didn't know you'd have a *detective* at your disposal, so I tried to make it easy for you to find me."

Caught off guard by the unexpected quip, Veronica laughed aloud. "Was that a joke, Edison?"

A reluctant smirk soon faded from his hardened features. "Do you want to hear about this or not?"

"Sorry," she replied. "Go ahead."

Raymer resumed his story. "Given the history of the house, Father McCallum advised the Archdiocese to purchase it as a precaution. To keep it off the market. When he discovered my interest in the house, he not only facilitated the transaction, but he put me to work as well."

"Doing what, exactly?" Veronica asked.

"Hunting and staking vampires."

Veronica's eyes widened. "You're kidding me, right?"

"No," Raymer shook his head. "He's been my informant for the last two years."

"So, wait a minute. You're telling me you're working for the Church? For some kinda secret society?" Veronica raised an eyebrow.

"Look, our arrangement is simple. McCallum gives me a lead, and I track it down." He pointed to Alderson. "Just like a detective, only none of my suspects are left alive. If I need something to complete a mission, such as military grade hardware or a gym bag full of silver stakes, Father McCallum makes a call. It goes up *his* chain of command, and I'm given everything I asked for within a matter of hours."

"So, who gives *him* orders?" Veronica asked. "How does he know where you can find vampires?"

"That's a question I can't answer," Raymer responded.

"Can't or won't?" Veronica pressed him.

"Both."

"Are you the only one working for him?" Alderson joined the conversation.

"No, there are others," Raymer told him. "But we all work alone unless there's a particularly large or dangerous mission. In that case, reinforcements can be called in. But we are instructed never to use names."

Veronica was stunned. She inched closer to the edge of the sofa. Alderson met her glance and appeared to be just as taken aback by the former anthropology professor's revelation.

"I know it sounds outlandish," Raymer said, "but the Vatican has known about the existence of vampires for centuries. Obviously, they're not going to advertise that they have a cabal of vampire killers at their disposal. Nevertheless, every new pope receives a sealed letter informing him of our existence and purpose. With that, we are given *carte blanche* to carry out our work in secret."

"I've gotta say, Edison, you're just full of surprises these last few days." Veronica ran her fingers through her hair. "This is crazy."

Raymer shrugged. "Only a few select men like Bill McCallum have ever really known what a vampire truly is. The myths and folk superstitions have come down through the ages, but as I'm sure you will be very interested to know, Veronica, writers like Féval, Le Fanu, and Stoker—as well as the hacks responsible for early penny dreadfuls—were anonymously given pieces of legitimate information regarding these creatures to include in their writings. Those fragments came from priests and hunters during each respective era. Just enough, but not too much."

"Why?" Alderson asked. "What was the point of leaking this info to the public?"

"Simple. To keep the legend of the vampire alive in a world where belief in the supernatural was being explained away by science. But not enough to shock the entire human race with the realization it was no longer the apex predator of this world." Raymer slid a hand across his shaved head. "Nowadays, tawdry erotic fiction and ridiculous films marketed to teenagers suggest that plan has gone off the rails. Vampires have almost become *too* popular and commonplace. These are very dangerous creatures. They shouldn't be romanticized or admired. But as awful as some of this media is, the popularization of the vampire's various weaknesses has certainly saved the lives of many individuals who've turned down the wrong street or discovered a terrible truth about a loved one that mysteriously disappeared."

Veronica was captivated by her colleague's confession. Alderson's opinion remained unreadable to her.

"What's alarming is that they are growing in numbers," Raymer warned. "For now, intercession isn't necessary. We just stick to the shadows and kill the fucking things. But in the future?" He shook his head slowly. "It may not be a secret that can be kept for much longer."

The room fell silent as Raymer paused to collect his thoughts. Veronica was lost in thoughts of her own, as she ruminated over the cultural and spiritual implications of what Edison had revealed. It was Alderson who finally broke the silence.

"I can't believe this is the thing we saw in the woods."

Veronica glanced at Alderson to find him once again staring at the photograph of Charlotte. When he felt her gaze upon him, he appeared embarrassed and tossed the phone onto the coffee table. She frowned as he attempted to change the subject.

"So, what else did this priest have to say? Anything that will help us take her down?"

Raymer stood up and dusted off his trousers. For a moment, Veronica feared he was about to pontificate in the same way he used to when he taught his anthropology courses, but his demeanor suggested he was open to dialogue.

"My discussion with Father McCallum has led me to believe we have two options to take out this vampire," he stated. "The first is a completely hands on approach, and, believe me, I have a hundred percent confidence that my plan will work." Raymer glanced at Veronica, and then returned his attention to Alderson. "I've already brought everything we need. From a high-powered Mil-Spec sniper rifle to holy water, so rest assured, weapons are covered."

"Good." Alderson nodded. "Do you have a particular strategy?"

"Yes," Edison said. "Tomorrow, we go up there in the morning. We'll start at that tomb and sanctify it. Make it impossible for the vampire to return if she's using it for shelter. And if she's in there, we drag her into the sun and that's it. We go home. If not, we check the areas around the plantation house, especially along its foundations. Split up and scour those woods. Search the riverbank. Our objective is to look for any evidence of freshly turned earth. If we find a place where she's gone to ground? We dig her up and let the daylight burn her to ashes."

"And what if we don't find her before dark?" Veronica was compulsively wringing her hands with the confirmation they would be returning to the woods so soon.

"We'll be ready for her," Raymer insisted. "I propose we cast *three* protective circles. One for each of us. We'll set up well before sundown. There will be one circle front and center, and then two behind it. We won't be too far apart from one another. Nathan, you'll be in the forward circle."

"Heavily armed, right?" Alderson asked.

"Ever shoot a .303 Short-Magazine Lee-Enfield?"

"No, but..." The detective scratched his stubbled chin. "Haven't those been around since World War I?"

"Yeah, but the SMLE's a workhorse," Raymer assured him. "A bolt action rifle with a 10-round magazine. I have several charger clips loaded with silver-tipped rounds for you. The feed ramp is sufficiently polished, so there'll be no issues with reloaded ammunition. You still have to work the bolt, but you have considerably more cartridges to burn through than you'd get with a hunting rifle. Also, you'll get a backup weapon, and a bag full of stakes, a mallet, holy water, crucifixes, and provisions."

"And why am I in the front?"

"This vampire seems to be fascinated with you. It was McCallum's suggestion that you be put forward to draw her out and put her at a tactical disadvantage."

Alderson clenched his jaw. "I guess that works."

"And where will I be?" Veronica looked up at Edison.

"To the right rear of Nathan. Wearing night vision goggles. Your task will be to act as a spotter, but you'll also be armed."

"And you?"

"I will be rear left with a TAC-338 sniper rifle, prone position, under partial cover."

"You really think laying on the cold, damp ground is a good idea?" Veronica asked.

Alderson interjected. "That's a heavy-hitting sniper rifle he's talking about. He'll have to be prone to use the bipod. It'll certainly do a hell of a lot more damage than a crossbow bolt."

"How much more?" Veronica leaned forward, her curiosity piqued.

"Remember what the .44 Magnum did to her hand?"

She nodded.

"That model of sniper rifle can do the same amount of damage to her chest. And from how far away, Edison?"

"Well, a Navy SEAL killed an Iraqi counter-sniper from 2,100 meters. So pretty damned far. Add in the silver bullets, and she *will* drop. No question in my mind."

Alderson nodded with approval. For the first time since he arrived earlier in the day, Veronica noticed that he seemed animated and motivated by something other than fear or anger.

Raymer moved to change the subject. "Look, I owe both of you an apology for what happened out there. I let my hubris take over and thought this was gonna be an easy kill, especially since there were three of us. No one in this room is at fault for that whole mess but me, and me alone. I promise it won't happen again."

Veronica eyed Raymer with surprise. "There's no need to apologize, but I do have one question."

"And that is?"

"What if this doesn't work?" she asked.

"I don't foresee that happening," Raymer answered.

"But if it does?" Veronica sat on the edge of the sofa. Her hands were clutched tightly between her knees. "What if you're oversimplifying things again?"

"OK, if she somehow manages to resist our attacks, which again, is *highly* unlikely, then I'll take over. Father McCallum strongly advised that if all else fails, we consider the other option, which is ceremonial magic."

"Wait, what?" Alderson shot a dubious glance to Veronica. Her jaw tensed, and the color drained from her cheeks. The skeptical detective turned back to Raymer. "A priest... a Roman Catholic *priest* advised you to do that?"

"Yes, Nathan." Raymer met his incredulous gaze. "Now if you'll let me explain."

"Why are we even talking about something so absurd?" Alderson was now on his feet. He took a few steps toward Raymer. "We don't need fucking... *magic!* We just need a shit-ton of silver! You already said she was poisoned so why can't we just finish her off?"

Raymer stood rooted in place and stared down the detective. "I'm not going to ask you again. Let me finish."

Alderson paced toward the other side of the room. As he passed Veronica, he refused to meet her pleading eyes.

"Alright, think of it like this," Raymer continued, his thick fingers rubbing the bridge of his nose. "A vampire is basically a spirit inhabiting and animating a corpse. We know, for example, that these creatures can teleport and move very quickly, but they can't turn into bats or wolves. They don't command the weather or any of that nonsense. All fiction. What we *do* know is that certain vampires—especially older ones—can master the ability of leaving their bodies. Either while sleeping during the day, or by sinking into a torpor at night. The spirit can manifest itself the same way a ghost might, but it's directed by the vampire's conscious will. It can go wherever it wants, which could explain why you saw the Brennen vampire trailing Tyler Marshall's spirit during your séance."

"That makes sense." Veronica nodded. Out of the corner of her eye, she could see Nathan fighting to control his temper.

"So, this ability will give us an opportunity to fight it on different grounds," Raymer said. "But at the same time, it puts us at an incredibly dangerous disadvantage."

"How so?" Alderson asked, his frustration boiling to the surface.

"It enables certain vampires—the really malicious and spiteful ones—to wage psychical attacks on their victims. They can influence thought, enter dreams, or hypnotize their prey."

Alderson's pacing came to an abrupt stop. Both Raymer and Veronica looked up when his movements suddenly ceased. Recognizing their scrutiny, he resumed his back-and-forth motions, his head hung in thought.

Raymer's lips tightened as he glanced at Veronica. She shrugged her shoulders, but her gaze pierced his. They both frowned.

Edison resumed the discussion. "I think it's more than evident that this vampire has these powers."

Veronica turned so she could face the anxious detective. "Nate, I've already been thinking about this, too." She spoke softly, with the hope of calming him down. "This would explain how she knew your son's name." She swallowed hard, fearing an angry outburst at the mention of his son. "Based on what I learned today, I think she singled you out because of your loss."

"Veronica's right," Raymer added. "She's already been in your head. That alone isn't something you need to worry about. But if she decides to take up residence there, then we have a problem."

"That's not gonna happen," Alderson responded.

Raymer narrowed his eyes. "Well, if it does, you need to tell us. As soon as possible. Otherwise, you risk falling completely under her control. At worse, it's comparable to demonic possession. At best, she'll manipulate you to the point you may not be able to tell fantasy from reality."

"She tasted *your* blood, too!" Nathan stood riveted by the bar cart. "So how do we know she hasn't started doing this shit to you?"

"She hasn't," Raymer affirmed. "But I know how to protect myself. There's no need to be defensive. We're trying to help you."

"Look, I'm tired." He lifted both of his hands before letting them fall back to his sides. "I'm... I'm hungry. And both of you have had two years to adapt to all this shit. It's been like two *days* for me. This is a lot to process."

"We understand," Veronica responded. "Look, let's take a break. It's after dinner time. Why don't we take a breather? Order some food?"

Raymer nodded. "That's a good idea."

"Agreed," Alderson said. "Listen, I need to use the bathroom. I'm sorry."

"It's OK." She stood up and stretched her stiff legs and pointed toward her staircase. "Bathroom's upstairs. You can't miss it. We'll wait and order something when you get back."

He nodded and skirted past them. Both Raymer and Veronica watched as Alderson disappeared up the steps. When the bathroom door closed, Veronica was the first to speak in a low whisper.

"He's fucked."

Raymer nodded with concern and lowered his voice. "We need to keep an eye on him."

"Listen, before he gets back here, I've gotta ask. What the hell kind of ritual are you planning to perform?"

"A binding ritual," he said. His eyes were still watching the stairs.

"So that's why you needed her name."

"Yes."

"OK, but what kind of binding ritual are you gonna try? Do you even have diagrams of the sigils? Christ, whatever verses or incantations you need?"

"No, but—"

"And I guess you lost all your grimoires and other points of reference when you sold your books for guns and whatever the hell else you bought."

"Like I said before, I don't need books."

"Of course you need books for this, Edison! And you know you have to prepare for weeks before you can do something like this. You need to fast, there are certain astrological considerations, not to mention—"

"McCallum said that much of the formal preparation can be circumvented. Besides—"

"What the fuck does he know? He's a goddamn priest!" Veronica's whisper intensified to a harsh rush of sibilance.

"Shhh!" Raymer held a finger to his lips. The toilet flushed in the distance. They could hear the tap water running upstairs. "McCallum knows what he's talking about. Besides, you know as well as I do these things are all a matter of willpower. It's simply mine against hers."

"Yeah, well, in any other situation, I'd say your stubborn ass would be unbeatable, but this thing is on a completely different level."

Raymer pursed his lips. "I'll improvise."

"And compromise the efficacy of the binding? *Are you fucking serious?*"

"Look, we may not have a choice!" He drove a fist into his palm. "But like I told you both earlier, we have enough fire power to blow her back to the Civil War. The ritual is simply a backup plan that may not even be required."

"Fine, but in order for this to *actually* work, you need time."

"The only thing I *need* is something that once belonged to her. Something personal."

"Damn it," Veronica muttered. "There was a dried flower pressed between the covers of one of the daguerreotypes. A lily. I'm sure Charlotte put it there. Had I known what you were up to, I suppose I could've taken it."

"I'm hoping I can find some of her hair, or a scrap of her clothing when we go out there tomorrow. That way—"

"I already have something," Alderson interjected from the top of the stairs.

Raymer and Veronica glanced up in surprise to learn their conversation had been overheard.

"Did you pick up something this morning?" Raymer asked. "What is it?"

"No, not this morning. I found it at the scene of Tyler Marshall's murder. I bagged a scrap of her dress, but never submitted it to evidence. I'm sure it's a piece of those filthy rags she was wearing."

"Are you sure? Because if I use that and it's not hers..." Raymer trailed off.

"I'll bring it tomorrow when we meet up. You can see for yourself. Feel it. Whatever. It's hers," Nathan assured them as he began to descend the stairs. "But since you both decided to have your top-secret discussion while I was gone, you wanna explain to me exactly why you need it?"

Alderson nudged past them and returned to his favorite spot beside the chair. Raymer turned to follow him and picked up where he left off.

"Well, as I was saying earlier, if vampires are in essence souls trapped in physical bodies, their spirits are subject to the laws of ritual magic and they can be bound. With her name, I can invoke her. Furthermore, I can chastise and *command* her. With a personal object, I can utilize its essence to forge a psychic conduit with her. There's a whole bunch of other mumbo jumbo that informs a *disciplined* ritual binding, but I only need to elicit one piece of information from her."

"And that is?"

"Where her resting place is," Raymer responded. "We can force her to reveal where she hides by day, find her, and destroy her when she's vulnerable. I could spend hours, days, whatever, forcing her to reveal *all* of her hiding places, if I'm up to the task. Magic is basically nothing more than a battle of wills."

"That's another very dangerous oversimplification," Veronica warned him. She crossed her arms against her chest.

"What if she lies?" Alderson asked.

"She can't."

"Why?" Nathan replied. "You gonna bind her with some kinda magic fucking lasso?"

"In theory, yes. But the binding isn't *literal.*"

The detective shook his head in disbelief. "What happens if you can't *bind* her? Or all these shortcuts you're taking prevent the ritual or whatever from working?"

Raymer rubbed his chin and glanced toward the window. A moment of silence fell between them, and the bells of St. Luke's began to ring again a few blocks away.

"Then we all die."

23

THEIR DINNER ARRIVED WITHIN AN HOUR. AFTER TIPPING the delivery driver, Veronica carried two large brown paper bags of Chinese food to her dining room. She began unpacking take-out boxes of steamed vegetables, fried rice, egg rolls, sweet and sour chicken, Szechuan beef, Lo Mein, and a two-liter bottle of Coke. The aroma of the food caused her stomach to rumble. She couldn't remember the last time she had eaten anything.

The professor placed napkins, silverware, and plates on her dining room table and set places for herself and her guests. In lieu of the usual pillar candles, antique handbells, and other Spiritualist paraphernalia, Veronica placed several small packets of soy sauce at the table's center. She also opened a bottle of Pinot Grigio. Within a few minutes the three of them were absorbed in the task of preparing their plates and drinks.

Veronica took a moment to appreciate the sense of normalcy. It felt wonderful not to be alone. With her glass of wine in hand, she cleared her throat and addressed her guests.

"At the risk of sounding corny," she began, "I know this whole situation is fucked up, but I'm very grateful that both of you are here."

She raised her glass timidly and forced a smile to each of them. Nate lifted his glass of soda and nodded. Raymer reached over to clink his wine glass against her own.

As her eyes passed from Raymer to Alderson, she momentarily focused on the dark corner where the shadow of Charlotte Brennen had observed her séance. The professor's heart sank as an inevitable sense of doom reasserted itself.

They spent several minutes eating in silence. The food was satisfying, but Veronica felt a cold, hopeless feeling creeping over her, and began to fear they had no chance of victory against their opponent. Desperate to drive these thoughts away, the professor turned to speak to Raymer.

"I've been meaning to ask you," she began with some hesitation. "What exactly is your exercise regimen? Is a gym membership part of this gig you have with McCallum?"

Raymer paused a moment as he finished chewing his food. "Not exactly. I took a job with a construction outfit when I first settled in up there. I still had some of Bartsch's cash at my disposal, so money wasn't an issue. I did it partially for the cover, primarily for the hard work. I thought because I'd been lifting weights and hitting the heavy bag, I could just step right into it." He shook his head. "I was dead wrong. The first few days of breaking concrete nearly killed me. But after a month or two, I was conditioned to it."

"Well, you look great," she said while loading a fork full of vegetables. "I have to admit, I kinda like the new Edison Raymer."

"I'm happy to see that you're also doing well for yourself," he replied, dabbing the corner of his mouth with a napkin. "And that you haven't abandoned your studies."

Nathan's fork clattered against his plate as he reached for his soda. Sensing his discomfort, Raymer turned to include him in their conversation.

"I never thought I'd be sitting down to break bread with a detective from the Williamsport Police Department, but you're a good man, Nate. You've kept an open mind about all of this, and you've handled it better than anyone could expect."

"Thanks," he said, fidgeting in his seat. "I never thought I'd be having dinner with a wanted man who moonlights as a vampire hunter and a psychic lit professor that cusses like a goddamned sailor. But life's funny like that."

"I'm not psychic," Veronica said with a smirk. "But it's awfully flattering of you to think so, Nate."

As she observed Alderson, Veronica felt incredibly protective of him. He stared at his plate while slowly picking at his food. She agreed with the compliments Raymer had just paid him. He was brave and honest. But he was also drowning. She could see the emptiness overtaking his gray eyes. The flashes of anger and his eagerness to kill the vampire were the only things tethering him to this world.

If we make it through this, I'm going to help him. Even if he won't let me. I'll call his wife and have her over for tea. I'll insert myself in the middle of the whole mess without a moment's regret. Whatever it takes.

That's what you do for your friends, isn't it?

Raymer's deep voice drew her back from her thoughts.

"Listen, I don't want to spoil the mood, but we need to make sure we're prepared for anything that might come to pass tomorrow."

They spent the next few minutes outlining their plans. Raymer ran down a list of items he brought with him and asked Alderson to bring along a few additional tools from his garage. Veronica jotted down a list of essentials to pick up from the grocery store before they departed in the morning. The professor underlined two things she was especially adamant on obtaining: bottled water and more cigarettes.

Soon Alderson and Raymer lapsed into an impenetrable, jargon-heavy discussion about guns and ammunition. The constant barrage of abbreviations, letters, and numbers was almost as obtuse as a theory-laden academic paper. Veronica took the opportunity to clear the table, pack up the leftovers, and load the dishwasher. By this point the two men had quieted long enough for her to return to her seat at the table and change the course of the discussion.

"I think we need to talk about the other elephant in the room here." Veronica looked hesitantly toward Alderson. She feared setting him off with further talk of the vampire. "There are things about this creature that don't make sense to me. And before either one of you say it, I know—all we need to do is kill her. But in the interest of *understanding* our enemy, *if* in fact we need to resort to plan B, there are a few things we should try to iron out."

Alderson sat with his elbows on the table, his hands propped under his chin. Raymer folded his arms and leaned back in his chair. "What's on your mind?" he asked.

"Well, first of all, why do you think she's so fixated on the crossroads?" Veronica asked. "There's clearly some kind of significance, but the European beliefs concerning suicides or pacts with the devil don't really seem to be relevant. So do you think we should be looking at African customs instead?"

"Of course," Raymer answered. "She was a slaveholder. What else could she have picked up on?"

"Well, she could have been dabbling in *many* things," she responded. "I mean, she did come from Scotland. Maybe—"

"Sorry, I didn't mean for that to sound condescending," he apologized. "No, the European myths you probably thought of first, like the Faust legends, are going to lead you down the wrong path. Most likely, she learned of these ideas from the slaves on her plantation."

Alderson leaned forward and placed his hands on the table. He seemed eager for Raymer to continue.

"Although," Edison reflected, "it sounds like she was picking and choosing whatever aspects of these beliefs that best suited her."

"So, what's the basic gist of these legends?" Alderson asked. He finished the rest of his drink and pushed the glass to the side.

"Well, in Central and West African traditions, crossroads are thought to be gateways between worlds. The intersection of the dead and the living. The myths of these cultures were brought to our shores by the Transatlantic slave trade and handed down to successive generations via oral tradition."

"Right." Veronica took another sip from her wine glass and savored its slightly bitter taste.

"By the mid-nineteenth century," Raymer continued, "the waters had been so muddied by Christianity that the names of the deities said to preside over crossroads were all but forgotten. Or, they had been transformed into something else entirely."

"So, what do you think she was trying to *do?*" Veronica asked. "Offer her soul in exchange for her children to be... What? Returned to her? Restored to life?"

"Maybe," Raymer said. "But that's not how the crossroads ritual works. Adepts are said to bargain for a *skill* not a *favor*. And, at least among the West African legends, there is no exchange of souls. Only offerings. So, whatever she *wanted* may not have been what she *received*."

"Do you think that was how she was turned? The so-called skill or advantage she gained was vampirism?"

"Honestly, I don't think it was that literal. Another vampire may have just been at the right place at the right time. Or, it may have been impersonating the role of the Christian devil or a Hoodoo deity like Papa Legba. I'd venture to say whatever it was that turned her also *tricked* her."

"Interesting." Veronica paused to consider it all. "I never thought of the trickster angle. But that makes sense. If she kept going there expecting to see or reunite with her children, it seems something completely different eventually happened."

"One thing I can tell you," Raymer stated, "is that her kids weren't buried in that mausoleum. I think she buried them at the crossroads."

"Fuck," Veronica muttered. "Well, apparently she did take her last stillborn child out there. One of Jane's entries mentioned that. I don't think the infant's body was recovered."

"I'll bet she had the other ones moved there from the tomb," Raymer suggested.

"But why? Did she think it was like some magic burial ground? Like in that Stephen King novel?"

"Possibly," Raymer inferred. "It's clear in those journals you read that the deaths of her children pushed her over the edge. So who knows what—"

"That's the other thing that doesn't make sense to me," Veronica interjected. "With all the trauma and grief she endured from the loss of her children, why the hell would she turn around and kill other kids? Is it jealousy? Vengeance? You'd think she'd try to protect children instead?"

"What, like some goddamn vampire Mary Poppins?" Alderson shouted. "That's ridiculous!"

"Nate, I'm just trying to understand," Veronica said calmly. "Sure, she was stubborn and manipulative, but what made her become so *evil?*"

"Who cares?" He slammed his fist against the table. "I don't have any sympathy for this bitch. I get it, she lost her kids. It's tragic. Boo-fucking-hoo. But just because a few of her kids died doesn't give her the right to *kill* dozens more!"

Veronica pursed her lips and remained silent.

"Christ, we don't even know how many kids or people she *has* killed." He pointed a finger at Veronica. "You're turning up shit in books about babies she stole from cribs in the early twentieth century. It's fucked up."

"No one's denying that, Nathan," Raymer weighed in. "And I sure as hell don't have any sympathy for her either. But Veronica's right, there's no harm in trying to better understand the psychology of this monster. I needn't remind you that she can get into *our* heads, so we may very well have to get inside of hers to win this battle."

"All you need to know is that she's fucking crazy!" Alderson snapped back. "How the hell can you know what she was trying to do? Her behavior isn't rational. It wasn't back then, and it isn't now!"

"I agree," Raymer said. "There are some things about her that we may never know. But that doesn't mean we shouldn't try to figure it out."

Alderson rose to fetch the bottle of soda from the fridge, returned, and poured himself another glass. "OK, since you two insist on playing armchair psychologist, can one of you explain why the hell she created those things I found in the woods? Why did she kill some of them but then turned the other ones into vampires or whatever the fuck they were? Helpless *babies* for Christ's sake!"

Raymer folded his arms across his chest and grimaced. "I think she was trying to make surrogates," he speculated after a moment's reflection. He turned to Veronica. "Think about it. Remember what happened with Bartsch? He was drawn to Jennifer Stroud and then to Laura because they resembled his deceased wife."

"Hold on a minute." Veronica held up her hand as she tried to parse out Raymer's theory. "So you think she preys on kids that remind her of her children?"

"The picture of that boy," Alderson spoke up in a distant voice. "Although a few years younger, he resembled Tyler Marshall."

276

"But she killed him," Veronica reminded Nathan. "She didn't try to turn him."

"No, but I've said since day one that it looked like she was interrupted," he explained. "He was partially covered, and he was found some distance from the crossroads. My hunch was that she heard his mother coming into the woods and bolted before she could finish."

"But she only tried to *transform* the infants," Veronica stressed again.

"Not necessarily," Raymer said with an unmistakable tremor in his voice. "She may have turned several older children. The difference is the infants were too weak to rise."

"But you think the older ones did?" Veronica asked. "Jesus Christ, Edison. There could be dozens of them out there!" She ran her fingers through her hair. "This is seriously fucked up."

As soon as she spoke, the realization hit her. She lifted her eyes to Raymer, and he met her gaze with trepidation.

"The Aston house girl," she whispered.

Raymer nodded in preoccupied silence.

"It's possible," he eventually said. "But we really have no way of knowing. On the other hand, these things are incredibly territorial. She may have grown tired of having to share her hunting grounds, so she just killed them."

"True," Veronica added. "I was also thinking about the ages of her victims. None of her children lived past the age of three. So, it makes sense that the ones she turned were so young. The other victims were too old to serve as replacements. So, she killed them when she didn't recognize them or when they proved *not* to be the kids she was looking for."

"Either way, I suspect we'd have run into more of the Brennen vampire's progeny if they were still at large. And the Aston house vampire likely has no relation to her."

"OK, hold up." Alderson lifted his hand to stall the conversation. "That's at least the second time tonight you two have mentioned this 'Aston house' vampire. What's the deal?"

Raymer sighed. "She was the first vampire I ever encountered. Back when I was in graduate school."

"I know," Alderson said. "Veronica told me that part. But I get the sense you're not telling me something. What else was so significant about it?"

"Two things," Raymer said. "First, the vampire was an eleven or twelve-year-old girl. Second, she was able to cast her spirit from her body. In particular, she moved through mirrors. Until you two came to me with the story of the Brennen vampire's appearance at the séance, I never encountered anything else like her."

Alderson reflected on what Raymer had just told him. "So, what happened to her?"

"I don't know," Raymer admitted. "I've been living in that house for almost two years hoping to lure her back, but she's never returned."

A temporary silence fell over the conversation. Veronica noticed that Nathan still seemed agitated when he suddenly spoke up again.

"OK, I've got another basic question neither of you has explained to me yet," he said. "How exactly are these things made? Obviously, it's not just through a bite. You told me that this morning. But you never explained *how* they are made."

Grateful to change the subject, Edison responded to the detective's question. "They are created through the *exchange* of blood. This is something McCallum confirmed when we first began working together. The vampire drains its victim to the point of death, and then it shares a portion of its own blood with its prey. When they awake the following night, they have completed the transformation."

Veronica shot Edison a worried glance and then turned her attention to Alderson. "Nathan, I *did* explain that to you already. Remember? After you came back from the woods?"

Alderson regarded her with a blank stare. "Sorry, I guess I forgot with all the other shit we've been dealing with the last few days."

"It's OK," Veronica said with a forced smile. "Like I said, it's a lot to take in. Do you have any other questions while we're at it? Anything else that's been *bothering* you?"

"What about coffins?" he asked. "Do they have to sleep in coffins?"

"No," Raymer confirmed. "The *need* to sleep in coffins or their native soil was just a myth perpetuated over time. But certainly, it's convenient for them to take shelter in coffins when they are first turned, as they make for effective hiding places from the sun."

Another short lull in their conversation prompted Veronica to reflect on Raymer's responses. She momentarily set aside her concern for Alderson when an awful and wholly unsolicited image suddenly flashed in her mind.

"What if turning those infants into vampires wasn't deliberate after all?" Her eyes lit up with horror. "What if it was an accident?"

Raymer narrowed his eyes. "What do you mean?"

Veronica swallowed. She felt as though she were going to be sick. "Think about it. It's thankfully rare for her to get ahold of children that young. But when she did, what's the first thing a mother would do to quiet a crying or hungry child?"

"She'd nurse them," Raymer stated.

With a loud scraping sound, Alderson slid his chair across the floor and stood up. "If this conversation continues in this direction, we're going to need something a little bit stronger than soda."

The frazzled detective returned from the living room with a bottle of Jack Daniels. He poured a generous measure into the small bit of cola remaining in his glass and then offered the bottle to Raymer.

The former anthropology professor declined as did Veronica—although she refilled her glass of Grigio to the brim.

Alderson threw back his drink, grit his teeth, and then poured himself another. Before sitting back down, he snatched up the bottle and placed it on the kitchen counter, so it would remain out of reach from his seat at the dining room table.

"I know my limits," the detective assured his partners. "I know I gotta be straight tomorrow. Anyway, here's another thing—among so many others—that I don't understand. How the hell has she survived this long? And stayed hidden?"

After careful consideration, Raymer offered a response. "I suspect she's managed to survive because she goes to ground and enters a kind of hibernation, or an extended period of torpor when prey is scarce." A frown caused his brow to crease. "Another rather unpleasant thing to consider is her tendency to prey on children. As you can imagine, the blood of a child is incredibly potent and pure. It would have a powerful restorative effect on her."

Alderson looked away in disgust. A chill rippled over Veronica's arms. "That's awful."

"Keep in mind though, she hasn't *only* been feeding on children. If she was that particular, she would not have survived this long. This vampire's limited to whatever or whoever she encounters in those woods. Therefore, she's likely sustained herself on the blood of animals and fed on carrion. The stray hunter, fisherman, or hiker. Anyone that might wander into the forest."

Veronica chimed in. "Before you got here, I was digging through some old books about local legends and hauntings. There are tons of reported sightings of a woman in black that could have been her. One story was about two fishermen that came across her. They lived to tell about it, but think how many *didn't?*"

"Why Williamsport?" Nathan asked, his hand curled around the base of his empty glass. "Not only her, but obviously Bartsch was here too. Was there some kind of connection between them?"

"Not that I'm aware," Raymer said. "But the fact that there have been two prominent vampires in a small city like Williamsport ought to put this whole thing into perspective for you, Nate. These things are every-fucking-where. I'd venture to say in the Tidewater region alone, we've extinguished somewhere between thirty or forty of them in the past few years."

"Jesus," Alderson muttered.

"Whether she *chooses* to remain confined to the forest to be near her children or if she simply doesn't know any better because of her mental instability, I honestly can't say. But the fact that she *does* confine herself there narrows down the places we may find her."

"Well, at least we have *one* advantage," Veronica sighed. "Although, those woods and riverbanks go on for miles."

"There's something else I think it's important for both of you to understand about this particular vampire," Raymer warned. "Not only does she appear to possess psychical powers, but she has made absolutely no effort to blend in with society. Most vampires, like Matthias Bartsch, for example, are very clever in how they manage to disguise themselves. To maintain their secrecy, they must be very careful not to leave a trail of bodies to their proverbial doorstep. So, they have to exercise great discipline when it comes to choosing their victims."

Raymer paused and crossed his arms over his chest.

"But this thing is a different story. She's adapted to the wilderness rather than the world of humankind. She seems to have intuitively learned how to dispose of her victims, which has kept her from being discovered. My guess is this section of the James River is a graveyard that would rival the one you suspect is all around the crossroads, Nate."

"What the hell are we going to do about all those graves?" Veronica asked. "We can't just leave them there."

"I'll handle that," Alderson replied. "After we take her down, I'll get a forensics crew up there. Even if it costs me my badge."

"I'm not sure that's a good idea," Raymer said. "We may need to keep this between the three of us. Think about what would happen if the truth about her got out."

"Can't McCallum's people clean this up?"

"They could," Raymer said. "But if that's the route we want to take, then I'd advise not complicating matters by bringing in your colleagues or the FBI."

Alderson nodded. "Let's table that issue for now. What else do we need to know about this thing before we go out there tomorrow?"

Raymer exhaled heavily and picked up where he left off earlier. "You both just need to remember that she's unpredictable. She has no moral compass or code. She was mad in life, and she remains mad in death. Therefore, like a rabid dog, she must be put down."

Veronica crossed her arms and spoke next. "You know, she seems more like a revenant in that respect. Her behavior hearkens back to all the reports of vampires in eighteenth-century Europe."

"Well, yes and no," Raymer countered. "First of all, those tales were true. There was no way the Church could have covered up all those outbreaks of vampirism in Eastern European villages. It spread like a virus," he trailed off. "But unlike the typically mindless revenant, this vampire is cunning. As your research shows, Veronica, she is incredibly tenacious."

Veronica took another sip of wine. The anxiety was branching out in cold waves from her stomach.

Raymer leaned forward and slid his arms along the table. "Also, when these things only feed on animals or the dead, they degenerate into ghoulish, deformed creatures that are extremely feral in nature."

Veronica shuddered at his description. Her gaze fixed on him as he continued.

"I ran into a coven of these things up in the Jersey Pine Barrens a few months ago. They were living in the woods up there. Park rangers kept finding animal carcasses. They chalked them up as wildcat or coyote attacks, but the tell-tale sign was the conspicuous absence of spillage or blood staining the ground. So, armed with my crossbow, some night vision goggles, and a dozen silver stakes, I spent two nights tracking them through the woods. I found them burrowing under the floorboards of a dilapidated woodshed."

Alderson's eyes widened. He listened as Raymer continued his tale.

"They're quick, they're ferocious, but they're predictable," Raymer noted. "It wasn't easy, but I made sure that each of them was dead by sunrise."

"Fuck, Edison," Veronica responded. "That's terrifying."

"Father McCallum has intimated that these fiends are also common in the Appalachian Mountains," he said. "But he's got another unit that keeps watch on that region."

Both Veronica and Alderson sat in mute awe. Edison also fell into an uneasy silence, as if replaying his encounters in his mind, before he continued.

"My point is the Brennen vampire exhibits *some* of these feral and ghoulish characteristics. You saw how she was when we were out there. She just kept coming at us. So obviously, we can't underestimate her strength. But since she has retained a significant aspect of her personality from before her death, we have to be wary of her intelligence as well."

"Alright," Alderson interrupted. "I don't mean to be rude, but I don't know how much more of this I can take."

Raymer met the detective's weary glance. "Let's call it a night then. We have a very difficult day and night ahead of us tomorrow, and we need our rest."

"Agreed," Veronica said. She stood and pushed in her chair. Alderson went past her into the living room. She glanced at Raymer and nodded surreptitiously to the detective. They turned to follow him into the room.

"Listen, Nate, you're welcome to stay the night if you'd like," Veronica offered. "The sectional is comfortable, and I have plenty of extra blankets and pillows."

He addressed her from the foyer. His rigid posture loosened a bit and he spoke with sincerity. "I appreciate that, but I don't think it's necessary." He paused a moment before adding, "I'll see you both here tomorrow morning. Bright and early."

Veronica nodded and looked to Raymer, who was moving over to the couch, where he had left his duffle bag.

"Hold up a second, Nate." Raymer lifted the bag onto the sofa and unzipped it. He withdrew a crucifix and a handful of silver crosses attached to thin chains. "Take these home with you. Put one on and keep the others near you at all times."

Alderson held out his hand to receive them without objection. "Thank you," he said and carefully placed the smaller items in his pocket. He snatched his coat from the rack, slipped it on, and stuffed the crucifix into an interior pocket. Glancing at Veronica, he forced a weary smile. "Thank you for dinner. You're a great host."

She returned his smile and wished him goodnight. With a final nod to Raymer, Alderson turned, unlocked the door, and departed.

"Goddamn it," Veronica hissed under her breath. She glanced at Raymer, who stood scratching his chin with his back to the front door.

"She's already working on him," he said. "I wouldn't be surprised if he's already started having visions of her."

"Then we shouldn't have let him leave!"

"I think he'll be OK for one night," Raymer said. Veronica had the distinct impression he was trying to convince himself as much as her. "Besides, he has to keep up appearances. His wife might become suspicious if he doesn't come home tonight."

Veronica placed a hand on her hip and shifted her weight. "Christ, what if we put *her* at risk?"

"I don't think she's in any danger," Raymer said as he locked the front door. He returned to the living room with a contemplative look on his face. "At least not yet."

24

AFTER QUIETLY TURNING TO CLOSE THE DOOR LEADING from his garage, Nathan Alderson crept into his kitchen. The house was quiet and dark, save for a wash of yellow lamplight coming from the adjacent dining room. With her straight blonde hair swept up in a loose bun, Kelly Alderson sat at the dining room table, her small hands cupping a mug of tea. She was steeping the tiny bag and had yet to raise her eyes to her husband.

"I'd ask who she is, but emotional availability is not exactly your strong suit," she said. "So, I doubt I have any reason to worry on that front."

"No, you don't," Nathan replied. He stood in the entry way, still partly enveloped in shadows.

"I've been calling you all day." She lifted her head to observe his reaction, but her voice remained low. "Left about a dozen voicemails. Sent about a dozen texts. You couldn't find the time in your busy day to reply to just *one* of them?"

Alderson took a step into the room. He stood looming over the table. Kelly turned her eyes away and stared into her tea. The steam and scents of clove and chai wafted into the air.

"My phone is dead," he explained. "I'm sorry."

"Did it ever occur to you to *charge* it?"

"No, that's not what I meant," he corrected himself. "It's bricked. I dropped the damn thing. The whole screen is cracked, and I can't get it to work."

"Well, that's convenient." She lifted the heavy mug and carefully sipped its spicy contents. Finding it was still too hot to drink, she winced and set it back on the table.

"Not really," he said. "If you don't believe me, you can go see what's left of it in my nightstand upstairs. Anyway, I have to get it replaced. And the last thing I wanna do is waste two hours at the goddamn Verizon store. So no," he added. "I wouldn't say it's convenient."

"Well, I guess that explains why McCain's been calling the landline." Kelly sighed and shrugged her shoulders.

"Oh?" Alderson stiffened. He hadn't checked in with his partner for days. With the previous few days an incoherent blur, he couldn't even remember when he had last spoken to him. "I'll call him in the morning."

"So, where the hell have you been?"

"Working."

"Where?" She continued to press him. "Have you been out in those woods? Are you making any progress?"

"Some," he said. "But I'd rather not discuss it. I know it upsets you," he added with a trace of sympathy that sounded entirely foreign to her.

"Have you eaten anything? I could reheat some chicken in the crockpot for you. Lots of butter. The way you like it."

"No," he shook his head. "I've already eaten."

"Where?" She leaned forward and blew upon the surface of her tea. "You can't live on fast food and coffee all the time."

"I'm fine," he insisted. "I just want to go to bed. I'm exhausted, and I have another long day ahead of me."

She nodded, her hands still surrounding the hot mug of tea. Her wedding ring glistened by the dim light of the table lamp.

"I miss you, Nathan." She tilted her sharp chin upward to study him.

"I know," he said and turned away from her searching gaze. His eyes lingered over the heavy drapes veiling the dining room window. The night beyond was pitch black. His stomach churned as he remembered the vengeful thing that haunted the moonlit forest just a few miles from his home.

He turned his attention back to his wife. Rather than make another promise he was uncertain he could keep, he decided to lie to pacify her anxiety.

"I'm very close to cracking this case," he said. "I'm working with some people. We just need a little more time."

"What people?" she asked. "All of McCain's messages sound as if you've left him in the dark."

Too late to retract his words, he frowned and wished he hadn't let his guard down.

"Never mind that," he said. "I'm gonna head up to bed."

"Fine." She folded her arms across her chest. From losing so much weight, her favorite Wonder Woman t-shirt now seemed oversized. The juxtaposition of the faded gold emblem against the fragile frame of his wife looked absurd and depressed him.

Alderson slowly walked through the dining room and drifted toward the staircase. In the shadows of the entry way, he slid off his shoes, removed his overcoat, and quickly tucked the crucifix Raymer had given him under his arm. With her back to him, his wife was unable to see the conspicuous object he had smuggled into their house.

"I'll be up later," she called after him.

Nathan offered no reply.

The hallway he ascended to was dark, but he instinctively made his way to use the bathroom. He then flipped on the light switch to disperse the waiting shadows of the bedroom. He placed the crucifix on the nightstand and fished the tangled mess of silver crosses from his pants' pocket. Glancing over his shoulder to ensure his wife had not quietly followed him up the stairs, he untangled one of the necklaces and slid it over his head. He quickly placed the rest of them under his pillow and tossed the heavier crucifix in the top drawer of the nightstand.

Nathan removed his shirt and pants, carefully folded them, and placed the clothes atop his chest of drawers. Standing in his boxers and socks, he padded back to the entry way, flipped off the light switch, and waited for his eyes to adjust to the familiar gloom. Stumbling back to his side of the bed, he turned down the sheets, and slipped onto the cool, firm mattress.

As Alderson laid on his side, he struggled to fall asleep. His mind continued to race but in time, his body began to relax. He was just on the cusp of sleep when the bedroom door issued a slow, drawn-out creak.

His heavy-lidded eyes opened slowly to the dark. Still on his side, the detective tuned his ears to the quiet. Outside, he could hear the rustling of the leaves as a light wind swept over the trees beyond the bedroom window.

The door swung on its hinges yet again. Ever so slightly, but enough to elicit another strained groan.

It's just a draft. Goddamn house has shitty insulation.
Go to sleep.

Nathan adjusted his lean body along the cushioned mattress top, settling into a more comfortable position. The springs squeaked beneath his weight, and the house fell silent again. With his left hand under his pillow, he could feel the thin cold chains of the crosses curling around his fingers.

A muffled *thump* from beyond the bedroom door caused him to open his eyes to the dark a second time.

He listened carefully but could not place the sound. From far away, he heard tap water running and the sharp sounds of the ceramic teacup and saucer as Kelly rinsed them and placed them in the sink.

Once more, the house went quiet.

And once again, Alderson heard another *thump* somewhere on the upper floor of his house.

Nathan threw back the covers and darted to his feet. His eyes now adjusted to the darkness, he quickly stepped toward the half-open door. A cursory inspection revealed nothing amiss. He stood in the entryway of the bedroom and took a tentative step into the shadowy hallway.

Thump.

The sound had come from his deceased son's bedroom.

With his pulse racing in his ears, Alderson sped down the hallway and hesitated before the door. His heart heavy, he gripped the cold knob, and flung the door open. He slid his hand along the smooth wall until he felt a plastic switch. The room was suddenly flooded with light from a motionless ceiling fan above.

"Nate?" Kelly called out to him from downstairs. "I thought you went to bed?"

He surveyed the room, taking in the crisp, colorful bedspread that tightly conformed to the twin mattress and pair of pillows propped against the headboard.

"Just getting some water," he shouted back. His dry throat was parched, and his voice was unsteady.

He continued to scan the collection of objects neatly positioned around the room. Posters of superheroes and cartoon characters stood out against the white walls. The blank screen of a small TV sat under the window. An Xbox console and a pair of wireless controllers were crammed onto the shelf below. A set of tall white bookcases loomed on each side of the window. Boxes of board games, rows of DVDs, and slim video game cases lined the shelves. Action figures stood poised for battle beside a sleek 1966 Batmobile. He had assembled it for his son from a vintage model-kit only months before he died.

Alderson glanced toward a closet to his left, but it was firmly shut. On the door was a large poster of Spider-Man swinging between a pair of skyscrapers. The maniacal Green Goblin—with explosive pumpkin in hand—pursued him from the rear.

The room was exactly as his wife had left it after she spent a harrowing afternoon cleaning and arranging it less than two months ago.

Nathan took a step backward and was reaching to flip off the light switch when a cluster of small metallic objects caught his eye. On the floor in front of one of the bookcases lay three Matchbox cars. Two were positioned on their roofs, with each of their four wheels facing upward. The third had fallen right-side up.

Alderson cautiously approached the displaced objects as the door slowly swung inward behind him. As he bent to retrieve the cars, he was unable to see the shadowy outline of Charlotte Brennen standing erect in the full-length mirror mounted on the back of Cody Alderson's bedroom door. By the time the heartsick father had stood up with the toys in hand, she had disappeared.

Nathan carefully placed the wayward cars on the shelf from which they had fallen. A cold chill suddenly rippled down his spine, causing him to spin on his heel and look behind him.

Nothing was there.

To Nathan's right, a six-inch Superman figure had fallen backward onto its shelf, prompting the detective to shudder involuntarily. He could discern no reason for the toy to have fallen. He stared at it, the pair of bright red boots pointing to the shelf above, the red fabric cape curling around its blue muscular legs. He couldn't bring himself to touch it.

Alderson hurried out of the room, extinguished the light, and closed the door tightly behind him. With a quaking hand, he reached up to grasp the silver cross dangling from his neck and sped down the hallway back into the darkness of the master bedroom. He approached his side of the bed with caution and sat down on the edge of the mattress. For several minutes he did not stir. The wind had picked up outside the house, and he could hear the leaves as they were driven through the yard below.

The house around him had settled back into silence. Still he waited, listening, anticipating, and dreading any further disturbances. Eventually, he allowed his weary body to fall onto the mattress. Nathan pulled the covers tightly around his shoulder. Soon enough, he fell asleep—clutching the crosses he had placed beneath his pillow.

25

ALDERSON ARRIVED AT VERONICA'S HOUSE JUST AFTER SEVEN the next morning. Raymer greeted him at the front door, once again clad in black. Veronica was already dressed and finishing up a light breakfast in the dining room. Both had already donned silver crosses around their necks. Alderson handed Raymer a small evidence bag containing a piece of the vampire's tattered dress, which he placed within his duffle bag after careful examination.

After loading their respective vehicles, Veronica made a quick stop at the local grocery store. Less than an hour later, they parked their trucks in the clearing near the crossroads. They sorted their weapons and supplies on the tailgate of Alderson's truck. Veronica left the various snacks, protein bars, fruit, aspirin, and first-aid kits within the grocery bags. Each of them brought a heavier jacket, but left their coats in the trucks, trusting that their constant motion would keep away the morning chill.

Raymer opened the hatch and tailgate of his Scout while Veronica and Alderson circled around him. Each of them grabbed a musette bag filled with crucifixes, crosses, rosary beads, communion wafers, and multiple ampules of holy water, as well as a snub-nose .38 revolver—loaded with silver-tipped bullets. Raymer buckled the straps on the first bag and handed it to Veronica.

"That's your .38." Edison pointed to the bag as Veronica glanced inside to check its contents. "I took the liberty of cleaning it and reloading it for you." He then explained there was more holy water and ammunition in his truck. Finally, he pointed to a large carton containing six unopened boxes of communion wafers blessed by Father McCallum, which they would use to cast the protective circles.

After he and Alderson collected their bags, Raymer leaned into the truck and lifted an army poncho. Laid carefully on padded foam was the .303 Enfield rifle and the formidable McMillan TAC-338 sniper rifle. Veronica was taken aback by the latter weapon's night vision scope, bipod, and desert camo paint job. Raymer covered the long rifles again and explained that the .38s in each bag would be sufficient until nightfall.

Alderson clipped his badge to his belt in case they encountered anyone in the woods and were asked to show identification. He withdrew a Mossberg 500 12-gauge shotgun from his truck—not for vampires, he explained, but for any shady locals that might give them trouble. With the 12-gauge in one hand, and a hefty sledgehammer in the other, Alderson was ready to proceed.

"Let's start with the tomb," Raymer directed.

The three of them traversed the slick clearing, wading through tall grass as they made their way to the burial vault. The sky above was overcast, and the fresh morning air was brisk. The wind was low. The woods were alive with the busy sounds of active birds. A train whistle blew far in the distance. The crunch of leaves regulated their pace as the chimneys of the ruined Brennen plantation loomed ahead. Veronica shuddered as she looked upon the brick smokestacks.

With only a preliminary glance at the foundations of the house from several yards away, Alderson led Raymer and Veronica across the field to the vine-wrapped mausoleum at the edge of the next clearing. Once they stood before the entrance to the worn structure, Raymer stepped in front of them and gestured for Alderson and Veronica to stay behind him. He withdrew a crucifix from his shoulder bag.

"Be ready for anything," he whispered as he crept toward the rusted door. The interior of the tomb was dark, but his trained eye could penetrate the gloom. Alderson aimed a heavy flashlight over Raymer's shoulder, but Edison quickly turned and shook his head, prompting the detective to switch off the light. Raymer continued to step forward until he stood at the center of the mausoleum.

He quickly scanned each of the vaults to his right and left, then reached into his pocket for his own penlight and examined the narrow crypts to confirm they were empty. His eyes were drawn to the sealed placard to his lower left: WILLIAM BRENNEN, BELOVED SON, 1851–1854. With the crucifix still in his right hand, he squatted down in front of the face-plate and held up his left hand. He splayed his fingers wide to test for any cold drafts emanating from the vault. Certain the vampire was not resting within the tomb, Raymer emerged from the musty structure and nodded to his companions.

"I think it's clear," he said. "But let's leave no room for error."

Alderson passed his shotgun to Raymer and stepped into the mausoleum. He gripped the heavy sledgehammer in his hands. With his back to the portal, Alderson bent his knees, swung his arms, and brought the blunt instrument crashing against the oxidized plaque. With one blow the seal was shattered. He quickly stepped back into the light of day in anticipation of what might emerge from the vault.

There was only silence.

Fishing through his shoulder bag, Raymer re-entered the tomb. He withdrew a handful of hosts and crumbled them in his fists before blowing the consecrated powder into each of the eight vaults. He then crumbled more wafers to draw heavier lines at the mouth of each of the slotted crypts.

After dusting the chalky residue from his hands, he reached into the musette bag for a vial of holy water. He uncapped the small ampule and began tracing the sign of the cross. Thin streams of blessed water splashed the interior walls of the tomb. As before, he moved from each slot to the next, consecrating them with the purifying water.

Finally, he withdrew a small hammer and dug through his shoulder bag in search of a packet of carpenter's nails. He drove a single nail above each of the eight slots, from which he suspended a silver cross or crucifix. He then tossed handfuls of plastic rosaries into each of the vaults.

Veronica stood watching from outside the structure. As Raymer emerged, he beckoned for her to inspect the tomb for herself. She shook her head and turned away, her arms still tightly folded against her breasts.

"As I suspected, the boy's tomb was empty," Raymer said. "All I could see inside were traces of sand and a couple rusted hinges. She probably weighed down the coffins with sandbags before burying the bodies at the crossroads."

Alderson peeked into the shadowy mausoleum to admire Raymer's handiwork. Veronica stepped forward to address her colleague as he stood with his eyes already scoping the ruins of the plantation house.

She pointed a thumb back to the burial vault. "Do you think she was using that place as a sanctuary?"

"Honestly, no, I don't think so," Raymer said. "But she won't want to take refuge in there now. I've made it completely uninhabitable to her."

Alderson caught up with them. "Can't she just reach in there and pull all those rosaries out? Or tear all the crosses down?"

"Possibly," Raymer shrugged. "But she'll be significantly burned in the process."

"What about the holy water? Won't it dry up?" Alderson pressed. "Isn't all that wafer dust just gonna blow away."

"She'll be dead by the time that happens," Raymer asserted, his dark eyes malicious and determined. "Now let's go check out the house."

Veronica and Alderson trailed behind Raymer as he walked toward the ruins of the Brennen plantation. He signaled for Alderson to go left while he scanned the foundations to the right. Veronica lifted her head to study the leaning chimneys. A cold feeling washed over her as she stood gazing upon the decaying grounds where the vampire had once lived. An empty, weed-choked shell of its former glory, the colossal structure still possessed an ominous aura of dread.

Alderson and Raymer each circled the perimeter of the house twice but found nothing out of the ordinary. Raymer made a pass through the overgrown interior—liberally splashing streams of holy water on the unhallowed grounds. He returned moments later convinced the house warranted no further investigation.

Edison led them back to his Scout, where he produced three e-tools from the truck bed. Alderson tossed his sledgehammer into his truck and took up one of the compact shovels from Raymer. Veronica wrinkled her brow as she accepted the light-weight instrument from her partner. "What's this?"

"It's called an e-tool, or entrenching tool," Raymer explained. "Less cumbersome than a regular shovel. It's also collapsible for easy carry and storage."

"So, what are we gonna do with these?" she asked.

"We're going to split up and scour these woods." Raymer gestured to the forest surrounding them before he turned back to Alderson. "Nate, since it's less of an issue if someone spots you, check out all the paths leading down to the school. Then make a few passes through that section of the forest."

Alderson nodded, his hands clasping the e-tool and 12-gauge. The detective's steely eyes betrayed his eagerness to continue the hunt.

"Where do you want me to go?" Veronica asked.

"Stick around here and cover those two trails. Look for any loose or freshly turned soil. Don't wander too far from the trucks. If you see anything out of the ordinary, call me on my cell. It seems like we still get decent reception here. I'm going to head down to the riverbank." He glanced at his wristwatch. "Let's meet back here in no more than two hours."

Each of the three hunters went their separate ways. With the e-tool tucked under his arm, Raymer stood for a moment at the mouth of the path leading down to the river. He placed the crucifix in the partially unzipped musette bag, checked the .38, and began to walk.

Taking long strides, he descended the path quickly, passing under the canopy of oaks and river birches. Most of the trees still retained a fair portion of their leaves. As he scanned his surroundings, the brilliant yellows and rusty oranges against the gray sky above was striking. But Raymer could only think of how these dense thickets would transform at nightfall, and how the seemingly endless acres of woodland provided the vampire with too many places to hide.

Before long Edison's heavy boots began to sink into the marshland, and the river stretched out before him. To his right was the area he had assigned to Alderson, so he headed left, away from the Williamsport city line.

After choosing his direction, Raymer walked along the river's muddy edge for nearly thirty minutes before he began to slow his pace. He gripped the compact shovel, his fingers wrapped tightly around the handle. As he crossed the terrain, he kept his head bent to examine the ground, looking for any signs that the earth had been disturbed. McCallum's words played through his mind.

"They don't need to breathe, Edison. The riverbanks are soft and easy ground for them to burrow under and rest undisturbed."

Raymer let his eyes study the imposing waters of the James River. Daunted by its width, concerned with its depth, and utterly crushed when he considered its length, Raymer began to feel as though the task of finding the vampire this way was hopeless.

She could be bedding down somewhere in the middle of the river. But where?

He continued to walk, looking for footprints—bare footprints—to indicate any place where she may have waded into the waters.

It's not like there was going to be a neon sign with an arrow pointing to her grave. "Here lies Charlotte Brennen."

You're a hunter. Now hunt.

Raymer wished he had more time to observe and track his prey. He wondered if he was skilled enough to follow the Brennen vampire through the woods, and trail her to one of her resting places. With enough practiced stealth, could he remain hidden? Or would she inevitably sense that he was behind her?

Raymer grew more frustrated with each step he took. By now he had likely traversed two miles of riverbank. He glanced at his watch and decided to press forward. The wind began to pick up, skimming across the rippling surface of the James. It was at least five degrees colder this close to the river. His eyes momentarily stung but the wind eventually died down.

The riverbank had narrowed for some time now, so he was careful where he stepped. His boots were soaked through and caked with mud. A slight bend in the river ahead caused the bank to widen once more. He turned to his left and his pulse quickened to see a dilapidated shack with a rusted metal roof. It looked like an old tobacco curing barn and was nestled within a copse of river birches. Through the tall reeds and cat tails of the marsh, he spied a haphazard bridge crafted from rotting duckboards.

I've got you now.

Raymer slowed his pace and carefully crossed the marsh, following the boards onto dry land. As he crept up the slope toward the old shed, he reached for the .38 and brought it to bear in his right hand. His left hand gripped the e-tool like a makeshift club. The leaves were especially thick around the foundations of the shack, but nonetheless, he probed the ground with the collapsible shovel. After a thorough inspection, he turned up no sign of the vampire's presence.

He stopped, took a breath, and used the head of the e-tool to pry open the barn doors. As daylight flooded the ramshackle building, a strong animal stench overpowered him. His pulse quickened and his grip on the pistol tightened. As he checked the corners, he noticed patches of fur among the dried bloodstains on the floor. Piles of antlers and bones were stacked against the wall. A frayed rope hung from the exposed rafters. He realized that local hunters had been using the shack to field dress deer.

He scowled as he surveyed the old floorboards. He probed a few with the heel of his boot, and all of them seemed to be loose and dry rotted. Raymer pointed the pistol at the floor and brought the e-tool down with his left hand. The board splintered easily.

Dropping to his knees, he set the pistol aside and used the sharp end of the shovel to pry up as many boards as possible. He bent forward to examine the crawlspace beneath the shack. After a cursory inspection with his unaided eye, he withdrew his penlight to scan beneath the floorboards. He found nothing but flattened, hard-packed soil.

Edison re-emerged from the shack, eager to breathe in the fresh open air. A sheen of sweat covered his smooth brow. A feeling of defeat clung to him worse than the stink of the hunter's den. He slipped the pistol into his bag and scraped the edges of his e-tool against the barn door to clean it. Coarse, matted fur and dirt fell to the ground.

He looked at his watch. Considering the time it would take him to retrace his steps, Raymer decided it was best to head back. With the wind at his back and frustration spurring him forward, he was climbing the semi-steep hill to reach the crossroads in a little less than an hour.

Alderson and Veronica had already returned from their respective walks. Nate stood with a bottle of water in hand while Veronica sat smoking with her legs dangling over the side of the tailgate.

"Any luck?" Raymer called out, slightly winded from his ascent up the gradual hill.

"Nothing," Alderson replied. Veronica shook her head and exhaled a plume of bluish smoke. "But I do have some good news," the detective said.

Nathan beckoned for Raymer to follow him around to the passenger side of his truck cab. He opened the door to reveal the .44 magnum resting on the dashboard.

"I found it near the edge of the clearing. It needs a thorough cleaning, but I can handle that."

"Good work," Raymer replied. "I've got the cleaning kit in my truck. But before we do that, did you happen to bring any more evidence bags with you?"

"Sure," Alderson noted. "There should be a few in my glove compartment. Why? What do you need them for?"

"In case we need to resort to plan B," Raymer said cryptically. He gestured for Veronica to join them before he continued. "Let's look over the area where we tackled her the other night. See if we can find any more scraps of her dress. Fingernails, strands of hair, hell, if anything's left of her fingers that the animals haven't dragged away since we were here."

Veronica grimaced but accepted the gruesome task. Alderson returned from his truck and handed each of them an evidence bag. They spent the next half hour collecting anything left behind by the vampire. Between the three of them, they bagged a strand of hair knotted around a twig, a few more scraps of her dress, a shattered metacarpal bone clotted with blackened gore, and a splintered fingernail. Raymer also gathered a handful of soil from one of the vampire's footprints.

"Christ," Veronica said, as she continued to scour the underbrush for further evidence. "Do you think she's been wearing the same dress all these years? It looked like the same mourning gown from the daguerreotypes."

"Who the hell knows?" Alderson answered. "It sure as fuck *smelled* like it."

Their musings were soon interrupted by Raymer. "Alright, let's get moving on those circles." He paced heel-to-toe and came to a stop halfway into the clearing. He used his foot to carve an X in the soil. "Nathan, get everything you need from the trucks and hustle back up here."

Having collected the evidence bags, Raymer handed them to Veronica and told her to put them in his gym bag with the original scrap of evidence Alderson had given him earlier that morning. Before she walked away, he also asked her to bring the boxes of communion wafers from the truck.

In a few minutes, they rejoined Raymer at the center of the clearing. With the Enfield rifle slung over his shoulder, Alderson carried the dirty .44 Magnum and a gun cleaning kit in his free hands. His musette bag rested against his hip. Raymer instructed him to sit on the ground where he had made the mark.

Raymer then etched two additional marks behind the detective's position. He instructed Veronica to start casting a large circle around Alderson. She unzipped the bag, tore open a box of wafers, and began to crumble them in her fists.

"Nate," Raymer called out. "I'm coming back with the bag of provisions and will give you enough food and water to last the night. Is there anything else you need?"

"No," Alderson replied.

"Once she closes that circle, you're in it 'til dawn," Raymer reminded him.

After a moment's hesitation, Alderson placed the .44 on the ground, stood, and wandered toward the tree line to empty his bladder. Veronica kept working on the circle as Raymer headed for the Scout. He made multiple trips until he returned with his rifle and poncho. Raymer then paced behind Alderson's circle and made two marks in the dirt.

Once Veronica finished casting the circle around Nathan, Raymer set the rifle down on the X he had furrowed to the detective's rear left, closest to the trucks. He then returned to one of the bags he had fetched and carried extra crosses, a bag loaded with a hammer and several stakes, and charger clips with silver-tipped ammunition for the .303 to Alderson.

When Raymer looked up, Veronica caught his attention and pointed to the right rear X. "Is this where you want me?"

"Yes, so put everything you need on or around that mark and come over here."

She did as he instructed, stocking up on bottled water, trail mix, and protein bars. She also placed her coat, purse, and her own bag of holy weapons to be bound within the circle. When she returned, Raymer reached into a gym bag and handed her a pair of dual-tube, high-resolution night vision binoculars attached to a head harness. He helped her put the apparatus on and clipped the final strap under her chin. "Now, here's all you have to do to disengage the goggles."

The expensive binoculars were mounted on a locking swivel, and Raymer showed Veronica how to swing them upwards away from her eyes, lock them in place, and return them into position. Once she was used to them, she pushed the binoculars upwards and heard them click into place.

"I bet I look ridiculous."

"You don't," Raymer replied. "And, tactically, you have the most important job here. You're our spotter."

"What do you want me to do?"

Raymer explained that Veronica would need to keep constant watch around their position. Although he hoped the vampire would arrive from the same direction as their previous encounter with her, Veronica was to alert them if it attempted to switch its angle of approach.

Raymer beckoned Veronica to follow him to his designated spot, where he laid on the ground and began sighting the sniper rifle. "All that's left now is for you to make a circle around me and finish up with your own. Then, we wait until nightfall."

Veronica began to crumble the wafers as Edison retrieved another large bag and his army poncho. He resumed his prone position, draped the poncho over himself, and removed a bottle of water from the bag. As he opened it, Veronica bent forward and began sprinkling the powdered dust around him.

"Well, it looks like you covered all our bases here, Edison." Veronica stepped to her left and drew another portion of the circle. "I'd say we definitely have the advantage over her this time. Hell, we're even better prepared than when we took down Bartsch."

At the mention of the German vampire's name, Alderson turned in his circle to face them.

"There was nothing slipshod about our fight with Bartsch and Laura," Raymer said. "We hit them with everything we had and as quickly as we could. Keep in mind, Matthias was a trained soldier who fought for one of the most ruthless and disciplined armies in history. Also, both of our opponents were armed. We had the element of surprise, and—"

"No. We got lucky." With a fist full of hosts still in her hand, she stepped back to face him. "The only reason that went half as well as it did was because we sucker punched them."

Raymer glanced up to study her changing expression. He withheld his reply as he sensed Veronica had more to say.

"Look, I've gotta ask. Do you feel *any* remorse for what happened to Junior and Laura?"

Raymer resumed checking the sights on the rifle. "Junior was an old man who lived a full life. He knew exactly what he was getting into. I'd venture to say the death of Bartsch was a victory for him. He found his peace."

"I wouldn't be so sure of that. We dumped his body in a hole in the middle of the woods!" She gestured wildly behind her. "Probably not too far from where we are now if I have my bearings right."

"Look." Raymer lifted his dark eyes to her. "I didn't want the man to die."

"Well, I think he still had a few more years left in him. It's a goddamn shame." Veronica placed her right hand on her hip, leaving a white smudge from the hosts. "So, what about Laura? She was one of your students. You knew her for years, and what's worse, she looked up to you. Trusted you."

Raymer sighed and considered his response. "Obviously, that wasn't the way I wanted things to go down. But again, like Luttrell, she knew what she was getting into. I briefed her on the whole thing over the phone and she insisted on coming down from the Annandale Institute."

"How could she have really known what she was getting into? She probably thought you were full of shit and came down here just to see so for herself."

"Either way, once Bartsch got ahold of her, she seemed to take pretty quickly to her new lifestyle. She could have gotten away from him and come back to us. But she never did."

"Presuming she *could* have gotten away," Veronica corrected him. "Even if she did, she was probably afraid to come back and figured you'd kill her on the spot. You were pretty goddamned cruel about the whole thing."

"You're right, I would have killed her," Raymer admitted. "But it wouldn't have been out of spite. I would've been doing her a favor. Sparing her from what could have been an eternity of guilt. Last but not least, you need to stop and think of all the lives we saved by taking her and Bartsch down." He finally took a long swig of water from the plastic bottle.

Veronica wanted to say more but decided any further discussion was a waste of valuable time. She silently finished forming the consecrated circle around Raymer, then went to her own position and began to break up more wafers. Alderson sat quietly and began his task of cleaning the .44 pistol. Within twenty minutes, all three of them were sealed within their strategic positions and protective circles.

"Not much longer now." Alderson lifted his eyes to the darkening sky. He stood, dropped the cleaning kit, and shoved the .44 into his waistband. Raymer adjusted the night-vision scope mounted on this sniper rifle one last time, while Veronica used a half-empty bottle of water to clean the grime from her hands.

Above them, the hazy gray sun that had followed them all afternoon had disappeared. Heavy clouds began to roll faster along the dark purple horizon. The wind picked up and sent dead leaves and stray powder from the circles whirling around them. Flushed with fear and adrenaline, night had at last fallen and they awaited the arrival of their enemy.

26

MORE THAN TWO UNEVENTFUL HOURS PASSED WHILE THE hunters sat within their protective circles. Veronica had already burned through half a pack of cigarettes while acclimating herself to the night-vision goggles. She was unsettled by how otherworldly the forest looked through the green-tinted lenses. Holding the .303 steady, Alderson paced within the confines of his circle, and kept his eyes trained on the woods surrounding them. Meanwhile, Raymer studied the terrain through the scope of his high-powered rifle, on alert and ready for attack.

Lost in their own private and anxiety-ridden thoughts, time passed quickly for the band of hunters. Conversation was minimal, and the forest hypnotized them with its persistent, heavy silence. The plastic grocery bag of provisions Veronica kept at her side occasionally flapped in the breeze, causing her to stir at the irritating sound.

It was close to midnight when a twig snapped in the distance. A rustle of leaves and a pair of louder cracks to their right triggered adrenaline to rush through their veins.

"Get ready," Raymer whispered. He slithered forward to adjust his position against the cold ground. Edison tightened his grip on the stock of the rifle and scanned the perimeter of the trees before him.

Now on her feet and already short of breath, Veronica quickly spun in the direction of the sound. "I don't see anything."

Alderson was poised with the .303's rear stock cinched into the hollow of his shoulder. With the tendons of his forearms taut and his finger indexing the rifle's trigger, he prepared to fire.

Another swish of leaves indicated that something large was quickly approaching them several yards ahead, to their right. Her chest tight with anticipation, Veronica strained to discern any sign of their enemy. Her heart pounded as she expected to see the tall, shadowy form of Charlotte Brennen sneaking through the woods.

"Do you feel it?" Raymer called out, his voice strained and hissing between his teeth. "That chill from the other night?"

Alderson continued to aim at the yawning path directly ahead of him. "No," he replied, his eyes locked on the shadows.

"Veronica?"

"What!"

"Do you feel her?"

"I don't... I don't think so," she stammered.

Another loud crack caused each of them to shiver involuntarily. Raymer clenched his left eye. At last he saw movement in his crosshairs. Through the rifle's night-vision scope, he could see a shadowy shape moving through the thickets. As it drew closer, Raymer recognized the glowing, seemingly phosphorescent eyes of a skittish deer leaping toward the path.

"False alarm," he muttered.

Veronica gasped in relief as the powder-brown doe darted past them. Alderson lowered the Enfield rifle with disappointment.

"Don't let your guard down," Raymer called out. "Something down by the river may have spooked that deer to make its way up here."

Veronica was quick to readjust her goggles. She continued scanning the tall grass, swaying pines, and birches enveloping them on all sides. Several minutes passed as the forest once again settled into silence.

Alderson remained on guard, his back to Raymer and Veronica as he stood firm at the edge of his circle.

Veronica waited and eventually lowered herself back to the ground. Poised on her knees, she reached into her purse for her pack of cigarettes. With an unsteady hand, she cupped the smoke dangling from her lips and repeatedly flicked the small plastic lighter. A heavy gust of wind suddenly swept through the forest. After several unsuccessful attempts, she finally managed to ignite the tip of her cigarette. She inhaled the sharp smoke into her lungs and exhaled heavily, her fingers cold and still shaking.

Veronica settled back down into her circle and savored the comfort of her cigarette. To keep himself agile, Alderson ran through a series of bends and stretches. He continued to pace to keep his blood flowing, while Edison retained his prone position. The disciplined hunter was entirely subsumed by his surroundings.

The wind picked up, whipping past Veronica's face with a high-pitched moan. Her hair was tousled wildly and became tangled in the straps of her headset. The professor pulled the stray locks free and took another drag on her cigarette. With her knees drawn up, she watched as the wind began to disturb a portion of the protective circle. Through the enhanced vision of her goggles, she could see fine white granules of powder forced away from the rigid curve, dispersing upward into the air around her.

"The wind is starting to fuck up my circle," she warned her partners. She quickly snuffed her cigarette on the ground and flicked the butt away. "Are you guys OK?"

"Yeah." Alderson glanced down to see that his circle was still intact. "Raymer?"

"Fine."

With her night-vision goggles now disengaged and locked upwards, Veronica reached into the musette bag and withdrew a few more wafers. After crumbling them in her fists, she crawled forward to reinforce the breach in the circle.

In a low voice, Raymer addressed Veronica. "Keep those goggles down."

"Sorry," she said and snapped them back into place. "I was fixing the circle." She turned her attention back to Alderson. "You sure you don't need to check yours?"

"Don't worry about it," he called back over his shoulder.

Now sitting, Veronica brushed the residue from the hosts on her knees and smoked another cigarette. Alderson squatted down in his circle for some time before the tension in his leg muscles forced him to sit down.

The wind rustled the poncho spread over Raymer's back. He reached up to reposition it and continued to stare ahead. Each of them fell back into the quiet rhythm of the woods—but there was no sign of their target.

The night was now alive with the sounds of the trees swaying above, behind, and beyond them. The tall narrow trunks bent with the persistent breeze. The air had grown much colder and sharper, prompting Veronica to reach for her wool coat. She stood against another barrage of wind, pulled the coat around her, and quickly fastened the buttons with ice-cold hands.

Alderson was up and pacing again to ward off the chill. Before long, he also bent down to snatch up his camouflage hunting jacket. He swung the coat over his shoulders, slid his arms through the padded sleeves, and zipped it halfway up his chest. The wind whipped through his blond-red hair and caused his eyes to dry up.

Raymer steeled himself against the cold and looked at his watch. "It's almost one AM," he announced.

"Christ," Alderson cursed. "Where the fuck is she?"

"I don't know," Raymer replied. "But it can't be much longer now. She showed up pretty late the last time. We just need to be patient."

"We've been here all day and night!" Alderson shouted over his shoulder. "I'm running out of patience."

"We got here a lot later that night," Veronica reminded them. "I guess that made it seem like things happened faster."

Raymer grimaced and pushed himself up on his elbows. "She's biding her time. Waiting for us to drop our guard. Stay sharp. I go through this every time I hunt these things in the wild."

With their eyes fixed ahead, the monotony was disrupted by a foghorn blowing in the distance. The mournful sound had reached them from some unseen ship cruising on the wide river. Not long after, Raymer thought he heard the hooting of an owl. Veronica noticed it as well and tried to detect the bird through her night-vision goggles. Its low trill continued for another twenty minutes before it moved out of ear shot.

Veronica lit another cigarette, hoping to distract herself from not only the cold, but from the pressure building up in her bladder. She jumped slightly when Nathan's voice called out to her. "You wanna toss me a candy bar or something?"

"Sure." She dug through the grocery bag and sorted through its contents. "We've got a couple granola bars, a few packages of peanut butter crackers, a Snickers. Uh, let's see, what else?"

"Whatever." Alderson huffed and pushed himself up off the ground. "The Snickers sounds fine." The detective approached the edge of the circle with his hands out to receive the candy bar. Veronica softly pitched it to him and was surprised when Nate caught it on the first try.

"Well, how 'bout that," she muttered to herself. She withdrew a red apple from the bag and decided the sugar would do her well. "You need anything, Edison?"

"I'm good," he replied. He reached into his own small bag of provisions and unwrapped a granola bar. "Just stay alert, people."

Veronica spent the next several minutes preoccupied with her apple. The light snack only proved to intensify the hunger pangs she had so far managed to ignore. She tossed the core into the high brush and took a sip from her bottle of water. Veronica drank sparingly, hoping to delay the need to relieve herself. Although the night-vision apparatus was relatively light, her neck began to hurt from the unfamiliar weight. The cold was also doing no favors to her aching joints. Wishing she had brought a pair of gloves, Veronica blew into her hands but her fingers remained numb. She lit another cigarette, having now smoked nearly an entire pack of Marlboro Lights since early that morning.

The trio lapsed into another dull silence. The combination of cold air and adrenaline kept them awake, but their extended vigil was beginning to take its toll. Raymer maintained his covert position, his wounded forearm pressed into the earth. His hands tingled from the lack of circulation, and he knew he'd have to stand soon and walk off some of the stiffness.

The smell of woodsmoke from houses across the river and near the school had drifted up to them. Veronica adjusted the magnification of the binoculars. Through the green haze, she could discern pinpricks of light as she glanced toward the distant river.

It was Alderson who broke the long period of steady silence. "Do we really have to stay in these circles all night?"

Raymer breathed heavily through his nose and fought the urge to roll his eyes. "Yes. I'd think that would be abundantly clear after what happened here last time."

"Yeah, but why can't we just get back in if we see her coming?" Alderson persisted.

"Because we might *not* see her coming," Edison replied. "And as I'm sure Veronica can explain just as well as I, the circles must remain unbroken *if* they are to provide us protection against her."

"OK, but seriously, I've seen fucking vampire movies." Nathan strode from one edge of his circle to the next. "You already told us some of that shit wasn't true. So how do we know this isn't just another myth?"

Raymer scoffed. "The evidence is clear from Tuesday night. She *did not* cross the circle. She never once breached it, even though she repeatedly tried. If it didn't work, Nate, we'd all be dead."

"Well, *you* left the circle!"

"Because I was desperate," Raymer reminded him. "And I had no other choice if I wanted to save *you* and Veronica."

"Save me?" Alderson was livid. "Oh, I see how it is!"

"Look, if you want to leave your circle, be my guest." Raymer called back in a cold, even tone. "See what happens."

"That's enough!" Veronica shouted. "Nate, what the hell's gotten into you? You know the deal with the circles. Christ, I'm either gonna piss my pants soon or you two are about to witness a very unpleasant peep show. Staying put is a pain in the ass, but we have to!"

"Fuck this," Alderson said. "I'm willing to lure her out at this point. If that's what it takes. We've been sitting here doing nothing for what... *eight* hours?"

"Nathan, I strongly advise against that half-assed strategy," Raymer responded. "We're getting closer to the time she appeared the other night, and I need you on point. Please, settle down and be patient."

As if on cue, the wind tore through the trees. The grocery bag next to Veronica slid toward the edge of her circle. The harried professor quickly reached out and slammed her fist against the bag to keep it from drifting further.

Raymer glanced up at the sky and noticed dense, heavy clouds moving rapidly above the unsettled trees.

"Was that a rain drop?" Veronica called out.

"No, no, no!" Alderson kicked the duffle bag of weapons beside his booted foot.

All at once, a steady drizzle began to fall.

"You gotta be fucking kidding me!" Nathan shouted.

"Stay put!" Raymer yelled. "A little rain isn't going to hurt us. Christ, Nathan. I thought you were an outdoorsman. Act like it!"

"I swear to God, Raymer. Don't push me right now."

"Cool it! Both of you!" Veronica interjected. "Just tell me one thing, Edison. You came up here with every weapon and provision under the sun. *Please* tell me one of you checked the goddamn weather app on your phones."

"My phone's broken," Nathan shouted. "Raymer? How about you? Did you think to check the weather this morning?"

"No," he answered. The drizzle turned into a cold, steady shower of rain. "Although, it wouldn't have deterred me from coming out here. It'll pass."

"You'd better fucking hope it does!" Alderson was already drenched. His hair was plastered against his forehead.

Veronica staggered to her feet and pulled her coat close. She turned the collar up, but the cold rain slid down her neck and back. The lenses of the goggles had fogged up, and she tried to wipe them down with the cuff of her peacoat. With her head bent to keep the rain from her face, she paused to take stock of the ground at her feet. What she saw made her heart sink.

"The fucking rain is washing away my circle!"

"This is ridiculous!" Alderson cried out. "We need to bail. She's not gonna show up in this."

"Don't move!" Raymer replied. "This is *exactly* the kind of distraction she may have been waiting for!"

"It's freezing, Edison," Veronica whined. "It's not going to do us any good to catch fucking pneumonia out here."

"I said stay put!"

Soon enough, the rain was coming down in torrents and was already puddling on the muddy surface of the forest. It had completely dissolved the outer edge of Veronica's circle and the perimeter of Alderson's was no longer visible.

Veronica turned and estimated there was roughly a hundred yards between where she stood and the pair of parked trucks. She bent down, grabbed her purse, and picked up the soaked bag of snacks.

"I'm gonna make a run for it!" she called out against the raging storm.

"Don't!" Raymer roared. "Don't fucking do it, Veronica!"

She was poised to break into a run when she felt a strong arm curl around her waist. Veronica screamed as Alderson clasped her and led her toward the trucks. Caught off guard, she stumbled alongside him and almost planted her face into the ground. Nathan prevented her fall and guided her forward. Before long, she found herself grasping at the door handle of Alderson's truck. Winded from the mad dash for cover, Veronica slumped inside the empty cab.

Soaking wet, she slammed her fingers against the armrest to lock the door and groaned when she remembered the truck wasn't running. She flinched as the driver's side door flung open and Nathan slid behind the wheel.

"You OK?" Nathan propped the Enfield rifle against his seat. He quickly rubbed his face on the back of his coat sleeve and pushed his hair back from his eyes.

"Yeah. Thanks for the assist." Veronica was a little winded and terribly uncomfortable in her drenched clothes. "Will you please help get these goddamn goggles off of my head?"

After sliding the key into the steering column, Alderson revved the engine to activate the windshield wipers. The heater and defroster also came to life. He punched the small light embedded in the roof of the cab so he could better see the cumbersome apparatus Raymer had strapped to Veronica's head. After a few false starts, Alderson removed the goggles and placed them on the dashboard.

"Thank you." Veronica rolled her wet head from side to side.

A loud metallic clanging caused them to jump. Something loud and heavy had just been tossed into the back of the truck beside them. Nathan glanced into his rear-view mirror to see the silhouette of Edison Raymer jogging back to his circle.

"Christ," the detective muttered and slapped his hand against the steering wheel. After a minute passed, he craned his neck to watch Raymer struggling to slide the TAC-338 into the rear of the Scout. Alderson turned to Veronica. "I can't leave him out there by himself. I'll be right back."

Alderson flung open the door and leapt into the rain, which was pouring down in heavy sheets. The squall made it nearly impossible to see. "Raymer!" He cupped his hands around his mouth to help project his voice.

"Get back in your truck!" Edison commanded. He swung his arms and tossed another heavy gym bag into the rear of the Scout.

"Did you get everything?" Alderson yelled out over the furious storm.

"I said get back in your fucking truck!"

Alderson fumbled for the chrome handle, flopped back into his seat, and slammed the door shut. "Asshole!"

Veronica sat still, afraid to say anything that would further enrage the detective. The rain hammered on the roof of the cab. The windshield wipers swept back and forth as water ran in thick waves over the windows. Behind his gun rack, the rear window was completely fogged up.

To his left, Alderson saw a short flash through the blurred window. The dome light of Raymer's cab had briefly lit up. It fell dark again after the sound of a slamming door. Alderson lowered his power window and called out to the man parked beside him.

"So what do we do now?"

After a moment, Raymer leaned across the seat to wind down his passenger-side window. "What'd you say?"

"I said what do we do now?"

"We wait and see if she shows up," Raymer shouted back. "It won't be dawn for at least four more hours."

"Are you serious?" Veronica called out from beside Alderson. "This is a bust, Raymer. She's not gonna show!"

"I'm not leaving!" he yelled back. "You two can do whatever you want!"

He quickly rolled his window back up and turned on his truck. Alderson was confused when he heard the Scout's tires sputtering in the mud.

Raymer recklessly backed up his vehicle and swung it around to face the dark woods, as if to resume his vigil.

With a sigh, Alderson followed suit, and maneuvered his truck alongside the rusty Scout. He engaged the parking brake with a trembling hand.

"Just let him calm down," Veronica said. "He's the most stubborn son of a bitch I've ever met. Although I gotta say, you give him a run for second place."

"What the hell did I do?"

"I was kidding, Nate." Veronica began picking at the thin plastic enclosing another box of Marlboros. She finally managed to open the slippery box and had a cigarette lit moments later. "This whole fucking night was a waste."

Alderson stared forward through the blurry windshield. The forest ahead was completely obscured by the unrelenting rain. The heat seeping out of the vents offered some comfort but made their eyes heavy. On the dashboard, the digital display revealed it was 3:06 in the morning.

"I'm not sitting here 'til sunrise." Alderson gripped the steering wheel. Veronica withdrew her lighter and another cigarette and handed them to Nathan. The detective accepted the professor's offering, immediately lit it, and savored the burning deep within his lungs. He felt mild relief as he blew out the heavy smoke.

About twenty minutes later, Raymer flashed his penlight and signaled for Alderson to power down his window.

"I can't see shit," Nathan shouted before Raymer could address him.

"Neither can I."

"So, are we coming back tomorrow night?"

"No," Raymer said. "She called our bluff. If she's not gonna come to us, then I'll make her come to me. I'm heading home to start the binding ritual. Right now."

Alderson clenched his jaw. "What are we supposed to do in the meantime?"

"You two go home. You've both done your part—the rest is up to me. I know what I'm doing, and I don't have any time to waste." He began to crank up his window when Alderson called out to stop him.

"No way!" he shouted. His elbow was getting soaked resting on the door frame. "I'm not sitting around again so—"

"We don't have time to argue!" Raymer yelled. "Now do as I say and wait 'til you hear from me."

"Do you at least want these weapons back?"

"Sure. Fine. Whatever," he replied. Alderson passed the .303 to Raymer through the open window, followed by the .44 and the night-vision goggles.

Before he wound up his window, Edison offered one final warning. "Remember what I said, stay home. Lay low the next few days. Keep up appearances with your wife. Go to work and be seen. Once I get the information I need from the ritual, we will need to act quickly. So, get your phone replaced so that Veronica and I can contact you."

With that, Raymer rolled up his window and began driving down the trail. Nathan released the brake and followed. Once they emerged from the woods, he turned onto Route 619, following Raymer's lead. The pair of trucks parted ways at the intersection of Route 10.

Veronica brushed a strand of slick hair away from her eyes. Nathan broke the silence as he pushed his boot down on the gas pedal. "Do you know anything about this ritual or whatever he's talking about?"

"A little," she replied and leaned against the damp armrest of the passenger door. "Basically, he's going to use magic to force the vampire to reveal its resting place."

"And then what?"

"Then *we* go to that location—presumably by day—and destroy her while she's vulnerable."

Alderson frowned and slowed to obey a red light. "Do you think this'll work?" The light turned green and bathed his countenance in an eerie glow.

Veronica shifted in her seat and stared ahead as the truck continued along the empty road. "I hope so. I mean, in theory, it's actually pretty goddamn smart. But there are many variables."

"Such as?" Alderson activated his signal and turned down a residential street.

"Well, *proper* preparation for a binding ritual takes a long time. So, the efficacy of the ritual may be compromised if Raymer doesn't adhere to it by the letter."

"Great." Alderson made another turn and inched toward the professor's driveway.

"However, as Raymer implied before, the ritual doesn't necessarily *have* to follow a formal procedure. In fact, it may be more powerful if he imagines and directs it himself."

"Does he actually know what he's doing?"

Veronica paused. "Yeah, I think he knows enough to be dangerous. Like I said, that stubborn streak of his'll go a long way here. But there are other complications beyond just the formality of the ritual itself."

"Like what?" Alderson threw the truck into park and cut his lights.

"For starters, I doubt she's going to give us GPS co-ordinates to her grave or hideout or whatever," Veronica replied. "If we don't find it fast enough, she could move to another location, and then Raymer would have to repeat the ritual all over again. But hopefully, if he manages to force her to reveal *multiple* hiding places, we might be able to level the playing field somewhat."

"This is ridiculous." Alderson shook his head. "Not to mention hopeless."

"Yeah, well, unless we sit out in the woods every night until she shows up, we really don't have another choice."

"Sorry, but I don't agree with that." Alderson leveled a frustrated look to Veronica. "Why the hell wouldn't she be out there tonight? Or tomorrow night? We have, or rather *had,* all that ammunition. Why can't we just try again and lure her out somehow?"

"She might've gone to ground, Nate." The exhausted professor shrugged. "And if that's the case, it could be weeks, months—fuck, even *years*—before she returns. But if she *has* gone into hibernation, and Raymer times the ritual right, he'll be able to learn of the location in the day. We can strike *before* she wakes or moves to another spot."

"That sounds pretty fucking convoluted," he said, drumming his fingers against the steering wheel.

"It is," she said, "but this shit doesn't always lend itself to logic. We're dealing with vampires and black magic. Most of what we think we know goes out the goddamn window when the supernatural enters the equation."

"How long do you think it'll be before we hear from him?"

"I don't know," she admitted. "Maybe a few days? But one thing is for certain, and you have to *promise* me, Nathan."

"What?"

"Do not go back out there alone."

Alderson exhaled heavily and didn't answer.

"Promise me," she repeated. "In the name of your wife and son. I'm begging you. Don't do it."

"Fine."

"Get some sleep," she advised him. "If you go anywhere, make damn sure you're home before nightfall. If you want to hang out at my place, I sure could use the company. But I understand if you can't."

Alderson nodded. "I'll be in touch."

Veronica studied Alderson's expression carefully. Despite her better judgment, she gathered her purse and bags, opened the truck door into the rain, and hurried to her front door. Once she was safely inside, she watched the detective's truck back out of her driveway and disappear down the street.

Veronica Upham would never see Nathan Alderson again.

27

ALDERSON WAS LESS THAN A BLOCK AWAY FROM HIS HOUSE when he was forced to bring his truck to a slow crawl. Through the blurry windshield the detective beheld a confusion of flashing red and blue lights just outside of his home. Several squad cars were parked along the street. An ambulance was blocking his driveway.

What the fuck is going on?

Nathan pulled his truck along the curb, cut the engine, and sprung from the cab. The rain continued to pour from the sky. As he jogged forward, he noticed bright yellow barrier tape flapping in the wind. The Williamsport Police Department had cordoned off his neighbor's front yard—the tape stretching from Alderson's mailbox to a telephone pole across the street. Standing behind the barricade, Alderson could make out the figure of Frank McCain. His partner stood with his collar up and a large black umbrella in hand. Nate could see the red glow of a cigarette dangling from the older man's mouth.

"Frank?" Alderson called out. "What the hell's going on?"

McCain flicked his cigarette into the rain and bent to maneuver himself under the crime scene tape. As Alderson rushed to meet him, McCain barreled forward, collided with his partner, and swung him hard against a squad car along the curb. With his forearm pressed against Nathan's chest, McCain bared his teeth just inches from Alderson's face.

"Where the *fuck* have you been?"

316

Nathan lifted his hands and tried to shove his partner backward. The heavier man stood his ground, leaning forward to place additional pressure against Alderson's sternum.

"Don't make me ask you again," he sneered. With one final thrust, McCain took a step backward and adjusted the umbrella over their heads. The rain washed over the nylon fabric in waves.

"I've been working the case," Alderson rasped. He adjusted his jacket and took a step away from the squad car.

"That's not what I meant, and you know it!" McCain fired back. "Where the hell were you that you're comin' home at four-thirty in the morning?"

"I was in the woods." Alderson caught his breath. "The woods by the school."

McCain narrowed his eyes. "Doing what?"

"Looking for clues. Trying to solve this goddamn case."

McCain snapped his umbrella aside and glanced up at the sky. With a frenzied gesture, he slid the umbrella closed and slammed it on the roof of the squad car. Once again, he leaned his body into Alderson's and pressed his partner against the driver's side door. The heavy rain drenched the pair of policemen. "Stop bullshittin' me and tell me what the hell's goin' on with you!"

"Back up, Frank. I'm warning you. I'm about to lose my patience."

"You ain't doin' shit!" he roared. "Where've you been all week?"

"I told you! I've been working the case."

"What the fuck does that even mean, Nate?" McCain's voice cracked. Rain and spittle dripped from his chin. "I've been calling you for *days*. You haven't shown up for work. D'Amato's *furious*. He's had to bullshit his way through two press conferences while his lead detective's MIA."

Alderson was distracted by the flashing lights surrounding him. A pair of EMTs steered a gurney onto his neighbor's lawn. Ash Townsend and the entire WPD forensics team were examining something close to the cable box.

"How long's it gonna take you to think up another lie?" McCain reached up to adjust his hat. Rain spilled over the brim.

"I broke my phone," Alderson finally confessed. "I dropped it when I was out in the woods."

"And I guess you had Kelly screenin' the landline? Try another one."

"No, I wasn't home. I didn't have a chance to call you back because *I've been working the goddamn case!* How many more times do I have to say it?"

"None," McCain replied. "You're full of shit. I don't know what you've been doin'. All I know is you're done. You hear me? You're off the case."

"What the fuck are you talking about?" Alderson lunged forward. His tendons stood out in his neck. "This is *my* case!"

"Not anymore." McCain shook his head and leveled a disgusted look at his partner. "D'Amato pulled you and put me in charge of this fuckin' mess." He glanced down and pointed to the badge affixed to Nathan's belt. "You'll be lucky to still have that after tomorrow morning."

Alderson glanced over his shoulder at the commotion in his neighbor's yard. The EMTs had collapsed the gurney and were crouched next to Townsend. Wilkins and Hoffman—two forensics technicians in Tyvek suits—crossed the yard to meet their supervisor by the cable box. Hoffman was carrying an empty body bag.

"What's going on here, Frank?" He nodded to the forensics team and the medics. "Who the hell's on that stretcher?"

"You tell me, Nate." McCain reached over Alderson's head and snatched the umbrella. He shook it off, popped it open, and swung it above their heads. "She was your neighbor."

"What?" Alderson squinted his eyes in confusion. "Who?"

McCain reached into his pocket, withdrew a pack of Camels and a Zippo, and lit up. He kept his eyes locked on Alderson as he blew a cloud of smoke in his face.

"Emma Sullivan. Eight years old. Parents tucked her in around nine-thirty. The mother said she read her a bedtime story for chrissakes." McCain spit and took another drag on his cigarette before exhaling. "No signs of forced entry. Parents didn't hear a thing. The kid must've gone outside willingly."

Alderson felt a knot tightening in his stomach.

"The father got up to take a piss around one-thirty. Walked past the girl's room and noticed she wasn't in her bed."

The blood drained from Nathan's face. He knew McCain was studying every tick and twitch of his eye. He couldn't bring himself to meet his partner's gaze.

"He searched the house, but there was no sign of her," McCain continued. "Then he noticed the front door was slightly ajar. That's when he went outside to find his daughter torn to fuckin' pieces on the front lawn."

"Jesus Christ," Alderson muttered. The flashing lights and rain made him dizzy. He felt his stomach clenching and forced himself to suppress the urge to vomit.

McCain's knuckles were white as he gripped the wooden umbrella handle. As he spoke, his voice grew louder, and he inched his face forward until he was nose-to-nose with Alderson. "They found her right next to *your* house, Nate. Just a stone's throw from your fuckin' driveway. How's that for a coincidence? Huh? And it just so happens... *it just so happens* that your *wife* hasn't seen you all night and you conveniently come rollin' in, utterly oblivious to it all. Just in time to see them load whatever the fuck is left of her onto that goddamn stretcher!"

"I swear to God, Frank, I had no idea. I wasn't here, I told you I was up in the woods."

"Yeah, you was up in the woods." McCain sucked his cigarette between his teeth. Its orange glow cast a hellish glare on his face. "Up in those woods *with no alibi,* soaked to the skin, waitin' for the killer to show up and politely surrender? Fuck off, Nate." McCain turned and pointed at the house beside them. "I wanna know why the *fuck* we've got another body on that lawn! I wanna know why the killer just laid a dead kid on *your* goddamn doorstep!"

"I don't know, Frank," Alderson said. "I don't know. I wasn't here. I had no idea this was gonna happen."

"Was it Bartsch?" McCain narrowed his eyes. "Is he tryin' to send you some kinda message? You need to level with me here. Clearly you got a target on your back. Your fuckin' *wife* could be in danger."

"It's not Bartsch," Alderson insisted. "I can tell you that for sure."

"How do you know?"

Nathan hesitated. "I just do," he sighed. "I'm telling you, it's not Bartsch. You gotta trust me, Frank."

"No, I don't." McCain cocked his head. "Who's Veronica Upham?"

Alderson flinched. He cast his eyes away from his partner before proceeding with another half-truth. "She's a professor at the college. What the hell does she have to do with this?"

"You tell me."

Nathan forced himself to lift his eyes. He noticed the gloved EMTs were assisting Townsend's crew. They carefully loaded Emma Sullivan's remains into the long zippered bag laid out on the gurney. Technician Wright put down a plastic marker with the number '1' on its shiny surface. Alderson returned his attention to Frank.

"OK, remember how D'Amato sent me on that wild goose chase following up on Pettit's piss-poor notes?"

"Yeah." McCain wrung the last bit of life from his cigarette.

"I went to see the dean of the college. Bartsch isn't a student there. Never was. The dean told me to go talk to this flaky literature professor. She was sleeping with that *other* professor who burnt down his house and left town."

"And?" McCain tossed the spent butt and immediately lit another. His jaw remained firmly clenched and his eyes betrayed nothing but contempt.

"And it was a dead end," Alderson insisted. "She hasn't heard from this Raymer guy in two years. That's it."

"Huh." McCain nodded with a wicked gleam in his eye. "That's funny. 'Cause we got a call on the Crime Line from some hipster bookstore clerk up in Richmond. And this jackoff claims he went to a séance last Saturday night. Guess who hosted this morbid soirée?" McCain shouted. "That's right, Dr. Veronica Upham."

"I told you, Frank. She's a flake. When I—"

"But it gets better, Nate, 'cause this prick says Dr. Upham channeled the spirit of Tyler Marshall. The night after we found him dead in those woods. Now this Sandoval kid says he spent the next few days scared shitless until his conscience got the best of him and he decided to call us."

"And you believe him, Frank?"

"Sandoval also said he hasn't been able to get ahold of Upham all week," McCain added. "That's awfully suspicious, don't you think, Nate?"

"No, I don't." Alderson struggled to formulate a counterargument in his head. "She's not a goddamn suspect. I tried to tell you a few minutes ago before you interrupted me. I went to see her that afternoon."

Nathan swallowed hard as he saw the EMTs zip the body bag. The pneumatics on the gurney whined as the flat top slowly rose from the ground. He looked away from Frank to watch Ash Townsend place a gloved hand on the stretcher, then nod for the EMTs to go. In the meantime, Wright put another placard next to the cable box. The two medics began pushing the gurney across the Sullivan's muddy lawn, towards the open doors of the ambulance.

Alderson met McCain's stony gaze once again.

"You were saying?" McCain said. "What happened when you went to see Dr. Upham?"

"She fed me the same bullshit, Frank. Played me some amateur video of her séance and claimed Tyler Marshall was killed by a fucking ghost." Alderson leveled a finger at McCain. "Now, do you think I should've passed that information along to Chief D'Amato? You think it would've helped him prepare for his next press conference?"

"That's not the—"

"And don't even try to act like you wouldn't have laughed in my face if I came to you with a story like that!"

"So why was your truck parked outside of Veronica Upham's residence on Wednesday night?"

"What?" Alderson blinked in disbelief.

"I spent some time cruisin' the neighborhood Wednesday afternoon," McCain explained. "You know I like that bakery over on Randolph Street. The one next to that corner store near Copperstone Drive."

Nathan exhaled heavily. He was numb to the rain as it ran over his face and clung to his eyelashes.

"Imagine my surprise when I see your truck parked along that street for hours," McCain said. "No sign of you anywhere so I had it figured you must've been inside somewhere. After a bit of detective work, I concluded it musta been Veronica Upham's residence you were visiting, from the late afternoon, well into the evening. And to add yet another layer to this mystery, some rust bucket with stolen plates was also parked in her driveway."

Alderson grit his teeth and stared past his partner's grim face.

"So you wanna think up another one, Nate?" McCain took a heavy drag, waited, and exhaled. "I know you're not sleepin' with this woman, because you're a gentleman and you've got a lonely wife at home cryin' her eyes out waitin' for you to stop playin' hero and start actin' like a husband."

A loud commotion suddenly broke out to their right. Alderson turned to see Bev Sullivan racing toward him. A wide-eyed police officer trailed behind her, uncertain if he could restrain the frantic woman himself or call for backup.

"Where the fuck were you, Nate?" Her voice was shrill with grief. Her body trembled with rage. Dark rings ran under her eyes and her t-shirt was stained with her daughter's blood. "This isn't supposed to happen in a place like this! My baby's gone! She's dead! Where the hell were you?"

Bev managed to swing her fists against Nathan's chest several times before she was accosted by the police officer. The hysterical woman continued her barrage of verbal abuse as she was dragged away.

"Why the *hell* did he come after her? What'd my baby do to him? We're supposed to be safe. We live next door to a policeman! A fuckin' cop!"

The uniformed officer forced Mrs. Sullivan to turn around. He threw a heavy blanket around her shoulders, then cast a steely glance to Alderson and McCain.

"Now she's dead! Just like Cody!" Bev Sullivan screamed over her shoulder. "Guess you couldn't save him either! What the fuck good are you? Huh? What good are you?"

The distraught woman's screams soon lapsed into a fit of sobbing. The police officer coaxed her across the lawn, out of the rain, and back into the house beside Nathan's.

"Don't think that little interlude's gonna let you off the hook," McCain said and resumed his interrogation. "If it isn't Bartsch, then who the fuck is it? And what the fuck kinda game is he playin' with you? That girl's dead, Nate. And I'm absolutely *certain* it's because she had the misfortune of bein' your next-door neighbor."

"Frank, if I told you, you'd never believe me."

"Now that's the first thing you said all night that wasn't bullshit or poorly rehearsed."

"It's not Bartsch," Alderson repeated, "but whoever it is, they've been doing this for years. I tried to tell you before but none of you would listen to me. I told you those missing kids from the '90s were connected to this. And when I talked to Tom Carpenter from Archives, he told me kids have been disappearing in those woods since the late 1950s."

"Not this idiocy again." McCain scoffed. "I mean, you're talking about a killer that's gotta be pushin' eighty years old!"

Alderson ignored his partner. "That whole goddamn forest is littered with *graves*. I asked Townsend *and* D'Amato to get a forensics crew up there with more advanced equipment and they shot me down."

"Because it's bullshit!" McCain shouted back. "It's a hare-brained theory and—"

"So, I had to take matters into my own hands and find out for myself."

McCain grit his teeth. "What'd you do, go up there with a shovel and start digging? Get the fuck outta here."

"Yeah," Alderson replied. "That's exactly what I did. And I barely scratched the surface."

Frank McCain narrowed his eyes and lowered his voice. "Are you tellin' me you found a body up there and haven't reported it?"

Alderson withheld his reply. The detective shivered as the rain streamed over his face and shoulders. Nearby, one of the EMTs closed the rear doors of the ambulance with two sharp *bangs*.

"So now you're withholdin' evidence." McCain nodded emphatically. He flicked his cigarette and took a few steps back from Alderson. "You're done, Nate. I told you last week you weren't ready to be out here yet. It's a goddamn shame you didn't listen to me."

"Save it, Frank," Alderson said with a sour look distorting his face. "I don't need your pity."

"You're not gonna get it," he shot back. "Go home. Clean yourself up. Get some sleep. Because tomorrow mornin', you need to get your ass down to the station and face D'Amato. Maybe he'll cut you a break. If I were you,

I'd keep my mouth shut about those woods and tell him you're having a nervous breakdown or somethin'. Get your shit together. And when you're ready to tell me the whole truth, you know where to find me."

The older detective turned his back on Alderson and returned to the crime scene. He ducked under the tape and joined Ash Townsend as she pointed toward a dark spot on the ground and verbally directed Hoffman to inspect it. The lead forensic tech shot a look of disapproval at Alderson and turned back to McCain. They wandered further into the heart of the crime scene and disappeared from view.

Alderson leaned against the squad car. He watched Wright set down more numbered placards around the cable box. The technician was now up to '12.' Townsend remarked loudly about trying to preserve the integrity of the crime scene in the rain. The engine of the ambulance roared to life, and the bulky vehicle drove away with Emma Sullivan's remains inside.

You need to get that shoulder bag from the truck.

Nathan quickly retraced his steps back to his pickup. He opened the driver's side door, reached in, and grabbed the musette bag from the passenger seat. He slammed the door, sprinted through the rain, and stumbled up the sidewalk to his front door. He reached to retrieve his keys from his pocket, but his wet jeans were too tight to accommodate his hand. He tried the knob and was surprised to find it unlocked. Alderson braced himself and stepped inside his house.

Closing the door behind him, he struggled out of his boots and hung his drenched jacket on a coat rack. He dropped the musette bag off to the side of the door.

"Nate?" Kelly called from the dining room.

"Yeah," he replied. "It's me."

He heard his wife's light footsteps padding across the carpet. When she entered the living room she immediately froze at the sight of her weather-beaten husband.

"What the hell happened to you?" she gasped. "You need to get out of those clothes!"

Nathan merely stood rigid in place, a pool of water forming around his feet.

Suddenly his wife rushed toward him and threw her arms around his back. With her face pressed against his damp chest, she began to sob uncontrollably.

"Please don't go." Her voice was weak and breathless as she wept. "I can't do this without you. I can't."

Alderson wrapped his arms around his wife. He pulled her closer and ran his fingers through her hair.

"I'm sorry, Kel," he said softly. "I was just trying to do my job. And I failed."

"Your job is to be my husband," she said. "That's it. That's all. And you can still do that."

Nathan rested his stubbled chin against his wife's hair. It had been months since he was this close to her. Somehow everything felt right again, and he had the presence of mind to pause and cherish it before she continued.

"What happened to Emma?" Kelly withdrew from his arms and reached up to wipe the tears from her eyes. She exhaled heavily and rubbed her nose on the back of her hand.

"I don't know, exactly," he replied. "But she's gone."

"It's the same killer, isn't it?" Her eyes were shimmering with fear. "What's he doing *here?* Nate, what's going on?"

"I'm sorry, Kel." Nathan swallowed hard and stared into the dining room. "I really don't know."

She glanced up at him, her eyes searching his blank face and defeated stance. She took a deep breath and pushed a lock of stray hair behind her ear.

"Just tell me one thing," she said. "Are you hunting this killer, or is he hunting *you?*"

"Both," he admitted. "But we're gonna find him. I promise. McCain's taking over the case. D'Amato's likely gonna suspend me or fire me, I have no idea. I'll find out tomorrow."

"Good," she said. A tight frown creased her brow. "You need to walk away." She turned and drifted toward the dining room. "I called off tomorrow. I'm gonna make you some tea. I'll bring it up in a few minutes, so go upstairs and get out of those wet clothes."

Alderson slowly climbed the stairs. He entered the bathroom, slid out of his clothes, and tossed them onto the floor. He got a quick hot shower, brushed his teeth, and walked into the bedroom. After flipping on the light, he put on a fresh pair of boxers and sat down on the edge of the bed. Around his neck hung the silver cross he placed over his head the night before. He reached up and rubbed his thumb along its smooth surface.

"Where'd you get that?" Kelly stood at the edge of the bed, a saucer and cup in her hand. She eyed the cross with a nervous and perplexed look.

"Just something I picked up," he said quietly. "I don't really wanna talk about it."

"Drink your tea," she said and carefully extended her delicate hand toward him.

Nathan reached up and took the plate and mug in hand. The steam wafted from the cup and carried the aroma of chamomile.

After switching on a small lamp beside the bed, Kelly returned to the doorway, flicked off the overhead light, and turned down the covers. Nathan sipped his tea and sat with his feet firmly planted on the cold bedroom floor.

"She was Cody's first crush," Kelly said softly as she slid into bed. Alderson turned to look at his wife. Her back was firmly against the headboard and a faint smile had tugged at her lips. "Do you remember?"

With the teacup in hand, he turned so he was fully facing his wife. He waited for her to continue.

"It was after his seventh birthday party," she reflected. "I asked him what his favorite present was, and he said, 'the picture Emma drew me.'" Kelly laughed and a silent tear slid down her face.

Nathan forced a smile and shook his head. "I didn't know he was already noticing girls."

Kelly tightened her lips and looked away. "Yeah, she was a cute kid." She sniffed and wiped the tear from her cheek. She watched her husband as he sipped his tea. "I really miss him."

"I do too." Nathan placed the teacup and saucer on his nightstand. He pulled down the covers and crawled into bed, laying on his right side to face his wife.

"It's been an awful year," Kelly said, fighting off another wave of tears. She reached for the lamp, switched it off, and turned over on her side. Nathan slid forward, stretched his arm around her hip, and pulled her closer to him. With her back tight against his chest, she closed her eyes, and savored his warm embrace.

"I love you, Nate."

"I love you, too, Kel."

The rain continued to fall outside, drumming on the roof and driving against the windowpanes. The wind howled and rattled against the back of the house—shielded from the disturbing red and blue lights that continued to flash long past the arrival of the dawn. In the warm shadows of their bed, Kelly and Nathan Alderson drifted into sleep, entwined together, breathing in unison, and wholly unaware of the spiteful presence gathering around them.

28

I T WAS JUST AFTER DAWN WHEN NATHAN ALDERSON OPENED
his eyes. The curtains had been pulled over the windows. A thin
border of pale light framed the dark drapes as they hung to the floor.
The house was silent. A gray haze seemed to permeate the bedroom.
Mired in a groggy daze, Nathan let his eyes sweep the room. Various objects—lamps, mirrors, furniture—were blurred and indistinct. The door was
firmly shut. At the foot of his bed stood the tall figure of Charlotte Brennen.

Nathan's heart began to race. He attempted to rise but could not move.
His lean body was rigid, and his limbs were paralyzed at his sides. An unseen
weight pushed on his chest as he struggled to draw breath. He managed to
bend his head slightly, straining his eyes to see if his wife still slept beside
him. Her customary place upon the mattress was empty.

His attention was drawn to the woman looming at the edge of the bed.
Her pale face was blank of expression and her cold eyes bore into him. She
stood as motionless as a figure hewn from marble. Gone were the blackened
scars and layers of forest grime. The rank, tattered dress had been exchanged
for a pale nightgown—a shade or two darker than the white skin of her
throat. The fabric clung to the curves of her full hips, while her smooth
white arms hung at her sides. Thick blonde hair was swept back from her
forehead and twisted into a neat chignon. Two loose tendrils framed her
face, and her eyes remained fixed on Alderson.

You can't be here. It's daylight.

In a slow, languid motion, she lifted her hand to unfasten a pearl comb. With a shake of her head, her blonde hair fell over her broad shoulders, cascading in thick serpentine waves. She crossed her hands over her stomach and pulled the thin gown over her head and let it fall to the floor.

No.

Charlotte stood before him, bathed in the faint gray light of morning. Her full breasts were partially veiled behind her hair, which swept across the skin of her soft belly. Beneath the curve of her stomach was a nest of full golden hair. Her legs were slightly parted, and the front of her thighs were inches from the mattress.

I said no.

She took a step closer and lifted her knee upon the bed. The edge of the mattress sank with her weight as she slowly crawled forward, her right hand stretching out, her white fingers splayed over the covers. The mattress creaked as she crept toward him, her heavy breasts swaying slowly.

Goddamn it, I said no!

She slid both of her hands along Nathan's legs and wrapped her fingers around the edge of the comforter. As she began to pull the blanket toward her, her fingers clutched the waistband of his boxer shorts. With one fluid motion, she removed his underpants with the comforter and tossed them behind her.

Still unable to move, Alderson forced his eyes shut and gasped for breath. His lungs burned and his rigid limbs were numb. When the mattress sank again, he opened his eyes to see she had mounted the edge of the bed and was pawing her way toward him.

No. Please, no.

With her knees straddling Alderson's calves, Charlotte slid over his lower body, her long hair brushing his legs. With her eyes still locked on his, she lowered her head and inched forward. Alderson winced as he felt her breasts graze him, followed by a rush of her hot breath on his scrotum. His body tensed in revulsion as he felt her wet tongue slither along the shaft of his stiffening cock.

You're not real! You're... dead. You can't be here!

NO!

He tried to scream but there was no breath in his lungs. His arms were useless, and his legs were forced together. He shivered as her hands slid over his stomach to press hard against his chest. He opened his eyes in terror to see her leaning just above his face. Her eyes were wild with hunger. Thick waves of flaxen hair fell forward to frame them. She parted her lips with a sly smile. Her breath smelled of honey, blood, and cinnamon.

I said no!

"Lie still."

Alderson's pulse pounded in his ears. He fought to look away, but his eyes were riveted to hers as she grasped his shoulders and pulled herself forward. As she lowered her hips, he could feel the hot pulse of her sex against his own and he wrenched his neck to turn his face away.

Her white hand caressed the side of his stubbled cheek, forcing him to meet her penetrating gaze. All at once the air flooded his lungs and he gasped for breath. She slid her finger over his lips and eyed him steadily.

"Lie still."

Nathan felt the blood rushing through his limbs. Numb and tingling, he gradually began to regain control of his hands. With her weight still pinning him to the mattress, Charlotte slid her hands along his torso and placed her palms against his stomach. She slowly rocked her hips so Nathan could feel her swollen sex spreading to receive him.

NO!

Nathan's hand wandered around the curve of Charlotte's hip. He placed his palm against her smooth lower back and let it cup her full buttocks while his left hand clutched the side of the mattress. He strained to bend his elbow and slowly inched it toward his pillow.

Please God. Please. Please help me!

Alderson managed to slide his fingers upward until he felt the cold thin chains of the crosses he had placed under his pillow. He closed his fist around them and thrust his hand upward to press the tangled mess of silver against the vampire's skin.

But his arm locked in place and a darkness shadowed the face of the woman above him. Alderson's heart sank as the chains slid through his fingers. Against all reason, his palm was filled with thin, writhing serpents.

They slid up his forearm, wrapped around his wrist, and slipped through his fingers. He cried out as one of them sank its fangs into his flesh. The other snakes fell in tangled clumps on his stomach and then slithered to the floor.

Charlotte grasped his empty hand and guided it around her hip. Hypnotized by her ice-blue eyes, Nathan lifted his chin in defiance and spit into her face. Once again, his limbs felt heavy and he could only move his fingers. He dug his fingernails into her flesh, but the vampire thrust her arms forward and pushed his shoulders into the mattress.

"Lie still, Nathaniel."

Her voice in his mind sent ripples of fear and desire through his rushing blood. Alderson let his eyes wander over her parted lips, her milk-white throat, and her breasts as they slowly swung forward with her subtle movements. He felt compelled to bend forward and kiss them—to suckle the rose-pink nipples and nestle his face in the musky hollow between them. He could hear her heart inexplicably beating against her chest.

Nathan gripped her hips tighter and arched his back beneath her. Charlotte leaned backward and clawed her fingers down his chest. Nathan met her gaze as she lifted her soft stomach and slid her hand over the plump, fleecy mound below her belly. She reached between her legs and guided him inside her. With a soft grunt, she thrust her hips forward and began to rock slowly.

Alderson strained to force himself deeper and felt her melting around his cock. He sighed and gripped her hips, eager to quicken the pace of her movements. But Charlotte steadied herself and moved her full body in a slow, torturous rhythm. She pressed her sweaty palms against his chest, forcing the air from his lungs. Charlotte tossed her head backward and opened her mouth to issue a series of low moans. Nathan traced the blush of crimson across her throat and chest. Beads of perspiration glistened between her breasts and along her freckled brow.

Charlotte continued to buck her hips, now quickening the pace of her undulations. She bent forward, taking Nathan's face between her hands. Her hair fell forward again, enveloping them as she panted against his mouth. Nathan slid his hand along her slick back and behind her neck. He pulled her downward and opened his mouth against her lips, his fingers tangled within her wild golden hair. He felt her hot tongue sliding against his own, her honeyed breath filling his mouth and lungs. He dug his fingers into the flesh of her shoulder and kissed her deeply, her hips now snapping hard against him.

All at once his mouth was filled with a foul miasma. The scent of her flesh filled his nostrils with a rank, putrid odor. Nathan attempted to pull away, but she spread her lips over his mouth and pushed her face against him. His lungs contracted as if she were sucking the air in gulping waves from his chest. His eyes opened, but he could only see darkness. Her hair hung stiffly about him, coarse and wet like seaweed rubbing against his skin. He pounded his fists against her back, but she would not relent, crushing him beneath her leaden weight.

At last, she broke their rotten kiss and leaned backward, still writhing desperately. Her full breasts had shriveled and drooped low above a distended stomach. They slapped against her bloated belly with her frenzied movements. Her flesh was gray and stiff, marred with sores and scars. Black veins branched beneath her cadaverous skin and ran along the sagging flesh of her arms.

Alderson frantically pushed against her, but the grotesque hag pinned his arms against the bed. She opened her mouth to expose jagged, brown teeth and emitted a shrill, drawn out scream. Nathan's flesh crawled and he fought to slip out from under her. He tried to call out but there was no air to empower his cries.

"Lie still!" she shrieked as Alderson began to weep. The ghastly creature continued to ride him, his cock still swollen and nearing its climax. He could smell the stench of her sex as it quivered against him. The haggard vampire shook and grunted in lustful abandon as Nathan Alderson spilled his seed into her barren, stinking womb.

The undead thing straddling his hips began to cackle, still thrusting and milking every last drop from him. Alderson roared and broke away from her grip. He slid his hands around her neck and began to squeeze. The vampire's mocking laughter deafened his ears as Nathan thrust himself upward and flipped the succubus onto her back. He withdrew himself from her withered cunt and pressed his thumbs into the hollow of her throat. Gritting his teeth, Nathan wrung his hands around her neck, his eyes clenched as the taut muscles in his arms and back rippled. The vampire beat her hands against his back, spurring him to tighten his grip.

When Alderson opened his eyes, he gasped to see the discolored face of his wife, her mouth a rictus of shock and pain, the veins stiffening along her forehead. Her ice-blue eyes were wide with terror. Nathan immediately relinquished his grasp, rolled to the other side of the bed, and jumped to his feet in confusion and horror. He bent over, clutching his stomach as a stream of vomit exploded past his lips and splattered on the bedroom floor.

From the other side of the room, he heard Kelly desperately sucking in mouthfuls of air. He stood to see her back against the far wall, gasping for breath. At last, a flood of tears burst from her eyes. She scrambled to her feet, pulling herself up with the window ledge. Still hyperventilating and racked with sobs, she ran out of the room wearing only a t-shirt and yoga pants. Alderson could hear her stumbling down the steps. Seconds later he heard the jangling of her keys and the slam of the front door.

Nathan collapsed on the edge of the bed with his head clutched in his hands. In the distance, he heard the ignition of Kelly's car and the squeal of tires as she peeled out of the driveway. He lifted his eyes to stare into the mirror above Kelly's vanity, but he no longer recognized the broken man he saw reflected within it.

29

F RANK McCAIN PULLED INTO THE ALDERSONS' DRIVEWAY
shortly after 9:00 Friday morning. It had been less than four
hours since he stood in practically the same spot. The rain had
let up, but the veritable shitstorm had not. He had barely begun
to draft his report on Emma Sullivan's homicide when Kelly Alderson
burst into his office in hysterics, claiming her husband had tried to kill her.

Now, he stood gazing up at his partner's two-story suburban house
wondering what awaited him inside. He slammed the car door, secured his
hat, and was about to draw his duty weapon when a familiar voice called
out to him from the house next door.

"Frank?" Sergeant Fernanda Perez stood on the front stoop of the
Sullivan residence. "What's goin' on? What're you doing back here already?"

McCain beckoned for Perez to come closer, so she crossed the yard to
meet him in the driveway. He stepped around her so his back was to the
neighboring house.

"How many other officers are still over there with you?" McCain asked
her.

"Uh, just me, Sinderson, and Mitchell," she replied. "Townsend and her
crew left shortly after you did. Why?"

"Yeah, she and the coroner are performin' the autopsy as we speak,"
McCain confirmed. He glanced over his shoulder and motioned for Perez

to move toward the front of his unmarked cruiser. "Listen, we may have a bit of a situation here, but I wanna try an' keep things on the down low, OK?"

"Sure." Perez nodded with an anxious frown. "Not that long ago, Kelly Alderson came barreling out of the garage and drove away like a bat outta hell. I almost went after her but—"

"Yeah, she came to see me," McCain interrupted. "She said Nate attacked her."

"What?" Perez's eyes widened. "What do you mean attacked her?"

McCain shrugged, "She says she woke up and he had his hands around her neck."

Perez was stunned. She could only manage a single confused word. "Why?"

"That's what we need to find out," McCain answered. "You up for this?"

Perez swallowed before nodding her head. "I guess so."

"I don't know what we may be walkin' into here," McCain warned. "But remember, he's one of our own. Let's keep this quiet."

"Understood." Perez released the strap on her holster. She followed McCain's lead as he approached the front door. He glanced over his shoulder to make sure none of the neighbors were watching and then tried the brass knob. It was unlocked.

With his Glock 32 drawn, McCain inched his way inside, quickly scanning the living room. "Clear," he muttered as Perez followed behind him, her gun also drawn. She leveled it towards the floor at a forty-five-degree angle and awaited instructions from the detective.

"Nate!" McCain called out. "Are you in here?"

There was no response.

McCain motioned to Perez to secure the living room and first floor. "Check the garage too," he whispered. He pointed upstairs indicating his intention to check the second floor.

With his weapon aimed ahead, McCain slowly mounted the carpeted stairs to the upper floor. The narrow hallway was dark. McCain tallied a total of four doors, and estimated they opened to a narrow linen closet, a bathroom, a further bedroom—likely Cody Alderson's room—and the master bedroom. Three of the four doors were closed. The door to the main bedroom was closest to him and wide open.

"Nate?" McCain tightened his grip on the Glock. A bead of perspiration trickled over his brow. "It's me. Frank."

When there was no response, McCain cautiously placed his left shoulder beside the perimeter of the door frame. He counted to three in his head and then spun inward, his eyes rapidly checking the corners of the dim bedroom and his pistol thrust forward.

McCain noticed his partner sitting on the edge of the bed. He appeared to be unarmed and was wearing only a pair of boxer shorts and some kind of necklace. McCain squinted and recognized a plain silver cross hanging from a thin chain.

"Are you armed, Nathan?" McCain asked.

Alderson didn't reply. The elder detective inched forward—his gun still trained on his former partner. At last, the man on the bed lifted his head and appeared to recognize him.

"Frank?" Alderson asked in a dry, weak voice.

"Yeah buddy, it's me." McCain lowered his weapon and continued to edge toward the window, where he opened the heavy curtains. "Why's it so dark in here?"

Alderson offered no explanation. With the overcast morning light now seeping in, McCain let his eyes sweep the room to piece together a story. He glanced up at a motionless paddle fan. The light bulb was missing. A table lamp had been overturned next to a nightstand. Vomit had congealed on the floor. The bedclothes were rumpled and half hanging from the mattress.

"Do you know why I'm here, Nate?"

When he didn't answer, McCain backed away from the window and skirted around the bed to its opposite side. As he passed the wall, he flicked the light switch on and off but to no avail. He made his way to the other side of the room. Once again, he opened the closed curtains veiling the opposite window. A pile of thin silver chains on the floor next to the bed caught the detective's eye.

"I think I fucked up, Frank." Alderson's voice drifted into the gloom.

"What makes you say that?" McCain slid his Glock into his shoulder holster.

The dazed man seemed unsure of his words. "I don't know... just a feeling."

McCain noticed a bandage on Alderson's shoulder. The detective pointed to it and asked, "What happened there, Nate?"

Alderson seemed bewildered. He continued to stare ahead as if he hadn't heard the question.

McCain's instincts momentarily put him on alert when he heard footsteps creeping up the steps.

"Perez?"

"Yeah?" The sergeant's voice trembled.

"We're in here," he said. "You can lower your weapon."

Perez cautiously entered the room. She had donned a pair of nitrile gloves and carried a black shoulder bag in her left hand. Her eyes swept the scene as she stood by the door. She seemed almost hesitant to take any further steps into the room.

"Downstairs is clear," she confirmed. With an uneasy glance, she thrust her left hand forward. "But you need to take a look at this."

McCain withdrew a pair of disposable gloves from his pockets. Once his hands were protected, he reached forward to receive the musette bag and carefully placed it on top of the chest of drawers. He first withdrew the .38.

"Serial number's been filed off," Perez whispered and pointed to the stock. "It's also loaded... with uh, what look to be silver-tipped cartridges. They look like they came from a reloading press, but I didn't see one in the garage. He must've gotten those rounds from someone else."

McCain opened the chamber to inspect the weapon for himself. To his dismay, Perez wasn't mistaken. He carefully emptied the bullets into his palm and set them with the unloaded gun alongside the bag.

"Is this your weapon, Nate?" McCain asked. "Where'd you get this gun?"

Alderson's eyes were fixed ahead on the wall. As before, he offered no reply.

Perez gestured to McCain. "There's more in that bag, Detective."

He pried open the flaps, reached inside, and withdrew a handful of rosaries and crosses. "What the hell's all this shit?" He removed a pair of small glass vials, which he placed with two muffled *thumps* on the surface of the dresser.

Fuckin' holy water? Maybe?

Finally, he pulled a large crucifix from the bag, along with an unopened roll of communion wafers wrapped in thin plastic. Frank bumped his hat and scratched his forehead. He glanced at Alderson and then back to Perez, to whom he pointed in the direction of the pile of silver chains on the floor. Perez took the cue and reluctantly approached the nightstand. She bent to inspect the items and carefully gathered them into her gloved hands.

"More crosses," she said with a grim expression.

McCain slipped her an empty evidence bag. Perez quickly began to drop the objects into the bag, sealed it, and handed it back to McCain. He placed it beside the other esoteric items on top of the dresser drawers and turned to the silent figure poised at the edge of the bed. He took a few steps forward and bent his knees until he was eye-level with his partner.

"Alright, Nate," McCain said with a heavy sigh. "I need to ask you some serious questions. Do you understand me?"

After a brief delay, Alderson lifted his eyes to his partner's and nodded weakly.

"Good," McCain said. He winced as he rose to his full height. Perez holstered her pistol and stood at the doorway with her arms folded against her chest. She eyed Nathan with suspicion and fear.

"Why'd you try to hurt Kelly?" McCain narrowed his eyes and awaited Alderson's response with dread.

"Kelly?" He seemed confused.

"Yeah," McCain repeated more forcefully. "Your wife. She says you tried to hurt her this mornin'. Is that true? Do you remember that?"

"It wasn't Kelly," Alderson said in an even tone.

McCain tilted his head and glanced at Perez. "What do you mean it wasn't Kelly?"

Nathan repeated himself, but this time, his words were barely a whisper. "It wasn't her."

"Then who was it, Nate?" McCain pressed. Perez clutched her arms close to her breasts and studied Alderson with wide eyes.

Nearly a minute passed but Alderson never clarified his response.

"Who was here, Nate?" McCain pushed further. "Did someone come in the house? Someone who wasn't supposed to be here?"

Alderson's arms tensed for a moment, but he avoided his partner's searching glance. McCain took a step forward and caught Nathan's attention. He pointed a thumb to his fellow officer as he spoke, "You remember Perez, right? Sergeant Fernanda Perez?"

"Yeah," Nathan said. He turned his head toward the woman standing in the entryway. His eyes seemed to pass right through her.

"That's good," McCain said. "Perez has been next door for several hours now. Did you see anyone come into Nathan's house, Sergeant?"

"No, sir, I did not," she replied.

"You wouldn't have seen her." Nathan shook his head.

"Wouldn't have seen who, Nate?" McCain took a breath to maintain his patience. "Who are you talkin' about?"

Alderson just continued to shake his head. His jaw had tightened, and his thin lips were taut and colorless.

"What's with all the crosses, bud?" McCain steeled himself. "Why're you wearin' that cross around your neck?"

"Protection." Alderson raised his head, looking first to Perez and then back to McCain. "But it doesn't work, Frank," he said with a laugh that made Perez's skin crawl. "It doesn't work *at all.*" Alderson's discomfiting laughter sank into a series of low sobs.

McCain's stomach was in knots. His palms were slick with sweat, and his heart was racing as fast as if he were held at gunpoint. "Protection against what, Nate?"

"Oh, no, no, no, no." Alderson shook an accusatory finger at McCain. "I... uh, I can't tell you that."

Perez brought the tips of her fingers to her forehead and discreetly crossed herself.

"Nate, we're here to help you," McCain replied gently. "If you don't tell us who, then we—"

"You can't help me!" he shouted.

Perez jumped and let her hand hover above the grip of her holstered weapon. McCain raised his hands to calm both of them.

"Take it easy, Nate. We just wanna talk to you."

"I tried to tell you," he said, short of breath. "I tried to tell *all of you.*"

"Tell us what, Nate? We're listenin'."

Alderson's eyes were glassed over. A thin line of drool spilled from the corner of his mouth. His angry outburst appeared to have been short-lived. McCain waited for his partner to continue.

"I tried to tell you *what* was in those *woods.*"

McCain took a step forward. Alderson's head was low, and his shoulders were drooping. He appeared to be fixated on the floor.

"Yeah, I remember," McCain said. He wasn't looking forward to hearing the same line of bullshit he had already heard from Alderson just hours before.

As if on cue, Perez interjected with her own questions for Alderson. "What was up in the woods, Nate?"

McCain shot her a disapproving glance, but the uniformed officer kept her attention on Alderson.

"Graves," Alderson whispered. "Dozens and dozens and hundreds and hundreds of *graves.*"

"Whose graves, Nathan?" Perez continued. "We only found Tyler Marshall out there. I think you might be mixed up."

Alderson lifted his eyes to the unsettled policewoman. "No, you just haven't found them yet," he said. "There are children buried there. Kids. Babies. Infants." A tear slid down his face. He cast a look of bitter sorrow toward Perez. "And all your saints won't protect you from the thing that put them there."

"Alright, Nate." McCain stepped in front of Perez. "That's enough of that. It's time we get goin' now."

"Listen to me, Frank," Alderson said. He reached out and loosely grabbed the edge of McCain's coat. He pulled his partner close to him. "When you go up there, promise me you'll go by day."

McCain gently unfastened Alderson's fingers from the hem of his coat and took a step backward.

"You have to go by day, Frank. You have to." Alderson began to chuckle as a fresh flood of tears streamed down his face. "You'll all see. You gotta go by day and there'll be *a big surprise*. When you dig them up, you'll see."

McCain clenched his teeth as he spoke to Perez. "I need you to get him some clothes."

Sergeant Perez stood fixed in place, her eyes riveted to Alderson.

"Don't go by night, Sergeant," Alderson warned her. His lips quivered, his eyes red and pleading. "Frank. You're not ready to go out there at night. *None of you* are ready to go up there at night."

"Perez!" McCain hissed and pointed to the closet. "I said get him some goddamn clothes. Now."

The sergeant broke her gaze and quickly made her way to the closet. Her unsteady hands reached in and wrenched the first piece of clothing from a plastic hanger. She then turned and began rummaging through the top drawer of the bureau. A moment later she returned with a dark green flannel shirt, a pair of gray socks, and a worn pair of blue jeans.

"Nathan, I'm going to help you get dressed now," she said and took a tentative step forward. Alderson remained frozen at the edge of the bed. McCain snatched the flannel from Perez and began to coax his partner's arm through the loose sleeve. Perez knelt down and carefully slipped a sock over Alderson's cold right foot and then followed up with his left. She slid both of his quivering legs into the jeans.

"Can you stand up, Nate?" Perez asked softly. "And finish pulling on your pants for me?"

Leaning on McCain, Alderson slowly stood. For a moment he staggered and threatened to fall forward, but Frank caught him under the arm and steadied him. Perez stood to his right and offered her arm to assist him. After a few awkward minutes, they managed to finish dressing the detective.

"Did you see any shoes down there?" McCain whispered to Perez. "When you were downstairs?"

"Yeah," she said, slightly winded. "There are a couple pairs of tennis shoes and dress shoes by the door."

"Good." McCain nodded, his face red and glistening with sweat. "Let's get him downstairs. Carefully."

With their arms looped through his, Perez and McCain led Alderson forward. McCain descended the steps ahead of them to block any potential falls—or worse. Perez led him one step at a time until they reached the bottom, where she directed him to take a seat while she fetched him a pair of shoes.

McCain watched his empty-eyed partner with a mix of fear, pity, and sadness. Perez once again knelt before him. Within a few minutes, she had managed to get both of the tennis shoes on his feet and had tied the long white laces.

What the fuck happened to him? What the hell rabbit hole did he fall into? And where the fuck did he get all those goddamn crosses?

"Hold on a sec," McCain mumbled to Perez. "Before you lift him up." Frank walked to the front door and opened it with a creak. He peeked his head out to ensure there wasn't a neighborhood full of nosy onlookers about to witness Nathan Alderson's departure from the house. Satisfied that the street was quiet, he turned back to Perez with one final directive.

"Not a word of this to anyone, Perez." McCain slipped his nitrile gloves off and shoved them in his coat pocket. "I know it's only a matter of time before everyone at the station finds out what he did and what happened. But don't you dare breathe a word about *anything else* you heard him say in that bedroom."

"I won't." Perez removed her gloves as well. "Swear to Christ, I won't. But you need to level with me, Frank. What the hell is going on around here? First the Marshall boy." Perez sighed in frustration and corrected herself. "I mean the *Stroud* girl, then Marshall. That girl next door, and now this. It can't all be a coincidence."

Perez and McCain turned to glance at Alderson, who still sat passively on one of the lower carpeted stairs. He was slowly rocking forward and backward, his arms tightly clasped around his chest and his hands tucked into his armpits.

"It's not." McCain cleared his throat and gestured to Perez to help him guide Nathan to the car. "It's not a coincidence. But I don't know *what* the hell it is."

Moving slowly, they managed to lead Nathan to the backseat of Frank McCain's cruiser. He cursed under his breath when both Sinderson and Mitchell emerged from the Sullivan house just in time to see Alderson ducking his head under the doorframe.

"Go back inside!" McCain shouted. "There's nothin' to see here!"

Perez pointed a finger at the two wayward officers and echoed McCain's command. "I'm going with Frank. You two stay here and keep an eye on Bev and Jason. They just lost their only daughter, for chrissakes."

Once she was inside the car, McCain turned over the engine, reached into his coat pocket for his cigarettes, and quickly lit one. He cracked the window and offered a smoke to his passenger. Without a second thought, Perez accepted, lifted it to her lips, and lit it with a trembling hand. She then buckled her seat belt around her wide hips and glanced at Alderson in the passenger-side mirror. "You OK back there, Nate?"

Alderson didn't reply, but McCain could see his red-rimmed eyes in the rear-view mirror. As he exhaled a puff of smoke, he fought the urge to let his emotions get the best of him. Instead, he adjusted the angle of the mirror so he wouldn't have to see his partner's dazed expression.

McCain stopped the cruiser to make a left turn out of the neighborhood. A parade of outside broadcast vans from the local TV channels cruised past them, *en route* to the crime scene.

"Looks like we got him outta there just in time," Perez whispered. "There's so many of them."

After the last of the vehicles passed, Frank McCain gave a curt nod to Perez, spun the steering wheel, and continued the short drive to the station. "Fuckin' vultures," he muttered.

30

VERONICA WOKE WITH A START. SHE HAD BEEN DREAMING but was grateful that she couldn't remember the details. Reaching beside her bed, she tapped her cell phone to discover it was only a little after 10 AM.

After Nathan dropped her off earlier that morning, she threw her wet clothes into the washing machine and left a voicemail for Susan Watkins explaining that she would have to cancel her morning class once again. Veronica considered telling Sue to assign one of the adjuncts to finish out the rest of the semester but held her tongue. It would be unwise to give Dean Ritter any further ammunition against her.

Now fully awake, the professor got out of bed and meandered through her morning routine. After swapping her clean clothes from the washer to the dryer, she made her way into the kitchen and prepared the teakettle. When she discovered her bread had traces of mold, she tossed it into the wastebasket and settled for a bowl of flavorless cereal.

After preparing a second cup of tea, she took a seat at the dining room table and booted up her laptop. She shook the wireless mouse to life, clicked on the browser in the lower left corner of the screen, and loaded MSN on her homepage. Below a small cloud icon denoting the local weather, she saw a large stylized photo of a strip of yellow crime scene tape. When her eyes scanned the headline, her heart began to race.

"Child-Killer at Large in Eastern Virginia College Town."

Veronica clicked the link and began to read breathlessly to herself. She lifted her left hand and instinctively covered her mouth. Her bloodshot eyes raced over the small print, which reported that Emma Sullivan, age eight, had been found murdered in the front yard of her Williamsport, Virginia home early Friday morning.

Goddamn it, no!

Veronica's eyes began to water. She continued to read, muttering aloud to herself. "This marks the second homicide within a single week in the college town, where the body of seven-year-old Tyler Marshall was discovered in the woods beside South Williamsport Elementary School..." Veronica quickly skimmed over the text and picked up after a few sentences. "In a press conference held earlier this morning, Chief Dominic D'Amato, of the Williamsport Police Department, advised citizens to continue adhering to a strict five o'clock PM curfew and to report any suspicious activity..."

That's why she wasn't in the woods.

Jesus fucking Christ, she went into town.

And killed another kid.

"This is our fault," she finished aloud. "And it's on the national news." As Veronica hurriedly scanned the rest of the article, one of the final lines stood out to her. "Detective Francis L. McCain has been newly appointed to lead the current investigation."

What the fuck?

She scrolled to the top of the page to see if the article had an accompanying video. To her simultaneous relief and regret, it did. She clicked on the play icon and watched as the news report began. It was comprised of a voiceover with shots of the house and the front yard where the little girl was found. These scenes were followed by photographs of Emma Sullivan and Tyler Marshall. The report then cut to an interview with the girl's hollow-eyed father.

"We didn't hear anything," he said in an unsteady voice. "I woke up and noticed she wasn't in her bed." Jason Sullivan's composure broke before he added, "That's when I found her on the lawn."

The interview immediately segued to a wide shot of a brunette news reporter clad in a wet raincoat. The Sullivans' house and a taut line of police tape could be seen over her shoulder. As she walked forward along the street, the reporter reminded viewers that the police had no suspects for either crime, encouraged them to obey the curfew, and repeated the number of the Williamsport Crime Line. Just before she rattled off her name and the news station's call numbers, Veronica gasped when she saw Alderson's truck parked along the curb to the left of the reporter.

Where the hell did this happen?

The professor reached for her cell phone and cursed in frustration when she remembered Alderson's phone was dead. She frantically opened a new tab on her browser, typed 'Nathan Alderson' into the search engine, and slammed the enter key.

"Fuck!" she shouted again and attempted to control her racing thoughts.

What the hell ever happened to actual phone books?

She then searched for 'Virginia Tidewater Phone Directory,' and found two results for 'Nathan Alderson.' The first hit was too far north. The second was a residence in Williamsport.

She took a deep breath and dialed the number. After several rings, the call went to voicemail and Veronica hung up. Annoyed with her own ineptitude, the frazzled professor cleared her throat and redialed the number. She paced along the perimeter of her dining room as she waited for the answering service to activate. Before long, an unfamiliar woman's voice came through the speaker.

"Hello, you've reached Nathan, Kelly... AND CODY!"

Veronica closed her eyes at the sound of the deceased child's voice before Kelly instructed callers what to do next. Her knuckles white, Veronica waited for the tell-tale sign to leave her message.

"Hello. Detective Alderson, this is Dr. Veronica Upham from Williamsport College. I'm calling to let you know I may have additional information regarding the whereabouts of Edison Raymer. Please return my call at your earliest convenience. Thank you. Goodbye."

Veronica quickly terminated the call and caught her breath. She returned to the dining room table, and nearly knocked her teacup over when she bumped the protruding edge with her hip. In a daze, she stared at the computer monitor.

I have to get ahold of him. Then I gotta call Raymer. Fuck, what the hell are we gonna do? She could go after someone else tonight. Or one of us. Goddamn it, I have to find Nate.

After opening another tab, she searched for a general line for the Williamsport Police Department. Taking another deep breath, she punched the number into the keypad of her phone.

"You've reached the Williamsport Police Department. Sergeant Edward Tozier speaking. Is this an emergency?"

"Um, no, hi, this isn't an emergency," Veronica began. "I was wondering if I could speak with Detective Nathan Alderson."

There was a pause on the other end of the line. "May I ask who's calling?"

"You may, but I just need to speak directly to *him*," she replied. After another pause, she quickly filled the silence by adding, "I'm a professor from the college. He's expecting my call, as I have some important information he's asked me to obtain for him."

"Well, how about you leave me your name and telephone number and uh, I'll see if someone can get back to you."

Veronica sighed. "I don't want to speak to just *someone*. I want to speak to Nathan Alderson. Is he there?"

"Ma'am, I'm going to ask you to please remain calm," the desk sergeant said. "Detective Alderson is unavailable. If you'd like, I can transfer you—"

"What I'd *like* is for you to connect me with Nathan Alderson!" The professor raised her voice and knew she was about to lose this insipid battle.

"I can transfer you to Detective Frank McCain," the man finished, struggling to manage his own temper.

"Listen, Sergeant... Tozier was it?"

"Yes, ma'am. I don't believe you've given me *your* name?"

"So, how about a little *quid pro quo.*" She attempted to level-set her tone. "My name is Dr. Veronica Upham. I am an English Professor at Williamsport College. I spoke to Detective Alderson on Monday, no, Tuesday, no wait Monday afternoon. Whatever." She took a quick breath and resumed. "I've been helping him with the case he's working on. You know, the one involving the Marshall boy."

The desk sergeant cleared his throat but offered no reply.

"Now I just saw on the news…" She paused and swallowed hard. "I just saw on the news that another little girl was found this morning. And I *really* need to talk to Nate… I mean Detective Alderson."

"I'm sorry, ma'am, that's not going to be possible." Sergeant Tozier breathed heavily into the phone.

"Sergeant, I'm begging you. *Please.* I'm a friend of his. I know Kelly. I knew his son Cody before he died. *Please.* I need to talk to him."

"Alright, look," Sergeant Tozier began. "You can't talk to Nathan Alderson because he's currently in custody."

Veronica furrowed her brow. "Wait, what?"

Tozier sighed into the phone again. "He's been put on a psychiatric hold because he strangled his wife this morning. We don't know if Mrs. Alderson is going to press charges or have him committed."

Veronica sank into her dining room chair as the room began to swim and distort around her. A nauseous feeling welled up from her stomach. "What the hell are you saying? You're joking, right? You can't be serious."

"Ma'am, I assure you I'm not joking," Tozier responded. "In fact, the whole department is pretty much in shock, and I *really* cannot divulge any more information to you than I already have. Now Mrs. Upton, if you'd like me to, I can have Detective Frank McCain return your call sometime later this—"

Veronica ended the call. Before she could process the information she had just received, she had already tapped on the entry for 'Ray Edwards' in her favorite contacts. Mercifully, her colleague picked up after only a few short rings.

"Veronica? What is it?"

"Raymer, Jesus Christ, where are you?"

"I'm at Father McCallum's," he replied. "I stopped by to borrow a few books and discuss the ritual with him. What's going on? What's wrong?"

"Edison, she's killed another kid." Veronica began to stammer. "And… And Nate's gone. She killed a little girl in town. I think it was his fucking neighbor. I just saw it on the news. And I called the police station and they said… they said that Nate was in custody and—"

"Veronica, please hold on." Raymer said. He must have placed his hand over the mouthpiece for his voice was suddenly muffled. "Bill, turn on the TV." Suddenly his voice regained clarity. "Veronica, what happened to Nathan?"

She steeled herself and quickly relayed what Sergeant Tozier had just revealed to her. "She must've gotten to him, Edison. We should have stayed with him! This is our fault. *All of it!* That little girl was killed *on our watch* while we were pissing around in those woods. She went into a fucking residential area and killed a kid in the middle of the goddamn suburbs. They found the poor girl on the front lawn."

She could hear Edison take a breath on the other end of the line. "I think I also heard you say she was Nathan's neighbor?"

"Yes." Veronica nodded and wiped her eyes. "I saw his truck on the news. It was parked outside the house next to where they found the girl." She cleared her throat and reached up to rub her nose on the back of her sleeve. "I'm sorry, I'm all fucked up."

"It's alright," Edison assured her. "None of us saw this coming. But listen, I'm with Father McCallum now. I'm gonna talk to him. He'll help me prepare for what I need to do."

"OK," Veronica said. She exhaled heavily and tried to steady herself. "I'm OK. I can be up there in about an hour."

"No, no, Veronica, listen to me," Raymer said firmly. "You need to stay put. I told you I need to do this on my own. You've done enough for now. I need to handle this part myself."

"Edison, please." Panic crept back into her voice. "I'm fine. But I can't stay here. It's not safe. What the hell am I gonna do after dark?"

"Lock your doors," he said. "I'm not trying to be a smart ass here but forget about the salt and line your windows with holy water, wafers, crosses. You've got everything you need in the musette bag," Raymer reminded her. "And don't forget you've also got the .38, which is loaded with silver bullets."

"Edison, you know I can't shoot. I couldn't fucking hit the side of a goddamn barn!"

"Veronica, listen to me." He paused to consider his words carefully. "Stay alert. Try to get some sleep until dusk. If that doesn't work, load yourself up on caffeine or hell, uppers if you have any. If she comes into the house, wait for her to come to you."

"What? What the hell are you saying?"

"Let her come to you, Veronica. Let her bite you," he said with a peculiar emphasis. "And when she's feeding on your blood, empty all five of those silver bullets into her stomach or chest or wherever you can push that gun against her."

Veronica was stunned. She had no idea how to respond before he continued.

"That much silver should kill her," he insisted. "But that many shots are going to wake up your neighbors. And since you'll be in close quarters, the noise of gunfire might even deafen you for a while. It will pass, but you need to have a bag packed and ready to go. Park your car in the driveway. As soon as she drops, get the fuck out of there and call me when the ringing in your ears subsides."

The professor clenched her eyes shut and nodded repeatedly. "OK."

"Now more than likely, it's not going to come to that," Raymer told her. "On one hand, I can't imagine she'll keep wandering that far away from the woods. On the other hand, she just fed, so she may be motivated."

Raymer paused as a distant voice said something Veronica was unable to make out.

"You're right," Raymer answered McCallum and then spoke to Veronica. "She may resort to a psychic attack, but you know how to protect yourself better than Nathan did. You need to be ready for anything."

"Why can't I just come up there and stay with you?" Veronica pleaded. "Please, Edison. I can help you with the ritual."

"Absolutely not," he replied. "You're forgetting that *you* are the last and most important piece of this puzzle."

"What are you talking about?"

"When I discover her resting place, you need to get to it. Immediately. Like I told you. We find where she's hiding, and we strike by day. Now I was counting on Alderson to assist you with that part but obviously, the plan has changed."

"Why the hell don't you just perform the ritual *here?*" Veronica countered. "I don't understand. She's already *been* in my fucking house!"

"Simple. Because the Aston house is charged with an incredible amount of negative energy," Raymer explained. "And I need to harness that to enhance the power of the ritual. I need to be where I am most comfortable and furthermore, I don't want to put you in any more danger than you're already in."

"But you're willing to let me go out to wherever the fuck she is and kill her myself?"

"Yes," Raymer asserted. "That's exactly what you're going to do. You're gonna get her just like you almost did the last time. Only if I time this right, all you'll need to do is expose her to the sun, stand back, and watch her burn."

Veronica reached up and clasped the back of her clammy neck. "Fine. I guess we have no choice."

"I have all the faith in the world you can do this," Raymer assured her. "Now. Get your bags packed. Be ready for either scenario. You likely won't hear from me again today or tonight. But keep your phone charged, and the ringer on. My call could come at any time, and you'll need to act quickly."

"I've got it." Veronica nodded and pressed her shaking palm against the table. "Edison, please. Be careful. Please try to call me as soon as you can. OK?"

"I promise, Veronica," he said. "Be brave. We're going to end her. I swear to you."

Before she could reply, Edison disconnected the call. For several minutes, she held the phone in her hand and simply stared at the dining room window. While her guilt threatened to derail her, she let her mind replay Raymer's instructions to drown out her feelings of doubt and hopelessness.

"Fuck this bitch," she mumbled to herself and shot to her feet. Veronica sped from room to room and began preparing for the inevitable arrival of night.

31

After ending his call with Veronica, Edison Raymer turned to see Father McCallum leaning forward in his recliner. He had muted the television and sat on the edge of his chair, his hands folded and hanging between his knees.

"I don't like this, Edison." He shook his head. "Not one bit."

Raymer moved to take a seat on McCallum's sofa. "Look, I know this is less than ideal, but—"

"Less than ideal? Please," the priest replied. "Edison, we've got another dead body on our hands. An innocent eight-year-old girl. Not only that, but this is now a *national* news story. Before this day is through, my phone is gonna ring and I'll have to answer for this. We absolutely *cannot* afford for anything else to go public."

"I understand that," Raymer said. "But we didn't know this would happen. We assumed she'd be out in those woods and would've come after *us.*"

"Well, she didn't." McCallum clenched his fist, which was crisscrossed with scars from his boxing days. "Not yet. I told you this thing was smart, and now it's clear that you're not going to be able to predict her next move."

"That's why I'm going to start the ritual. All I need—"

"Wait." McCallum waved his hand to silence his protégé. "You're forgetting that we still have the matter of this detective on our hands."

Raymer sighed and pursed his lips before speaking. "I realize that, but we don't know—"

"That's precisely the problem, Edison. You *don't know* what he's already told his colleagues. You *don't know* exactly what happened to him. What else did Dr. Upham tell you over the phone?"

"She said that Alderson strangled his wife this morning."

"But she's still alive?"

"Thankfully, yes."

McCallum nodded with a troubled expression. "Well, obviously it was the influence of the vampire. As long as he's alive, God help him, she's going to keep toying with his mind. Did you notice anything odd about his behavior after he confronted her in the woods?"

"A little," Raymer hesitated. "He seemed agitated. He never admitted it, but I had my suspicions that she was already working on him through his dreams."

McCallum narrowed his eyes. "What about you? Has she started working on *you?*"

"No," Raymer assured him. "She hasn't."

"Well, at least there's that. But I'd say it's only a matter of time before she does."

"I thought we had more time. And that once we took her down, he'd be free of her influence."

"Well, that was a mistake." The priest lifted his hands to his chin. "You shouldn't have left him out of your sight until you taught him how to guard himself against her psychic attacks."

Raymer fidgeted in his seat. "Look, Father, I know I've made some mistakes here. But there's only so much I could've done. We had to keep up appearances. If he started spending his nights at Veronica's house, people were gonna talk, and his wife would've gotten suspicious."

"People *are* talking!" McCallum pointed at the television. "Probably on fucking CNN, may the Lord forgive my French. And I'm sure Mrs. Alderson is not only feeling suspicious today but she's also lucky to be alive!"

"So, what do you want me to do?" Raymer asked. "That's what I came here for, Father. To ask you for your advice."

McCallum lowered his eyes and tapped his fingers on the arm of his chair. "Unfortunately, there's really nothing you *can* do in regard to Detective

Alderson," McCallum said. "She's already got her hooks in him, so the poor bastard probably can't tell fantasy from reality, which would explain why he attacked his wife. But that *also* means he could be sitting in a jail cell or an interrogation room right now ranting and raving about vampires."

"Well, more than likely, the cops aren't going to believe a word he says." Raymer glanced at the floor. "I should know, as I have some experience in that regard."

"Yeah, well, I'm afraid this situation is a little bit different because they've got two dead *children* on their hands," McCallum responded. "In short, this is a complete and total fiasco."

A heavy silence fell between them. The gray afternoon cast a formidable gloom and the small table lamp beside McCallum's recliner did little to illuminate the priest's modest apartment.

Eventually, McCallum leaned back in his chair and sighed. "I'm sorry, Edison, but this whole thing leaves me no other choice. I need to call in reinforcements."

"Bill, no!" Raymer shot to his feet. "Please, I've got this."

"I'm sorry," he repeated. "This is no reflection on you. It's my fault for not fully preparing you for this sooner."

"Father, listen, I just need more time. Once I've managed to bind—"

"Edison, please. Listen to me." McCallum shifted in his recliner. "I've made my decision. You can still lead the investigation, but I can't leave this up to one man and a well-meaning professor who's in *way* over her head. There's just too much at risk. We're talking about upsetting the very fabric of society as we know it. Too much has already come out." McCallum paused and glanced sideways at one of his bookcases. "I realize the existence of vampires is a secret that couldn't be kept forever. But I sure as hell hoped I would've already shuffled off this mortal coil before that day came."

Raymer stood with his arms folded and glared at the priest. "So what are you going to do?"

McCallum exhaled heavily. "I'm gonna make two phone calls. The first will be to someone with a significant influence on the police department, who can surreptitiously put a lid on the situation with the detective." The priest shook his head with genuine compassion. "I'm really sorry to say this, but I'm gonna make sure he's moved somewhere completely inaccessible to the outside world. That's the best I can do for him now. When we destroy this parasite that's latched onto him, maybe he can spend the rest of his days in some semblance of peace."

Raymer shook his head. A part of him wished the Brennen vampire had just killed Nathan, to ensure he would be spared any further misery.

"I told you. He's a good man, Father. None of this—"

"No one's disputing that, but he's also a liability. There's nothing further to discuss on that matter. Now," McCallum continued, "the second call I need to make is to our team up in D.C. I'll arrange for them to send a unit comprised of six to eight experienced vampire hunters to patrol those woods and be ready to take her down once you've discovered her location."

"That's not gonna work, Father." Raymer ran his hand over his shorn scalp. "I'm sorry, but that's the truth. We need a different strategy."

"So, what's your suggestion? You wanna send your lady friend into those woods alone just to get herself slaughtered?"

"No," Raymer replied. "First of all, we know the vampire's on the move. She's left the forest. So, your guys will be standing around there with their thumbs up their asses the entire time just like the three of us were."

McCallum moved to speak but Raymer raised a hand to silence him. "With all due respect, Father, let me finish." Raymer sat back down on the sofa and engaged his mentor with a pleading glance. "The vampire's no longer in those woods. Veronica said the girl she murdered was Alderson's neighbor. So that means she's bedding down somewhere outside the forest. The James River winds through half the state and there are woods and swamps stretching behind all those residential areas. She could be anywhere. Which is why I have to perform the binding ritual to figure out where she is."

"Edison, I never told you *not* to perform the ritual," McCallum reminded him. "I'm just calling in a team to assist you and your friend in the practical execution of the plan."

"But we don't need them," Raymer insisted. "If you want to keep this quiet, why bring more people into it? Why alert your superiors to a colossal fuck-up that we can handle ourselves?"

"I assure you, they're already aware of it."

"There are too many variables. I don't know these guys, so how can I be sure—"

"Again, the ship for discretion has already sailed. We just need to end this before it gets worse. And in terms of their capabilities, I wouldn't call them in if I didn't trust in their efficiency."

Raymer leaned forward. "Look, you're the one who told me I had two options. We tried the first plan, and it didn't work. But I haven't even had a chance to execute plan B as it were. *I'm* the one that has a personal connection with this thing. *I'm* the one who can cast the most effective spell, because there's nothing I want more than to see this thing destroyed."

McCallum looked away in contemplation before he returned his attention to Raymer. "Here's the deal, Edison. You have three days." He held up three thick fingers. "If the mission is not accomplished in that time, then I send in the cavalry. Do you understand?"

"Yes," Raymer responded. "That's all I'm asking."

"I still think you're making a mistake," McCallum added. "But I really don't want to complicate matters any further by bringing in another team." The frustrated priest shook his head and exhaled heavily through his nose. "And like I told you the other day, I have faith in your ego, and it's your ego that's going to empower this ritual."

Raymer nodded and waited for the priest to continue.

"But *do not* underestimate the importance of your commitment to this procedure. This isn't some parlor game, as these are seriously dangerous forces you're calling on."

"I understand," Raymer assured him.

"Now, about that." McCallum slapped his hands on his knees and rose to his feet. "I believe the purpose of your visit today was not to argue with me and defy my express orders, but to borrow some books. Is that not so?"

Raymer felt ashamed for a moment. "I didn't come here to argue with you, Father. That wasn't my intention."

"Relax, I understand. While this situation is 'not ideal,' as you so eloquently put it, it's nothing we can't handle."

The tall man approached one of his bookcases and bent to study his collection of magical texts.

"So, first things first, as I'm sure you've guessed, you need both *The Key of Solomon* and *The Lesser Key of Solomon,* or as it's also sometimes called, the *Lemegeton.*" He passed the slim hardback volumes across his coffee table and handed them to Raymer. "Those will instruct you on the most basic operations of summoning and commanding the vampire's spirit to obey your will. Now obviously the book refers to them as spirits or demons, but as I explained to you before, the vampire is beholden to the same laws."

"Yes." Raymer nodded. "I'm familiar with these. I used to own Mathers' translations before I sold off my books."

"One of your less inspired moments," McCallum quipped. He pointed to Edison and elaborated further. "The *Clavicles* also provide detailed descriptions of the preparations required for these operations." He paused and met Raymer's gaze. "While you'll have to forgo these preparations out of necessity, I *highly encourage* you to read and comprehend each of the steps you're supposed to undertake so that at the very least, the methodology can still inform your ritual." McCallum shrugged his shoulders. "To put it simply, pretend that you've performed these tasks and convince your conscious mind that you've already executed them."

The priest turned back to the bookcase and traced his finger along the various spines in search of a specific volume. "Next, I'd recommend the *Grimorium Verum,* which, for your purposes, contains information regarding the processes of evocation and most importantly, the *dismissal* of spirits. Rather than facilitate her departure, your goal is to delay and stall it. You must entirely exhaust her with your interrogations and keep her engaged until after the sun has fully risen."

McCallum selected another book from his collection and began perusing its table of contents. Raymer was momentarily enthralled by the cleric's knowledge of the occult. "It's not every day you receive these kinds of instructions from a Catholic priest."

"Yeah, well, as you know, I'm not your average priest." McCallum snapped the book shut before placing it back on the shelf. "And I imagine you also already know, Dr. Raymer, that these particular texts and procedures do not align themselves with the powers of darkness but are instead wholly dependent upon the intervention of God. So technically, the rites of black magic are simply secret forms of Judeo-Christian practices and therefore well within my area of expertise. But I digress."

Raymer waited patiently as McCallum searched for a specific title. "Ah, here it is." The priest turned and handed a heavy black tome to Edison. "*The Grimoire of Honorius.* This will likely be the most useful to you. It was falsely attributed to a twelfth-century pope, which makes for a great story and gives it an air of blasphemy that the uninitiated completely misunderstand. In fact, it is the most liturgical of grimoires and its invocations read like prayers or litanies."

Raymer held the book in his hands and began leafing through its pages. He wrinkled his brow as he stopped to study some of the complex seals and sigils.

"*The Grimoire of Honorius* is singular in that it includes more explicit instructions for the binding of spirits and the resurrection of the dead, all delivered under the pretense that these acts were sanctioned by the Church," McCallum explained with a hint of skepticism. "Now, the bits about necromancy make for fascinating reading, but you aren't attempting to *raise* the dead, you are attempting to *command* the spirit or soul inhabiting the vampire's corpse, which is an important distinction."

Raymer continued to scan the book's contents. "You're right," he noted. "At first glance, this *does* read more like a Mass than an invocation."

"Yeah but look ahead a little further." McCallum leaned over and pointed as Raymer thumbed through the thick vellum pages. "Check out the passage entitled 'Universal Conjuration.' That's precisely what it is. I'd recommend you use that as the basis for your own invocation. Read it, absorb it, internalize it, and then make it your own."

Edison's eyes pored over the provocative text. "This is very helpful. I remember seeing references to this grimoire when I first looked into Goetia as an undergrad years ago."

McCallum stood with his back to the bookcase and offered another suggestion. "Given the significance of crossroads to this particular vampire, you should also pay attention to the 'The Conjurations of the Kings of the Cardinal Directions.' That's another means in which you can personalize and tailor your invocation to resonate with her."

"Understood," Raymer said. He finished leafing through the fourth grimoire and then placed the books on the coffee table in front of him.

McCallum returned to his recliner and settled himself back into the worn, form-fitting leather. He continued to study his protégé's expression before he leaned forward and raised a finger toward Raymer.

"Giving you these books and encouraging you to take shortcuts with the meticulous preparations ascribed to these procedures is likely foolish if not downright irresponsible and *dangerous,*" McCallum warned. "But you don't have the time to follow the rules and perform these rites to the letter. I'm only lending you these books to serve as a guide." McCallum shot a quick glance at the muted television. "You need to *say what you need to say* to enforce your will and command this particular spirit. Do what empowers you and gives you the confidence that you need to impose your will. Choose an incense that appeals to you. Wear comfortable clothing. Play ambient music if it will enhance your concentration. Whatever it takes."

"It's a battle of wills," Raymer said. "Mine versus hers."

"Exactly. Think of it this way," McCallum suggested. "You knew how to command a classroom. Now you need to raise yourself to another level of consciousness and do the same thing as a magician. Can you do that, Edison?"

Raymer nodded. "I can."

"Good." McCallum locked eyes with Raymer. "But you must remember *above all else* that your state of mind, and your absolute, ardent, unwavering *belief* in the words you are saying is absolutely *crucial.* Any crack in the façade and the entire thing will backfire. At best, you'll fail. At worst, you'll open yourself to influences even more diabolical than this vampire you're hunting."

"That's a risk I'm willing to take," Edison said.

McCallum leaned forward and glanced down the hallway toward his bedroom. "You're going to need some additional tools. I presume you have a ceremonial dagger?"

"Yes, I have something that will suffice."

"Ideally, it needs to be made of silver or gold. You can't just use a hunting knife."

"Believe it or not, I happen to own a silver athame. Something I saved from my younger days. I've been using it on urban hunts."

"That's exactly what you need. Now, were you able to obtain any personal items of hers?"

"Yes, I've got pieces of her dress, a lock of hair, a fingernail, and part of a finger bone from when Alderson blew her hand off. I also gathered some soil from her footprints."

"Good. Do you have a suitable receptacle for these objects? Preferably a chalice or offering bowl?"

"I do," Raymer affirmed.

"Well, then that only leaves the scrying mirror, and I have just the thing." McCallum gestured for Raymer to remain seated as he rose from his chair and disappeared down the hall to his bedroom. A few minutes later, he returned carrying a medium-sized object wrapped in black silk.

"This is a highly polished stone of obsidian," McCallum explained. "As you will learn from the texts, you will place this mirror within a second smaller and carefully crafted circle. You'll find the appropriate dimensions and sigils in *The Key of Solomon* or the *Lemegeton*. Once you've worked yourself into the proper transcendental state, she will manifest in the mirror within your mind's eye. That is when you'll unleash your interrogation and keep her trapped there until after dawn."

Raymer took the heavy object into his arms and placed it on the sofa. He bent to the floor to retrieve one of his large gym bags and began loading the mirror and books. Once they were carefully arranged, he zipped the bag and rose to his feet, lifting the bag at his side.

McCallum walked with Raymer and clasped a strong hand on his back. "Be careful, Edison. Pace yourself, and don't waver in your focus or your conviction. Take this thing down, once and for all. But please," the priest paused just shy of his door and Raymer turned to face him. "Don't make me regret my decision to let you handle this on your own."

32

WITH SEVERAL DOZEN CANDLES ABLAZE AROUND HIM, Edison Raymer stood shirtless in the center of his basement. Clad only in a pair of black pants, his bare feet were firmly planted in the center of an encircled hexagram etched with chalk onto the concrete floor. The dimensions of the figure had been measured with exacting detail.

True to the instructions in the Solomonic grimoire, the topmost point of the hexagram—which he faced—represented the state of matter. Of all things feminine. Of water, to which he believed Charlotte Brennen was so inextricably linked. The lower point of the intersecting equilateral triangles met the curving circle behind him. Its meaning girded him in his righteousness, as the lowest point stood for the spirit, the masculine, and all aspects of heat and fire. To his left, he had inscribed the Greek letter Alpha, to his right, Omega. His feet straddled the letter Tau.

Almost touching the top convergence of the enclosed Macrocosmic Shatkona was a smaller chalk circle. At the center of the empty annulus was a narrow podium draped in white silk. Upon its slanted surface sat Father McCallum's obsidian mirror, angled so it could be viewed from a seated or kneeling position. Before the mirror, Raymer had carefully placed his athame next to a silver offering bowl. Inside the meticulously polished receptacle were all the vampire's personal belongings they had collected—the scraps of cloth, strands of hair, fingernail, finger bone, and soil upon which she had walked.

Before spending hours copying various cryptic sigils and letters into and around both circles, Raymer had taken the time to drape the basement walls with black tapestries. His workbenches had been similarly covered, so as not to distract him as he carried out the grueling task ahead. He had burned frankincense and myrrh to purify both circles, and the commingling scents still lingered around him.

Despite the exotic aroma, the air surrounding Edison Raymer was heavy with a sense of foreboding. Yet he was cognizant that this nearly electric tension was the intangible manifestation of his own will. Before dropping to his knees, he fixed his eyes on the center of the empty circle before him. "Elohim Gibor!" His booming voice repeated this admonition three times, as proscribed, to begin his work.

Once his knees hit the floor, Raymer finished the consecration of the circle. With his muscular back and shoulders stiff and straight, his eyes focused on the obsidian mirror. He spoke a simple yet powerful invocation. "O, Adonai most powerful, El most strong, Agla most holy, On most righteous, the Alpha and the Omega, the Beginning and the End—thou who hast established all things in thy Wisdom—I duly and truly consecrate these circles in thy Divine and Holy Name of Names!" He took a deep breath. "What is sealed under these symbols shall not be undone! So mote it be!"

Raymer knelt forward and reached for a leather scourge he had carefully positioned within the hexagram. With the whip in his left hand, he administered six quick snaps over his left shoulder. Edison winced but did not cry out with the pain. Shifting the lash to his right hand, he followed suit with six more sharp cracks over his right shoulder.

After placing the scourge aside, he took up a silver handbell and rose to his feet. He turned to face the east and with a sharp flick of his wrist, he began to ring the bell.

"O mighty King of the East, Magoa! By my labor! By my *will!* By the name of Him that sits on High! I beseech Thee, I call to Thee! Send unto me the Spirit of my enemy Charlotte Brennen! If she tarries on Thy paths, freeze her with Thy winds and render her unto me! I compel Thee with all the Virtue and the Power of the Most High!"

Raymer held the bell still and made a low bow in the direction of the east. He slowly turned to face the south and rang the bell again.

"O Œgim, Great King of the South! By my labor! By my *will!* I invoke Thee by the High and Most Holy Name of God. Make manifest the Spirit of my enemy Charlotte Brennen! If she hides within Thy bowels, expel her from Thy dust and make her answer unto me! I compel Thee! I beseech Thee! It is He who commands Thee!"

Edison silenced the bell and made another bow to the south. He turned next to face the west and began tolling the bell.

"O thou Bayemont, most potent King, he who reigns in the West! By my labor! By my *will!* I command Thee by the Virtue of the Most High. Seek out the Spirit of my enemy Charlotte Brennen! If she sleeps beneath Thy waves, spit her forth from Thy abode and drown her in my hate! I beseech Thee! I compel Thee! It is He who commands Thee!"

The ringing ceased. Raymer bent low to the west.

Edison turned to the north and rang the bell.

"O great King and Emperor of the North! Amaymon! By my labor! By my *will!* By the Virtue and the Power of the Creator! I beseech Thee, I call to Thee! Shine Thy light upon the Spirit of my enemy Charlotte Brennen! If she walks in Thy shadows, drive her forth into the flames of day! I compel Thee with all the Virtue and the Power of the Living God!"

Raymer silenced the bell and bowed to the north. He placed the handbell on the podium and stood with his arms outstretched, facing the obsidian mirror within the second smaller circle. In a loud, thunderous voice he called:

"Charlotte Gordon! Charlotte Brennen! I abjure you! I command you! Charlotte Gordon! Charlotte Brennen! My enemy! My adversary! I compel thee! I command thee!"

With his left hand to his brow, Raymer made the sign of the cross, touching his taut abdomen and then each of his shoulders.

"I, Edison Joseph Raymer, invoke thee, Charlotte Brennen! I, Edison Joseph Raymer, spurn thee, Charlotte Brennen! I, Edison Joseph Raymer, compel thee, Charlotte Gordon Brennen to obey my *will!*"

Raymer snatched the handbell from the podium.

"Come forth on the winds from the east!" Raymer shook the bell while facing east. "Appear!"

"Come forth from the earth in the south!" Raymer shook the bell while facing south. "Appear!"

"Come forth from the waves in the west!" Raymer shook the bell while facing west. "Appear!"

"Come forth on the flames from the north!" Raymer shook the bell while facing north. "Appear!"

The candles throughout the basement began to flicker and dim. Some of the wicks burned blue, while others grew large to devour the dense air around them.

"I conjure ye, Charlotte Brennen, from whatsoever part of the world ye may be. From the east to the south to the west to the north or in any place that comforts thee! Thou art *expunged!* I command thee, appear promptly and *bend* before my *will! Bow* in obedience! I conjure ye! I command ye absolutely, Charlotte Brennen, in whatsoever part of the universe ye may be! Appear!"

Raymer took a step toward the podium at the head of his circle. He raised the silver athame in his right hand. With his fingers tightly wrapping the black handle, he drew the sharp blade across the palm of his left hand. He watched as his blood ran in rivulets, dripping over the contents he had placed in the silver bowl. Next, he lifted the bloodied blade and cut the sign of the cross in the air above the altar.

"I conjure ye and most urgently command ye! Charlotte Brennen! I force, I constrain, I exhort, I rebuke, by the most Mighty and Powerful Name of God, of Elohim, of Jehovah! I demand you delay no more! Come forth with haste! I fear not thy noise! I fear not thy deformity! I fear not thy hideousness! I fear not thy rage! I fear not thy will! Appear!"

Raymer gathered the loose soil from the bowl into his hand. He smeared the blood-drenched contents over his face and then tossed what remained over his left shoulder. He then picked up a piece of the vampire's dress and shouted, "In the name of thy lost William! Appear!" He tore the tattered black fabric in two.

He reached for a taper candle and removed it from its silver holster in one hand, and then pinched the strands of Charlotte's hair between the thumb and index finger of his left hand. "In the name of thy lost Joanna! Appear!" He touched the tip of the candle to the nest of hairs and set them ablaze.

After placing the candle back in its holder, he took up the rotten finger bone. "In the name of thy lost Lilian! Appear!" With a quick snap, Raymer cracked the bone in half and placed the fragments back into the dish.

"I conjure you, Charlotte Brennen, I constrain ye, I command ye, with utmost Vehemence and Power, by that Most Potent and Powerful Name of God!"

Raymer reached into the dish to withdraw the fingernail and held it aloft. "Thou hast tasted of my blood, thus I devour thy flesh. As you seek to master me, I shall obliterate you! *Ex umbra in lucem!*"

He placed the fingernail on the bed of his tongue and then swallowed it whole.

"Tremble at my *will!*" he roared. Veins protruded from his temples. His smooth head was slick with perspiration. "Tremble at my command! For I shall lay your plans to waste! I shall drag you from darkness into light! I shall poison your blood with rivers of silver! I will dance upon the rotting bones of your children! I will defile them in their earthly slumber! I will see that you are never united with them in body, in spirit, or in mind!"

With the handbell aloft, he began to stalk the perimeter of the circle, the clangorous metallic chimes filling the air.

"May you be forever separated from William!

"May you be forever separated from Joanna!

"May you be forever separated from Lillian!

"May your ears be deaf to the cries of William!

"May your tongue be dumb to the pleas of Joanna!

"May your eyes be blind to the face of Lillian!"

Several candles to Edison's left were extinguished as a low wind moved through the basement. A rack of pillar candles fell forward and crashed to the floor. Raymer stood fast—his eyes now fixed on the face of the obsidian mirror.

"I shall constrain you, Charlotte Brennen, by the Holy Light of the Sun, which is the Eye of the Lord."

His bell continued to ring out as the candles were snuffed one after another.

"I fear not thy tricks nor thy deceptions! For by the seal of the Moon and the Stars, I shall bind thee, Charlotte Brennen. I force and compel thee to obey and execute my *will*. Appear before this circle! Without failure, without resistance, without delay! Appear!"

Raymer stood in pitch darkness—his eyes riveted to the blank polished stone. The temperature had dropped, and his sweat was cold on his skin.

"Be ye accursed, damned, and eternally reproved. Be ye tormented with perpetual pain, so that you may find no repose by day. So you may not walk by night, lest you *obey* my command! Appear! Within this circle I compel and conjure ye! Charlotte Brennen! Appear!"

Through the dense atmosphere, a long, groaning creak resounded through the blackness. A low yellow light originated from the top of the basement stairs.

Raymer turned to see a bare filthy foot slip into view on the topmost step. The wood bent beneath the weight of the shadowed intruder. A second foot—caked in mud, which clung to long curling toenails—came down upon the next step. Raymer saw the unmistakable fringe of black, tattered cloth swinging above a grimy ankle.

No. It's not possible.

The stench of rot and river muck overpowered the perfume of the incense. Another low *thump* came from the stairs as the thing shambled down two more rickety steps. A gnarled hand clutched the banister as Charlotte Brennen took another heavy step forward.

The bell slipped from Edison Raymer's grasp and clattered to the floor.

33

WITH A FEW HOURS UNTIL DAWN, VERONICA SAT AT HER dining room table. Her chair was angled to face the corner where Charlotte Brennen had appeared during the séance. Every light in the house was on, and the hum of her laptop's cooling fan broke the silence. She had placed her cell phone on the table before her, anticipating the moment when Edison would call to tell her that the binding ritual had been a success and he had discovered where the vampire was hiding.

Veronica knew she would have to act quickly once that moment came, but the clock kept ticking and the phone remained silent. She was beginning to worry, not just about Raymer, but about her own situation.

What if the ritual didn't work? Or she's impervious to whatever Edison cooked up with that priest? Maybe she's on her way here right now? It's not like she needed a formal invitation the first time she darkened that corner.

Veronica shuddered at the thought and tightened her grip on the snub-nose .38 Special. She lifted it and pointed the barrel at the place where the vampire had materialized barely a week ago. Veronica had no idea how much recoil the revolver would produce, or how she could steadily fire round after round into the fiend and keep a safe distance.

That's why Edison told you to let her bite you. No aiming involved. Just jam it into her chest and fill her full of silver.

The large heat register in the ceiling began to blast hot air as the furnace kicked on. With the sudden rush of warmth enveloping her, she found herself yawning uncontrollably. Veronica took a sip of lukewarm coffee from a nearby mug and contemplated taking a couple of No Doz tabs. Yet she could already feel her pulse pounding and decided not to take the caffeinated stimulants.

Her thoughts wandered back to the night when Nathan, Edison, and she had gathered around the table together. "The best laid plans..." she said aloud and yawned again. Little did they know what their adversary had in store for them. She wondered if Kelly Alderson had committed her husband. It was difficult to imagine him locked in a cell and doped up on tranquilizers.

As her mind continued to wander, her eyelids grew heavy. She blinked a few times and sat up straight, determined not to let sleep overtake her.

"That phone's gonna ring any minute now," she said aloud to no one. "And you have to be ready to go when he says it's clear." Veronica brought her left hand around to try a grip technique that Alderson had showed her. She aimed at the corner and indexed the trigger.

Soon enough, she had slumped back in the chair and was fighting the urge to sleep again. "I'll just close my eyes for a few minutes..."

Exhausted, Veronica slumped forward, and her breathing began to slow. She was subjected to a series of unsettling images.

Nathan Alderson led a funeral procession through the forest. Six uniformed police officers carried a coffin on their shoulders. They placed the casket at the center of the crossroads. A young girl with strawberry-blonde ringlets awoke and rose from the coffin. She wandered along the forest path until she met a solemn boy wearing an ill-fitting suit from the last century. They clasped hands and made their way to the riverbank. Charlotte Brennen slowly emerged from the black waters of the James, her dress soaked and muddy. River weeds clung to her limbs, her long hair drenched and partially veiling her white face. In her left hand she gripped a silver stake. A large mallet was clasped in her right. Edison Raymer lay writhing on the riverbank. Laura McCoy and Matthias Bartsch knelt beside him, their eyes shining black in the moonlight. They each pinned Raymer's arms and legs to the ground as Charlotte approached, her bare feet leaving footprints in the mud. Raymer fought and struggled against them as Charlotte bent forward to place the point of the stake into his mouth.

Veronica forced herself awake. She leaned back in the chair and tried to erase the disturbing visions from her mind. On unsteady legs, she pushed herself upward to stand. The .38 slid out of her hands and onto the surface of the table.

She popped two No Doz tablets and chased them down with the remainder of the coffee. But it was no use. Veronica hadn't had a good night's sleep since the séance, and her circadian rhythms were out of sync. It was only a matter of time before the constant wakefulness and anxiety caught up to her. She sat back down and hoped the sudden jolt of coffee and stimulants would shock some life back into her.

Just as she sat down and picked up the pistol, her eyelids started to close again. She tried the same trick as before and sat up straight, but this time, something very strange occurred. A small patch of shadow began to spread across the wall and darken.

Veronica shook her head and flexed her fingers around the pistol grip, but her hand was empty. She looked from left to right, but the gun was gone, along with the entire dinner table and its contents. In mute horror, she looked up to see the walls had been consumed by an impenetrable darkness—a black so deep that no light reflected from any point around her.

Seconds, minutes, and hours had passed but Veronica was none the wiser. The terror that had gripped her earlier ebbed away as a ripple of concentric circles broke the eerie murk before her eyes. Naked and sweat-soaked, Edison Raymer stepped out from the surface patterns and began to walk toward her, but there was no ground beneath his feet. His face was stony, and his eyes pierced her the same way they did when they first met years ago.

Veronica felt that she was still sitting, but as Edison drew closer, his face and gaze were on the same level as hers. She moved her lips to speak, but Edison slowly raised his arm and rested his index finger against his lips. Veronica had lost the ability to measure time, as Raymer didn't flinch, nor did he breathe.

Suddenly, a rotting hand—scarred and blood-stained—emerged from behind him and grasped his shoulder. A withered arm bereft of its hand snaked around his torso from the other side. Edison Raymer was pulled back into the void before she could reach out to save him.

Veronica toppled out of her chair onto the floor beneath her dining room table. The pistol, which had been back in her grasp, slid away from her as she hit her head against the wall.

She sat up in a daze. The muted gray light of the sun was obscured by clouds and streamed in through the windows.

What time is it?

She reached out and used the table leg to stand. Forgetting about the gun, she took up the phone with trembling hands and checked for missed calls. There were none.

It was already 11:30 on Saturday morning.

He should have called hours ago if the ritual had worked. He was only supposed to keep her bound 'til after dawn.

Veronica stooped to fetch the pistol and set it down before her. Still weakly clutching the phone, she called Edison's number. It rang six times and went to voicemail.

Goddamn it, he can't still be in the middle of it. If it didn't work, then why the hell didn't he call me?

Veronica redialed the number. It rang a half-dozen times before going to voicemail a second time.

That wasn't a dream.

It was a plea for help.

The musette bag Raymer had given her hung on the back of another dining room chair. She snatched it up and withdrew a vial of holy water, a roll of communion wafers, and a silver cross on a beaded chain, which she draped around her neck. Veronica stumbled into the living room, her cell and the small bottle in one hand and the pistol in the other. She shoved the items into her purse and slung it over her shoulder. After grabbing her keys and a coat from the rack in the foyer, she bolted out the door and slid into the driver's seat of her Volvo.

Veronica cranked the engine and put the heat on full blast to ward away the autumn chill. Without checking the mirrors, she pulled out of her driveway and headed down the winding residential street. In a moment's time, she turned onto Route 10 and put the aging car's pedal to the floor. The car sped out of Williamsport in the direction of Richmond.

Her thoughts raced as she drove along the highway.

What if he's just sleeping? What if he's still bound in the circle interrogating her? What if I interrupt him? What if he's mad that I came? What if the door's locked? What if he sends me home?

The haunting vision of Edison in the black void flashed through her mind.

What if he's hurt? What if he needs help?

What if he's dead?

She thrust her foot on the gas and gripped the wheel, exceeding the speed limit by at least twenty miles per hour. She arrived at Dutch Gap Trace in no time, thanks to the light weekend traffic and lack of speed traps.

When she reached the cul-de-sac, she swung her Volvo around and pulled along the curb in front of the Aston house.

It's Raymer's house.

Not the goddamn Aston house.

"Who are you kidding?" she mumbled to herself as she snatched her purse from the passenger seat, threw open the car door, and turned to face her destination. "It'll always be the Aston house."

The wind blew her hair into her eyes as she slammed the car door shut. She brushed her disheveled hair behind her ears and eyed the house with apprehension. From the street, it looked dark, still, and uninhabited. Her heart jumped when she noticed the front door was slightly ajar.

With her hand on the butt of the .38, she hurried along the sidewalk. As she raced to the door, she failed to notice the muddy footprints leading into the house—nor did she see the bloody footprints leading out of it.

Veronica paused before the door, withdrew the gun from her purse, and took three quick breaths before forcing herself to go inside. She spun to her left and entered the dim living room. The sparse furniture had been upset—table lamps were overturned, the chairs and sofa were out of place, a glass-topped coffee table had been smashed. Shards of broken glass crunched beneath her shoes as she crept along the carpet.

A foul odor hit her as she made her way through the dining room and into the kitchen. For a moment, she feared the vampire was in the house. But her eyes began to water as she realized the stench was... *fresh.*

Please God, no. Let me wake up from this. I'm still sleeping. Head down on the dining room table. Please.

Veronica placed the back of her hand under her nose and over her mouth, the pistol still weakly thrust ahead. She nervously used the gun to swat at a cluster of flies that buzzed around her face. The door to the basement was open. She reached around the wooden frame into the darkness, feeling blindly along the wall until the tips of her fingers ran over the light switch.

Her instincts rebelled but she knew she had no choice but to descend the basement stairs. Halfway down the steps, Veronica stopped. Her eyes grew wide, and she covered her mouth and nose with a shaking hand—partly out of fear, but mostly out of revulsion.

Two narrow hopper-style windows were broken. Misshapen cracks had spread across the panes like spider webs. Black tapestries, which had been fastened to the walls, were torn to ribbons. Some were pulled down to reveal the racks where firearms and weapons were once neatly suspended. The tools of the vampire hunter's trade lay scattered on the floor.

Splayed out on the concrete was the mutilated body of Edison Raymer. He lay on his side, contorted unnaturally, his fingers frozen as if clawing at the legs of an invisible assailant. He had been torn open from throat to groin, his ribs cracked and shattered. Slathered in blood and bile, his innards had spilled onto the floor. It was impossible for Veronica to distinguish his heart from his lungs or his liver as the organs had been stomped flat and smashed beyond recognition.

The concrete was stained with glistening blood, mud, and feces. Gore ran down the walls as Raymer's congealing blood dripped down a drain in the center of the floor. A handful of teeth were stuck along the mouth of the ventilated cover.

Veronica grasped the handrail tightly. "Edison," she whimpered. "Jesus fucking Christ... No!" She fought the urge to retch and held her breath, unable to turn away from the gruesome reality before her.

Raymer's mouth gaped open—slack-jawed and hanging from his face. The flesh of his throat had been shredded and torn. His dead eyes stared up at Veronica—as if he'd had just enough life left in him to watch his murderer leave his broken body behind and ascend the basement stairs.

Flies swarmed on his dark skin, and the copper stench of blood mixed with the foul smell of waste finally succeeded in overwhelming her. She turned away on tremulous legs and mounted the stairs, two at a time, until she stood in the middle of the kitchen, gasping for fresh air.

I can't leave him like this.

I can't.

After shoving the .38 into her purse, Veronica edged her way to a wall-mounted telephone. She pulled a paper towel from a nearby rack, used it to cover her hand, and picked up the receiver. With a bare knuckle, she dialed 9-1-1.

When the operator asked, "what's your emergency?" she blurted out the first words that came to mind. "M-my neighbor has been murdered. His address is, uh, 1596... 1596 Orkney Springs Court... in... in the... in Dutch Gap Trace."

"Ma'am, could you—"

"His name is Edison Raymer." Veronica flinched as she said his name aloud. "Please. Send someone! Quickly!"

Before the operator could continue, Veronica dropped the receiver and let it dangle above the kitchen floor. She ran to the front door with the paper towel still balled up in her free hand. Veronica crumpled the evidence and shoved it in her coat pocket. She nearly tripped over the front stoop and stumbled onto the walkway. She righted herself and froze when she noticed the footprints along the sidewalk trailing to and from the house. She staggered back to her car, ripped open the door, and threw herself behind the wheel. With her hands shaking, she fumbled with her keys until she found the right one and jammed it into the ignition.

Wasting no time, she revved her engine and peeled out of the cul-de-sac. In less than two minutes, she was already southbound on Route 10. A Chesterfield County police cruiser came barreling past her, its lights flashing and siren wailing, with an ambulance not far behind.

What the fuck are they gonna think when they find him?

And what the fuck am I gonna do when she finds me?

Veronica drove toward Williamsport. The digital clock on her dashboard displayed 1:27 PM. She leaned over the steering wheel to glance up at the cloudy sky and slumped back in the seat.

"Fuck!" she cried out and slammed an open fist against the wheel. The tears came hot and fast, blurring her vision.

Where you gonna go, Veronica? She'll find you. She'll come to your house or wind up invading your dreams. Clearly, she can go wherever the hell she wants. There's nowhere for you to hide. You're not safe anywhere.

You're dead. Your life is over.

You only have a matter of days before someone finds you torn apart in your goddamn living room.

Flashes of Raymer's mangled corpse assaulted her as she struggled to focus on the road. She next thought of the footprints—indisputable proof of the vampire's physical manifestation.

How did she get all the way out there? And so quickly? How was she actually there? She obviously couldn't do that to him in... in spirit form. Could she? Can she project herself somewhere as a spirit and then manifest in a wholly physical form?

How the hell is that even possible?

How is any of this fucking possible?

Veronica suddenly swerved the Volvo back onto the road as she failed to follow a curve along a small bend. She glanced in her rear-view mirror to ensure no cops were behind her. Suddenly her cell phone began to ring in her purse.

"Fuck," she shouted and turned her attention away from the road. As before, she began to drift onto the shoulder, the Volvo's alignment pulling the car to the right.

"Damn it!"

All your friends are dead. Let it go to voicemail.

The incessant ringing of the phone threatened to erode whatever was left of Veronica Upham's waning sanity. She grit her teeth and continued speeding back to Williamsport—back to her empty life, to her doom, and to her inevitable death.

"What the fuck am I gonna do?" she cried aloud. With one hand still on the wheel she reached up and wiped the tears from her eyes.

What can I do?

Veronica clenched her jaw and continued to drive. Her pulse pounded—her breathing was short and labored.

Should I try to find Father McCallum?

Veronica assumed she'd be able to find a phone number or address for the mysterious priest, but the idea of approaching him made her nervous.

Would he even help me? I have no idea how much Raymer told him about my involvement or what I know. Besides, all that secret society shit is creepy. I don't trust him. Any of them. And it's not like I have time to track the son of a bitch down anyway.

I need to handle this on my own. I can't let her win. Not after what she's done. To Nathan. To Raymer. To Tyler. To Emma.

To the countless other kids that are buried in those woods.

I have to find a way to stop her. Before she kills again.

The professor struggled to steel herself. Their weapons had failed them. And she no longer had access to most of them. Besides, she wasn't comfortable handling guns and was more likely to shoot herself than her target.

She pounded the steering wheel as she envisioned the police hauling Raymer's illegal arsenal from his house, tagging each of the weapons as evidence of some criminal conspiracy, where they'd sit in some cluttered room in the back of the local police precinct.

What a waste.

But you still have the .38. You can wait for her. Like Raymer said. Let her get close enough and then fill her corpse with silver.

Or you could just let her kill you.

Veronica weighed the merits of what appeared to be her only viable option.

You think it matters if she does? You still think you're gonna roll into class Monday morning and resume teaching Wuthering Heights? And let's see, what's next? George Eliot? Wilkie Collins? Oh, how about Arthur Machen and then you can end it all with a bang from Bram himself?

"Just in time for Halloween." Veronica began to laugh through her tears and wrung her fingers around the sticky steering wheel. "Today, we're going to begin our discussion of *The Great God Pan* and the Yellow Nineties!"

Suddenly the idea hit her like a thunderbolt.

Her brow furrowed and she began to wonder to herself.

Could it work? Seriously, could it?

Maybe I can convince her to destroy herself.

Just like Villiers or whatever his name was tried to convince Helen Vaughan to kill herself in Machen's story.

What do I have to lose?

"Fuck you, Charlotte, you insufferable cunt."

Veronica eased up on the gas pedal as she entered a residential area. She was now within five or less minutes from her house, but she ignored the turn and kept driving, her knuckles white and her eyes wide and contemplative.

Ten minutes later, she eased her Volvo into the nearly empty parking lot of the Williamsport Historical Society. With her tires straddling the lines of the designated spot, she cut the engine, grabbed her purse, ducked out of the car, and slammed the door behind her. She quickly walked across the lot and pulled open the door to enter the quiet building.

Winded and wind-blown, Veronica approached the front desk in search of Joyce Lambeth. The elderly woman emerged from a small office and was adjusting her spectacles.

"Oh, hello Veronica!" Mrs. Lambeth appeared to be both surprised and glad to see her. "What brings you in today?"

"Hi Joyce," the professor replied. "I was hoping I could see the Westcott archives again." She caught her breath and pushed a lock of matted hair behind her ear. "In particular, those daguerreotypes. The pictures I took on my phone aren't very good, and I promised my student I'd come back and retake them."

Veronica's flushed face and the traces of tears along her cheeks had not escaped the observant historian—nor had the conspicuous silver cross hanging around her neck. Joyce reached up and removed her glasses and spoke candidly. "If I may say, you seem a little worse for wear. Can I get you anything else? A glass of water maybe?"

"That won't be necessary, Joyce," Veronica responded. "I'm in a bit of a hurry."

"Well, you seem a bit distraught," the older woman replied.

"It's nothing. I was afraid maybe you were closing soon and that I wouldn't make it. And I know you're closed on Sundays so—"

"Oh, no, I'll be here until at least five and I'm happy to stay a bit later if you need time to do your research. I was just reading a novel back there, something you probably know by—"

"Thank you, I appreciate that very much." Veronica swallowed and tried to regulate her breath and pounding pulse. "I shouldn't be too long."

"Fair enough," she said. "Come along and I'll get you set up."

Veronica followed Joyce into the special collections room and took a seat at the same table she had occupied just a few days earlier. She reached for her purse, took out her cell phone, and placed it on the surface of the table. Before the historian returned, Veronica made sure to stuff the .38 deeper into her purse so that Joyce wouldn't see it. Mrs. Lambeth returned with the jewelry box and a frown only a few minutes later.

"Do you want to look over any of the letters or the diary again while you're here?" Joyce asked. "I'm sorry to say we haven't made any headway on the transcription of the diary. Unfortunately, Barb had a family emergency." Mrs. Lambeth lowered her voice to a whisper. "That poor young girl they found yesterday morning was her niece and she's incredibly upset."

Veronica blanched at the mention of Emma Sullivan and kept her eyes forward on the ornate box of the vampire's memories. "I'm very sorry to hear that," she managed. "I heard the news yesterday. My heart goes out to her and her family. I wish... I wish there was something I could have done."

"Oh, bless you, Dr. Upham," Joyce said sadly. "What could you possibly have done to help that poor girl? We were all so shocked when we heard what happened. I just can't imagine what's happening around here."

No, you most certainly can't. And you don't want to, Joyce. You don't want to know.

The historian continued to linger as Veronica's heart pounded in her chest. She lifted her red-rimmed eyes to Mrs. Lambeth and said, "I shouldn't be too long. If I need something else, I'll be sure to come find you."

"Well, if there's anything I can do, just let me know," Joyce responded with a peculiar emphasis. "I mean that. I'm here if you need to... talk if anything's... *troubling* you."

"I appreciate that," Veronica said, fighting back a new wave of tears. "I'll be fine. Just give me about half an hour or so."

Mrs. Lambeth nodded and made her way to the door. Once she closed it firmly behind her, Veronica exhaled heavily and leaned forward with her head in her hands. She ran her thin fingers through her hair and clutched the back of her neck. The room was silent and heavy. She listened for several minutes, hoping that Joyce had gone back into the office and resumed reading her book.

Suddenly, she heard a phone ring from the main room. Joyce answered the call after only one additional ring. Veronica listened as she heard the curator's muffled voice beyond the door. She immediately jumped to her feet, tossed her phone into her purse, and picked up the box. Veronica approached the door, cracked it just an inch, and listened to make sure the historian was still preoccupied on the phone.

With the jewelry box cradled against her chest, she crept into the hallway and glanced down the darkened corridor that led to the restroom. Still encouraged by the sound of Joyce's low voice responding to queries on the telephone, she hurried through the shadows, past the bathroom, and made her way toward another door that led to the garden behind the building. Her sweaty fingers slipped on the knob and she scrambled to unlock a small brass bolt before she swung the door open and emerged breathless into the light of day.

She dashed around the right side of the building and ran to her car. Within seconds she was behind the wheel, and the stolen box of daguerreotypes was resting on the worn gray leather of her passenger seat. She turned over the ignition, threw the car in reverse, and drove out of the parking lot. Within a matter of minutes, she had steered her Volvo into the parking lot of South Williamsport Elementary School.

Veronica sat behind the wheel of the car and stared through the filmy windshield. She scanned the area to ensure there was no one at the playground or lingering outside the school. As far as she could see, the grounds were unoccupied and barren of visitors. The dashboard clock read 3:18 PM.

Dusk was more than three hours away.

She reached into her purse for a pen and withdrew the crumpled paper towel from her coat pocket, which she spread across the center of the steering wheel. In large block letters, she wrote the following words: IF YOU FIND THIS, I AM DEAD.

Veronica placed the message on the flat surface of the dusty dashboard, grabbed her purse and the jewelry box, and exited her vehicle. She slammed the door without bothering to activate its locks.

The cold October wind kicked up, as if to impede her progress as she crossed the wet soccer field. Veronica continued to stride forward, her tennis shoes and the cuffs of her blue jeans already damp and soiled with mud. She shifted the weight of the jewelry box and held it under her left arm. As she approached the dark mouth of the path leading into the forest, she lifted her eyes to the gray sky above. She had the distinct, unquestionable feeling that there was nothing above looking down upon her—favorably or otherwise. With a sick heart and her skin crawling with fear, Veronica Upham entered the woods to face her enemy for the final time.

34

WITH HER KNEES DRAWN UP AND A CIGARETTE BETWEEN two thin fingers, Veronica sat within the center of the crossroads. Night had fallen more than three hours earlier, but there was no sign of the vampire. The woods remained cold, dark, and quiet. As her eyes adjusted to the night, the waning moon cast enough light for her to see. Besides the silver cross around her neck, she had only the .38 and a single vial of holy water for protection. She hadn't bothered to cast a circle around herself and had no other weapons at her disposal.

She placed the bottle of holy water directly in front of her. The jewelry box containing the daguerreotypes sat unopened at her side. She smoked cigarette after cigarette while rehearsing what she planned to do once the vampire arrived—presuming she *would* arrive before the night was over.

As the evening wore on, Veronica struggled with the traumatic memories of the past few days. She was assailed by horrific images of what she found in the basement of the Aston house. In the lonely silence of the forest, she felt the full weight of her loss. Despite their recent estrangement, Edison had been her closest companion and her lover for years. She had admired his presence, his sharp mind, and his unwavering certitude. And now he was gone.

Her thoughts turned to Nathan Alderson, a man she had only known for a few days. But he made a deep and lasting impression on her. He believed her. He listened to her. He treated her as an equal. He was driven to solve this case but had no idea what he was up against. Yet he adapted as best he could until the vampire got into his head.

As her tired eyes swept the familiar tree line and clearing of the forest, scenes from their previous confrontation replayed in her mind. She stood over the vampire's thrashing corpse while Raymer and Alderson held it down. The stake was in her hand, the tip above the monster's heart. All she had to do was bring the hammer down. She was one blow away from ending the nightmare once and for all.

But she hesitated.

And now, Raymer was dead. The ritual had failed. Nathan had been driven out of his mind. His wife now grappled with the loss of her husband and her child in the span of only a few short months. And Veronica's conscience refused to allow her to forget the death of Emma Sullivan. The little girl was taken from her family before she had a chance to really begin her life, leaving a void that could never be filled in the hearts of her mother and father.

All of it could have been prevented.

If only I had acted faster and hadn't faltered, none of it would have played out like this.

Veronica shivered as the wind picked up. She pulled her coat around her body and wrapped her arms around her legs. She rocked back and forth to keep warm. After smashing the butt of her cigarette into the ground, she lit another and reminded herself of one indisputable fact.

You may have fucked up and choked when you had the chance to kill her. But there's only one thing to blame for all this.

Veronica took a heavy drag on her cigarette and blew the smoke into the cold air around her.

Charlotte Brennen.

The minutes slowed as she silently cursed the name of her enemy. She pictured the vampire's face in her mind and imagined it consumed by fire, the decrepit fiend's body devoured in flames. Veronica saw herself driving a stake through the vampire's breastbone, piercing its heart, and pinning it to the earth. She relished the monster's defeated screams and yearned for its mouth to grow slack and silent. She visualized the total destruction of

Charlotte Brennen and willed it to take shape before her, channeling what little energy she had left into this one singular wish.

Veronica forced her mind to go blank. She stared at the bottle of holy water she had set before her. Her eyelids grew heavy. The cold and the steady silence lulled her into a false sense of calm. She could no longer fight against the insistence of sleep. Fearing that she was on the brink of dozing off, she reached into her purse and withdrew the roll of communion wafers. After casting a medium-sized circle around her, she let her body relax. Veronica slid her legs out to her side and stretched her arm along the ground. The bait was set, and she fell into a deep sleep.

✝

Hours later, she was awakened by an abrupt *crunch*. Veronica slowly opened her eyes to focus on the ground beneath her stiff body. She pushed herself upward on unsteady hands and rolled onto her side. Glancing around quickly, she remembered she was at the crossroads. Veronica gasped when she realized she was no longer alone.

"Stay back!" she shouted as the vampire loomed above her. Charlotte had stepped on the bottle of holy water that must have rolled out of the circle while Veronica was sleeping. The vampire was grinding the shards of broken glass beneath her bare foot. Smoke wafted up between her toes. Veronica frantically used the tips of her fingers to close the small breach in the circle. With her head bent downward, Charlotte fixed her cold eyes on Veronica.

The scarring that had marred the vampire's face had already begun to heal. Veronica could still discern the faint impression of a cross along Charlotte's forehead, but the skin had already softened and regained some of its pallor. Veronica felt sick to see that the blood of Emma and Raymer had fulfilled so heinous a purpose. The vampire's crippled arm was curled tight against her chest. A rounded nub of tender flesh had closed over the bone.

Charlotte stood rooted to the ground only a few feet from Veronica, eyeing her with curiosity. "Why are you here?"

The professor's heart raced when she heard the vampire speak. Veronica lifted her head to meet the gaze of her enemy. Her mouth was dry, yet she forced her lips to part.

"Charlotte Gordon!" Veronica watched as a ripple of recognition passed over the monster's features. "I know you. I know *everything* about you."

The vampire took a step toward her. Veronica retreated a few inches, but kept her eyes locked on Charlotte.

"You were born in Scotland and came to Virginia after you married *Henry Brennen.*"

Her brow furrowed and she took another step forward.

"And then you lost *William,*" Veronica said. "When he died of a fever."

The vampire froze, her face a mask of confusion and anger. Veronica reached for the jewelry box and held it aloft with trembling hands.

"Take it," she commanded. "Take it and look inside. It once belonged to you."

Charlotte bent forward and extended her right arm. She gripped the lid of the box and snatched it from Veronica's grasp. The vampire held it close to her chest, her uncertain eyes still studying Veronica.

"Open it!" Veronica gestured to the container and then slid a few feet backward.

With the bottom of the box resting on her withered arm, the vampire retreated several steps before sinking to her knees. She placed the jewelry box on the soil, lifted the lid, and withdrew the daguerreotype of Henry Brennen. The vampire's face darkened. She cupped the photo in her hand and slammed it hard into the ground. Veronica flinched as she heard the thin glass shatter.

Charlotte then took up the photo of William. She balanced the portrait against her arm and caressed it with spindly fingers.

"That's him, isn't it?" Veronica said, fighting to remember the dates she had read in Jane Westcott's journal. "William Brennen. Three years old. He died in 1854, didn't he?"

Charlotte continued to stare at the photograph. She tilted her head and examined the image of her departed son. Her taut features had softened, and her eyes glistened in the darkness.

"They're all in there," Veronica reminded her. "Joanna. Lillian. Do you remember?"

Charlotte carefully placed the photo of William beside her. She then returned to the box and withdrew each of the remaining daguerreotypes one after the other. The withered lily slipped from between the covers of the hard-shell case and drifted to the ground. Veronica watched as the vampire picked it up between her fingers, only to let it fall once again.

"I know you lost another child," Veronica said. "A fourth baby. In the winter of 1859. Did you ever name it?"

Veronica waited in silent dread, but the vampire ignored her question. She was enthralled by the faces of her long dead children. Charlotte slid forward on her knees to inspect the antique photographs, which she slowly spread out in front of her.

"Do you remember Jane Westcott?" As before, the vampire offered no response. Charlotte continued to pore over the daguerreotypes. She bent forward, her long tangled hair sweeping the earth, her fingers now splayed in the mud. The desiccated flower lay discarded off to the side of the open cases.

"Jane Westcott," Veronica repeated. "She was your friend. Your *only* friend. She comforted you after William died. She was there for you when Joanna died. She saved these pictures for you. But you *abandoned* her. You turned your back on your only friend. Didn't you?"

Charlotte slowly lifted her head and cast a spiteful glance at Veronica. Long-forgotten memories began to stir within the vampire's disordered mind.

"And her daughter, Molly. You were needlessly cruel to her. Just as you were to Richard Westcott. That doctor saved your life countless times, but you repaid him by casting his wife and daughter aside as if they meant nothing to you."

Charlotte narrowed her eyes and stared at Veronica. She leaned backward, still kneeling on the earth. Her fingers continued to curl in the mud as she eyed her prey.

"He should have left you to die," Veronica said. "He should have let you bleed out on your bed when you failed to bring Joanna to term."

Veronica reached into her coat pocket and withdrew her cigarettes. She met the vampire's gaze with defiance. She flicked her lighter and thrust it outward. Charlotte recoiled as the unexpected flame emerged from Veronica's fingertips.

"Yeah." She lit a cigarette and exhaled a puff of smoke into the air. "A lot's changed since 1859." Veronica folded her legs under her and pointed a finger at the vampire. "I know everything, Charlotte. I know that you named your daughter after the poet. Joanna Baillie. Let me guess. Your favorite play was *De Montfort*. Am I right?" She exhaled another plume of smoke into the air.

Charlotte was unmoved. She ran her fingers across her tattered dress in a vain attempt to smooth its creases.

"I know everything," Veronica challenged her. She tapped her cigarette, causing its ash to drift to the ground. "I know each of your children died, and I know you buried them here." Veronica slammed her fist onto the ground. "At these godforsaken crossroads!"

Charlotte shifted her weight as her hand pawed at the mud.

"And for what?" Veronica asked. "What did you bargain for? They've been rotting here for nearly *two hundred years*. They never returned to you. And they never *will*."

The vampire swept the empty jewelry box aside and crept forward. Veronica held her ground and took another drag on her cigarette.

"Do you know what year it is, Charlotte? It's 2016. Think about that. Let it sink in. Two. Thousand. Sixteen. That's about one hundred and fifty-seven years since you murdered your husband. Since you tore his throat out in the nursery." Veronica pointed beyond the trees toward the ruins of the Brennen plantation. "What's left of your grand estate is just over those trees. That and the empty tomb where you filled the coffins of your children with bags of sand. I told you. I know everything." She paused. "Well, almost everything. The one thing I *don't* know is how the fuck you became what you are now. But that doesn't matter. The only thing that *does* matter is that you should be *dead*."

Veronica pushed herself to her feet and flicked her cigarette into the nearby brush. The vampire remained crouched low to the ground, watching her with keen interest. Veronica took several brazen steps to the edge of the circle and continued to chastise Charlotte in a forceful voice.

"Let me tell you about the last century and a half of pain, torment, and hell *you* are solely responsible for," she shouted. "Let me tell you about the dozens upon dozens of innocent *children* you murdered in cold blood! The helpless *infants* you buried alive, the ones you cursed with your poisonous blood, and *nursed* with the sour, curdled *slime* that seeps from your breasts!"

Charlotte hissed and began to stagger to her feet. Indifferent to the protective circle, Veronica lunged forward and shoved the vampire backward.

"No! You're gonna listen to me!" The professor's eyes gleamed with fury. "You're gonna heed every fucking word I have to say!"

Veronica clenched her fists, bent forward, and shouted into the face of the crouching vampire. *"You murdered all of them! You killed scores of innocent children!"* Veronica shook with rage. Scalding tears flooded her eyes and began to stream down her face. "Think of all their mothers! Think of all the lives you ruined! Think of all the parents who mourned for their lost children. Just as you had done! What was the *point?"*

Charlotte's eyes bore holes into Veronica, but the professor stood firm.

"You stole them from their homes! You lured them into these woods. And you killed them. Slaves. Soldiers. Hunters. Fishermen. *Children!* Whoever you could get your filthy hands on. You killed them. *And for what?* What have you gained? You have gained *nothing!"* Veronica thrust her head forward, while the rest of her body remained stock still. "You fattened yourself on helpless human beings and gorged yourself on scraps of dead animals to prolong your miserable existence for *nothing!* You will *never* see William again. You will *never* see Joanna! You will *never* see Lily! And you don't fucking *deserve* to see *any* of them!"

Charlotte rose but did not move to attack or subdue her prey. Veronica maintained her position and resumed her barrage of abuse.

"And what of poor Tyler Marshall?" she cried. "You dragged him to his death in these woods just over a week ago. Did you even know that was his name?"

Veronica slid her right hand into her coat pocket. Her fingers wrapped around the grip of the snub-nose .38. She stretched her index finger along the trigger and took another step toward the vampire.

"While you were sucking the blood from his veins, tell me... did you hear his *mother* calling him?" With her free hand, Veronica pointed in the direction of the elementary school. "Did you hear her desperate pleas echoing through the woods? You vile, despicable *leech! Did you?!*"

Charlotte snarled and bared her teeth. She took a step forward as Veronica tightened her grip on the compact revolver.

"But that wasn't enough, was it?" Veronica said. "When we nearly *beat* you in these woods, you had to have your revenge. You were too much of a *coward* to come back here and face us. So, you went after that little girl. Her name was *Emma Sullivan*. She was eight years old. And you killed her! Just to spite us. Like a petulant child, you threw a tantrum and took that girl's life. Another mother childless. For *nothing!*"

Charlotte edged closer. Veronica relinquished her grip on the pistol, reached up, yanked the cross from around her neck, and thrust it forward. "I said stay the fuck back!"

The vampire swung her fist and knocked the cross from Veronica's hand. The professor retreated several steps.

Undeterred, Veronica slid her hand back into her coat pocket. "I'll tell you this, you loathsome cunt. You got to Nathan. And you got to Raymer. But you're not taking me down so easily. You have no power over me. I don't fear you. I *despise* you."

With her hand clenched at her side, Charlotte began to close the distance between them.

"You aren't fit to exist! You're an abomination! You've spent decade after decade haunting these woods like some witch in a fairy tale, lost in your grief, lost in your vengeance, but not anymore. You can go ahead and kill me, Charlotte. Go ahead. I'll be dead. I'll be gone. But you'll *still* be here." Veronica indexed the trigger of the concealed pistol. "Without your children. And without the solace of your perpetual ignorance. You will never forget my words! You know what you are! Every step you take in these woods is a step away from peace. Whichever way you fly is hell, 'cause you are damned forever. You *are* hell, and you deserve to die."

Veronica threw back her shoulders and spit into the vampire's face. As Charlotte reached up to wipe the saliva from her chin, the professor braced herself for the attack she was counting on. Blinded by rage, the vampire charged forward.

Veronica clenched her eyes shut as she felt Charlotte's arms slip around her. The fiend's cold hand grasped the back of her neck. With her fingers tangled in the roots of her hair, the vampire yanked Veronica's head to the side and sank her teeth into her throat. The professor thrust the .38 against the vampire's stomach and pulled the trigger. The blast was staggering. She managed to fire a second shot as they both fell backward and hit the ground.

Pinned beneath the vampire's weight, Veronica cried out and emptied the cylinder of the .38, one deliberate trigger pull at a time. Five silver-tipped bullets were now lodged in Charlotte's chest. Black blood poured from the gunshot wounds. Veronica shoved the vampire's body aside and rolled out from under her.

Drenched in the creature's blood, Veronica crawled away, leaving the empty .38 smoking on the ground. She pressed the sleeve of her coat against the wound in her neck and grit her teeth at the pressure and the pain. Her right hand stung from the recoil and she was still half blind from the muzzle flashes. The back of her hand was black with powder burns. Veronica's ringing ears were hollow as her head throbbed with the rush of adrenaline and terror.

She tore off her coat and crumpled it against her neck. Bending forward, she struggled to catch her breath and center herself as the forest spun around her. Using the bottom of her coat, she frantically wiped the vampire's blood from her face and hands.

Charlotte lay face down on the ground. Her crooked spine arched as she tried to push herself up, but her limbs collapsed beneath her. She stretched out her arm and dug her fingers into the mud and attempted to pull herself forward.

Veronica staggered to where Charlotte slithered along the ground. With a muddy foot she forced the vampire onto her back. Charlotte groaned and clutched her stomach as streams of slick black ichor gushed between her fingers and over the stump of her crippled arm. Her face was contorted in agony and fear. Fresh blood stained the vampire's teeth, mouth, and chin. Her legs slid through the mud as her feet curled inward.

Veronica stared down at her, still pressing her blood-drenched coat to her neck. "Stay down!" Her words were muffled and distant. "You're finished. Those were *silver* bullets, which is... which is poison to you and your kind."

Veronica wheezed as the pain in her throat continued to throb. Charlotte thrust her weak hand outward and grabbed for Veronica's ankle. The professor stepped aside and nudged the vampire's feeble arm away with the tip of her shoe. "Give up," she whispered. "There's nothing left for you."

Charlotte gnashed her teeth and emitted a low, animal snarl. A pinkish foam oozed from the corner of her mouth. Her black eyes glistened with fear.

"The sun is on the rise." Veronica pointed to the sky above them. "And when it comes shining through the trees, you're finished."

Charlotte thrust her head into the mud. Her eyes rolled back into their sockets as oily blood ran from her nostrils. The veins along her temples protruded and darkened. Her body convulsed and she continued to claw helplessly at her bleeding chest. The livid flesh of her breast was exposed as she pulled away strips of her dress. The blood-drenched rags slid from her body. Her stomach and torso were riddled with holes. Blood oozed like black mercury from her wounds.

Veronica watched as the vampire's movements became more sporadic. In time she lay perfectly still, barring the occasional twitch of a finger or toe. Her eyes stared upward—fearful and defeated.

"Only a matter of time now," Veronica said hoarsely.

She pulled the coat away from her wound. Although the bleeding seemed to have slowed, she was dizzy from the loss of blood and the mild vertigo caused by the gunshots. Veronica settled herself on the ground facing Charlotte. Her ears continued to ring, but the sounds of the forest were becoming clearer. She glanced at the sky above and noticed it was beginning to lighten.

Charlotte stared up through the canopy of trees overhead. Her rigid body lay framed in mud, and her wounded arm was stretched out at her side. The vampire's right hand lay instinctively over her heart.

Veronica kept looking to the sky. The minutes dragged as the clouds slowly rolled along the horizon. The trees swayed softly in the breeze. Her heart skipped when she heard the trilling song of a bird awakening in its faraway nest. Another bird answered its cry and before long, the entire forest came alive with a chorus of chirping. Beyond the trees, the black sky was turning deep blue, while a flush of pink began to creep along the edge of the distant tree line.

Charlotte had not moved as Veronica eagerly waited for dawn. The professor rose to her feet and began to pace restlessly, repeatedly lifting her gaze to assess the changing sky.

The firmament above was now a swirling dome of dark blue, rose, and gray. A yellow-orange light presaging the arrival of the sun roiled along the eastern horizon. Birds flew above the treetops. At last, the rim of the sun began to crest through the clouds.

Charlotte thrashed her head from side to side. The panicking vampire watched as the sky faded to colors she hadn't seen in more than a century and a half.

Veronica saw that the area where the vampire lay was still shaded by the heavy treetops above her. She spun to her right and noticed the sun was already flooding the open area of the clearing just beside the crossroads.

Ignoring the pain in her throat, Veronica grasped Charlotte by her ankles and began to drag the heavy vampire toward the clearing. Unable to sit up, Charlotte weakly kicked her legs and flailed her arms. Veronica adjusted her grip, grit her teeth, and continued to pull the vampire's body forward. Charlotte dug her fingers into the ground, hoping to arrest her progress. But Veronica tugged her forward, adrenaline coursing through her slender frame.

With sweat glistening on her brow, Veronica stepped backward into the sunlit clearing. As the warm golden rays swept over Charlotte's feet, ankles, and calves, the exposed flesh began to blister and smoke. With a desperate groan, Veronica yanked Charlotte's body further into the clearing until her torso and face were directly exposed to the morning light.

Veronica stumbled but quickly regained her balance. Gasping for breath, she watched in spellbound horror as Charlotte extended her arms outward. The vampire issued a hideous shriek as her skin began to burn. Thick waves of acrid smoke rose into the morning air. Veronica jumped when flames erupted from the vampire's chest and spread to consume her face, arms, and shoulders. Choking on the rank smell of charred hair and burning flesh, Veronica turned away until the worst of it had passed.

Charlotte's terrified screams came to a sudden halt. Veronica shielded her face with her hands as flames rose several feet into the air. Glowing cinders eddied on the wind. Soon enough, the fire receded until only a few fading embers remained.

Veronica rushed forward to inspect the pile of smoldering ash and bone. The horrid stench was powerful but somehow invigorating. The strange alchemy that had played out before her seemed a bizarre and feverish dream. Although she had witnessed the death of Matthias Bartsch by the same means two years ago, it continued to astonish her that something so simple as the light of the morning sun could vanquish such a persistent threat. Within a matter of moments, the centuries-old nightmare that had plagued Williamsport was no more.

Veronica turned away from the scorched pile of smoking gore and stumbled back to where she had left her purse and other belongings. She winced as the strained muscles in her back locked and nearly prevented her from bending over. With her blood-stained coat over her shoulder, she knelt to gather the daguerreotypes scattered on the ground. After returning them to the jewelry box, she picked up the empty .38, shoved it into her purse, and hurried along the path leading to the elementary school.

When she reached her car, she opened the door and tossed the items onto the passenger seat. She snatched the note she left on the dashboard, crumpled it into a ball, and shoved it into a plastic cup holder between the seats. Veronica glanced in the rear-view mirror to examine the wound on her neck. It was still too clotted with blood to discern its depth. She fished her keys from her purse, found one that fit the ignition, and turned over the Volvo's engine. Within minutes she was on the road and driving back to her house on Copperstone Drive.

As she gripped the wheel, the magnitude of what had just taken place began to overwhelm her. The vampire was finally destroyed, but Raymer was still dead. Alderson's life was over. Kelly faced nothing but emptiness and loss. Tyler, Emma, and all the other children were gone forever.

The world was crawling with vampires. No one was safe. She and Raymer had only managed to destroy a small fraction of them. But what was that in the grand scheme of things? What was that in the face of the numberless dead secretly moldering in unmarked graves? Not just in the woods along the James River, but all over the world?

Veronica eased her Volvo into her driveway and threw the car into park. When she killed the engine, the initial silence deafened her. She peered through the hazy windshield of her car to see the early morning sun reflected on the panes of her living room window. Birds continued to sing beyond the confines of the car. The bells of St. Luke's began to chime just blocks away. Veronica gathered her belongings, opened the car door, and wandered into her quiet, empty house.

35

Veronica spent most of Sunday morning standing in the shower. Hot water poured over her aching body as heavy steam flooded the small bathroom. She couldn't tell whether it was day or night and for at least a short while, the false and busy world beyond the damp walls seemed to no longer exist.

She had already emptied an entire bottle of hydrogen peroxide over the wound in her neck. Her anguished screams had resounded along the smooth ceramic tile lining the walls of the bathroom. The sounds of her weeping afterward were drowned by the constant stream of water from the showerhead as it soaked her body and splashed into the tub below.

She eventually forced herself to turn off the shower, reached for a towel, and emerged into the swirling steam. Once she had dried herself off, she swept the condensation from the mirror and squinted her eyes to examine the wound. She was unable to recognize whether it was superficial, infected, or in need of stitches. After fumbling through the medicine cabinet, she lazily affixed a piece of gauze to her neck with two Band-Aids. Then she gathered her soiled clothes from the night before, balled them up tightly, and shoved them into a small garbage bag. Returning to the medicine cabinet, Veronica swallowed four tablets of Ibuprofen before wandering into her bedroom. She donned a faded t-shirt and a pair of sweatpants, then staggered to her kitchen to prepare herself a cup of tea. The ceramic cup and saucer remained untouched as she sat slumped in her living room chair.

Without the aid of booze or drugs—prescription or otherwise—Veronica managed to silence her mind. She simply sat stoic and frozen in place. She wondered for a moment if she was experiencing the symptoms of shock but made no effort to counteract it.

It was well past noon when her trance was interrupted by the doorbell. Her uninvited guest rang twice more and then issued a series of heavy knocks. Slowly, she rose and approached the front door. Taking her time with the locks, she eventually swung the door open. A tall man in a trench coat, tie, and black hat stood on her porch. He was accompanied by a short, heavy-set Latina in a tight-fitting police uniform.

"Yes?" she managed, bereft of both energy and civility.

"Dr. Veronica Upham?" the man asked. His eyes dropped to survey the bandage on her neck.

The professor leaned against her doorframe with tired eyes. "Uh-huh."

"Detective Frank McCain of the Williamsport Police Department." He flashed his badge and pointed a thumb to his colleague. "This is Sergeant Fernanda Perez. May we come in?"

Without a word, Veronica spun around and returned to her living room. McCain and Perez followed, closing the door behind them.

"I left you a voicemail yesterday, Dr. Upham," McCain called out as he studied the mix of antique and modern furnishings throughout her living room. "Since you never called me back, I figured we'd just pay you a visit."

Veronica withdrew her cigarettes and lighter from her purse and then took a seat on her sofa. She half-heartedly directed her guests toward the chair and sectional. "What can I do for you?"

"Well, you called us," McCain said as he lingered behind the wingback chair. Perez stood behind him with her arms folded across her chest.

"Did I?" Veronica lit a cigarette and reached for her cold cup of tea. She gulped down its contents in order to create a makeshift ashtray.

"Yeah." McCain narrowed his eyes. "On Friday. You called the station looking for Nathan Alderson. Gave Sergeant Tozier hell from what I understand."

Veronica nodded with indifference. "So?"

"So?" McCain's façade almost slipped before he regained his composure. "Well, I was a bit upset, you see, 'cause I was hopin' to talk to you. A few days before you called us, I got a call from some kid up in Richmond who says you—and I ain't makin' this up—*channeled* the spirit of Tyler Marshall at some kinda séance last Saturday night. Is that correct?"

Veronica blew a heavy cloud of smoke into the stagnant air. "I'll be damned if I'm doing this all over again."

"Excuse me?" McCain took a step around the chair. "I didn't quite catch that."

"Let's cut the bullshit." Veronica set the teacup on her coffee table and leaned forward. "What Eric Sandoval has to say is the least of your worries. I know you're Nathan's partner. And thanks to Sergeant Tozier, I know he had a mental breakdown and tried to kill his wife. So, what are you doing here now? Today?"

McCain exhaled heavily and cast a wary glance to Perez. The diminutive woman gave an encouraging nod in response.

"Earlier today," McCain began, "I decided to go see Nate in the psych ward over at the hospital. Yesterday we got word he was bein' transferred to Eastern State. Now, I don't know who gave that particular directive, but when I arrived this morning, he was already gone. The nurse on duty said an unmarked van showed up, driven by a pair of uniformed security guards brandishin' the proper insignias, paperwork, *et cetera.*" McCain reached up and scratched his chin. "They scrawled an illegible signature on the sign-out sheet and off they went with Nathan in tow."

Veronica nodded and flicked an ash into her teacup. A look of sadness spread over her features as she imagined the fate awaiting Alderson.

"Now somethin' about this just didn't ring true to me," McCain said. "Call it a hunch, intuition, whatever. So, I made a call over to the Peninsula and they knew nothin' about it. No record of the transfer, and no patient in their care by the name of Nathan Alderson."

Veronica sighed and stared at her coffee table. "That doesn't surprise me. Not one bit."

"Why, Dr. Upham?" Perez interjected before McCain resorted to a more heavy-handed approach. "What makes you say that?"

The professor lifted her weary eyes first to Perez, then to McCain. "Do you really wanna know?"

Perez swallowed and nodded with a fearful expression. McCain stood motionless beside the chair.

"I told Nathan everything when he came to see me." Veronica struggled to remember the day of the week. "It must've been Monday. He came to the college. I was teaching that day." She trailed off and adjusted her position on the sofa. "He didn't believe me at first. Not until he went up in the woods the next day. Then he came back and asked for our help."

"Hold on a sec," McCain said. Perez shot him an irritated glance. "He didn't believe you about *what*? And what happened when he went up in the woods? You talkin' about the woods by the school? What did he find there?"

"Bodies," Veronica responded without hesitation. She took a final drag on her cigarette and dropped it with a light *singe* into the teacup. "Although... it was a bit more complicated than that."

"OK." McCain clenched his jaw before he spoke more forcefully. "You need to elaborate a bit more, Dr. Upham. These half answers aren't gettin' us—"

"You said Nathan asked for help," Perez interceded again. "What kind of help? And who else did you mean when you said 'our?'"

Veronica lit another cigarette and tried to arrange her thoughts. "Nathan turned to me for information that would help him catch Tyler Marshall's killer. And when it became clear who or *what* we were dealing with, we went to see Edison Raymer."

"Seriously." McCain took several swift steps forward and leaned over the coffee table. "I'm gonna give you one more chance to start makin' some goddamn sense. It's your turn to cut the bullshit. Quit bein' vague and tell us *what the hell* is goin' on around here!"

The professor remained unmoved by McCain's bad cop routine. She eyed him with pity and blew a mouthful of smoke from the side of her mouth.

"You sure you're ready for that, Detective?" Veronica asked softly. Dark circles curved under her eyes. Her complexion was wan and sickly. "I'm not sure you are."

"Try me," McCain responded and folded his arms.

Perez sighed and took a seat on the sectional. "Can I bum a smoke from you, Dr. Upham?"

Veronica turned her attention back to Perez. She placed her lighter and pack of cigarettes on a small saucer and slid it across the coffee table. She then glanced to McCain. "There's an ashtray on the porch. Why don't you go get it and make yourself comfortable? This is gonna be a long story, and I need you to quit pacing around my living room."

McCain scoffed and maintained his position beside the coffee table. "Nate warned me about you. He told me you were a flake and that you said a ghost killed Tyler Marshall. That the story you're about to tell?"

"No," Veronica responded coolly and blew another cloud of smoke into McCain's eyes. "It wasn't a ghost. A vampire killed Tyler Marshall. And he told you I was a flake and dismissed me because that's what he had to say to pacify people like you. People who can't see beyond the obvious. It's why these things can *literally* get away with murder."

Veronica suddenly rose to her feet and took a step toward McCain. She reached up and tore the bandage from her throat.

"You see that?" Veronica pointed to the wound Charlotte had left on her neck. "Tyler Marshall's killer was named Charlotte Brennen. She did this to me last night."

"Nice try," McCain shot back. "You prolly did that shit to yourself. I've seen creeps do a whole lot worse to score some cred and come up with an alibi."

"Where's this Brennen woman now?" Perez asked. "If what you're saying is true, how'd you manage to get away from her?"

Veronica turned to regard Perez. "Well, first I filled her full of sil-ver-tipped bullets," she said flatly. "Then I dragged her body into the sun just after dawn this morning. She's dead now, but she wasn't the only one of her kind. There are hundreds, if not thousands, of these fucking things out there. You could probably go so far as to say they're *legion*."

"You're so full of shit," McCain leered. "You even hear what's comin' outta your mouth right now? Nate got it half-right when he said you was a flake. But you're fuckin' delusional."

"You don't believe me? Then haul me off to jail. I've got nothing left to lose and no reason to lie to you." Veronica pointed at him with her cigarette.

"But if you wanna *learn* something, and you *really* wanna know what's going on in this city, go get the goddamn ashtray and take a seat in that chair. It was your partner's favorite. He *listened* to me when he sat there, and we saved ourselves a lot of time because he *trusted* me. You think you can find it in yourself to show me the same courtesy?"

McCain met her eyes but still refused to move. "And look what happened to him when he listened to you."

"Frank," Perez shouted from the couch. "Go get the fucking ashtray!"

"Alright already!" McCain adjusted his hat and leveled a steely glance at Perez. "Watch your mouth, Sergeant. Just 'cause it's likely D'Amato's gonna promote you don't mean you're a detective yet. So I still outrank you." He reached into his coat pocket for his own pack of cigarettes and his Zippo lighter.

"Thank you, Detective." Veronica sank back on the sofa and slapped her hands against her thighs. "This room is gonna stink like a pool hall by the time we're finished, but who gives a fuck?"

She leaned back into the cushions and waited for McCain to return from the porch. He tossed his trench coat over the back of the chair, sat down, and slid the ashtray onto the coffee table. After he adjusted his hat, he lit a cigarette and turned to Veronica with a jaded stare.

The professor began by describing how she became acquainted with Edison Raymer. She explained his obsession with vampires and relayed his experiences at the Aston house. When she started to recount their discovery of Matthias Bartsch after the attack on Jennifer Stroud, McCain leaned forward and began to listen more carefully.

Veronica unburdened herself of their experiences in the autumn of 2014. Raymer's enlistment of Laura McCoy to serve as bait, the arrival and corroboration of Junior Luttrell, all the way through the staking of Matthias Bartsch, the unceremonious burial of Junior in the woods, and Laura's death at the hands of Edison Raymer.

She paused to let Perez and McCain take stock of what she revealed to them. Perez was engrossed but fidgeted uncomfortably on the edge of the sectional. McCain tossed his hat on the table and loosened his tie.

"So Bartsch's been dead since 2014," he said with a faraway look in his eyes. "And you're sayin'... you're sayin' he was the real deal. A kraut soldier from fuckin' World War II that hadn't aged a day since 1944."

Veronica nodded. Before she lit another cigarette, she rose, parted the curtains and opened the living room window.

"Can I get either of you a drink? Coffee? Tea? Water?"

Perez requested a glass of water. McCain eyed the professor's bar cart but thought better of drinking on duty. "I'll take a soda or somethin' if you got it."

Veronica returned with their drinks and another cup of tea for herself. She could tell McCain wanted to ask her several questions.

"Go ahead, Detective," she said. "I'm listening."

McCain took a deep breath and rubbed a bead of sweat from his forehead. "I don't even know what to say. It's incredible." He glanced up at Veronica. "And I mean that literally. It's hard to believe." He shook his head and ran his fingers over his thinning hair. "But I... I've heard and seen a lotta shit the last few days."

The professor nodded. "I know it's hard to believe but think about it this way. How many cases have you worked over your career where it seemed as though something was off? How many murders have you investigated where things just didn't add up? Chances are," she said, reaching for the cup of tea she placed on the coffee table, "it was one of these things."

McCain sat silent for a minute. He took a sip from his glass of Coke and then spoke to Perez. "You remember that trailer fire a couple years ago? Out on 619?"

"Vaguely," Perez said. "The murder–suicide?"

"That's the one," McCain said. "I had to go out there a few times owin' to Jack Stiles. Every once in a while, he'd go on a bender and rough up that pretty wife of his. Christ, what was her name? Alice? *Allie*," he remembered. "He was just some drunk shitkicker, but she was sweet as pie. Now, I wanted to knock Jack's goddamn teeth out for how he treated her, but it was just your typical backwoods trailer park saga. When we got that call sayin' that Allie shot Jack and turned the gun on herself, I couldn't believe it. Even after all he put her through, I didn't think she had it in her, let alone to set the place on fire."

"You said it was on Route 619?" Veronica asked.

"Yeah."

"That's where we found Bartsch holing up with Laura in that cabin."

"Jesus Christ," McCain muttered. "I'll be damned."

A brief lull fell over their conversation as the detective and Sergeant Perez mulled over the significance of Veronica's revelations. Perez swallowed a mouthful of water and clutched the glass with trembling hands. After a few minutes, McCain broke the silence with more questions.

"So, Edison Raymer didn't burn down his house and skip town to collect on the insurance. He did it to hide the evidence of Laura McCoy's body. Just like Bartsch did at the trailer?"

Veronica took a deep breath and exhaled. "That's correct."

"Where's Raymer now?" McCain asked.

"Dead," Veronica said.

"Dead?" McCain failed to conceal his surprise.

Veronica nodded with a grim expression. "I haven't... I haven't gotten to that part yet."

"Jesus. I'm sorry." McCain was temporarily speechless. Eventually, he cleared his throat. "Let me make sure I got everything straight before you continue, OK?"

Veronica nodded again and wiped a tear from her eye.

"So, you two never reported the death of the fella from Poquoson?" McCain asked.

"No," Veronica admitted. "We buried him near the cabin." She shook her head and took a drag on her cigarette. "That wasn't our finest hour."

McCain sighed. "I'm afraid that's some serious shit we're gonna have to sort out here, Dr. Upham. Withholdin' evidence, aidin' and abettin' a fugitive, accessory to murder..."

"Seriously, Frank?" Perez slammed her empty glass on the coffee table.

"Nathan said the same thing," Veronica told them. "Look, I get it. We broke some laws. *A lot of laws.* But now you know why, or at least you will by the time I'm done here. By law, Edison and I are without question a pair of fucking criminals. But man-made laws don't apply here. Consider them outmoded. They're gonna need to be revised. Our whole fucking way of life is gonna need some serious reevaluation."

"Good luck tellin' that to a judge," McCain quipped.

"Yeah, well, you two know any good lawyers?" Veronica replied with a wan smile. "I'm giving it to you straight, as I promised I would. That's all I can do."

McCain nodded and resumed his questioning. "You said Luttrell came to see Raymer after he went to the police? You remember who he talked to?"

"I'm pretty sure it was Nathan's predecessor," Veronica suggested. She took a sip of tea and clutched the cup tightly with her pale hands.

"Rudy Pettit?"

"Yeah, that's it. Alderson mentioned him to me as well."

McCain looked at Perez and she shook her head.

"So he knew?" McCain wrinkled his brow. "Why the fuck didn't he say something? Why would he hide it?"

"Because he was just days away from retiring," Perez answered. "C'mon, Frank. I know you worked with him for years, but Pettit was a lazy bastard." She reached for McCain's crumpled pack of cigarettes. "Besides, who the hell would've believed him?" She lit a cigarette and blew the smoke outward. "I'm starting to sense a theme here."

Veronica nodded. "Well, maybe that's a tradition the two of you can break. Nathan would have. If things hadn't gone the way they did."

"So what happened to Nate?" Perez asked eagerly. She leaned forward and locked eyes with Veronica. "When we found him... he was... he was terrified. He had crosses all over his bedroom. We found a satchel full of holy water, rosaries, communion wafers. He also had a gun loaded with silver bullets. He said..." Perez pursed her lips to prevent her emotions from getting the better of her. "He said the crosses were for protection. But they didn't work."

Veronica took a cleansing breath and closed her eyes. "Did he say anything else?" she asked. "The last time I spoke to him was late Thursday night or I guess technically it was early Friday morning. He dropped me off at my house. We had gone up into the woods. I'm getting ahead of myself here, but we were searching for the vampire. She didn't show because..." Veronica trailed off and swallowed. "Because she left the woods to kill Emma Sullivan."

McCain was taken aback. "Christ, you're right!" He was silent a moment as the connection between the deaths of Tyler Marshall and Emma Sullivan fully dawned on him. "Obviously it was the same killer," he said half to himself. "But I been so caught up in your story here, I guess it just didn't hit me yet." McCain sighed and rubbed his forehead.

"The vampire did it to spite us." Veronica hung her head low. "I'll explain what happened in a minute, but we fucked up the first night we went up there and she got away. I'll never forgive myself for it, because if we'd killed her then, Emma would still be alive."

"The whole thing's a mess," McCain confessed. "Bev Sullivan's still a fuckin' wreck. Chief D'Amato's breathin' down *my* neck now for answers." He looked up at Perez and then to Veronica. "I don't wanna be the one to have to tell those kids' mothers what you're tellin' me."

"I don't envy you," Veronica said softly. After a moment's reflection, she leaned forward and broke the silence. "What else can you tell me about Alderson? About his behavior that night, or that morning?"

McCain snapped out of his unhappy musings and nodded slowly. "Right, so as I guess you already know, the Sullivans live next door to Nate. So, he showed up at the crime scene around four-thirty in the morning. It was pissin' down rain and the son of a bitch said he'd been out canvassin' those woods."

"He tried to tell you, Frank," Perez said quietly.

"Watch it, Fernanda." McCain sneered at the uniformed sergeant. "He didn't tell me *everything,* and I could tell he was dancin' around the truth from the moment he rolled up in his truck. *No one* would've believed him. Even though he was fulla shit, he wasn't fucked up or crazy. He was lucid, and he was still Nate," McCain insisted. "But the man we found later that morning?" He leaned back in the chair and shook his head. "That wasn't my partner. He was *gone,* Dr. Upham. He saw somethin' that scared the shit out of him."

"What'd he say?" Veronica pressed. "Do you know what really happened that morning?"

McCain tried to recall Alderson's exact words. "He just kept sayin' it wasn't Kelly," he said. "I think that whoever he *thought* he was attackin' was someone else. Nate would've never laid a hand on his wife, that's for sure." McCain swallowed to fight back his emotions. "They was goin' through a rough patch, as you can imagine. After Cody drowned, they weren't dealin' with it... together, you know?" McCain looked to Veronica for understanding. "That kinda shit always tears couples apart. Kelly was tryin' to get Nate to see a shrink, but he just wanted to work. When the Marshall boy was found, it was like he became possessed. He *had* to solve the case. I dunno, I ain't a psychologist but I think he was tryin' to make up for not bein' able to save his son."

"We were all worried about him," Perez added. "We thought it might've been too soon for him to be back in the field."

"Yeah, but I thought stayin' focused would've helped him deal with his grief," McCain rationalized. "He might've been on edge, but what happened by Friday was *beyond* fucked up."

"He had no idea what he was getting into," Veronica explained. "Look, I'm only half-way through the whole story. Let me get the two of you up to speed. I think I can fill in a lot of gaps for you. In particular, I need to tell you more about the thing responsible for those kids' deaths."

She lit a cigarette and told them about the séance and affirmed that she had both video and audio evidence she was willing to turn over to them to corroborate her story. She recounted her first meeting with Alderson and paused after detailing Nathan's discovery of the infants in the woods.

Perez's face had acquired an ashen hue as Veronica described what happened when Nate unearthed the dormant vampires. McCain was also visibly shaken. He lit another cigarette with unsteady hands. "Obviously, he didn't tell me what he found up there." He turned to Perez and added, "You remember what he said in the bedroom? He told us to go up there in the daytime. That's what he meant when he said we were in for a surprise."

Perez was stunned. She ran her fingers over her arms and muttered a quiet benediction under her breath.

Veronica added that Nathan also found the remains of another child, which he believed had been killed sometime in the 1990s.

"Nathan had footage of everything on his cell phone," Veronica confirmed. "Now again, I'm skipping ahead, but when we confronted the vampire in the woods on Tuesday night, his phone was broken in the skirmish."

"Yeah," McCain said. "He told me it was broken, but he never said *how*. I was callin' him for days, but it kept goin' to voicemail."

"Right, well, don't forget he had an iPhone," Veronica reminded them. "So, any pictures or videos he had on there are likely stored on the cloud or whatever the fuck it is. Your people can probably hack into his account and you can see the evidence for yourselves."

McCain nodded his head and puffed on his cigarette. "He tried to convince Chief D'Amato and Ash Townsend to get a crew up there. He went through Pettit's old files, and Christ, he talked to that old bastard in Archives who said somethin' about kids goin' missing back in the 1950s and '60s. And I told him he was nuts. That the killer would've been eighty years old." McCain swallowed with wide eyes. "But he was right. If we would've listened to him and gone up there, we could've uncovered all the evidence. But D'Amato kept stallin' and—"

"This goes back *way* further than the 1950s, Detective," Veronica said ominously before she resumed her story. "It started almost a decade before the Civil War."

Perez and McCain sat in rapt attention as Veronica explained how they reconnected with Raymer, and then relayed their confrontation with Charlotte in the woods, followed by a brief summary of what she learned about the vampire's history from Jane Westcott's journal.

Although deeply disturbed by the history of the Brennen vampire, McCain was the first to speak up. "How the hell could she have been... *livin'* or whatever you wanna call it out there all these years yet no one discovered her?" McCain asked. "It's fuckin' crazy to think this has been goin' on so long. And it was right under our noses!"

Veronica pushed a lock of hair behind her ear and lit up another cigarette. "I've been a professor for going on twenty-five years now," she stated. "My area of specialization is Victorian literature, but I always had a partiality to gothic novels, ghost stories, and supernatural fiction. Up until recently, my knowledge of these creatures primarily came from all my old books."

Veronica paused for a moment. "Anyway, there's a line in Stoker's *Dracula*. It's probably apocryphal and comes from one of the dozens of movie adaptations, but at one point, Van Helsing says, 'The strength of the vampire is that people will not believe in him.' That pretty much sums it up, Detective. These things have existed for centuries, but they blend in with society and they count on our incredulity and disbelief."

McCain leaned forward and snubbed his cigarette in the ashtray. "Yeah, I'm not much for readin' but I've seen my share of those movies. When we found the Marshall boy, none of us wanted to admit it, but we all saw what happened. If I remember correctly, when we realized he was drained of his blood, it was Nate that said the empirical evidence was starin' us in the face. Somethin' like that." McCain shook his head. "But we didn't believe it. Just like you said. We tried to rationalize it and find another explanation."

"Well, the Brennen vampire was an anomaly," Veronica explained. "She managed to survive in those woods undisturbed since the 1860s. When she couldn't get ahold of children, she likely fed on hunters, fishermen, and animals. I found stories in books about the Civil War and local legends that span the late nineteenth through the early twentieth century. Raymer suggested she probably spent years in hibernation. But in her sick quest to create or find surrogates for her children, she'd rise when she sensed a kid had gone into the woods. That's likely what happened with Tyler Marshall."

"It's ungodly," Perez said with a shudder and crossed herself. "I've never heard of something so... so *revolting*. All those kids. Why did she... why did she leave them in the ground like that?"

Veronica attempted to explain her theory. Sergeant Perez quickly wished that she hadn't asked.

"So, what happened next?" McCain asked. "After the confrontation in the woods. What happened to Raymer?"

Veronica lifted her hand and shook her head. "Before we get to that, I need to add one more important detail."

"OK," McCain said suspiciously. "What's that?"

Veronica turned back to Perez, "Forgive me if I'm being presumptive, but a few of your comments have led me to believe that you're a practicing Catholic, is that correct?"

"It is," Perez confirmed with some discomfort. "Why do you ask?"

Veronica explained all that she was able to piece together from Raymer's conversations about Father McCallum and the role of the Church in covering up the existence of vampires and sanctioning their destruction.

"The whole thing was news to me, as Raymer hooked up with these people after he left Williamsport. But it all makes sense," she admitted and eyed Perez with sympathy. "I mean no disrespect, but the Church has a pretty despicable track record when it comes to cover ups. In this case however, I genuinely believe their intentions are good. But at the same time, they'll go to any length to maintain their secret." Veronica turned to McCain. *"That's* what happened to Nathan. They couldn't risk him telling the truth. Even if no one believed him. They had to cover their tracks. So, they pulled some strings and more than likely, you'll never find him."

"This just gets more outlandish by the minute," Frank said defensively. "You're sayin' there's a goddamn world-wide *network* of vampire hunters? I've heard my share of conspiracy theories, but this is fuckin' nuts!"

"Listen." Veronica leaned forward and clasped her hands together. "I'm telling the two of you all of this for a reason. It's time we blow the lid off this whole fucking thing. I don't know how to get ahold of him but call your people up in Richmond. The priest's name is Father Bill McCallum. He lives in an apartment somewhere in the city," she noted. "And then, you need to call the Chesterfield County police." She took a deep breath before adding, "Ask for homicide, and they'll surely relay the details of what they found in the Aston house Saturday afternoon."

Veronica braced herself and explained how McCallum advised Edison to resort to ceremonial magic to bind Charlotte's spirit when she didn't turn up in the woods. She then relayed the gruesome details of her discovery of Raymer's body. After she described her final confrontation with Charlotte, she rose from the couch and momentarily disappeared into the dining room. When she returned, she carried the battered jewelry box containing the daguerreotypes. She handed the box to McCain first and explained what it contained.

The detective examined each of the antique photographs with a mixture of awe and terror. He passed them to Perez who seemed afraid to touch them. They placed the photograph of William with his mother on the table and stared at it together.

McCain eventually looked up at Veronica. His face was drained of color, and he seemed to be fighting a feeling of nausea or disgust. "So, what do we do now?"

"Like I said," she began, "we blow the lid off of this." She withdrew a cigarette, crushed the empty box, and tossed it on her coffee table. She sat back down, lit it, and clutched her lighter in the palm of her sweaty hand.

"OK." McCain reached up to scratch his head. He looked at Perez and stuck out his chin. "How the fuck are we gonna convince D'Amato all this is true?"

"I'll tell him," Veronica volunteered. "But you two need to back me up. I'll submit the daguerreotypes. You can bag my laptop with the séance footage and recordings." Veronica remembered her dirty clothes she left upstairs in her bedroom. "I'll give you the clothes I was wearing last night. They're covered in the vampire's blood. You can take them to your crime lab or whatever and they can run an analysis. Then you get someone to tap into Nathan's phone. After that, you need to find McCallum. And I'm sure the Chesterfield County police will have mountains of evidence from the Aston house. At least in regard to Raymer's weapons, which I guarantee you'll be able to trace back to the Church."

"You forgot somethin' else," McCain said to Veronica.

"What's that?"

"If what you're sayin' about this priest is true, then maybe we *can* find Nate. And we can get him the help he needs."

"Absolutely," Veronica nodded. For the first time in days, she felt a twinge of hope. "Once you get McCallum in custody, and if all this is gonna come out anyway, maybe he'll tell us where we can find Alderson."

McCain turned to Perez. "You up for all this?"

"We have to be," she said. "Not just for Nate, but... Christ, for *everybody*."

"I'll tell you this much," Veronica said. "You need to convince your chief to send the forensics people into those woods. Once that happens, there'll be no turning back."

McCain dug his fingers into the arm of the chair and nodded his head.

Perez rose from the sectional and approached Veronica with her hand outstretched. "We've got your back, Dr. Upham. You can count on us."

"Please, call me Veronica," she said softly and accepted the Sergeant's firm handshake. She remembered when she stood beside Nathan Alderson in practically the same spot in her living room. "We're all in this shit together now, and our college town is about to become the epicenter of the most significant discovery in modern history."

EPILOGUE

CHIEF DOMINIC D'AMATO HAD JUST CONCLUDED AN EARLY morning press briefing. He delivered a short, prepared speech and refused to answer any questions. After placing his cap on his head, he turned his back on the massive crowd that had gathered in the soccer field beside South Williamsport Elementary School. Frantic news reporters and civilians unleashed a barrage of questions regarding the investigation that was currently underway in the woods. A line of uniformed police officers and national guardsmen formed a barricade between the unruly crowd and the entrance to the forest. With their shields, batons, and tear gas at the ready, several officers shoved members of the press backward as they demanded answers no one was willing to provide.

Accompanied by Sergeant Perez, D'Amato ascended the long trail into the heart of the forest. When he reached the clearing, he made his way across the uneven ground. He searched for at least one familiar face among the mob of national guardsmen, FBI agents, technicians, and policemen.

Chainsaws roared as volunteers and paid tree service employees continued to denude the forest surrounding the crossroads. Military vehicles ferried teams of forensic archaeologists and cops to and from the dig site. News helicopters hovered overhead.

The forest had been cut back as far as the location where Tyler Marshall's body was found. To his right, D'Amato had a clear view of the James River, where police boats were anchored. A crime scene team in Tyvek suits and face respirators crested the ridge from the direction of the low-lying marsh. Each of the techs gripped the corner of a yellow body bag. The thick nylon receptacle sagged in the middle, suggesting it was filled with a carefully collected set of bones.

He slipped past three men in FBI jackets. One of them held an evidence bag with a blackened crucifix sealed inside. Over the din of engines and chainsaws, D'Amato caught a snippet of their conversation.

"...kids and adults are being exhumed *everywhere*. Mostly skeletal remains. It's unreal..."

D'Amato spied Frank McCain talking to Ash Townsend in the distance. He recognized Veronica Upham but was surprised to see Kelly Alderson standing nearby. She seemed unsettled by the constant activity and noise. With Perez by his side, the chief made his way toward them. He passed between two conversing guardsmen with carbines slung across their chests.

"...some idiot violated his NDA and already uploaded footage to YouTube..."

Shovels and picks clattered to the ground nearby. D'Amato glanced over at four men in Hazmat suits. They had just unearthed another half-dead baby.

"Get over here with the camera! We got another one!"

"It's burning! It's really fucking burning!"

Plumes of black smoke billowed into the sky as the latest unburied child let out a mewling wail. The sound pierced the clamor of buzzing saws and motors.

As D'Amato and Perez joined the rest of the group, Frank McCain nodded, dug through his pocket, pulled out a cigarette, and lit it with his Zippo. He took a drag and exhaled. Perez whispered a Hail Mary under her breath as Townsend stood in a daze.

Kelly stood off to the side, observing the chaotic scene around her. She jumped as Veronica placed a hand on her shoulder.

"We'll find out where they took him," the professor said, her auburn hair blowing in the breeze. "And we'll try to bring him back to you."

Kelly turned and buried her head against Veronica's shoulder. Bruises still marred the skin of her neck.

McCain adjusted his black fedora. Holding his lit cigarette, he surveyed the mass graveyard, knowing that there were more dead—and *undead*—to be disinterred.

"You were right, Nate," he muttered to himself. A sharp scream rang out from his left. Townsend hurried to inspect the source of the commotion. Another infant vampire was unearthed and caught fire in the sun.

Frank McCain shook his head and pulled his trench coat around his shoulders.

"Jesus fucking Christ."

THE FIRST HUNT.

Come Forth in Blood is Ryan Henry and Matthew Heilman's first collaboration and the precursor to *Lie Still The Dead*. Blending classic horror with realistic psychological drama, the novel introduces Edison Raymer, Veronica Upham, and the elusive vampire Matthias Bartsch.

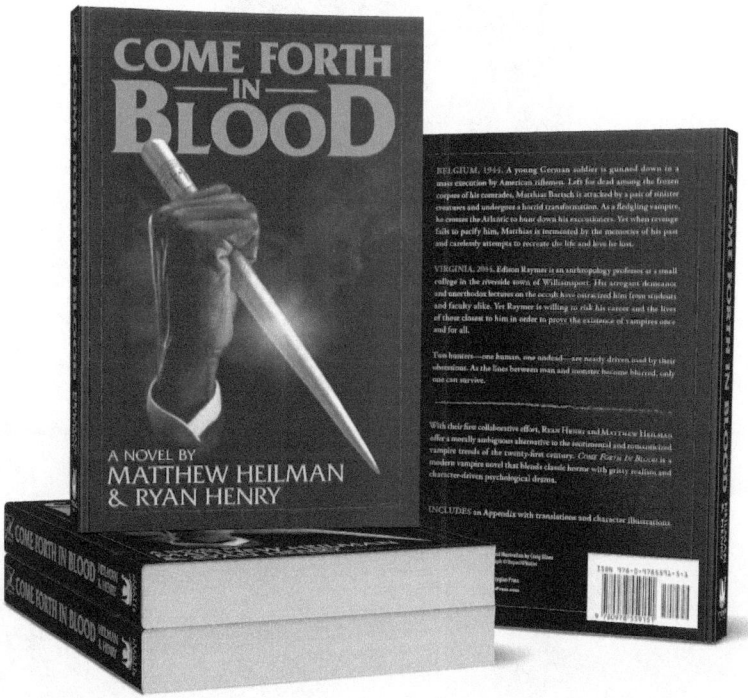

Available in Hardcover, Paperback, and eBook formats at your favorite bookseller.

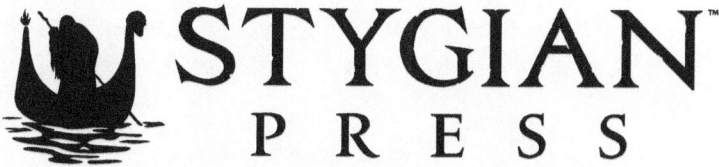

We want to hear from you! Please visit our website for more information about new releases, author updates, special offers, and more!

www.StygianPress.com

www.ingramcontent.com/pod-product-compliance
Lightning Source LLC
Chambersburg PA
CBHW020246120726
47904CB00001B/105